The
Mothers
of
Quality
Street

Also by Penny Thorpe

The Quality Street Girls

The
Mothers
of
Quality
Street

PENNY THORPE

HarperCollins*Publishers*

HarperCollins*Publishers*
The News Building,
1 London Bridge Street,
London SE1 9GF

First published by HarperCollins*Publishers* 2020

1

www.harpercollins.co.uk

The 'Quality Street' name and image is reproduced with the
kind permission of Société des Produits Nestlé S.A.

A catalogue record for this book
is available from the British Library

Hardback ISBN: 978-0-00-830780-6
Trade paperback ISBN 978-0-00-836377-2

Typeset in Sabon LT Std by
Palimpsest Book Production Ltd, Falkirk, Stirlingshire

Printed and bound in Great Britain by
CPI Group (UK) Ltd, Croydon CR0 4YY

MIX
Paper from
responsible sources
FSC™ C007454

This book is produced from independently certified FSC™ paper
to ensure responsible forest management.

For more information visit: www.harpercollins.co.uk/green

In loving memory of my cousin and fellow writer,
James José Martin Walker
1981 – 2019

Chapter One

The toffees for the window display had been carefully painted with strong poison. Mr Kirkby, the shop owner, didn't like to spoil good food like this because it was such a shameful waste, but in the early summer heat of that coronation year of 1937 it had been the only way to keep the ants at bay. Besides, the salesman from Mackintosh's had been very clear when he gave that particular box of toffees to Mr Kirkby, that they were inedible anyway. It was a relief to finally be throwing the casket away because the worry of having poisoned goods on the premises had weighed on his mind. He had warned his staff about them, and he was confident that none of them would forget and help themselves, but it had preyed on his thoughts as often as his wife had nagged him to throw them out.

As Mr Kirkby stood in the hot shop window, dismantling his display, mopping perspiration from his brow and his hands, he took another look at the casket of sweets and thought again how proud he was of his work. He was not as much of an artist as the confectioner at the Mackintosh's factory who had made the pretty sweets inside the silk-covered box with its golden trim, but he had painted the toffee fingers so delicately with a gloss of liquid cyanide syrup that, in the strong summer light, the difference was barely noticeable.

Mr Kirkby had, in fact, used rat poison. There was no sense going out and buying weak ant poison when he had enough Victorian rat poison in the cellar to kill an army. His wife was always telling him to get rid of the nasty stuff – it worried her having it lying about the place – but Mr Kirkby pointed out in return that you couldn't get rat poison like that any more; his mother used to put it down in the shop, and once they got rid of it they'd never be able to buy any more. Only the other day there had been a story in the newspapers about how the government were making a new law to restrict the use of it after an accidental poisoning down south somewhere; it was only a matter of time, Mr Kirby told his staff, before they outlawed fly paper and made you surrender your mousetraps.

Kirkby's Fancy Goods was very close to the Halifax Borough Market and they had always attracted more than their fair share of mice; despite being a very clean, high-class establishment. The laying down of poison was a routine he had inherited from his mother, and her father before her, just as he had inherited the shop. And although it was commonplace, on that occasion Mr Kirkby had been more cautious than usual, gathering all his staff and explaining to them personally that they were not to touch the new window display because he had added poison to the centrepiece to keep off the ants, and that when it was dismantled the casket was to go straight into the rubbish bin.

Mr Kirkby and his wife had invested a lot of money in this window display, but it had been worth it. The coronation of the new king and queen had brought brisk business, with all the neighbourhood coming in to buy bright bunting and party goods for their street parties. Yes, the spring of 1937 had been a boon for Kirkby's Fancy Goods. The window display had been done up in red crêpe paper and golden curtain cord to look like an enormous royal crown, and lengths of blue satin ribbon with 'God Save the King' on them criss-crossed a screen behind it.

Mrs Kirkby had overcrowded the window with examples of every line they stocked that could possibly be connected with street parties, patriotism, or His Majesty the King. Coloured card hats in the shape of coronets; pop-up theatres for kiddies illustrating the inside of the abbey; special coronation editions of magazines; knitting and sewing patterns for items of patriotic apparel; even a bouquet of carnations, artificially coloured to a burst of red, white and blue. Finally, nestled in the bottom right-hand corner on a velvet cushion, was the presentation casket of Mackintosh's 'Fancy Bonbons'. They were not one of the shop's usual lines, but oh, how wonderfully royal they made the window look. They were like a treasure chest or a jewellery box, sparkling in the late May sun.

Mr Kirkby often left open tins of toffees in his window and had never had cause to poison them before, but the sweets in the opened tins were usually safely wrapped in snugly twisted cellophane, or made from artfully painted plaster of Paris. These confections were naked, intricately decorated, and so very, very tempting.

'We wouldn't usually allow spoiled confectionery to leave the factory, but these were a special case. I mean, look at them,' the Mackintosh salesman had said, 'they couldn't just go straight into the bin. I said to my sales manager, I said, "Can't I let them go to a good home, just this once?" and I told them about the idea I had for making them part of your window display, and he let me bring them round.' The Mackintosh's salesman had sighed at the craftsmanship of the handmade bonbons. These were not the regular mass-produced toffees that he was used to dealing with – these were sweets of a premier class.

'They don't look spoiled to me, Mr Carstaff,' Mr Kirkby had said. 'I'll certainly take them off your hands – people aren't as fussy as you think. If I just mark the price down—'

'Oh no, not this box. People might not be fussy but at Mackintosh's we're fussy for them. This one is just for your window. I saved it for you, Mr Kirkby, as you've always been so good as to offer me such a lot of window space over the years. It's a sort of parting gift – my last window for you before I sail for Canada and my promotion – to celebrate the coronation. I've got a plan to make you a giant crown from crepe paper, with a ball and sceptre decorated with Quality Street cellophane. This casket will be the centrepiece, but it's only leaving the factory on the condition that it's absolutely not for consumption.'

Mr Kirkby admired the casket. 'If you don't mind my

asking, why aren't the toffees good enough for sale? I'm not complaining as they'd look lovely in my window, but I just can't see what's wrong with them.'

'Ah, well, our Head Confectioner, Mr Birchwood – that is to say, he *was* our head confectioner, they've let him go since this – he wore cologne on his hands while he was working on this batch. It's expressly against company regulations and he's tainted the product with it. Our director said he could taste it in the sweets and he wouldn't let them go out.'

'But what about the casket? It's very fine. Surely you must want to use that and refill it.'

'Can't be done, Mr Kirkby. Do you see that emblem?'

'Why yes, it's the lion and the unicorn.'

'It is indeed. I'll let you in on a secret, Mr Kirkby: we're expecting a royal visit to Halifax, and these sweets were a sample of what the head confectioner thought to make for the King, that's why the casket is emblazoned with the royal coat of arms. We couldn't possibly use it for anyone else so it will appear in your window for the coronation display, but that will be all. Our new confectioner will make another casket for the King.'

'King George? Here in Halifax? What an honour! And such an honour to have a casket with his coat of arms in my window. It will be a proud day for the town.'

'That it will, Mr Kirkby. That it will.'

As Mr Kirkby dismantled the coronation window display he was already planning its replacement. Halifax was still gripped by royal fever, and now the secret was out and the town knew they were getting a royal visit Mr Kirkby thought it would be prudent to plan a display which would honour the King and also tell the story of his family business; 'Kirkby's Fancy Goods Welcomes His Majesty' the display would say, and it would be resplendent in royal blue and emerald green. Oh, it would be a delight to construct.

Mr Kirkby had agreed that when he took down all of his coronation decorations he would give them to the local Brown Owl so the Brownies could put them to good use for the King's visit in July. The shop, however, would have a completely new look. Mr Kirkby had expected Brown Owl to call by that afternoon, but he had not expected half the Brownies to come with her, proffering thank you cards which they had made, and waving pocket money which they wanted to spend in the shop.

'Archibald!' Mrs Kirkby put her head of tightly wrapped curlers around the parlour door which opened into the shop and called out to her husband who, truth be told, would have known that she was there by the smell of setting lotion alone. 'Archibald, the Brownies are on their way!'

'Yes, dear. I've seen them.' Mr Kirkby sometimes wished his wife would watch their shop with the same enthusiasm she watched the road from their parlour window so that he wouldn't have to serve eight customers all at once.

'Have you got rid of that casket from the window yet?'

'I'm just doing it, dear.'

'Well, you make sure you put it well out of the way. I don't know why you insisted on poisoning them anyway. Nasty stuff to have about the place!' Mrs Kirkby's thoughts on the subject of her husband's vigilance against many-legged intruders was cut short when she saw the Brown Owl almost at the door and she ducked away back into the parlour, leaving behind only traces of hair ointment and disapproval.

Mr Kirkby quickly scooped up the casket of poisoned sweets from their velvet cushion, snipped off the attractive gold tassel on the top – he had a use for that – and put it on top of the rubbish bag beside the staff door, ready to take out to the bins in the alleyway when he had finished. Now that the casket was safely tucked into the refuse sack the incident was forgotten for him, and that was his first mistake.

Kirkby's Fancy Goods was suddenly very busy; along with the Brownies and their leader several other customers vied for the attention of the staff. Three old matrons had come in with their list of weekly orders; a harassed-looking mother was searching for a birthday gift for her daughter; and Steven Hunter, the handsome teenaged son of the wealthy Hunter family, had ostensibly come in to supervise his much younger sisters, Gracie and Lara, while they spent their pocket money, but in reality he was just there to make eyes at pretty Marilyn Parkin across the counter when she was supposed to be serving customers.

Mr Kirkby didn't mind letting Marilyn enjoy the attentions of the Hunter lad; he remembered only too well what it had been like to be young and in love, and rather than call her away to help serve customers, he himself climbed out of the window to deal with the flood of Brownies. They had brought pocket money to buy sweets, which they all wanted to pay for at the same time, and some of them wanted to take the children's toys down off the shelves to take them apart and investigate them while they waited for their leader to walk them all back to the church hall for their meeting.

In amongst the busy, noisy, happy throng, six-year-old Lara Hunter and her newly adopted sister, Gracie, both a year too young as yet to be Brownies, had seen the gold embossed lid of a casket of sweets glinting in the summer sunlight. The box had slipped from the top of the rubbish sack onto the floor and the little girls hoped they could buy it with their pocket money. They lifted it carefully into the shopping basket they were carrying together, and held out their pocket money, ready to offer it to the harassed shopkeeper behind the counter.

Most of the little girls didn't know enough maths to work out whether or not they could afford the items they wanted to buy and were calling out 'Do I have enough for this?' or 'Do I have enough for a quarter of Strawberry Creams?' The shopkeeper was attempting to carry on a conversation with the Brownie leader while also operating the till hurriedly, and he accepted that he might have given away a few free sweets by attempting to run the pocket money through the till without really checking who had paid for what and whether in fact they did have the right money.

'My wife is that excited about the visit,' Mr Kirkby told the Brownie Leader. 'I said we could just leave up the old decorations, but no, she won't have it. She says if the King passes by our window she wants him to see something fresh – she doesn't want him thinking that we've just kept up our coronation decorations.'

The Brownie Leader, delighted to be getting so much material for her own banners, thought it was too good to be true. 'But surely she'll want red, white and blue, the same as before?'

The little Hunter girls squeezed their way through the

Brownies, held up their handful of pocket money, and asked, 'Do we have enough for a pretty box of toffees?'

'Yes, yes, just a moment, you two, I'll come and help you choose one.' Then he returned to his conversation with the Brownie Leader. 'Not Mrs Kirkby, she's dressing the shop in emerald green for the Empire, and we're going to have a window display telling the story of the family business and the town.'

The little Hunter girls, having already chosen their box of confections and not needing any help choosing another, left their pocket money on the side of the counter near the till and wriggled through the throng back to their brother. They were very pleased with the pretty casket because they had been saving up to buy a thank you gift for someone who had been very kind to them both.

Steven Hunter noticed his sisters by his side and did his best to tear his eyes away from the lovely Marylin. 'Have you two got what you wanted?' he asked them.

The little girls nodded and followed him out of the shop with their purchase neatly tucked away in their basket. They called out a farewell to Mr Kirkby and he, assuming that they were coming back later when the shop was less busy, waved the little girls away, unaware that in their basket they carried the casket of deadly sweets.

Chapter Two

It was late, and the illuminated windows of Reenie's boarding house acted as a beacon to her young man, her cheerfully drunken father, and his long-suffering, peculiarly ugly horse.

'Reenie!' Her father called in a whisper loud enough to wake half the street. 'Reenie! Ruffian's thrown a shoe, Reenie.' Mr Calder hiccupped loudly and then sneezed. He was a little man and the force of both actions seemed enough to knock him off balance, but his nag, who waited with a martyr's expression, righted him with a light, well-timed head-butt. Ruffian was the master of the light, well-timed head-butt. 'Reenie! Can you come and take Ruffian?'

There was a rattling of locks, bolts, and chains before the front door of Mrs Garner's boarding house opened onto the balmy June night, heavy with the scent of lime tree blossom. It was Mrs Garner herself who opened the door; bleary-eyed, and tightly wrapped in as many layers of coats and dressing gowns as she thought appropriate for a respectable Yorkshire widow of advancing years when opening her front door at midnight. 'Peter McKenzie, whatever are you doing out of doors without a coat after dark? You'll catch your death of cold.' Mrs Garner knew Peter, of course, but she was used to seeing him call for Reenie in his smartest clothes, with his hair neatly combed. This sorry specimen was not in keeping with the Peter McKenzie she knew.

Peter looked at his sleeves in confusion, the knowledge that he had no coat only just dawning on him. 'I don't feel very well.' His lost expression made him look much younger than his nineteen years.

'You my Reenie's landlady?' Mr Calder was taking his cloth cap off his balding head and smiling politely in the general direction of the stone-fronted boarding house while leaning slowly away from it.

'Yes, but she's not home yet, Mr Calder. She's working a night shift down at the factory.' Jane Garner tried to keep her voice to a genuine whisper in consideration of the neighbours, who thought her far too lax with her boarders as it was.

'Oh.' Reenie's father's expression of disappointment was almost comical 'But I've got an 'orse, see.' He jerked up the hand which was holding Ruffian's makeshift bridle, in the manner of a marionette whose string had been pulled suddenly. Then he let it drop with a glum sigh.

Mrs Garner was a respectable woman, but she was no stranger to tipsiness. She could see that Mr Calder and young Peter wouldn't get much further that night and Mrs Garner had never in her life hardened her heart. 'You give that to me, Mr Calder.' She shuffled down the steps from her front door to the pavement in her flapping slippers, gently prised the rope from his hand and tied it around the railing above the cellar steps. 'Ruffian can bide here while you wait in the parlour.'

'No, I got a friend, see?' Mr Calder was telling his daughter's landlady as she pushed him awkwardly up the steps. 'I got a friend I know'll stand us a drink. Good old boy.' Mrs Garner didn't know if he was talking to the horse or about the friend. 'I just wanted Reenie to mind the 'orse.'

'Very wise, Mr Calder, very wise. Up the stairs now; you too, Peter.'

When Reenie arrived home an hour later she was confused to see a coat she recognized draped neatly over a hedge at the top of the hill, her father's horse in the street and the parlour lights lit down below the level of the street. Something was afoot.

'Don't wake them.' Mrs Garner intercepted Reenie as she came through the front door. 'You'll never guess who's sleeping on the parlour table.'

'Is it Peter and me dad?'

'How did you know?' Mrs Garner was helping Reenie out of her coat and hanging it up along with the coat Reenie had rescued from the hedge as she passed.

'Well, I've just found Peter's ulster in the bushes, which I thought might indicate he'd been passin' this way, and as for me dad, I can't help but feel the presence of his massive great workhorse in the middle of the street was a bit of a giveaway.'

'They said he'd thrown a shoe.' Mrs Garner was all concern and Reenie couldn't help but feel she was very lucky to have such a caring landlady.

'Thrown a strop more like – Ruffian kicks his front shoes off if he doesn't fancy a job; he thinks he's too good for farm life.' Rennie saw her father sitting at a chair in her landlady's kitchen parlour with his mouth hanging open and his cheek pressed against the tabletop. 'Come on, you.' She patted him on the shoulder. 'Time to go home to Mother. You can't sleep like that, you'll do your neck in.'

Reenie's father snorted awake for a moment, fixed his eyes on his daughter, squinted, rubbed his face, and then smiled. 'They made my daughter a manager.' He wobbled upright and proudly jabbed his finger into his own chest. '*My* daughter. *Junior Manager.*'

'Yes, Dad, I'm well aware of it. Now it's time to go home.' Reenie could see why girls whose fathers were in this state every night tired of it, but as it was only once or twice a year in her own father's case she couldn't help but find it comical. 'What have you done to my young man?' She waved an arm at Peter, who was snoring gently with his head on his folded arms and his straw-coloured, floppy hair a disorderly mop. 'I told you to bring him back in one piece.'

Mr Calder beamed with pride and told his daughter in a conspiratorial whisper, 'He's a cracking lad, he is. Cracking lad.' Then sighed contentedly back to sleep.

'Did I do the right thing?' Reenie's landlady asked with concern. 'Bringing them in to the parlour, I mean. I didn't like to let your Peter catch cold without a coat. And Mr Calder was ever so wobbly.'

'No, you did right. They're in no fit state to go home.'

At this, Peter's shoulders moved and he lifted his head very, very slowly. 'Please don't make me drink again.

13

Reenie, I don't want to drink again.' He looked sad and lost and put his head back on the cool, comfortingly stable kitchen tabletop.

'You were meant to be a good influence on m'dad! *"I'll go with him"*, you said. *"He'll only have a couple this year,"* you said. Now look at the pair of you. And what am I meant to do with the 'orse?' Reenie's questions were in vain as Peter had already begun to snore and Mrs Garner's cat was looking daggers at him from her place by the stove for making a noise while her kittens were trying to sleep.

'I didn't know your Peter drank,' Mrs Garner said.

'He doesn't, really; I think that's the trouble. Me dad asked if he could take him to the Ale Tasters' summer do. After their big do last October I thought it couldn't be any worse.' Reenie looked at her father and her young man, put her hands on her hips and huffed. 'There's me dad encouraging me to board in town so's I'm not riding back to the farm late after a night shift at the factory; there's him sayin', *"Oh no, Reenie, you're a manager now, lass. We can't have you run ragged helpin' on the farm when you've got a chance at Mackintosh's. You stay in town, don't mind us."* And I come home from a night shift, ready to crawl into me bed, and what do I find? Merry hell.'

'Should I fetch them a blanket each, do you think?' Mrs Garner's maternal instincts were strong. 'And maybe a little cushion for their heads?'

Reenie ruminated. 'All right, let's throw a blanket on each of them because I don't want the nuisance of nursing them through pneumonia, but I draw the line at a cushion.'

'What about a pitcher of water and some glasses? They

might wake up thirsty and be glad of them.' Mrs Garner shuffled busily round her kitchen-parlour in her flapping slippers, opening cupboards and humming cheerily as she looked for the tin of Carr's water biscuits, 'And just one or two little dry crackers.'

Reenie rolled her eyes 'You're soft on them, that's what you are.' But she smiled because she liked knowing that her father and her young man were in good hands. 'I'll walk the 'orse round to the factory stables and bed him down there for the night. If I'm not back in an hour you know I've fallen asleep on an 'ay bale.' Reenie checked for her latchkey in her pocket and then crept up the stairs to her own room to leave Peter's ulster on a hanger out of the way. Reenie almost missed the figure who was waiting in the open doorway at the other end of the landing. The young woman had evidently been woken by the noise downstairs and was now leaning against the door frame in her nightgown with her arms folded.

It was the factory colleague who boarded in the next room to Reenie, and she did not like to be disturbed. 'Are we quite finished for the night?' It was a sarcastically nonchalant question.

'Yes, Diana. Sorry. M'dad and Peter were just . . .' Reenie's voice trailed off; she was not known for holding back if there was an opportunity to give someone a bit of cheek, but Diana was not someone to whom anyone would dare give lip. 'I'll just go and take away the 'orse.'

As Diana turned back into her own room Reenie caught a glimpse of her orderly quarters. Diana was something of a mystery to Reenie; she was ten years older but never had gentleman callers, which always puzzled Reenie because Diana at, twenty-six, was of an age to be getting

15

serious, and she was the most beautiful girl that Reenie had ever seen. It was a mystery, too, that they were not better friends because though Diana might be older than Reenie, they had been thrown together in innumerable ways. From the moment of Reenie's arrival at the toffee factory nine months previously, they had worked together on the line; they had collaborated to help save the Norcliffe sisters from dismissal; they had been tried together at the same unjust disciplinary hearing that had nearly lost them their jobs – and they had fought to save the factory after they had watched it burn almost to the ground.

Now they were living under the same roof, but still not really friends. Reenie couldn't understand it; she seemed to make friends with everyone she met, but Diana was as distant as ever. Reenie might have put it down to Diana's forced separation from her family after the factory fire – the separation which had led her to seek lodgings – but Diana had been withdrawn even before those changes.

Diana was quiet, but never shy – she simply appeared to have little interest in anything except the gramophone records she had inherited from her father, or spending time with her young half-sister Gracie, who she visited at the home of Gracie's adoptive family every Sunday. Diana sometimes brought Gracie round to their boarding house for tea after they had been on an outing together and Reenie was hoping the little girl would be back again soon because when she was with Diana it was the only time she ever saw her fellow boarder smile.

Chapter Three

To see the Mackintosh's toffee factory from the outside
it would be difficult for a stranger to notice that anything
unusual had happened to the old Albion Mills building
in the last six months. Tens of thousands of people
regularly rattled past the factory by rail, and apart from
the telltale scar in a brighter brick where the gash in
the factory wall had been repaired, there was almost no
reminder of the terrifying fire which had nearly destroyed
the business. And if a busy traveller looked up from
their railway timetable at Halifax station and looked
across at the enormous toffee factory in the canal basin
below the platform, they would see a flash of fashionable
Art Deco offices, a steeple of a chimney in gleaming,
glazed white brick piercing the sky, a sea of white-capped
workers flooding into the gates, and rows of gritstone
Victorian mills reclaimed for the town's new industry,
disgorging scores of liveried lorryloads of Mackintosh's
Quality Street to be shipped to all four corners of the

globe. To the outsider, Mackintosh's Toffee Town appeared stronger than ever, unassailable by either competition or calamity. However, on the inside it was at breaking point; some thought they could not possibly survive the year.

Before the fire at Christmas Mackintosh's had come tantalizingly close to running the fastest confectionery production line in the world, but all that work – and, more crucially, all those machines – had been destroyed overnight. The floors which had survived were caked with thick soot, and water from the firemen's hoses had poured through their storerooms like a river. There had been no choice but to reopen their old factory on the Queen's Road. A relic of another age, the Queen's Road factory had been a partially mothballed warehouse for years, and without their machines they were forced to set up scratch lines, making their sweets by hand. The factory had called back retired married women to take up their old jobs on the hand-making lines and save the day, but they had all known that in time the factory planned to restore the old machines, line by line, and reopen the damaged factory as soon as they could.

Now the gabled production hall, where Gooseberry Cream was starch pressed and chocolate enrobed, had heard a rumble of gossip that their situation was about to change.

Emily Everard took it upon herself to spread the word during their morning tea break, striding up and down the rows of women sitting beside shut-down conveyor belts gasping down their well-earned, steaming hot cups of Assam. Mrs Everard was only a factory line worker herself, but she assumed an air of authority. 'They want to see all the married women at the end of the shift. We're to go to the canteen where there'll be an announcement.'

Young Siobhan Grimshaw looked up from her Mackintosh's monogrammed teacup with a worried expression. 'But I can't stop on at the end of the shift; I'll miss the Stump Cross tram. I've got to be home for the kids. Don't they realize what we have to do to be here? We've got lives outside of work, if they didn't know.'

Emily Everard pulled her white cotton wraparound overalls a little tighter across her capacious bosom. Emily had retired from factory life twenty years earlier, when she had left to be married, and was very proud of the fact that she could still fit into her old overalls. Her colleagues were too kind to point out that the overalls didn't fit if she had to keep pulling at them all the time. 'I wouldn't complain too loudly if I were you; rumour has it they're about to announce the first list of married women to be let go, and you don't want to sound like you're volunteering.'

'They can't be letting us go already! We've not been here five minutes.'

Old Mrs Grimshaw, mother-in-law to Siobhan, was philosophical, 'Some of us have been here five months – and they always warned us it would only be temporary. We knew this day would come.'

'Yes, but I never thought it would be so soon; I thought it would take them years to rebuild; I thought they'd need us at least until after the summer.'

'Until after you'd saved up to buy your lass a uniform for the grammar school?' Emily Everard asked.

'You heard about that?'

Emily nodded to Siobhan's mother-in-law who was packing Gooseberry Creams into cartons beside her on the production line. 'I've not heard anything else from this quarter! No one from Back Ripon Street has ever won a scholarship that I can remember – you must be very proud of her.'

'If I can't get the money for the uniform, she can't go, they've said as much.' Siobhan was keeping her eyes on Mrs Everard as she spoke, but her hands were moving with dizzying speed to pull pink, flattened card cartons from the rolling cage behind her, flick them open and fold them into shape before tucking them under her mother-in-law's elbow to be filled with sweets. 'When I sounded as though I wasn't going to be able to buy it they started to talk about withdrawing the scholarship offer.'

Emily Everard was appalled. 'They can't do that!'

'They can. Then I heard they'd lifted the marriage bar at Mack's and that they needed married women who'd worked here before to come back while they pulled together after the fire and I knew we were saved. I paid for a taxi cab, of all things, and went straight round to the school without wasting a minute and I told the head-mistress in person that I was one of the Mackintosh girls she'd heard about in the paper, and that I'd be working for Mack's again, and my daughter would wear the best uniform in the whole school.'

'What did she say to that?' Emily Everard did not like the sound of any child being excluded from a scholarship for want of a few clothes, and was already mentally composing a letter of complaint on Siobhan's behalf.

'Well, she said she'd be pleased if my daughter was as determined and resourceful as I am, and they'd be glad to see her in full winter uniform at the start of the term.'

'Well then, it'll be reyt,' Old Mrs Grimshaw said, exchanging two filled card cartons of Gooseberry Creams for empty ones.

'Only if I can get her the uniform, Mam! They have a summer uniform, a winter uniform, a gym kit uniform, and a speech day uniform! I'm on my way to the winter one, but I need another six months to save up, at least! Don't get me wrong, the money's good here and I'm not knocking it, but one month's pay packet isn't going to buy a gym kit, let alone a full uniform.'

'You're telling me.' Doreen Fairclough, a lady of Siobhan's own generation piped up from further down the conveyor. She had been almost in tears that morning as she had tried to get to work on time after her daughter had delayed her by announcing that her younger brother, Fred, had stuck a piece of bath sponge up her nose and now neither of them could get it out. The sympathy the other women had shown to her plight had given her the courage to join their conversation. 'It's almost impossible to put anything by. I'm feeding my two kids and the three next door who haven't seen a proper dinner since their dad lost his leg falling off a scaffold. I'd be feeding half the street if our Frank would let me, but he says we've got to save something to feed our two after this lot of work dries up.'

Old Mrs Grimshaw was glad of the money she could earn by being back at the factory, but for her it was about something more than the wages: for three decades she had watched with longing as other women walked through the gates of her factory to do the jobs that she had once done, and to live the life she missed so much. 'I've always known it wasn't going to last,' she said, 'and honestly, I always said I'd give my eye teeth to be back at Mack's, even if it were just one shift. I have loved every bloody minute of it, because I knew that any minute it could be taken away – but my God it hurts to know they'd let us go so easy! They don't know what it means to us to be back.'

Emily Everard leant over the conveyor belt to say confidentially to the other women, 'You know they sent Sir Harold Mackintosh hisself round to my mother's house to beg her personally to come in and work?'

Mrs Grimshaw laughed. 'Isn't she about ninety? They can't have been that desperate for staff.'

'She's seventy-six and she worked with Violet Mackintosh back in the day. She knows how to make toffee with nothing but a tea kettle and a Swiss Army Knife.'

'Did she say yes?' Siobhan was only thirty-two but even she was feeling too old to be back at work on the production line. Working a full week of packing shifts and then going home to feed and bath the kids before she staggered bone weary into bed, was tough enough on her but a woman of seventy-six?

'Of course she said yes. She nearly bit his hand off. They put her in charge of Queen's Road factory for the first two weeks of hand production and she taught forty girls how to make fudge in a barrel.'

The women smiled at the thought of someone whose love of the factory and the job went back even further than their own, getting her wish and returning to such a glorious welcome.

'I just can't bear to go.' Siobhan was shaking her head at the injustice of the idea that they could lose their jobs so easily. There were tears in the young woman's eyes and she tried to brush them away with discretion. 'I love my kids, and I'm not saying that I don't want to be at home while they're growing, but . . .'

'You don't have to explain yourself to us,' Emily Everard said, 'we know. We might be the only people who know.'

'I'd do anything for my kids – and I'm doing this for them, to put food on the table and save up for a uniform, to put something away for Christmas and pay off the doctor's bill from when my last one was born. But it's not just that . . .' Siobhan was exhausted, and the production line work was a heavy burden on top of all she had to do at home, but there was something that made her want to hang on and she knew it wasn't just the money for her daughter's school uniform.

The other young mother on the line knew what she meant: Doreen had re-joined the factory to put food on the table, but that wasn't her only reason. 'It feels like everyone's taking from us – and God knows Mackintosh's are taking just as much from us as everyone else – but when I'm on the line with you lot I don't think about that. When I'm on the line I'm more myself than I am anywhere else. There's something I'm *good* at; I've got a skill and it's like—'

'You know what my mother said it was like?' Emily Everard pulled her overalls tighter as she stuck her chin out with dignity. 'She said it was like witchcraft, turning sugar powder into toffee gold.'

'She's right, though,' Doreen said. 'It's like being able to do magic.'

'I hope to God they don't send us in the first round.' Mrs Grimshaw kept her eyes fixed on the line that she didn't need to see with her eyes to work quickly. 'I just want one more day.'

Chapter Four

Laurence Johns was nervous. He had been a Head of Department at Mackintosh's for some time and meetings like this one in the Mackintosh's boardroom were a common occurrence for him, but his department was International Affairs and he knew that he had been interfering in domestic matters which were not within his jurisdiction. This meeting was not a routine one, and he baulked at the thought that he was about to be forced to admit to his colleagues that he had made a rash decision which was putting their employees into immediate danger.

Departmental managers filed into the oak-panelled boardroom, some with their private secretaries, some with junior managers who were eager to take notes and prove themselves to the very people who might advance their careers. When the director was quite sure that everyone was present, he thanked them for attending at short notice and proceeded to business.

'We have run,' said Mr Hitchens, making a careful steeple of his fingers as he rested his elbows on the shining surface of the mahogany board table, 'into some difficulties which we need to address.'

Amy Wilkes looked over her delicately rimmed spectacles at him and asked, 'What kind of difficulties?'

The director gestured to Laurence to answer, which threw Laurence into renewed panic before he said, 'Difficulties of supply.'

There was a strained silence as the senior Mackintosh's managers looked around at each other's faces to see who looked the most like they already knew what was happening. There were a lot of puzzled expressions and that prompted more muttered concern.

Laurence continued, 'We have to cut supply from our main Irish factory.'

A young man in an over-starched collar who was taking notes for the factory's Chief Accountant, piped up, 'But what does that have to do with us? That's the Irish factory manager's problem, not ours.'

'It *is* our problem; they were making almost a third of our Quality Street.' Mr Hitchens' words silenced the room.

Major Fergusson looked very grave indeed and smoothed down his moustache with thumb and forefinger, before saying, not unkindly, 'I'm sure it can't have escaped your notice that Great Britain is in the midst of a trade war with the Irish Free state and has been for nearly five years. It has been mentioned in the newspapers. After the Easter Rising in 1916 and the Great War, there was so much anti-English feeling in Ireland that any English produce, including Mackintosh's toffee, would be seized by the general public, taken out into the street, and burned with the aid of paraffin. How could they possibly have made our Quality Street without drawing attention to themselves?'

Laurence Johns explained. 'Mr Sinclair, a Mackintosh cousin from America, is managing the exports of the toffees made at the Irish factory and masking the fact that the factory is under the ownership of English proprietors. Mr Sinclair has been very good at maintaining supply without revealing where the produce is going. The reason we asked you all to this extraordinary meeting is because we have been sent photographs this morning by the Irish factory manager by special courier.'

Laurence took the file of photographs from the secretary sitting beside him and tossed them carelessly across the table. The photographs had been enlarged to give as much detail as possible and showed the exterior of Mackintosh's principle factory in Ireland. On the walls, painted in huge letters, were the words 'Burn everything English except their coal'.

Amy Wilkes was a shrewd bird and could see the direction their problem was taking. 'So local people know the factory is secretly owned by Englishmen and the American manager is just a front?'

Johns took a sip of water and wished that he could have explained this in a written memo without having to face his colleagues. 'After the accident here at the plant we had to take desperate measures to ensure supply which is why we chose to have a Quality Street line set up in Ireland. We did the same in Ireland as in Halifax: we lifted the marriage bar and brought back skilled married women to work on a temporary line. They've made enormous sacrifices to save Quality Street – and we've put them in danger.'

The starched collar was not following as quickly as Amy Wilkes. 'Why would this risk the safety of the workers in Dublin? What's so dangerous about toffee making?'

'Because if Mackintosh's toffees can be seized from shops and burned in protest, what's to stop a raid on the factory itself?' Major Fergusson waved the picture of the Inchicore factory. 'Look at the photograph, man. It's a direct threat!'

Johns nodded. 'We had to stop production yesterday. Word got out that the product they were making was by appointment to the royal household and we couldn't allow the risk any longer, so we need additional girls to work at toffee making here in Halifax now that the Inchicore factory has had to return to normal production levels.'

Amy Wilkes narrowed her eyes. 'Just how many extra girls do you need us to find?'

'Five hundred and ninety.'

Amy could not respond at first – the number was too great to comprehend. If he'd said *twenty* she'd have told him he was expecting too much, but this many was impossible. They were already employing married women who they'd taken out of retirement as an emergency measure, and although there were plenty of unemployed labouring men in Jarrow and Clydeside, they weren't trained confectioners, and they weren't moving to Halifax in the morning to work for something as paltry as a woman's wage. Amy Wilkes shook her head. 'That's impossible, I'm afraid. We'll need time to recruit and train them up and even then we've taken on every girl we can get in Halifax.'

'What about the married women? I heard that they were being let go—'

'I don't know where you heard that.'

'News travels fast in the factory. You're making an announcement to them after the late shift tonight.'

'*That's* not what we're announcing. We have a bigger problem than you thought.'

'I don't mind that you got blotto with m' dad, that's not the problem – it's what you *said* when you were blotto.' Reenie was brushing down her horse in the factory stable and looking over his withers at Peter McKenzie who was sitting on a hay bale in a shady corner.

Peter was looking uncharacteristically sorry for himself and somewhat confused. 'But I'd never say anything bad to you—'

'You hardly said two words to me at all, but you said an awful lot to m' dad.'

'I don't really remember what I said to your dad. I know I only said good things about you, Reenie, I definitely sang your praises.'

'And?' Reenie folded her arms and raised her eyebrows to indicate that there was another matter which he really ought to remember.

'And I think I drank your health?' Peter looked worried; he rarely drank, and although he vaguely remembered spending a happy evening with Reenie's father, he was worried about what kind of a fool he might have made of himself, if only because he hoped he hadn't brought embarrassment to Reenie.

'And you asked m' dad for permission to take my hand in matrimony. Not only did you ask my dad's permission, but you asked everyone else in the pub what *they* thought. I'm getting a lot of comments on the factory floor and I am not best pleased.'

Peter's face blushed red. 'Oh, I . . . I didn't—'

Reenie interrupted his surprised and embarrassed stammering 'Do I need to remind you, Peter McKenzie, that I'm not seventeen until October, you're not twenty until August, we've not been walking out five months – and I'm not leaving my job at Mack's willy-nilly for a goose's bridle!'

'But we could have a long engagement?'

Reenie pursed her lips in disapproval. 'Why are you in such a hurry? Is this because you think I'll go to Blackpool with you if we're engaged? Because I've told you that I'm not having any hanky-panky until we're married!'

'No, no, I never thought that. When I said we should go to Blackpool I was never thinking of suggesting that – I just thought you'd like Blackpool. You could bring a friend as a chaperone, I wasn't suggesting—'

'Then why are you in such a hurry to be engaged if you're willing to have a long engagement?'

Peter was earnest. 'I just want everyone to know that I think you're wonderful.'

Reenie's shoulders relaxed a little and she felt a wave of affection for her young man. She softened her tone and said, 'Peter, that's not what you've made everyone in the Old Cock and Oak think; you've made them all think I'm in the family way, and now I've got to explain to everyone I see that I don't have a bun in the oven, I've just got a very healthy appetite.'

Peter's face went from pink to white as the blood

drained from it in embarrassment when he realized what he'd done. 'I'm sorry, Reenie. I didn't mean to—'

Reenie waved her hand to indicate it was forgiven and forgotten so long as he realized what he'd done. 'How's your head?'

'Awful. I only meant to have one, but they wanted me to try a bit of all of them.'

'That's the Ale Tasters' do, all right. You get down to the canteen and get a good rasher of bacon down you.'

'I don't think I could ever eat again.'

'Nonsense, you're just not used to the drink, that's all. Trust me and go and ask if they've got any bacon left and a bit of fried bread; it'll see you right.'

Peter raised bleary eyes to Reenie and looked even greener around the gills. 'I've got to go onto the line in ten minutes. I don't think my head can take the noise.'

'Which line, and what do you need to do? If it's observing and taking notes, you could always wait until this afternoon?'

'No, I'm meant to be teaching this week's new starters. I've got a dummy line set up and Women's Employment are bringing me twenty giggly fourteen-year-olds to learn how to deliver cellophane rolls to a wrapper.'

Reenie felt even more sorry for her young man. He was such an amiable, well-spoken, responsible gentleman; turning up to work with a hangover was as unlike him as she could imagine. 'You're in luck because I happen to know that it's Diana Moore what's bringing over the minnows to be trained, and my morning is all report writing from notes I've already done, so why don't you take my reports and I'll take your class and square it with Diana? She won't be fussed who teaches the young ones, so long as they're taught right. In fact, I think she prefers it when I teach them because she knows they don't listen to you.'

'Don't they listen to me?'

'No, they're too busy making eyes at you.'

Peter's colour rose again with embarrassment. 'You don't think Major Fergusson knows, do you? I wouldn't want anyone to think I encouraged it!'

'Everyone knows you don't encourage it, and Major Fergusson thinks it's very funny. I shouldn't worry; as long as Major Fergusson is head of department we'll both be reyt. I should think he's got a couple of years until retirement.' But there Reenie was wrong.

Chapter Five

'I demand to see Major Fergusson. I'm the daughter of a very important person and I've got a letter from Lady Mackintosh.' The arrogant girl at the factory gate was ignoring Diana Moore, who had come down from the factory offices to see what she wanted, and instead was speaking beyond her to the factory watchman.

The watchman, who had only stepped out into the doorway of his cabin to admire Diana as she walked past, was regretting his move. On the one hand, he couldn't ignore a request from someone with a letter from his employer's wife, but on the other hand, everyone knew that if you crossed Diana Moore she might chew you up and spit you out as mincemeat. The toffee factory watchman looked from one threat to the other with his mouth hanging open in nervous indecision.

Diana decided to put the man out of his misery and said, 'Go on, then. You've got a telephone in there, haven't you?' Her voice sounded intoxicating in contrast to that of the girl with the letter and she nodded to the shabby interior of his cabin with the grace and dignity of a monarch. 'Call the switchboard. See if they can get hold of the Major.'

The watchman looked as though he thought this might be some sort of trap, but he went back inside and picked up the heavy Bakelite receiver.

The girl with the letter was evidently not from a factory family; the girls whose mothers and aunts had done this job years before them kitted their daughters out with shoes or clogs appropriate for the hard slog on the line, and they had pinned back their hair tightly to stop it from catching in the machinery in the event they were too silly to avoid getting too close to it. The factory lasses wore plain cotton dresses under their white wraparound factory overalls, and they had the air of girls who have been raised with this day in mind since they were old enough to talk. The girl with the letter looked as though she'd fallen over in the chemist shop and landed face first in the make-up counter. She wore cheap, ready-to-wear copies of ugly, high fashion clothes, and she had plucked and repainted her eyebrows into such an unnatural shape and shade that her expression had that Jean Harlow look of fixed surprise.

The two young women studied the watchman through the window of his gatehouse hut as he made enquiries on his telephone, waited, spoke again, and then turned to them both in surprise while holding the telephone receiver at his shoulder. 'He says he wants to talk to you.'

The girl with the letter smirked in triumph and pushed her way forward but the watchman shook his head and said, 'Not you' and nodded towards Diana.

Diana moved inside the hut and reached out both hands for the telephone, turning her back to the window so that she could not be overheard. 'Major?'

'Ah, Diana!' Major Fergusson bellowed down the telephone from his office in the factory. 'Just the girl I needed to speak to! Fancy you being there too.'

'Yes. Fancy.'

'I hear that there is a young lady at the watchman's gate, the daughter of a very important person and she's been asking to see me personally to ask about a job in my department as a junior manager.' Major Fergusson was always pleased to encourage young people into the rewards of factory work, but he did not conduct impromptu employment interviews. 'Of course I'm flattered, but . . . well, you know that we have no vacancies in my department, but there are plenty on the production line. Could you, er . . . Would you mind awfully . . .?'

Diana frowned. 'I've already spoken to her, Major, and turned her down for a job. She refused to accept my word for it but said she'd wait until she could speak to you. And she's not the daughter of a very important person,' Diana said as she looked at the girl's letter of application. 'She's the daughter of the vicar at Stump Cross. She's applied to me twice and been rejected twice. The only reason her second letter to us saw the light of day is because it was accompanied by a missive from Lady Mackintosh, but I've looked at that letter and her ladyship doesn't ask us to give the girl a junior manager job – it's the girl herself who has the temerity to do that. Lady Mackintosh simply asks if we have a vacancy for "a girl with no factory experience". Lady Mackintosh knows very well that this girl is taking a liberty, but she's too well-mannered to say it in so many words.'

Major Fergusson was only too familiar with this sort of political minefield; many was the time when the factory had been forced to find a position for a young man whose father or uncle had local influence, only to discover that the lad was utterly useless. Sometimes they could let the young person go, but sometimes they were stuck with them for years on end, a drain on resources at best, and a thorn in their side at worst. 'What does the girl say? Does she offer some reason why she would be suited to the more senior position?'

Diana was sarcastic. 'Yes, she does. Principally, that she stayed on at school a long time and that she's a member of the middle classes. She thinks that this entitles her to leapfrog all the girls with real experience of factory work.'

Major Fergguson tried to assume the best of this determined new applicant. 'Oh, come now, there must be some other reasons why she would have the audacity to suggest we consider her for this kind of position at her age? Perhaps she's nervous of requesting factory work because she's worried she is too delicate for it. Perhaps she admires the physical strength of the girls in the factory and is simply too humble to suggest we start her off there.' The Major sounded more cheerful now that he had found a positive light to cast on the situation, but it was clearly not washing with Diana, so he said, 'We can't offer a junior manager job, but as I understand it we are very much in need of workers on the line. I'm sure that we can find a place on the Jaffa Toffee line. What do you think? If she's remarkable enough to warrant a manager's position one day, she'll work her way up in no time at all and the experience of the line will be grist to her mill. What is the girl's name?'

'Verity Dunkley,' Diana turned over the letter of application. 'But she prefers to be known as Dolly.'

'Oh dear, oh dear.' The Major's tone changed completely.

'Is something the matter, Major?'

The Major twitched his moustaches at the other end of the line. 'Well, this is most embarrassing. She applied for a position before and was seen by Mrs Roth before Mrs Roth was transferred to the German factory.'

Diana didn't dare to think what might have happened. Mrs Roth had been the most hated overlooker at Mackintosh's, and Diana's arch nemesis, until she took a transfer to the Mackintosh's troubled toffee factory in Dusseldorf. Mrs Roth was a bitter old tartar and it would not have surprised Diana if she'd given this Dolly Dunkley an unreasonably hard time. Diana's thoughts softened towards the girl; her letter might not be temerity at all, but rather a brave attempt to show some self-confidence after a barraging by Rabid Roth.

'Yes, as I remember she was very rude to Mrs Roth, very rude indeed. Snubbed her when she discovered that she was in the Salvation Army and refused to continue her interview with an overlooker, insisting on being seen by someone of a higher rank. Mrs Roth was most upset by the girl and didn't rate her abilities at all.'

Diana couldn't believe her ears; Frances Roth wasn't someone who took a slight lying down, and this sounded like it must have been quite a match. 'I suppose we have two questions: are we so desperate for workers that we will employ someone who is this badly behaved – and if we do, where are we to put her? I'm tempted to take her on at the lowest grade just because I don't want us to get caught up in a never-ending cycle of letters of complaint and recommendation just because a vicar's daughter wants a factory job and won't take no for an answer, but I also don't think Mrs Wilkes would thank us for taking on a troublemaker.'

The Major hummed down the telephone line in thought. 'I think you're quite right; we don't have time at present to fight a war of correspondence and if we don't give her a chance we might be caught up in one. She's young, and we were *all* troublemakers when we were young. Let's give her every possible chance and start her right at the very bottom, allowing her to work her way up. You've got some minnows starting soon, haven't you? Put her in with the youngest girls, on the easiest job, with the maximum training there's time for. We'll soon know what she's made of.'

Diana had personal reason to be glad that the Major was so compassionate towards even the most troublesome young employees, having been one of the troublemakers he had taken under his wing years ago, but if this Dunkley girl took advantage of the Major, Diana would personally see to her downfall.

'Follow me.' Diana summoned Dolly Dunkley and turned to walk back into the factory. The girl with the letter smirked in victory, clearly believing that the telephone conversation with the Major – which she had not been able to overhear – had involved a dressing down for Diana.

Diana Moore did not care if Dolly Dunkley thought she had scored a moral victory. She knew that she would learn her own place – and Diana's – soon enough. Diana was admired and feared in equal measure and she knew that almost every girl on the production line wished they had her life and that many of the men, young and old alike, wished they had the courage to ask her to a dance. Diana, on the other hand, hated the easy life she now led, working as a junior manager in the Women's Employment Department and living in a clean, respectable boarding house where she was safe, and cared for – and so very, very lonely.

The factory corridors which Diana had walked daily for the last decade felt familiar, but there was no comfort in them any more. Diana was sickened by the sight of everything and, no matter how hard she threw herself into her new work, the desperate pain she carried with her seeped into everything she saw and drained life of all colour and hope.

She had lost the love of her life, and she couldn't bear it. Six years earlier, when she was a carefree and careless nineteen-year-old, she had fallen pregnant with the child of a young man she had always known was trouble. That young man had been killed at Christmas and she had been emotionally unprepared for all the things she would feel at his loss – but he was not the love of her life. The child they had made, the child whom she had hidden and passed off as her half-sister with the help of her step-mother, the child she had nursed through illness and worked herself to the bone to keep, the little girl who was now known as Gracie Hunter was her everything – and she had lost her forever.

Calamity upon calamity had led to the loss of Diana's home, her stepmother, and her means of keeping Gracie with her. She had always known that their life together couldn't last forever, and she had never expected to be able to keep her as long as she had, but when the time came to give her up it had been worse than she could have ever imagined. The judge and the clerk of the court had known that she was Gracie's true mother, but to everyone else, including her own daughter, she had kept up the pretence that she was a concerned older sister, with a sister's love. The family who adopted Gracie were kind and wealthy and had children of their own, were able to give Gracie all the things that Diana could not: siblings, toys, pretty clothes, and clean air to breathe. The Hunter family had even been kind enough to adopt Diana, in their own way. They had invited her to visit their happy, rowdy house in a better part of Halifax every Sunday and they treated her as an extended family member so Diana lived for Sundays.

Now it was Monday morning, and Diana Moore walked against the flow of cotton capped girls on their way down the factory corridor to their shift. Dolly Dunkley walked beside her and Diana doubted she would last until dinner time.

Chapter Six

'All right, you rabble, simmer down. This isn't a real production line, it's a dummy line. This is where we run dummy sweets made of plaster through a new machine to test how the line works before we ramp up with real toffees and real speed.'

Reenie Calder was patient with the new girls; she remembered only too well what it had been like for her on her first day at the factory and she could feel the excitement of the new starters; they might be nervous, but they knew how lucky they were to be getting a chance at Mackintosh's. The difference between Reenie and these girls was that when Reenie had started work at Mack's the previous year she had been sixteen, and these girls were only fourteen-year-olds who had left school at Easter. It felt even more important to impress upon them how to work on the line safely before they reached it.

'Excuse me?' The much older girl with too much make-up on who Diana had brought in at the last minute waved her hand at Reenie while she interrupted her. 'I'm not here for all this rubbish. Just give me my job and I'll start.'

Diana, who had stayed to help Reenie supervise the new girls, feigned surprise. 'Worked in the factory before, have you?'

'No, of course not. Do I look like a factory lass?' She looked like a tart's handbag turned inside out, but Diana didn't give any indication that she thought this, or that she was insulted by the insinuation that there was anything the matter with looking like a factory lass. 'I stayed on at the grammar school until I'd matriculated. I would have thought it was obvious that I'd had an *education*.'

I'll give you an education, Diana thought to herself, and turned on a kind smile which almost reached her sparkling eyes. The younger girls appeared both impressed and nervous of the 'educated' young woman who was answering back, and Diana wanted that nipped in the bud. The Major might think it was worth giving Dolly Dunkley a trial, but Diana would be blowed if she'd let her get away with murder. 'If you don't want to listen to what Reenie has to teach you, then I'm happy for you to be taken straight down to the line. I'm sure it will be enlightening for these other girls to watch you work.'

Dolly Dunkley was so conceited that she believed it *would* be enlightening for the younger girls. They would see how simple it was for an educated young lady to pick up something as base as factory piece-work. The working classes made such a meal of these things as far as Dolly was concerned.

Reenie didn't like it. She cared about what happened

to these new girls, and she was the one who had spent months trying to persuade everyone who would listen that they ought to be using the dummy lines to teach the new girls before they went onto a line so that they wouldn't be thrown in at the deep end. However, Diana was ten years her senior and she knew that she had the final say in the matter. Reenie called out to the assembled girls, 'All right, we're off down the Harrogate Toffee line, and I want you to watch closely because you'll learn more from watching the other girls at work this morning than you've ever learnt in your life.'

Mary Norcliffe was working the Harrogate Toffee line with a level of skill unusual for a nineteen-year-old girl. The older girls did tend to be more competent than the younger ones, but Mary was by far the fastest worker on her line. She was not in a good mood that morning – if Mary could ever have been said to be in a good mood; she had overslept and felt infinitely worse for it. The morning tea break was fast approaching, and she was watching the painted tin hands of the cream enamelled clock with bone weariness. Mary was seated at a line which had, in part, been designed by her friend Reenie Calder. While the factory was recovering from the fire which had nearly destroyed it before Christmas a great many of their production lines were still being run entirely by hand, but here and there new lines had been established with new machines, and they were faster than anything the factory had seen before the fire.

Mary was working at two of the Harrogate Toffee twist-wrapping machines simultaneously, keeping them running with the grace of a magician making substance out of nothing. As ginger and lemon flavoured toffees whizzed naked down the narrow conveyor belt towards her machines, she juggled the rolls of gleaming foil and sparkling cellophane which had to be changed on each machine every few minutes, and the cartons brimming with finished toffees which the machine would disgorge. Mary's assistant had to dart back and forth from the cages at the edge of the production line to fetch fresh rolls of foil and cellophane, take the empty card inners of the spent rolls to the rubbish hoppers beside the cages, scoop up the cartons of wrapped toffees to stack on the pallets by the goods hoist – and try not to get in Mary's way while doing so.

Not only had Mary timed her machine to run in perfect, overlapping synchronicity, but each of the girls on her line had timed their machines to run in a wave with their neighbours, creating a perfect pattern of work. It was only possible because they all knew *exactly* what they were doing and loved it.

When Dolly Dunkley arrived on their line, Mary was just turning her stool on its side to sit down and take her morning tea. Like the machines on the line themselves, each of the workrooms had timed their own tea break to begin as the one next door ended, so that the tea ladies with their trolleys of boiling hot tea urns and soft iced buns would be able to deliver their wares to the girls with the same precision that the serving assistants delivered rolls of foil to their machine operators.

'Betty! Betty! I can see you!' The cry of a girl on the overhead balcony caught the attention of the production girls down on the line who had stopped the machines and were just settling themselves for a well-earned break.

Looking down on them from the iron staircase and viewing gallery, which ran around the top of the work-room, were a score of fourteen-year-old new girls on their first day, getting their first glimpse of a real factory line after so many years of hearing about life on them from everyone in the town. Some of the girls saw younger sisters, neighbours, or friends who waved down to them with enthusiasm and cried their names, others saw re-inforcements and were glad they'd soon have more help on the line because they were all run ragged and there was only so much overtime work a body could take.

'Mary, you've got a new assistant on the line.'

Mary turned abruptly around to find Diana almost at her side, with a tarty-looking girl in tow.

'Can she keep up? My assistant is pretty good and it took me a long while to train her – I don't want to swap her if I can help it.'

'It's only for a partial shift.' Diana turned to Dolly Dunkley, who was pulling back her shoulders and smirking; she looked as though she was enjoying the attention she was getting from the new girls up on the balcony and the suspicious girls on the factory floor. 'Dunkley, I'm going to give you a chance to change your mind. Do you really want to try to keep up with Mary on your first day?'

'I don't see why not.' Dolly cast a sly look at her audi-ence; she clearly wanted to showboat. 'Do I just do the same thing as these other girls were doing when we came in?'

There was a flicker of a smile on Diana's composed face when she heard Dolly use the word 'just'. 'Yes. That's all there is to it.' Diana was walking slowly backwards towards the exit, the beautiful iron-rimmed irises of her eyes fixed on Dolly's piggy ones. Diana had seen the time on the clock and knew what was going to happen next.

'I really can't see what all the fuss is about,' Dolly laughed and at the same time a whistle blew and the girls who had been at their tea breaks whipped their stools into the air, spun them back onto their feet in perfect synchronicity and restarted their machines in a cascade motion; each with an eye on the girl to the left of her, timing the motion of the machines perfectly. The assistants sprang into action, waiting with their first rolls of foil and cellophane like sprinters at the start line of a race. 'Hang on,' Dolly called out in exasperation over the noise of the machines, 'I wasn't ready; we need to start again.'

No one listened to Dolly's whining, and the machines whirred on, their operators building up speed and their assistants darting back and forth to points around the factory floor that confused Dolly and irritated her because they moved too quickly for her to understand the drill. Mary held out her hand for her first roll of cellophane, ready to make the changeover, but Dolly huffed and mouthed something indecipherable. Mary gave her short shrift and gesticulated angrily in the direction of the cage where the rolls of cellophane were kept, mouthing the word 'Go!' and throwing a look of irritation up at the gallery where Reenie and Diana watched along with the gaggle of new girls.

Dolly sighed and turned her back on Mary to mouth to the balcony with casual irritation that Mary wasn't listening to her, that they should start again. The minnows appeared sympathetic to Dolly, but Reenie and Diana were impassive.

Behind Dolly a problem was building up on the line; the reason the machines were all timed to run out of cellophane or foils at different moments was so that the steady supply of toffees running down the conveyor towards the wrapping machines would never build up a backlog. If one of the machines stopped wrapping toffees briefly while it was shut down for a roll change, the other machines would pick up the excess.

Mary leapt forward to catch the attention of the assistant on the next pair of machines along from hers; she could see that Dolly was floundering and turned to another who was at the cages, tucked her fingers under her front teeth and whistled loudly enough to pierce through the noise of the machines. The assistant clapped her hands at the girl by the cages to indicate she wanted her to throw her one of the rolls of cellophane which was there and it came soaring gracefully through the air like a golden bird. The assistant caught it, passed it to Mary who went immediately to the changeover on her machine, while the assistant indicated that the girl at the cages should throw her more of the rolls of cellophane and foil. However, the patch of gum arabic, which held the end of the roll in place came loose, and so did the roll of cellophane, unravelling like a streamer at a party and touching down across several feet of dusty floor. The assistant girl knew that the roll was now not clean enough to use, so kicked it under the nearest pallet to clear up into the rubbish hopper later. In the meantime she could see that she'd have to do her best to assist both her usual machine operator and Mary at the same time, although it couldn't last for long as the pile of finished cartons of toffees would soon pile up to a point which would make Mary's work impossible.

Dolly finally deigned to start work. Reluctantly, with a look of distaste on her heavily painted face, she picked up a small carton of finished, wrapped toffees and carried them to the place where one of the other assistants was carrying hers. This resulted in a telling-off from the other assistant who pointed out that she was taking her cartons to the wrong place.

Dolly looked to the gallery where the younger girls were now showing her far less sympathy. They were muttering to one another, and what Dolly could not hear was that they were all talking about what they would have done in her place. *Why doesn't she take two cartons to the pallet instead of one? Why is she doing everything so slowly? If she's going to stand still why doesn't she watch the other girls to see if there's a pattern to what they're doing and then imitate it? Does she realize how much money she's costing everyone in piece rates? Does she even care what she's doing to everyone else's wage packet?* As the minnows muttered Reenie looked to Diana to see if she was ready to stop this madness; Diana was not.

Dolly decided to keep working, but at a pace which sent a message to everyone that they ought to have stopped when she told them to. She got in the way of assistants coming back from the cages and tried to take their rolls of cellophane and foils from them and send them back to get more for themselves. Dolly slowed everyone and everything down while Mary and the other assistants did their best to work over the top of her. The overlooker came down from her high chair and took over the place on the line where Dolly was meant to be, but it was too late: the backlog of naked toffees had snowballed to the point where the overlooker was forced to admit defeat and press the button which would shut down the line and trigger a partial shutdown of the toffee-making line in the next workroom.

Shutdowns happened all the time, but they were an annoyance to everyone and cost the company money. The overlooker called up to Diana, 'I hope you're going to take this one on your department!'

Diana nodded. She showed none of the emotion of the overlooker and nor did the emotion of the room appear to touch her. 'Report it as a training exercise and mark it down to me.' Diana was not in the habit of wreaking havoc on orderly production lines, but she was confident that every one of the girls watching from the gallery would tell their friends about this and word would get around that you ignored the training you were offered at your peril. The machines had died down, but there was now the noise of the angry girls on the shop floor to compete with. Diana turned quietly to Reenie and said, 'Can you fix this one while they watch? I want them to see how fast you can work when you're not just keeping pace with everyone else.'

'But I'd need to be more than fast to pick all this up! I need to get Betsy Newman to move across to the—'

'Yes, yes, yes.' Diana waved her hand dismissively. 'Go and do whatever it is you that do and I'll make sure they watch and learn. Send Dolly back up – and don't be kind to her because she doesn't deserve it.'

'Oh, but you can't tell me not to be kind to someone.

That's unnatural. She might look thunder on the outside, but I bet on the inside she's right sorry.'

'I forbid you to show her any mercy, Reenie. And tell Mary I want to see her in the Employment office in her dinner hour; I need to speak with her.'

'I bet she'll want a word with you an' all after this one. She'll be spitting feathers. I'd batten down the hatches, if I were you – and whatever it is, save it a few days till she's got over this; you don't want to poke Mary when she's cross.' But then Reenie remembered who she was talking to and wondered if perhaps Mary ought to stay out of Diana's way. Mary was known for her fiery temper, but Diana was known for an icy one.

'You tell her I want to see her. I've got a surprise for her.'

Down on the production line, Dolly Dunkley was sulking. Diana watched with interest as the girl snatched a toffee from the stationary conveyor belt, screwed up the wrapper and threw it under the pallet and stuck the toffee in her mouth while looking daggers at her new colleagues. There was only a moment before the girls on the production line turned on Dolly in rage and indignation: how dare she take a toffee to eat when it was forbidden to eat on the line, and how dare she throw her litter on the floor? Diana thought Reenie would be lucky to get Dolly out of the workroom alive, after this, but if she did, then Diana knew *exactly* where she wanted to put Dolly. If she didn't hand in her notice before the day was out, then Diana had a job for Dolly to do, and Diana was going to enjoy watching her do it.

Chapter Seven

'Do you remember old Mrs Todmorden?' Diana did not give Mary Norcliffe the opportunity to complain about the fracas with Dolly Dunkley when the former stormed into the Women's Employment office during her dinner hour as requested. Diana did not believe in explaining herself if it could possibly be avoided; in fact, Diana did not believe in speaking at all if it could be avoided, and so she launched straight into her business with the younger girl.

'Is she all right?' Mary had just been on the point of opening her mouth to say something in anger when the mention of the old lady took the wind out of her sails. A look of dread passed over her pale face and she asked, 'Nothing's happened to her, has it?'

It was typical of Mary, Diana thought to herself, that she would worry automatically that something was wrong without any evidence to indicate it. Diana sighed and indicated that Mary should sit in one of the empty pine chairs beside her neatly ordered, but busy, desk. Diana had a pile of reference requests waiting for her to write to what seemed like every bank, boarding house, and building society in the district; then a meeting to take minutes at for Mrs Wilkes; she hoped Mary's worries could be dealt with more quickly than usual. 'There's nothing wrong with Mrs Todmorden; quite the contrary, in fact. She's not stopped banging on about how Harold Mackintosh went to her house and begged her to show you all how to make toffee in a barrel.'

'It was fudge in the barrel, not toffee. The toffee we did on—'

'In all honesty, I don't care. The important thing is that she rated you highly. She's still talking about you, and I'm in a fix, Mary. You know they sacked old Birchy the head confectioner for spoiling the toffees with his cologne? Well, Herr Baum, one of the confectioners from the German factory, has come over to fill in for three months and I have to find a new assistant for him. I'm looking at you.'

Mary slumped in the office chair and looked lost, her factory whites crumpling as she slouched her shoulders and crossed her arms in thought. 'Well, I don't know who you should choose. I mean, all the girls who worked with Mrs Todmorden did quite well and—'

'I don't want you to advise me on who to hire, you dummy! I want *you* to take the job. I need someone who I know will work fast, listen with their ears and not their mouth, and learn everything he's got to teach. You're reliable and I think he'd like the way you work.'

'But I'd have to leave Bess to work on her own and I need to stay on the line so that when my sister comes back to work I can keep an eye on her.'

'And how long will that be? She's been playing the invalid at home since Christmas—' this was perhaps uncharitable of Diana; Bess had been injured in the car crash which caused the factory fire, and although she was lucky not to have been killed, her injuries were still sufficient to warrant a stay in hospital and a long convalescence, 'and if she ever does come back how long is she gonna' last on the line before she's caught slacking like she did when we were all working the same line together? You can't risk helping her again, Mary, because if you're caught this time you'll both lose your jobs, and Reenie and I aren't on the line with you any more to tell you to watch yourself. This is a chance to do something you're good at and that no one else round here can, frankly.'

Mary appeared lost in thought for a moment, and anyone passing the glass-panelled partition which separated the office from the corridor would have thought that the stern but beautiful office manager was giving bad news to the factory lass in her crumpled overalls and tough work boots. They had the look of strangers negotiating an unpaid bill, not friends of some years who had spent one night last December believing all they held dear was lost, and building new lives together under the same factory roof in the months that followed. Mary said, 'That can't be true; we work in Toffee Town, there has to be more people who can assist the head confectioner. There's Mrs Todmorden herself, for starters.'

'Mrs Todmorden is older than God's dog – and the fact she lived long enough to teach you is one of the miracles of life that I will never pretend to comprehend.'

Diana fixed Mary with her steely eyes. 'You've got the skills necessary to do the job, so make the most of this chance – it might never come again. It'll pay better than your work on the line and if you pass up on this because you want to chaperone Bess I will not be best pleased with you.' Diana knew what she had to say to get Mary to take the job. 'If you leave it to me I'll find a job for her that will keep her out of trouble, but you have to leave it to me to put her where I think is best; I don't want you fussing about her when you should be working.'

Mary wrestled in her heart with all her nameless objections and realized the wisdom of the older girl's words. 'All right,' she said, and a flush of embarrassment made the strawberry mark which ran down her cheek like a crimson teardrop contrast even more strongly with her calico-pale skin and the violet circles below her eyes. 'Thank you.'

Mary excused herself; she needed to eat quickly and get back to the line before the whistle blew for the afternoon shift, and while the factory was flooded with so many extra workers with the rebuilding, it was near impossible to get into the canteen to eat. Mary would run all the way down to the old stables to sit and eat sandwiches she had made alongside her friend Reenie and Reenie's young man, Peter. Mary found herself looking forward to her chance to retreat to that quiet, safe place away from the bustle of work, where she could discuss what was happening to her. She pulled her shapeless white mobcap over her shapeless black hair and rose to leave the employment office. 'For the record, that Dolly girl wants sackin'.'

'So does the Prime Minister, but we've all got our crosses to bear – yours is Dolly Dunkley and the nation's is Neville Chamberlain.' Diana privately planned to make

Dolly Dunkley rue the day she'd ever been rude to her, but she didn't need to share that with Mary Norcliffe.

Mary slunk away like a guilty thing, even though she had just been given compliments, assurance, and good news. And Diana hoped to the God she didn't believe in that she could keep Bess from the kind of trouble she'd been in before. Diana had an idea how, but it wasn't going to be easy.

Chapter Eight

Reenie was sticky from her day in the factory. Unusually for her she was leaving early in the afternoon before most of her colleagues had finished their shifts, but she had tried to help with a blockage in a sugar siphon and had ended up covered down one side in powdered sugar, and Major Fergusson had let her leave earlier than usual to go home to Mrs Garner's boarding house to wash it out of her hair before it became too uncomfortable.

It wasn't often that Recnie left early. In fact, she usually stayed very late indeed. Only last December she'd left work at one o'clock in the morning just as a car was skidding on black ice into the side of the factory. She and Peter were the first to see the crash and the first on the scene to rescue the injured passengers before the car had burst into flames, engulfing the factory building. It had been an incredibly long night, but somehow she'd found energy and resources she hadn't known she possessed. These days, however, she was lucky if she could stay awake long enough to eat her tea and have a bath before she fell into bed. Reenie still adored the work she did, and she loved everything about being part of factory life, but she'd been finding more and more often that doing the right thing was an uphill struggle.

Reenie wasn't afraid of hard work, or long hours, or difficult jobs, but she was constantly bemused by the minefield of trying to work out exactly who to trust, who to help, and who to hide away from at Mackintosh's. It never ceased to surprise Reenie that not everyone wanted to see jobs done well and everyone made happy. At her school she'd been a bit useless academically, but they'd taught her to be useful practically because that always made up for it. But sometimes, at Mackintosh's, she could see a way that she could be useful, or helpful, or kind, and she would get a telling off for interfering or 'meddling' as one of the lady managers had called it. She'd been given advice by Diana Moore that she was to do her own job, and if she saw a way to help someone else with theirs she had to ask Diana first, because the way to get on at Mackintosh's was not the same way you got on at school or on the family farm.

Reenie knew that she was a fish out of water; she knew that she didn't have the fancy school certificates that Dolly Dunkley had, or Peter's posh upbringing; she didn't even have the age and experience of grown-up Diana, but she had thought she had a talent that made up for all that.

Reenie wished now she was going home to her parents' farm with her beloved ugly old horse Ruffian, but since her promotion from the shop floor to Junior Manager she'd taken the room in the boarding house beside the factory and the railway station because as long as Reenie was slogging her guts out doing her job and going between the Halifax and Norwich factories, she needed to be somewhere where she wouldn't be snowed in or flooded out, or that would be a pig to get to late at night if she was working after hours. Her parents worried about her leaving home so young and had only allowed her to move into a boarding house because they knew that Diana Moore was also taking a room there at the same time, and as another lady manager at the Mackintosh's factory she would be sure to keep it respectable. The fact that Diana had secretly given birth to a child out of wedlock and was passing her off as her half-sister was not something Reenie's parents – or anyone else – would ever have guessed.

'Mrs Garner, is there hot water for a bath?' Reenie called out to the landlady who she assumed was down in the basement which served as both kitchen and parlour. Reenie had agreed to meet Peter after his shift for a trip to the cinema so she'd have to be quick. She was lucky where she lived because they had a shared bathroom at the end of the landing with hot and cold running water and, unlike some boarding houses where you could only have one bath a week, Mrs Garner let the factory girls have a bath whenever they wanted one because it was often mucky work in the factory. The rents were rather higher at Mrs Garner's boarding house, but as junior managers, Reenie and Diana could afford to pay a little more than the production line girls who were lodging with poor families in the town, or even the girls who had to live at home and give their wages to their mothers.

Reenie didn't hear an answer from Mrs Garner, so she

tapped at the kitchen door which was a little ajar. 'Mrs Garner? Are you in?'

She heard a muffled cry for help from within, and pushed the door wide. There, wedged firmly into the door frame of the hatch to the coal hole at the far end of the kitchen, was the skirt of a cotton floral day dress beneath the familiar sight of Mrs Garner's fudge-brown calico housecoat. Reenie did not know where to look as she realized that her landlady had become stuck in the coal chute, and the only portion which remained visible was her rather round bottom.

'Are you all right?' Reenie called loudly as she crept awkwardly closer to the coal hatch and the undignified position of Mrs Garner, 'Do you want any help?'

''ull 'ee 'oot!' Mrs Garner called through from the other side of the tiny door frame, ''ull 'e 'oot!'

'I can't make out what you're saying, Mrs Garner, you're a bit muffled.' Reenie listened hard as Mrs Garner called again but couldn't really discern any clear instruction. 'Hang on a minute, Mrs Garner, I've got an idea!'

Reenie nipped out to the pavement at the front of the house above the level of the kitchen parlour where the other side of the coal chute was closed and fastened against the elements; sliding back the solid iron bolt and heaving back the wooden trapdoor Reenie was able to let some light into the coal cellar and peer inside. There, in the dim, soot-blackened depths of the cellar, Reenie thought she saw the outline of her landlady's pearly white arms and face, and some dark, wriggling smaller shapes between them; it was her landlady's kittens.

'Reenie, love, I'm stuck. The coalman is delivering any minute and the cat has dragged her basket into the coal cellar and all the kittens with her. I tried to get them out so that he can fill up, but I'm wedged in at . . .' Mrs Garner shied away from stating exactly which portion was wedged in. '. . . at the back!'

'Don't you worry, Mrs Garner,' Reenie was already pulling herself up and dashing back to the scullery, 'we'll have you out in a jiffy!'

A muffled cry came from the coal hatch and Reenie knew that Mrs Garner was telling her to hurry. Reenie looked around the kitchen parlour until she found what she was looking for; a parcel of fresh butter. Reenie grabbed it, ran back round to the front of the house and reopened the trapdoor to the coal cellar where she called down to her landlady, 'I've got you some butter, Mrs Garner! Do you think you could get yourself out if I pass you down some butter?'

'What on earth am I meant to do with butter? I'm stuck in the dark with the last of the coal, a cat, and three kittens – where does the butter go?'

'I thought you could rub it down your sides where you're wedged in and then—'

'Oh, just go round the other side and pull me through. I think I can hear the doorbell so there's someone at the door. You go and see and pull me out.'

Reenie balanced precariously on the edge of the trap-door, with one hand holding out the butter and the other clinging to the lip of the paving stone above as she strained to reach out across the darkness to her landlady. It was a hot summer day and in the warmth of Reenie's hand the parcel of butter had softened just enough to become difficult to handle. Before Reenie knew what was happening the parcel had slipped from her fingers, she had slipped from her perch and she was sliding quickly down through the dusty, black coal chute colliding with her landlady at the bottom with an almighty thud, freeing her from the offending door frame. The pair of them landed in a sooty heap on the terracotta tiles in time to hear the determined knocking a floor above at the open front door.

'That'll be Mr Torrance come to deliver the coal.' Jane Garner heaved herself up and tried to dust herself down, but she was soot black to the waist, and smudged down to her knees, 'Do I look presentable, dearie?'

Reenie held her breath as she looked at her landlady and struggled to think of a kind way to tell her that her hair was standing up like a broom end. At that moment Mrs Garner looked up from brushing her knees and saw Reenie's butter-smeared, soot-drenched, sugar-coated, cat-clawed dress, and her mucky face besides.

Mrs Garner guffawed and said, 'Oh lord! Do I look as bad as you?' She turned to search for a glimpse of her reflection in one of the glass panels of her china cabinet and laughed uproariously at what she saw. 'Well, it's a good job it's only Mr Torrence come calling. Go up and ask him to wait, would you? I need to coax the cat *and* her litter out before he can make his delivery or they'll all be squashed – and we don't want that!'

But although Mr Torrence was on his way to their street with his delivery, and although he would most certainly not have minded being greeted by the lady of the house covered in what he would have called 'good clean coal', he was not at Jane Garner's front door; the party who waited for them were part of the very poshest family of Reenie and her landlady's acquaintance, and as she reached the top of the stairs and saw them in the doorway Reenie couldn't help but let out a quiet, 'Oh lor.'

Waiting politely and patiently in the summer sunshine were three of the golden-haired Hunter children, like angelic beings basking in the glory of the heavenly hosts. Steven Hunter, the eldest son, home from his boarding school for the long summer vac, and at just a year younger than Reenie quite the man about town these days, had brought little Lara and their adopted sister Gracie on an unannounced visit to Diana Moore.

Steven Hunter did not give so much as a hint that he had noticed the riot of butter, soot, sugar, and cat-related chaos on parade in Reenie's apparel. 'Gracie wanted to bring Diana a present – chocolates or some such.' Steven waved an amiable hand in the direction of a bright straw basket that the little ones were carrying between them, and a parcel within wrapped in brilliantly clean white handkerchiefs.

The little girls smiled hopefully, proffering their basket to the big girl who they thought might be in fancy dress, admiring her immensely for it.

'Oh dear.' Reenie thought about apologizing for her appearance, but didn't know where to start so decided to try to be useful instead. 'I'm afraid you've had a wasted journey. Diana'll not be back for hours, but you can leave your present in the hall if you want to.'

The little girls conferred and appeared to be in two minds about handing the precious casket over. Reenie heard snatches of whispered words, *should we tell her that she can take one too if she likes sweets?. . . she is very nice . . . Diana doesn't mind sharing . . . there are lots of them . . . we should let her choose one . . .*

Reenie moved forward a little awkwardly, more conscious than ever of her odd appearance in front of these perfectly turned-out children, and tentatively reached towards them to take the basket which was intended for Diana. Gracie lifted the basket shakily by its handle with both hands because it was heavy, and usually when she and her sister carried it they carried it together.

Reenie looked down at the bright white napkins which lined it, and then at her own filthy hands and said, 'Oh, but you know what? I'm worried your present will get sooty. I don't dare touch it myself in case I make marks on it so I think your best bet is to hang onto it until you can see Diana in person. And she'll be ever so glad to see you – talks about you all the time, she does.' This was a cheery exaggeration on Reenie's part but although Diana rarely spoke if she could avoid it, she had once told Reenie very briefly (after much badgering from Reenie) that a child's drawing, which she had taped to her dressing table, was by little Gracie.

Mrs Garner's disembodied voice called out from below, 'Reenie! Could you come here and help me with something?'

'I'm sorry, I ought to go and help my landlady. We've had, um . . .' Reenie looked at the two children and then leant in and tried to say confidentially to Steven, 'we've had kittens.'

'Ah, say no more.' The young man nodded with understanding. 'Climbing the curtains yet?'

'Not yet – we haven't got them out of the coal cellar.' Reenie's eye was caught by a prancing pom-pom of butter and dust just behind the two little girls and she darted forward to catch it, but too late as Lara had also seen

the escaped kitten, scooped it up in her hand and immediately smudged her pinafore dress. A second kitten
arrived at the top of the stairs and was clumsily caught
by Gracie after a few moments' chase. Gracie clutched
her kitten to her chest, getting coal dust on both her dress
and her chin.

'Oh look,' Lara squeaked in delight, 'mine's licking my
hand!'

'Oh, he's yours now, is he?' Steven Hunter smiled at
them both with the indulgence of an older brother who
has been treated as an adult for the first time and is
enjoying the novelty.

'Well, they can have them if they want them.' Reenie
had grown up on a farm, and the adoption of vast menag-
eries was nothing out of the ordinary to her. She knew
that the kittens needed new homes and she thought of
the Hunters as the kind fairies with endless resources
who took on anything and anyone. Little did she think
that Diana would have an entirely different perspective
when she came home and heard what she'd done.

'Oh, can we?' Gracie's cornflower blue eyes lit up and
gazed hopefully on her newly-minted brother who wanted
to do everything he could to bring her joy.

'Yes, yes, I suppose so.' Steven Hunter feigned annoyance but a grin crept through. 'Are they old enough? I
mean, should we wait until they're . . .?'

'No, they're fine, help yourself. They need homing and
Mrs Garner says she needs shot of them sharpish. You
can have a box for them if you've got far to go.'

Steven Hunter appeared to be an old hand at the tricky
business of kittens and made light work of it. 'I expect
the girls will be able to put them in their pockets or

something until we're home. I say, thank you; this is jolly nice of you. Are you sure we shouldn't leave Diana's present here? Will you mind if we come back again some other time?'

Reenie looked back at the hallway where even now she could just see the top of Mrs Garner's head bobbing up and down below the edge of the stairs, waving her hand at Reenie to get the Hunters to leave so that they didn't catch her in a moment of dishevelment. 'Oh, I think come back later. Like I said, we're a bit busy the now.'

'Quite understand. Don't tell her what we called round about, though – I think they want to surprise her.' He gave Reenie a stage wink and then picked up the basket his sisters had brought with them to let them keep their hands free for the squirming kittens they had so fortuit-ously found. As he walked the little girls back towards the place where Reenie assumed a golden coach awaited him with footmen and white horses to take them to their fairy-tale home, she wondered how long that handkerchief parcel in their basket would stay so dazzlingly clean and white.

Chapter Nine

Diana had noticed the worried looks on the faces of the married women waiting in the factory dining hall to learn the fate of their jobs. If Reenie had been here, she thought to herself, she'd have jumped the gun and tried to reassure the women that they weren't about to hear the news they were expecting, but Diana had more patience and they'd know what was what soon enough.

'Ladies, I wish to extend my personal thanks on behalf of the firm of Mackintosh's, and of the people of Halifax.' The director was standing on one of the dining tables to be certain that he'd be seen and heard over the heads of the four hundred women who waited, worried, clutching each other's hands and holding back tears. 'In our hour of need you came to our aid and we owe you a debt of gratitude.'

Diana heard more than a few women muttering under their breaths, 'Don't send us home, don't send us home.'

'We now have one more request to make – and it is a matter of delicacy which I'm sure you will meet easily.'

Diana heard a woman a few feet away from her whisper to her colleagues, 'He's going to ask us to go quietly so we don't upset the unmarried girls and remind them what their fate is when they marry and have to leave here.'

'His Majesty the King has announced that he will be visiting Halifax shortly before the coronation and I have the pleasure to inform you first, among all our employees, that he will be visiting our factory as well as our town.'

There were gasps of surprise among the assembled staff and confused faces among the excited ones. Was he about to ask them not to petition the King for their jobs? Not to make trouble if they were still on the line at the time of his visit? Was there a chance that one or two of them would be chosen to be presented to His Majesty?

'To celebrate this great occasion we have decided that we will add a new sweet to the Quality Street assortment; we will call it the King's Toffee; and it will be the finest toffee we have ever made.' A dawning realization was appearing on the faces of some of the women – this was better news than any of them could have hoped for in even their wildest dreams. 'I don't need to explain to you how difficult it will be for us to create a new sweet and a new line to make it on in the limited time we have. We cannot leave a task like this to inexperienced workers and we need your skill and your trustworthiness. Ladies, I know we have already asked more of you than we can ever repay, and I expect many of you were unprepared for the length of time we were going to keep you from your families and your domestic duties, but your old firm has a heartfelt request to make of you: stay on until September and help us make the King's Toffee. Help us make history for our town.'

There were cheers and whoops as the women celebrated the news that they were not being sent home and that they would be making toffees for the King. But beside Diana an older woman turned concernedly to her friend. 'Will that give you long enough to save up for your Jenny's school uniform?'

'Close.' She forced a smile and said with a lilt that had an air of Dublin about it, 'I'll be one month short.'

Diana made a mental note.

The old boardroom was small enough to hear a conversation conducted at one end at the other, but Diana chose to sit apart from Major Fergusson and Mrs Starbeck who were standing beside the window, speaking in subdued tones as they waited for the other managers to come in to join them. Diana was present to take notes, and if she could use her lowly rank to avoid talking to Mrs Starbeck she certainly would. There was something about the woman which reminded her of Dolly Dunkley – both wore more make-up than was ordinarily accepted, and both wore very new clothes. In the case of Dolly it was all cheap and looked it but Mrs Starbeck had a cloying sort of glamour about her; she was a handsome woman, and well turned out. No doubt there would be many gentlemen who wouldn't have kicked her out of bed for eating peanuts, as Diana's late father would have said, but Diana couldn't like her. There was something too pristine about Mrs Starbeck, she was rather too charming, too clever by half. Her clothes and make-up alone must cost the woman more in a season than Diana earned in a year; and that wasn't even taking into account the little sparkle here and there of discreet jewellery which she

68

wore when she knew she wouldn't be visiting the production lines.

Mrs was a courtesy title, of course, used for all the permanent women workers of overlooker's grade or above at Mackintosh's. Married women could take on casual, seasonal work but, like almost every major employer in the country, there was a bar on employing married women as permanent staff. Cynthia Starbeck could not have risen to the post of Senior Time and Motion Manager, nor become Major Fergusson's second-in-command if she were a married woman. She had left the factory for a placement in the Dusseldorf factory before Reenie Calder had been introduced to her department, and Diana dreaded to think what Cynthia would now make of over-enthusiastic Reenie. Reenie believed the purpose of her department was to make everything better for everyone and have a go at improving everything, while Mrs Starbeck believed it was to watch the workers to make sure that they were doing the maximum amount of work possible for the minimum amount of money possible. Mrs Starbeck's clipboard and stopwatch were legendary and Diana hoped she wasn't back for long.

'I was so sorry to hear of the loss of your father and I don't wish to pry into your family arrangements, but should you need any assistance with putting his affairs in order . . .' Although Mrs Starbeck was not a close personal friend of the Major, their professional association was a long one. She had been his colleague for several years, had served as the treasurer of several local charities with which he had also served, and the Major had even asked Mrs Starbeck to be an executor of his will. There was a trust between them, though Diana Moore could not think why – as far as she was concerned, the Major was everything that was good and Mrs Starbeck was a cow.

'Thank you, Major, you're very kind.' Mrs Starbeck creased her brow but did not manage to squeeze out a tear. 'My father was an adventurous man and I'm glad to be able to say that he died as he lived. He loved his little boat and I don't think he'd have wanted to go any other way than sailing.' There was a dainty gold pendant around Cynthia Starbeck's neck on a chain, and she straightened it very precisely, with only the slightest movement of thumb and forefinger. Diana wondered if the adornment was associated with the recently deceased parent.

'And my father's solicitor is taking care of everything for me. It *has* been a shock. I had not expected to return from Germany for several months, but the solicitor was most insistent that I cut short my work on the continent. I hope I'll be able to settle my father's affairs within the year and then resume my work in Dusseldorf if that suits Mackintosh's?'

'We quite understand; these things take time. Have you managed to find lodgings nearby?' The Major knew that Mrs Starbeck had never liked Halifax, but he secretly hoped her time with their German factory had given her a new appreciation of the town.

'I shall be staying in my little flat in Hipperholme. I didn't let it out when I went over to Dusseldorf, I just had it shut up. I know it's silly of me, but I dislike the idea of someone else in my home while I'm not there.' Mrs Starbeck said this with the confident manner of one who does not care whether or not it *is* silly, because she can afford to do it and has no one to answer to but herself.

Diana was relieved when her own manager, Amy Wilkes, appeared for the meeting, along with several other members of senior staff. The chances were that Diana would be able to get away with taking notes and then leaving without having to say anything to anyone, least of all Cynthia Starbeck.

'What's the first point on the agenda, Mrs Wilkes?' the Major asked as everyone settled themselves into their seats.

'The confectioner's assistant, Major.'

'Ah, yes. Last one went to our competitors, didn't he? Did you have someone in mind?'

'Mary Norcliffe,' Diana said. 'She worked well at hand-making in the weeks after the fire and we know that she's a fast and reliable worker.' Diana had been planning a move to get Mary into the job for a while, and though speaking up at meetings like this one was against her own policy, she couldn't waste the opportunity.

'Oh dear me, no. You must excuse me for interrupting, Major,' Diana bristled that Mrs Starbeck was apologizing to the Major, but it was Diana herself she'd interrupted, 'but has it really come to this that we're employing women for confectioner's apprenticeships? We know that they always marry and leave, so is it really worthwhile to train a girl, when a young man would be much more likely to make a career with us?'

Diana wanted to point out that Mrs Starbeck herself was proof that female employees did *not* always leave to marry, and that the firm's founder and first confectioner, Violet Mackintosh, had been a married woman of immense dedication and talent. As a member of the Women's

Cooperative Guild it irked Diana to hear a woman failing to live up to all the Suffragists had lobbied for.

'Fortunately, that is one less thing for us to worry about, Mrs Starbeck.' Major Fergusson was charming and warm, though it was clear he was telling Mrs Starbeck to get back in her box. 'I understand that the Time and Motion department at our Dusseldorf factory have some control over their choice of staff, but here in Halifax you will remember that we are mercifully spared that additional trial. Mrs Wilkes and her colleagues in the Women's Employment Department still take care of all of that for us and have our absolute trust. In Time and Motion we merely plan the layout and working of the production line and request that Mrs Wilkes hires us the requisite number of staff. Although, at present, this may be more troublesome than usual with our acute shortage of staff.'

'I'm pleased to report, however, that we have found a replacement Head Chocolatier, Major. Mrs Roth recommended a man from among the Dusseldorf staff. They had two trained confectioners and were able to spare one for three months.' Amy Wilkes glanced out of the corner of her eye, willing Mrs Starbeck to complain so that she could see her put in her place.

'Which confectioner is being sent here?' Mrs Starbeck looked put out. 'And I understood Mrs Roth was remaining at our Dusseldorf factory to manage the over-lookers; I didn't think she was coming back here to choose staff.'

'Mrs Roth is also recommending a list of German girls from the Dusseldorf factory who are already very experienced confectioners and will be able to start work immediately on arrival.'

'Well, I don't think we should be inviting foreigners to work at the factory if we have workers in Halifax who need jobs. It's not patriotic.'

'That is our problem, Mrs Starbeck.' Amy Wilkes had been delighted to hear a year earlier that Cynthia Starbeck had been promoted to a job in an entirely different country to the rest of them. 'We have done absolutely everything we can to employ every able-bodied man and woman available in the town – we have lifted the marriage bar and brought back septuagenarian grandmothers to make confectionery with their bare hands, but if we want our business to thrive in the coming months we need to bring in more workers, and I believe we've exhausted the possibilities locally.'

'What about hiring unemployed men and training them up? Building the necessary skills among British workers?' Mrs Starbeck flicked a lock of brassy gold hair from her brow the better to lock eyes with Amy Wilkes, her long-time nemesis.

'We're already doing that. You may not have noticed that Reenie Calder and Peter McKenzie have set up dummy lines to train over two hundred and fifty workers how to work on the line; they're coming from as far afield as Wakefield and Castleford and the youngest ones are barely fourteen. We have reached the limit of the local workforce – and if we want to remain in business to support that workforce, we will have to take outside help. I'm only too aware that when you left England we had hunger marches from Jarrow, but if you've been following the news from England during your time abroad you'll have seen that employment in the West Riding has since increased beyond anything we could have predicted and there is now a widespread shortage of skilled workers.'

Mrs Starbeck was wrong-footed; she had only been back in the country a week and she couldn't have known that the new munitions factories, preparing for potential war, had supplied a great deal of the work that men had been crying out for. 'I suppose if you particularly want girls from the German factory then I can draw up a list of potential—'

'Thank you, no, Mrs Starbeck.' Amy bristled. 'Recruitment of staff is still the prerogative of the Women's Employment Department. I shan't tell you how to set up a line on the factory floor and I would thank you not to tell me who to hire.'

'I simply offered because I know that Mrs Roth doesn't always see how unsuitable some of these foreigners are. If you're bringing them all the way from Germany I would have thought you'd want to make sure that you were hiring the right sort.'

There was a charged silence; Cynthia Starbeck did not need to say aloud what she meant, because everyone at the table knew what she was getting at only too well. Cynthia Starbeck was a well-educated woman from a well-known Yorkshire family; her father had been a member of Parliament, her mother's family had owned a coal mine, and Cynthia herself had served as treasurer for several charities. She was the picture of upper middle class respectability, and she was also a staunch supporter of Oswald Mosley's antisemitic British Union of Fascists, a far-right political party. As an ardent fascist, she had left for Germany in their Blackshirt uniform. However, the British Government had outlawed the wearing of political uniforms while Mrs Starbeck was in Germany so she had not been faced, as others had been, with the indignity of having to leave work on one day in her jet black British Union uniform and return the following day in mufti. There were a lot of Jewish employees in Dusseldorf and Amy Wilkes was certain that Mrs Starbeck did not want any of them in Halifax.

Mrs Starbeck carefully adjusted the gold pendant at her neck and plastered a winning smile on her face before turning to the Major to say sweetly, 'I always choose the girls for my lines. But if I'm making a line fit for a king to inspect, then of course I shall want to make some additional arrangements about decoration and the presentation of the girls. We must have everything looking nice.'

'Which line was it you were building, Mrs Starbeck?' Diana feigned innocence, but she was only asking to give her own manager the opportunity to cut Starbeck down to size while she watched.

'Well, the line for the King's Toffee, of course. Oh, I'm sorry – have I made a mistake? I just assumed you'd want me to take on that line, Major. I thought you'd want it to have a woman's touch and I am the most senior lady in the department.' It was said with such wide-eyed humility that it made Diana's teeth itch. The woman was angling to take on the King's line and to make everyone feel embarrassed about suggesting anything else. Diana knew that the Major was used to tricky customers and hoped he'd see through this blatant act of manipulation.

'That is very kind of you to offer, Mrs Starbeck, but I have decided this will be the perfect opportunity to make a showcase of the talent of some of our very own bright young things. I have Reenie Calder and Peter McKenzie in mind for this line.'

'But they're juniors!' Mrs Starbeck's voice shot up in disgust before she brought it under control again and flustered back to composure. 'I mean to say, neither of them are twenty-one yet. Can one really trust something so important to colleagues with such little experience?'

'They will report directly to me on this project. I want our younger workers to know that we trust them to take on big tasks, to learn, to grow, to strive. I want to give them all the chances I wish I had been given at their age; they are our future, Mrs Starbeck, and I'm sure I can count on you to rise to this challenge.'

Diana said nothing, but her eyes narrowed in delight like a cat. She had worked with Reenie Calder on Reenie's first day at Mack's, and although Reenie was impossibly naive, inconveniently determined, irritatingly well-meaning, and friendly to a point that gave most people a headache, Diana would always rather see Reenie win the day than Mrs Starbeck. The creation of this King's Toffee line was going to be very enjoyable to watch, even if a challenge for them all.

Chapter Ten

Dolly Dunkley toyed with the idea of telling Diana Moore to stuff her job so she never had to see the whole nasty lot of them again, but Dolly's appetite for retribution was always greater than her capacity for self-preservation. She threw her white wraparound overall into a crumpled heap on the floor of the girls' cloakroom and then waited in a huff at the door outside in the factory corridor where Diana had told her to wait to be collected. Dolly had expected to see Diana Moore again, but when another white-aproned girl, younger than Dolly, came to collect her and walk her to the front gates, Dolly was affronted. Who did this Diana think she was? Dolly was not someone to be treated like any common factory girl.

'Was there any message?' Dolly demanded of the poor girl who had only volunteered to walk Dolly to the gates as a kindness.

'Message about what?' The girl looked at Dolly in confusion and the watchman at the factory gate ambled out of his cabin to stick up for the girl if need be because this had the look of a sacking and he was used to these ending in harsh words at the gate.

'From that Diana girl, obviously. Where does she expect me to go now?'

'Well, just home, I suppose.' Her guide shrugged. 'She's letting you off work this afternoon, but you need to be back here tomorrow the same time as you were today.'

Dolly looked at the girl with withering disgust, which confused her because she thought she had been imparting some nice news.

'I mean, you don't have to come back if you don't want to. It's not everyone's cup of tea, and if you don't think you'll enjoy yourself then you don't have to come back.'

Dolly sucked her teeth and narrowed her eyes at the girl. 'Oh, don't you worry, I'll be back tomorrow.' And with that she turned melodramatically on her heel and marched quickly towards the tram stop at the top of the hill, huffing and puffing with annoyance like the wolf who thought he could blow a brick house down.

The tram was not so crowded as it would be later in the day when the rest of the workers left off their shifts, but being a young lady of leisure Dolly was used to taking her journeys at quieter times of the day and tended to feel put out if she had to share her tram or trolleybus with any other passengers at all.

Dolly was a girl who had seen the way very wealthy people lived and laboured under the delusion that she was of the same social class and entitled to expect a very comfortable style of living as her right. She thought of a lot of things as her right and spent her days in a perpetual state of frustration about the things she did not have, and rarely dwelt on the things she did. Dolly had been born into a relatively fortunate position; her father was the vicar of a large and pretty Church of England parish which came with a comfortable rectory to live in, and more servants to staff it than was usual for a rectory of their size in 1937. Although her father was not a rich man, he had been able to secure his daughter a place at a grammar school, give her a holiday in East Anglia once a year, and had found the time to tutor her himself so that she was almost able to keep up with the other girls in her class.

Dolly resented all of this. There was another school in the county she had wanted to attend and she often sulked over the fact that she hadn't been sent there. It was one she had read about in a posh ladies' magazine and was a girls' boarding school where the young scholars were given a horse each to ride for recreation when they weren't at their lessons; where they were taken to Switzerland to practise their French; and where the teachers treated the girls like little princesses and never had the temerity to scold them. It was a constant aggravation that her father had not had anywhere near the money for the fees. Her father had, however, earned enough to allow Dolly to stay on at school until she was eighteen, and had never thought of suggesting that she leave education any earlier to go into work.

The vicarage was supplied by the parish rent-free and there was room enough for Dolly to live without the need to contribute a wage herself, so a couple of years had passed since she had completed her final school examinations, and her father had not hurried her to think about her future. As long as the Reverend Dunkley was a widower living alone, it suited him to have his daughter about the place (especially as it kept his church congregation from any gossip about his two female servants), and he gave Dolly a small allowance to spend on her wardrobe and entertainments. As a young girl she had always spent more than most children on bags of sweets and dresses for her dolls, but her spending had now reached a point which would have shocked her father's staff. For instance, recently she had spent fifteen shillings on a bottle of slimming lotion to rub on her skin to counteract the effects of the box of chocolates which she had eaten in one sitting, which had cost her seven shillings. The two things together, intended to cancel each other out, cost more money than their char lady earned in a week.

However, time had wrought its changes in the Dunkley vicarage; what had been a nice income and large house for the two Dunkleys was now stretched to capacity as the Reverend Dunkley had fallen in love and married a pretty young widow from his parish who brought with her a brood of small, rowdy children from her first marriage. The Reverend Dunkley delighted in his happy and likeable little stepchildren, but Dolly resented their very existence, especially when her father had to say that he could no longer afford to give her such a large allowance. With the expense of his other children they all needed to tighten their belts. To Dolly this was unthinkable; she had never expected to work for a living, but she had a taste for make-up, cosmetics, magazines and new clothes – she could not possibly make economies of the sort her father expected. With reluctance (and some trepidation because his daughter frightened him more than he cared to admit) the Reverend Dunkley suggested that Dolly might think about getting a job.

It was a horrible blow and Dolly had cried and slammed doors and kept the house awake with her sobbing through the night for an entire weekend, but eventually she came around to the idea that she would work for a living until she had a husband to take care of her. Her father assured her that it couldn't possibly be for very long as she was bound to be snapped up by a handsome young man before Christmas. It could only be suggested that the Reverend Dunkley was a little over-optimistic in his time-scales; devastating good looks might have been enough to blind a suitor to her personal failings for a time, but Dolly was not Katherine Hepburn, or Vivien Leigh. Dolly had once had a plain face which had caught a pretty glow when she smiled in kindness, but since her latter schooldays she had taken to shaping her eyebrows in what the magazines called the 'candy box style', and wearing every type of face make-up the Tokalon company sold until she could not smile (in kindness or cruelty) because her face would crack and the make-up would crumble off it in little powdery lumps. To those who had known Dolly when she was small there was something very sad about the girl's situation; she had so many positive qualities to offer, but instead she seemed to cultivate the unpleasant ones. An act of defiance, perhaps, against the world which had not given her all the things she felt she deserved in life.

The toffee factories had never held an appeal for Dolly as a workplace, but she had always wanted to visit one on a guided tour. It was only recently, when she heard that Irene Calder, one of the former Sunday School girls from her father's parish, had secured a junior manager position at Mackintosh's (thanks in part to a letter of reference from her father the vicar) that she started to feel that she had more of a right to that management job. Dolly knew the sort of girl her father had recommended, so to Dolly's mind it would be an easy thing to waltz into the factory and snap up a management position for herself. After all, Dolly had spent more time at school, she was confident that she was a harder worker (many was the time she had watched the servants in the vicarage clearing up after her or doing her laundry and had known instinctively that she could have done a better job herself if she had been in their place), and she was quite obviously 'the right sort'.

Dolly's father was relieved when Dolly stopped slamming doors and came around to the idea of working for her spending money, but he felt that launching herself straight into a factory career would be too hard on her. The Reverend Dunkley suggested that he might get her a nice genteel job as a private tutor to some parish children who were sitting the grammar school entrance exam. 'After all,' her father had reminded her, 'you don't need to earn a full wage; you have no rent to pay, and no household bills; you just need to earn a little for your pin money, something to pay for your lotions and potions.'

But Dolly would not hear of it. She was burning with jealousy at what she felt was the injustice of a lower-class girl from her father's parish being hailed a success by the local gossips. Dolly wanted that adulation and attention – and she wanted that job. She had already begun to glamorize the life of a factory manager in her mind and to fantasize about the likelihood of meeting one of the

Mackintosh sons and marrying into their impossibly enormous family wealth. And once she had set her sights on it, nothing would dissuade her. It was a shock, then, when she received a letter of rejection to her application. There had been more angry slamming of doors in the Dunkley vicarage, and this time a door was slammed on the charlady's foot as she was trying to leave the sitting room with a bucket of ash from the fire. Between Dolly's growls of rage, the char's howls of pain at her corns, and the new Mrs Dunkley's profuse apologies to the charlady, the Reverend Dunkley knew that he would have no peace at home until Dolly had got her wish. With a heavy heart and a sense of foreboding, he had written to a woman with whom he was barely acquainted and asked if she might do something to help his daughter. The woman in question was Lady Mackintosh, and the letter was a headache that seemed to have no end.

Now Dolly Dunkley sat on the rattling tram beside a little boy and his nanny who were looking out of the window and pointing out places they knew. The boy had an open paper bag of toffees at his side and, as Dolly brushed past him to alight at her stop, she nonchalantly stole one of his sweets and hopped off the vehicle before he could look round in anger. Dolly unwrapped the sweet, popped it into her mouth without thinking about what it tasted like, and threw the wrapper into the hedge of a private residence as she passed it on foot.

Dolly was in a very bad mood indeed and she felt very hard done by. She was already turning over all of the things she would say to her pen pal when she wrote to tell her how cruelly she'd been treated by those awful factory girls, and how desperately hurt she had felt. They were such bullies – how was she to have known that it was forbidden for workers to eat sweets in the work-rooms?

'You there!' a Germanic voice called out. 'What do you think you are doing?' An angry gardener in his overalls chased after Dolly as she trotted down the pavement towards the vicarage. As she turned to see what the commotion was, she realized that he was angrily shaking his fist at her.

'I don't know who you are! I don't know what you want!' she blurted out and looked around her for help as this frightening man, red in the face with rage, and saying unintelligible things in his native tongue, drew closer. He had a long beard on his neck but not his chin which gave him the look of a Quaker, and Dolly would have known that he wasn't an Englishman even if she hadn't heard him speak.

'You threw this sweet wrapper in my hedge!'

Dolly looked at the sweet wrapper the man was bran-dishing and gulped down the sweet she had just stolen. 'It wasn't me, I didn't do anything.'

'Don't you lie to me – I saw you throw this in my hedge when you got off the tram. People are always throwing rubbish in my hedge when they get off.'

'Well, if everyone does it you ought to provide a waste bin. It's your own fault.'

'Are you admitting it, then?' By this time the man's angry shouts were drawing the attention of passers-by and Dolly was flushed with fear and shame. 'Are you admitting you threw this into my hedge?'

'Of course I didn't! I'm not that sort of person. If it fell out of my hand then I didn't realize it had happened.

It could happen to anyone, it was an honest mistake.' Dolly tried to evade the gardener, but the path beside the tram stop was narrow and he didn't seem minded to do the gentlemanly thing and step out of her way. At that moment a trolley bus clattered to a stop near the pavement beside them, and a group of rough-looking young men dismounted from it, shouting abuse at the conductor who had thrown them off for being rowdy. Dolly looked at the young men in desperation and before she could utter a word they intervened.

'What have we 'ere then?' The ringleader sized up the man in gardening clothes, 'Another bloody foreigner harassing English girls? Go back to your own country – we don't want you here.' And he shoved the gardener backwards into the hedge of the nearest garden and guffawed with laughter. The other youths with him guffawed too, and shouted insults at the law-abiding man, while they absorbed Dolly into their pack and continued on. 'What's your name, love?'

'Dolly,' she said, delighted to be drawn away so easily. 'Thanks for getting that man away from me – I didn't know what I'd do.'

'What did he want with you, anyway? Trying it on, was he?'

'I really don't know. He seemed quite mad – it was terrifying.' And in that moment Dolly convinced herself that what she was saying was true, that she hadn't stolen a child's toffee, that she hadn't thrown the wrapper into someone's garden, that she hadn't lied when she was confronted about it. To Dolly, she was once again the victim of people who treated her cruelly.

'Well, you stick in with us,' the ringleader of the youths

told her, 'we'll look after you. I'm Harry Speight, and these are my friends. We're Blackshirts, we are, members of the British Union and we're on our way to a meeting. You come with us and we'll make sure you don't have no bother from no one.' Harry swaggered along at the centre of the smug posse of roughs whose necks had been shaved especially for the occasion.

Dolly held her nose a little higher. She was the centre of attention and people were talking about looking after her; it was an uplifting feeling. 'What sort of a meeting are you going to? Is it a lecture?'

'Summat like that. One of our members has been in Germany and she's just got back. She'll tell us what's happening over there cos they've got the right ideas – plenty of jobs and all the trains running on time. You come with us and see what she's got to say.'

'Would I need to be a member? I mean, would I need to join the British Union and follow Mr Moseley's fascists? I'm not a member, you see.'

'Don't you worry about that,' Harry drawled, 'you just come along and hear what our Mrs Starbeck has to say. You'll be begging to join once she's finished telling you what she's seen.'

Chapter Eleven

Reenie's younger sister Kathleen was sitting at the kitchen table of the Calder family's farmhouse making a banner for the Sunday School procession planned for the day of the King's visit to Halifax. Kathleen was not a gifted seamstress, but she hoped that if she ran up something cheap and cheerful she might get away with missing a couple of Sundays come the summer term. The Sunday School Mistress was tough on non-attenders, but she was sometimes willing to accept acts of work in lieu.

'So then,' Reenie told her mother, 'she just kicked her toffee wrapper across the floor and she didn't get sacked, or anything. I'm meant to be teaching these new girls good habits and making sure they learn fast, and then the likes of her come along and shut down a line and she gets to stay. It's not right and it's not setting a good example.'

Mrs Calder was bringing Reenie and Kathleen cups of cocoa which she'd made with fresh milk with a little square of chocolate melted into it that Reenie had brought home with some toffees as a special treat. 'Is it gettin' you down, love? Do you want to leave the factory? You know your father and I are ever so proud of you for doin' so well, but we'd neither of us be angry with you if you wanted to come back home. We miss you, and there's plenty of work to do on the farm if factory work is losing its appeal.'

'I miss you all too. And the dog, and the cat, and the horse and the geese – but I love my job, and even though some of the people are difficult, mostly everyone is lovely.'

Kathleen put down the needle and cotton which she had been attempting to thread with the tip of her tongue clamped between her lips. 'Reenie, I'm not being funny, or nothing, but what exactly *do* you do?'

Mrs Calder gently chided her younger daughter. 'Kathleen, you know very well what she does, she's a junior manager in the Mackintosh's factory.'

'Yes, but what does she *dooooo*?'

Reenie didn't mind being asked; in fact, she worried that the other Time and Motion managers didn't know what she did and she wished they'd ask her so that she could explain.

'Well, it's like this, see; in the factory you've got all these different production lines with girls making sweets, and wrapping sweets, and packing sweets into cartons and tubs and tins. They've all got to work as quick as they can because there's a minimum amount of work that they can do without getting dismissed. Everyone has to make their minimum, and if you don't make it once or twice you might be all right, but if you never make your minimum you're out.'

'Is that why Mam told you to make sure you were quick when you went on your first day?'

Mrs Calder hooked an iron out of the range, ready to attack the pile of clean shirts she was ironing for Reenie to take back to her boarding house with her. 'I didn't realize she'd try to break the factory record, I just meant don't dawdle.'

'Well, the faster you work the more you earn, so I wasn't going to let the grass grow under my feet. If you work ten per cent faster than the minimum you get paid ten per cent more, and if you work twenty per cent faster than the minimum you get paid twenty per cent more, and so on, all the way up to the maximum you can get paid. And when you get to the maximum you can do as much work as you like, but you won't get paid any more.'

'And,' Mrs Calder put in pointedly, 'if you work over your maximum you put all the other girls' noses out of joint because then the Time and Motion department see that it's possible to work faster and so they put *everyone's* minimums up, but for the same pay, and everyone has to work faster for the same money. That got your sister into trouble more than once, so you remember that if ever you go to work at the factory.'

Kathleen's ears pricked up. 'Can I go and work at the toffee factory?'

'Not yet, you're too young. You've got to get your matriculation certificate at school and then we'll see about where you're going to work.'

'Yes, but think about it, Mam – if I go and work at the factory I can earn as much as Reenie and then we can get a motorcar.'

'We don't need a motorcar, we've got Ruffian and he

can pull a trap in all weathers. Motorcars get stuck the moment it rains.'

'Ruffian keeps kicking his front shoes off.' Kathleen wasn't to be put off easily. 'A motorcar would never do that.'

'Well, you're still too young.' Reenie didn't say it unkindly, she remembered how desperate she had been to start work and when she got her job at Mackintosh's on her sixteenth birthday, it was a dream come true. 'The youngest you could join is when you're fourteen, and even then you'd be best off choosin' an apprenticeship, so you'd still have to go to the college every now and then. You're as well stoppin' on at school.'

'Your sister was a prodigy,' their mother said, 'and they made an exception for her when they promoted her to Time and Motion. If you went to work there you might just be on a factory girl's wage and you'd wish you hadn't left school for it.'

'Yes, but what does Time and Motion actually *mean*? What do you *do*?'

'Well, we look at the way that the lines run and the time it takes for the girls to do their job and we look for ways of doing everything better and safer and quicker so that everyone has a better time, really. I get to help plan where all the machines and the people are going to go when they make new lines, and I get to come up with lots of ideas, and sometimes I get to go to meetings in other departments just to tell them what I think. I went to a meeting the other day which was run by the buildings department and they were sayin' that they were gettin' ready for the King visiting and they wanted to put flagpoles all along Bailey Hall Road, and I told them they ought to be careful with that because you've got to 'ave plannin' permission for flagpoles round here, and they got all excited and asked me to come back to their next meeting because they didn't know about that.'

Mrs Calder sighed. 'Reenie, what have I told you about gettin' mixed up in things what aren't your job? Just keep your head down and stick to doin' whatever the other people in your department do, and no more. I don't want you to get a reputation for going off and marching to the beat of your own drum. You're a good girl, Reenie, but sometimes, when you try to help, you get into trouble.'

'Honestly, Mam,' Reenie said as she went to rummage in the stoneware bread crock for something to eat, 'I haven't been in trouble since before Christmas and it was only once, and Peter stood by me—'

'Don't let Peter get you in trouble!' Kathleen piped up, mischievously.

'Kathleen!' Mrs Calder scolded her youngest, and then asked, in an unnecessary stage whisper given that they were at home, 'Where did you learn about girls getting into trouble?'

'Oh Mother!' Reenie rolled her eyes. 'We grew up on a farm; did you really think Kathleen wouldn't know where babies came from at twelve years old?'

'She's far too young to be hearing about that!'

'I'm not!' Kathleen folded up her biblical banner in two quick movements and swept it under her elbow, ready to settle down to some family gossip. 'Tell us how you're getting on with your Peter. Have you kissed him yet?'

Reenie gave her mother a look that said it wasn't her fault that her sister was asking these things, and then said, 'I let him kiss me once a week on a Friday evening when he walks me home from the pictures and sees me to the door of my boarding house.'

Kathleen appeared satisfied with this answer, but her mother looked horrified. 'I didn't know that he was taking you to the pictures. Since when has he been taking you to the pictures? You're not alone there, are you?'

'No, Mother, the cinema's full of other people. You can't get a cinema to yourself on a factory wage. And what's wrong with the cinema? Everyone goes to the cinema. It's the *cinema*.'

Mrs Calder ironed her washing pile with renewed aggression and looked from one daughter to the other, clearly wrestling with too many opinions to voice them all at the same time. She thought for a moment more and then said pointedly to Reenie, with another dose of the partial stage whisper, 'Well, don't go getting carried away. Plenty of girls get carried away – they think they won't, but they do.'

'Speak for yourself,' Reenie said, arching an eyebrow at her mother. 'From where I'm standing it's three-nil to you.'

'Hey! I was married long before you three were born, so I'll have none of your sauce, Reenie Calder. I just want to make sure that I'm doing a mother's duty and keeping you on the straight and narrow.'

'With my young man or with my employment at Mackintosh's?'

Mrs Calder put down her iron with a heavy thud and looked as though she were about to burst into tears. 'I just worry about you all so much. Especially after you got into trouble at work last year, I just . . . I just dread to think what could have happened.'

Reenie realized it was time to drop her teasing; her mother was clearly finding it hard to be separated from her eldest daughter. 'Honestly, I won't get into trouble. I've got Major Fergusson to look out for me. As long as he's around he'll always stick up for me.'

'And what about when he retires? He's an older man, if I remember rightly.'

Kathleen cleared her throat. 'Mother, if I remember rightly we've had this conversation before and if Reenie had taken your advice a year ago she wouldn't have been promoted to Junior Manager – she might not even have been kept on past Christmas and when the factory burned down they might not have been able to build another line so fast. So, in actual fact, whatever it is that she does she's probably better off just doing it and ignoring all the people who don't like it.'

This, thought Reenie, was why her little sister did so much better than her at school: she was a clever girl and had an old head on her young shoulders.

'Now, I'm still waiting to find out what you actually *do*.' Kathleen folded her arms and sighed at her elder sister.

Reenie shrugged. 'In a nutshell, I try to do the right thing and then I get in trouble.'

Kathleen nodded sagely. 'I think you should crack on with it. Keeping your head down is boring. After all, you only live once and you've got the farm to come back to if they kick you out.'

Mrs Calder looked at her daughters and smiled; they might not be scholarship material, but she was proud of them. She only wished she could make the world the way they saw it, instead of how it really was. She hoped against hope that this Major Fergusson wasn't thinking of retirement. As far as she could tell he was Reenie's only champion – and clever and talented though Reenie might be, she needed someone to stick up for her when she found she couldn't do right for doing wrong.

Chapter Twelve

'Why do we have to ask permission off anyone anyway?' a young man in a cheap brown jacket appeared to be asking the posse at large as they tramped along the road, spilling over into the gutter, but it was his friend Harry Speight who answered.

'Precisely. It's discrimination, int' it?' Harry Speight was leading his young followers, including the credulous Dolly Dunkley, up the hill from the Stump Cross tram stop towards the welcoming glow of Crabley Hall in all its antique glory, where two men wearing black shirts under their light-coloured suits were standing sentinel at the gothic gates, checking the credentials of anyone who entered. 'Everyone else is allowed to march through their own streets without so much as a by-your-leave. The Trade Unions, the Band of Hope – even the bloody Sunday School makes banners and have their march through Halifax for 'igh days an' 'olidays, but the British Union have to go, cap in hand, to every man and his dog, begging permissions and licences and warrants just to peacefully march through the streets of their own home towns. It's a disgrace.'

'But didn't the British Union of Fascists start a riot in London?' Dolly was very pleased with herself for remembering and being able to point out the obvious flaw in her new friend's argument. 'I saw the newsreels – they called it the Battle of Cable Street and the police said—'

Harry Speight interrupted her. 'All right, all right; we all know what the newsreels said, we don't need any of that repeated, especially not at the meeting.' They were getting closer to the hall now, and although Harry enjoyed the thought of the approval that bringing so many new members would give him, he didn't want any of them showing him up. 'Look, I think you've been listening to the wrong people, so because you're new I'm gonna' explain where you're going wrong, but if you turn out to be one of those Socialists—'

'Oh no! I'm not a Socialist. They want to take all our money and spend it on poor people who haven't earned it. I'm not one of *them*.' Dolly was lucky that, since membership of the British Union had begun to wane, they were desperate for new recruits, and so her feeble assurances were accepted as sufficient to excuse her.

'Well, that's more like it; now you're sounding more like one of us. Look, if you want to join us you've got to stop watching those newsreels; they're all phoney. Everything you read in the news is phoney. What you heard about Cable Street, it wasn't true – the British Union were peaceful and it was the Communists and the Socialists who got violent. We was pure as the driven snow, we was.

96

And another thing, we're not the British Union of Fascists any more, we're just called the British Union, so you don't talk about Fascism. We've got a lot in common with our fascist brothers and sisters on the continent, but we're something new, something British. You follow?'

'Oh, yes.' Dolly was too busy gazing in dumbstruck admiration at the venue for the meeting to pay proper attention to the distinction – if there was one beyond the name – between European thugs and British thugs. Although it almost fell within the boundary of her father's parish, Dolly had never been inside Crabley Hall before. She hadn't even been able to get inside the grounds. Like most people in Halifax she had seen the weatherworn stone griffins perched high on the gate-posts, looking menacingly out at the road, and the groundsman who lived in the gatehouse and looked akin to the griffin; but she had never been able to see through the trees to the sweeping drive beyond the gate, let alone the Restoration grandeur of the hall itself. The summer sun was low in the sky behind the hall and a silhouette of darkness had drawn round the seventeenth-century stones of Crabley, but as Dolly walked nearer she could make out the shapes here and there of gargoyle water spouts on the gutters, mullioned windows, and gable bays. Sophisticated-looking people, all dressed in chic black, stood out in strong relief through the brightly lit windows.

Dolly felt immediately that this was just her sort of place.

'We're planning a march in Halifax, same day as Oswald Moseley's next march in London. And I don't care whether we get permission or not.' Harry Speight looked round at his gang of angry young misfits. 'We're gonna' to take to the streets either way.'

It did not escape Dolly's notice that these young people were not overawed by the grandeur of Crabley Hall; they were not in raptures over the large rose window above the porch they were being ushered through, or even the thought that they would be among exalted company if they were being welcomed into the country home of Lord Mayhew, seventh-generation owner and occasional occupier of Crabley. Dolly saw two of the girls in their company of seven hold out their coats to be taken by the servants without looking up from their conversation – they had obviously been there before.

'Is this where the BUF always meet?' Dolly waved around at the oak staircase, carved with vines and black-ened with age, and the tight-lipped housemaids waiting to take their coats and show them into the ballroom where rows and rows of wheel-backed mahogany chairs had been set out, their fawn velvet seats waiting for Dolly and her new friends.

'Don't let Harry hear you call us the BUF again,' one of the girls hissed, 'it's the British Union. And yeah, Lord Mayhew is a member, so meetings are here.'

This didn't feel like the Women's Institute meetings which huddled in her father's shabby church hall on wobbly, utilitarian benches; this was luxurious, intoxi-cating. Dolly was hooked even before the meeting began – and when the Halifax District Steward stood to intro-duce their speaker for the evening, Dolly felt her stomach lurch with excitement. She had finally found her people.

Dolly didn't care that the wearing of political uniforms had been outlawed in England – she was too busy admiring the stylish cut of the coal-black shirts with stand collars and gleaming buttons which were appearing one by one as newly arrived guests removed their well-fastened civilian rain jackets and handed them to silent servants who scurried away. Behind closed doors, and seemingly far away from the law, well-to-do men and women were smugly displaying the lightning bolt logo of Oswald Moseley's fascist party.

The speaker for the evening was a woman who had recently spent time living and working in Dusseldorf and as she rose to the stage Dolly saw the person she was convinced she would one day grow up to be: privately wealthy, but with a career for stimulation and status among her circle; she wore make-up, but applied with taste and sophistication – and, most importantly, she had an audience, and a power over that audience.

To Dolly's immense delight this new role model turned out to be an employee of Mackintosh's, in the very department she had hoped to work in. Dolly knew what she had to do next – she had to make this woman her supporter. Her name was Cynthia Starbeck – and she bellowed out to the assembled audience that she was a committed fascist.

Chapter Thirteen

'Coming to me for advice!' Major Fergusson sprang from his burr elm desk with an energy that would have done credit to a younger man. 'This is a turn-up for the books.' He ushered Diana Moore into his office overlooking the factory yard and closed the ornately carved door behind her so that she could speak freely. Major Fergusson could tell by her expression that she wanted a confidential discussion. Not many people could honestly say that they were able to gauge anything from Diana's habitually aloof countenance, but Major Fergusson knew more about the girl's past than most, and he was not fooled by the mask she wore.

'I don't see that it's so very unusual.' Diana raised an eyebrow and lowered herself gracefully into a balloon-backed chair in front of the desk. 'I'm sure lots of people come to you for advice.'

'They do, but you don't, and that's the turn-up for the books. But I can see that you don't like my teasing, so I shall be serious because I am always glad to see you.' And the Major said it with such sincerity that not only could Diana not fail to believe it, but she felt her hardened heart warm. 'And you know that you can always rely on me. Come, tell me what's troubling you.'

Diana took an exasperated breath. 'I have two girls who possibly want sacking, but Mrs Wilkes thinks we need to take all the able-bodied workers we can get and that I'm too fussy when I'm interviewing applicants, so I'm trying to give them both the benefit of the doubt.'

'Ah, not always an easy task. Although I have done it myself once or twice in my career.' Major Fergusson smiled knowingly, 'I do remember a young tearaway who almost succeeded in—'

Diana cut him off before he could make her blush with memories of her early days at the factory before her father had died and she had lost her zest for life and her taste for trouble. 'Yes, all right, you don't need to remind me that I benefitted from it when I first started on the line.'

The Major beamed at the memory of the trouble Diana had caused, creating her own posse and lording it over the other girls. It was amusing now at the distance of so many years. 'And more than once! Now who are the lucky recipients of our mercy on this occasion? How can I be of assistance?'

'I need to find somewhere to put Bess Norcliffe. She's utterly useless on a line, but there's no harm in her – and as long as we keep her out of trouble we can keep her sister, who has talents we desperately need.'

'Good Queen Bess! Is she coming back to us? Is she quite recovered from her injuries? Will she be strong enough to return?' The Major was kind enough not to suggest that even before Mary's younger sister had been hurt in the car crash which caused the factory fire, she was still a bit of a wet blanket.

'As strong as she ever was, but where do I put her?'

'That *is* a problem, but don't you know a problem solver?'

'Reenie Calder?' Diana was puzzled. 'I can't leave her to work with Reenie – she'd slow Reenie down.'

'No, I'm suggesting that you might ask Reenie how she would solve the problem of where to put Bess. Reenie thinks of solutions to problems that wouldn't occur to most people, but she is becoming more and more reticent of doing anything that Mrs Starbeck might consider to be "meddling". I don't want to see her lose her flair for problem-solving just because Mrs Starbeck has been a little hard on her. Give her this problem to solve and see how it turns out. Sound about right?'

'Fair enough, I'll sound her out, but I don't think there is anywhere we can put Bess.'

'Then come back to me if Reenie draws a blank. Nothing ventured, nothing gained. Who is next on your list?'

'You remember the vicar's daughter from Stump Cross who we agreed could have a chance at working her way up from the bottom?'

'Ah, the letter writer. Yes, how is she faring? Has she lived up to her own opinion of herself?'

'She was the one who brought the Harrogate Toffee line to a standstill by showboating.'

'Was she indeed? Has she learnt her lesson?'

'Not a bit of it. And she's threatening to write more letters. She's hanging on like grim death. I thought of putting her on cleaning.'

'Good idea. I should give her a job she doesn't want to hang on to. I think a spell as a cleaning lady will either teach her humility, or elicit her letter of resignation. Then you have proved to Mrs Wilkes that you are willing to give every applicant a more than fair chance, but you have also demonstrated that you are a good judge of character. Not to mention bringing the campaign of letter-writing to a neat close.'

Major Fergusson had known Diana for many years, and he knew that there was something else on her mind. 'If I'm not mistaken you have brought me your problems in order of importance, and the third problem – the problem which you are holding back – is the real reason for your visit.'

Diana was silent for a moment, weighing her words. Major Fergusson was patient and did not do anything to make the silence feel strained; he knew that not everyone wanted to blurt out everything they knew.

'Why did Mrs Wilkes agree to take me on as her assistant?'

'Because you asked for the position.' The Major was mildly surprised; he hoped that Diana didn't want to return to her old job on the production line. Although she had been something of a troublemaker in her early years at the firm, she had suddenly grown up around the time of her father's death, and since then had shown immense promise. The management of the firm had kept an eye on her career, and she had been offered a promotion to the grade of overlooker every year, but had always turned it down saying that she didn't want the extra hours if it meant she couldn't be at home in the evenings to look after her little half-sister. Shortly before the factory fire the firm had improved their offer and suggested that Diana might take a short transfer to their German factory where she could put her special skills to good use. However, she had turned *that* offer down for the same reason. Then, shortly after the factory fire, her younger sister was adopted by a wealthy local family and Diana had marched into the office of Amy Wilkes, the Head of Women's Employment, and demanded a promotion to the grade of junior manager, and a job as her assistant. Mrs Wilkes had not been advertising any such position, but she had accepted Diana on the spot.

'Yes, but I didn't really think I'd get it.' Diana had not known at the time what had made her ask for the position; she wondered if she'd been spoiling for a fight after the loss of Gracie and had hoped to get one with the only woman at Mackintosh's who she'd considered equal to her. 'Now I've got it and I'm twiddling my thumbs.'

'Twiddling your thumbs?'

'I work office hours so I'm finished here by half past four and I've got too much time on my hands in the week.'

The Major understood. After all these years of caring for her half-sister she was unlikely to have any hobbies. 'Had you thought about charitable work? There are plenty of organizations who'd be glad of your administrative skills. I was approached by a Quaker organization this week who are raising money for children of the Basque region in Spain; you could use the typewriter in your office to—'

'I doubt Mrs Wilkes would be pleased to see me using company property.'

'On the contrary, I think it might endear you to her.

Your manager has quite a soft spot for women with children; hadn't you noticed? Amy Wilkes always says that in Women's Employment you are always in the business of child rearing, either directly, or indirectly. The decisions we make as managers about what time a shift finishes influences the time a child is fed and bathed; the decisions we make on how much piece rates to pay the mother influence what the child is fed and how well they are clothed; the decisions we make on how fast the women must work on the production line influence how much energy and patience they will have for their children when they arrive home. Indirectly, we are raising the children who will become our workforce one day so we need to raise them well. If you wish to impress your head of department, then might I suggest using your spare time to work for a charity which benefits children?'

'I'll certainly give it some thought, Major.' And she thanked him politely.

The Major nodded sagely. 'You and I have known each other a long time, haven't we? What has it been? Seven years?'

'Eleven.'

'My goodness me, how time passes when you are enjoying your work!' The Major smiled and Diana thawed a little more. 'If you will forgive an old man for saying so, I think that in the time I've known you I have seen you make some remarkable sacrifices, and achieve remarkable things. You have held yourself to very high standards, and you have met them. But perhaps now is the time to think about what you *want* to do, rather than what you have a duty to do?'

But Diana didn't know what she wanted to do; all she

had ever wanted, since her daughter was born, was to keep her safe, and now her place of work was somewhere where she just killed time until they could see each other again. If there were some work she could do to bring her closer to Gracie she would do it, but she mistakenly thought that the Major wouldn't be able to help her there.

Chapter Fourteen

'This would not happen in the Dusseldorf factory.' Mr Baum surveyed the chaos of the Head Confectioner's kitchen and frowned. His brow did not crease easily because it was not natural for the man to frown; the lines at his eyes gave the impression of a man who had smiled so much he had prematurely wrinkled. Albert Baum, the Mackintosh's German Chocolatier, had a chocolate look about him; cocoa-coloured eyes, cocoa-coloured hair, and a smile white as fresh milk. He seemed a young man to have risen to the position of head confectioner, but he had learned his craft from his grandfather in his youth, and with only two years to go until his thirtieth birthday he had already surpassed the success of his forebear. Albert Baum's talent, diligence and cheerful disposition might have been enough to bring him success in a business of his own by now, but his home country would not allow it; as they entered their fifth year of Nazi rule, Albert Baum felt lucky to still have a job at all. 'We have a great deal of work to do, and before we can do it we must have a big clean, yes?'

Mary Norcliffe didn't know how to respond. She was ashamed that this foreigner should see a part of the Halifax factory looking in such disarray and she wished that Diana had brought her round first to put the place in order – but in all honesty it looked as if it would take at least a week to get the kitchen into any kind of working state. And not only was the place a mess, but as they looked through the cupboards to find out the state of the ingredients they found half-empty bottles of spirits hidden away in all kinds of places. There was no possibility that these were for making liqueur chocolates because the Mackintosh family were strictly teetotal Methodists, and their business was based on their religious principles – this hoard had clearly been for personal consumption.

'Are you a drinker, Mary?'

'Me, sir?' Mary was horrified at the thought. 'No, sir! They're not mine!'

'I know they're not yours, Mary. I have heard already about my predecessor; he spoiled his toffees with cologne, did he not? That is the typical mark of a secret drinker; they think they mask the aroma of their spirits with cologne, but it is the fallacy of the drunkard. This is a sad sight, is it not?'

Mary nodded. She had seen the ruin that heavy drink could do to a working man and it was always a tragedy to see talent crippled by dependency.

'We cannot help the man now, but we can help our firm. We have a great deal of work ahead of us and I will be relying on you to know the factory. We need to clear out all of these old ingredients and bottles, and half-finished things. And also these caskets which are lying empty.'

Mary was quick to try and say something helpful. 'Oh, but these are new, sir. They haven't been used at all and they are from the box-making department here. I think they could still be all right if we put them to one side.'

'No, we sweep the room clean and start afresh. Every item we use will be thoroughly cleaned and we will throw away and start again wherever we can. There will be no more making fudge in barrels!'

'Oh dear, no sir,' Mary looked worried at the thought that this very proper man thought that she had countenanced sub-par manufacturing standards, 'I would never have made it unless I'd been expressly asked to. And it was Mrs Todmorden who did the real making, sir, I just assisted. And I can assure you that it was a very clean barrel and that I helped to scrub it myself. Everything we did was done in a very orderly fashion.'

'Oh, Maria, you would make an excellent German, I think. You are very correct in your work, you like to stick to the rules. I will be very pleased with you. You learned many things from this old lady, I think.'

Mary felt a blush creep up her neck when he called her Maria; it suggested an intimacy that made her tummy flutter a little. 'It was an emergency, sir. The fire burned down half the production lines and we had no choice but to move into the old warehouse and start making all the sweets by hand. We wouldn't do it ordinarily, only in an emergency.'

'But what a way to learn. This is very good for an apprentice.'

'But I'm not an apprentice, sir. I'm just an assistant. I haven't had—'

'You will be my apprentice. I will teach you everything I can in the time allowed.' Mr Baum suddenly looked a little crestfallen. 'I am afraid that I cannot give you your indentures for a real apprenticeship because I will only be here for three months and then I must return to the Dusseldorf factory and my family, but perhaps when they find a new confectioner for the factory you will get your indentures with them. You would like that, I think, yes?'

'Oh, yes, very much, sir.' Mary was not usually chatty or inquisitive. She wished she could be more like Reenie and ask questions and strike up a friendship with people she'd only just met, but that went against the grain for Mary. However, as she bustled about the kitchen, scooping up armfuls of half-empty card cartons to put in the rubbish sacks, she steeled herself to ask the confectioner a question about himself. 'Have you left behind a large family, sir?'

'No, not a large family. I have a little boy who is five – Maximilian – and a daughter who is three; she is Greta and she is the apple of my eye. I have left them with my sister in Dusseldorf and I write to them each day to tell them who I have met in England.'

'Has their mother come with you to Halifax then, Mr Baum?'

'No.' Albert Baum was solemn. 'My wife died two winters ago. But I think she would have liked Halifax. It has many old buildings and great history.' Mr Baum opened a cupboard door and tutted. 'What is this I find? Eggs so old they could walk beside the hen that laid them! This Mr Birchwood who was dismissed, he kept a disorderly kitchen. You and I, Maria, we will make this as clean as a carrot!'

Mary tried not to burst out laughing; she'd never heard 'clean as a carrot' before, and supposed it was a German expression. It was the first time she'd felt like laughing in a long time, and as a smile spread across her face she felt a weight lift from her shoulders. Mary thought working with Mr Baum would be wonderful and she forgot for a moment that as long as she was working with Mr Baum, no one was keeping an eye on her sister. Mary tried to think of another question to ask her new boss. 'What's the Dusseldorf factory like, Mr Baum?'

'What is it like?' Albert Baum blew out his cheeks in thought. 'Well, it is very new and this is good because when we build it we plan what we will need to run a good factory. This factory you have here is made of very many old buildings which were built for other purposes and this is no good. It is better to build with the use in mind. But I tell you, Maria, your English factory will last longer than my German one.'

'Really?' This intrigued Mary. 'Why is that?'

'Because the people who are running my country are going to run it into the ground. They are madmen and they are arresting everyone, seizing property and closing things down, crippling businesses with their demands for bribes. And everywhere there are the Schutzstaffel, the SS, in their uniforms and their jackboots. The Schutzstaffel are like your Blackshirts in England, but worse. In Germany they are not just fanatics, they are fanatics with power and they use it to do terrible things.'

'But can't someone do something about it? Can't the

government tell them to stop? In England the government told Mr Mosley's Blackshirts that they weren't allowed to wear uniforms any more, and there are lots of other things they've been told to stop doing. Couldn't your government do something about them?'

'The government in my country created them. They encourage them. This is how it is now. In Spain and in Italy and in Austria it is the same – the fascists have taken over. The best I can hope for is that when I go home to my family we will find a way to leave, but it is not simple, there is nowhere else to go.'

'But can't you bring them to England? You could come and live in Halifax and then you could be the new confectioner.'

'I wish it were so simple. Your government will give me a permit to work here for three months, but no longer. After this I must go home.'

'But surely if you tell them what it's like in Germany they'll understand and they'll let you stay. Haven't you told them what it's like in Germany?'

He shook his head. 'They already know. They know that children in Germany are suffering under the Nazis and they do not let them in unless they have money, but how can a child have money? Good people in your country raise money to sponsor European children to buy them permits to come here where they are safe – but this kindness is a tiny drop of water in a great ocean.' Albert Baum sighed. 'I am sorry, Maria. I have become cynical. Perhaps I should be more hopeful like you.'

Mary didn't think she had ever heard herself called hopeful before; this must be how Reenie Calder felt all the time. She desperately wished she could find a way to be one of those good people who were helping refugee children and she wished she was more like Reenie; she wished she knew where to start being good.

Chapter Fifteen

'Come into the drawing room, but do excuse the dinosaur.' It was the sort of comment only Mrs Hunter could
have made. When Diana had allowed the adoption of her
daughter Gracie she hadn't dared to hope that she would
be able to see her again, but the family who adopted
Gracie were only too happy to see plenty of the girl they
believed was Gracie's older half-sister. They were a
wealthy family with eccentric ways and when Mrs Hunter
mentioned the dinosaur, Diana assumed she was speaking
about Mr Hunter. However, as she entered the room she
saw, to her surprise, an articulated dinosaur skeleton the
size of a small pony, and glass cabinets filled with neatly
arranged bugs and butterflies were now stacked against
every wall, hiding the delicate wood panelling and eggshell
paint. The drawing room was now unrecognizable from
the one she sat in most Sundays and she wondered if
Mrs Hunter had gone mad.

'We're having such trouble finding space. The British

Museum were quicker than us; they started planning for war far earlier than we did. Our plans only started in '33, and when we began in earnest—' Mrs Hunter stopped, seeing the puzzled look on Diana's face.

'The Museums are at war with each other?' Diana asked, confused but imagining some kind of strange war game between museum staffs where they hid their exhibits in unusual places and tried to track them down, like a crazy treasure hunt.

'Oh, my dear, no.' Mrs Hunter laughed and offered Diana a seat on the comfortable settee. 'Well, you know I am a trustee of the Natural History Museum in London? Now, I may not work as hard as a factory girl but I don't like to be idle and we all know that war is coming and have known for some time. Whitehall has told the museums to be ready, and we've been allocated budgets to move the collections wherever we can. The British Museum have already taken the prime spots in all the principle country houses, and we're resorting to putting delicate specimens in damp church vestries and below-stairs cupboards. Now we're trying to store dinosaurs in people's homes, for goodness' sake!' Mrs Hunter waved her hand in the direction of the fossilized iguanodon and then did a double-take as she realized that, while her back had been turned, a small black kitten, like a puff of soot, had attempted to climb to the creature's angry-looking ancient skull. 'Oh dear!' Mrs Hunter picked up the kitten with one gentle hand and called out, 'Lara! Gracie! You have lost Herodotus!'

Diana's eyes darted to the door; she needed to know if what Mrs Hunter was saying was serious, but she didn't want her little daughter to hear them talking about war. 'But it's just a precaution, isn't it?'

'Yes, yes, a precaution against bombing. If the museums are bombed from the air we want to make certain the collections are safe in the countryside.'

'No, I mean it's just a precaution against a war that will probably never happen, isn't it?'

Mrs Hunter had been bustling around with her head full of museum problems and lost kittens but now she saw Diana's real concern and it gave her pause. 'I'm sorry, Diana.' She softened her tone sympathetically. 'I know that you'll have been around Lara and Gracie's age during the last war, and I know that this must be very difficult for you to hear, but war *is* a real threat and all of the government departments are making preparations.'

Diana felt as though a cold wind had blown past her neck. She had read a great deal in the newspapers about the preparations for war, knew that munitions factories were being built all over the country; she knew that questions were being asked in parliament about how much money the government was putting aside for air-raid precautions, and how much food they could stockpile, but she had assumed it was all just scaremongering. A lot of hot air from a lot of hotheads who were jostling for power and needed to stir up panic to justify their jobs. This was the first time that someone she respected, someone with connections to really powerful people, had talked to her as though war was inevitable. She felt like a child playing 'What's The Time Mr Wolf', who has turned their back a fraction too long and looks back to see that they are about to lose the game. As Diana sank back into her chair in shock, two pairs of little stockinged feet rumbled into the room.

'Didi!' Diana's daughter Gracie was carrying the tortoiseshell sister to the black kitten, and ran to embrace the woman who had always been known to her as a big sister. 'Look at our kittens!'

'They are very lovely kittens,' Mrs Hunter said, indulgently, 'but if you can't keep them from climbing the dinosaur we're going to have to cover it up and spend all our days craning our necks to talk to each other around a packing crate.'

Diana looked down at her daughter's feet and noticed that, although she was wearing expensive lace-knit socks, they did not match. One had been knitted with a pattern resembling butterflies, and the other flower petals. 'Gracie, what have you put on your feet? Your nanny will be terribly put out if she finds you have put odd socks on.'

Diana knew that Gracie was safe with her adoptive family; she was healthy and she was well-fed, but it pained her to realize that no one had time for Gracie the way that Diana did back in the days when they had all lived together in her stepmother's house. The change in their circumstances could not have been more pronounced; Gracie wore clothes that Diana could never have afforded to buy her when she was on a factory wage and trying to make ends meet at her stepmother's house, and now that she herself was a junior manager and boarding at Mrs Garner's, she had more disposable income than she knew what to do with. For the first time in her life Diana Moore had an account at the Building Society and savings piling up. She'd have given them all and more to be able to dress her daughter every morning, and listen to all the things she had to say.

'I haven't got a nanny any more,' Gracie said, and then, imitating some adult she must have overheard, she said, 'It is *so* difficult to get staff these days.'

Mrs Hunter smiled at Gracie and then said confidingly to Diana, 'I've put my name on a waiting list with a Mother's Help Bureau, but really it isn't at all urgent. I can always leave them playing in the garden if Cook is in the kitchen to keep an eye on them, and the older children take it in turns to mind the younger ones; we're really managing much better than I ever thought we would.'

'But what happened to Nanny Bateman? I thought she was very good.' Diana was trying not to pry into the childcare arrangements for her secret daughter, but she could not help but worry about her. It was a dull ache in her heart when she was at work, rising to a crescendo of fear and pain in the small hours of the morning when she lay awake and alone, hating herself for not fighting harder to keep her little girl.

'Nanny Bateman gave us all quite a shock. We were sitting round listening to the wireless one evening, and Nanny Bateman was sitting in her chair by the window sewing nametapes into Emilia's gym knickers, when suddenly she put down her sewing and said, "I *must* go to Spain." Well, you can imagine our surprise, but it turned out that Nanny Bateman had been following the news for months about the civil war in Spain and the struggle against the fascists, and it had been eating away at her conscience because, lo and behold, she had been a Red Cross VAD medic on a battlefield during the last war, and she felt it her Christian duty to throw up her job here with us and go over there to nurse small children in the Basque region.'

Diana didn't know what to say to this. She could sympathize to a certain extent with people who felt they had a duty to do something which others might think difficult or distressing, but she thought Nanny Bateman's primary duty was to her existing employers. Diana disguised her disapproval and tried to ask the sort of question which someone of Mrs Hunter's own class might pose. 'Were you very put out?'

'Not a bit of it! I think it's wonderfully brave of her, and I admire her immensely. I took her straight down to the Army and Navy Stores and bought up everything she could possibly need, then took her, heavy laden, to the boat train myself. But gosh, we all miss her. She was such a hoot – and, to be perfectly frank, I need her now more than ever. I feel as though I'm never at home these days because I'm on so many different committees and none of them are frivolous things I can just throw up. I'm helping the Quakers to sponsor children from Spain to come here as refugees; I'm planning an aid detachment to travel over with medical supplies and tinned milk; and since I'm a trustee of the Natural History Museum I've been roped into the emergency preparations for war which, if you ask me, have been left far, far too late. Putting dinosaurs in people's drawing rooms, I ask you! This was not how I expected to spend the summer of 1937. I only hope war doesn't reach England as soon as I fear it will.'

Diana hugged Gracie even tighter than usual. She remembered what the Major had said to her about helping a charitable cause. She saw her chance. She took it. 'I'd like to help you raise money for the Spanish children.'

'Oh, but really, my dear,' Lydia Hunter was apologetic, 'I didn't mean that you should feel pressed to—'

'No, I want to do something.' Diana was already thinking about the myriad ways that this would help her to stay close to Gracie, and give her an excuse to visit the Hunter house even more often. 'I spoke to a colleague at the factory about it. He suggested I might volunteer my secretarial or organizational skills to a charitable enterprise and use the office typewriter. Perhaps I could help you? Reply to some of your correspondence, or print pamphlets.'

'Well, if you really could spare the time I could certainly use you.' Mrs Hunter was already scratching around for her appointments diary to find the date and time of her next committee meeting so that she could invite Diana. She was so engrossed in her search that she barely registered that her adopted daughter was chattering away to Diana, let alone what she was saying.

'I have a present for you,' Gracie whispered to Diana with wonder and love in her eyes. 'I have a sweetie for you.'

'You eat it, darling. I get lots of sweeties where I work. Next time Cook tells you that you have been a good girl you have that sweetie.'

Chapter Sixteen

'I bet we'll be gone by then. They won't keep us on that long.' Emily Everard enjoyed making pronouncements, whether they were based on firm evidence or not. She was speaking to the other married women on the Gooseberry Cream production line as they changed over the starch moulds and starch trays. Gooseberry Cream was one of the last lines still being made entirely by hand while they waited for a new mechanized line to be fitted out. The handmaking workrooms were much quieter than the mechanized rooms because the hum of machinery was almost entirely absent. It left the married women more opportunity to chat to each other and to make the most of the camaraderie of the line, and they were loving it.

Mrs Grimshaw, as one of the older women, saw it as her duty to keep morale up among the mothers of the Quality Street department. 'If they say they're keeping us on for the King's visit then I believe them.'

'But would they want the King to see that they're the type of business which employs *married* women? I think not. We'll be out on our ears the Friday before he comes, you mark my words.'

'What do you care, Emily? You said you'd never recognize the new king. You told me that you'd be loyal to King Edward to the end.'

'Well, that was before he chose to go away with that American woman. I can't forgive him for leaving his country.'

Doreen Fairclough, much softer-hearted, responded as she piped sugary soft centres into gooseberry-shaped hollows in the tightly compacted starch mould trays. 'But it was love, wasn't it? He couldn't help who he fell in love with, no one can. I'm loyal to the new king, but I feel sorry for the old one. It must be awful to have to give up your crown for love.' Doreen's own love for her children was tested on a daily basis, and that morning they had made her late for work by flushing a shoe and a pinafore down their newly installed indoor lavatory as an experiment, but her little ones had taught her how powerful love could be, and she couldn't hold the former king's decision against him.

Emily Everard clattered the wooden starch trays together with rapid efficiency. 'Wallace Simpson was a married woman when he met her. He can help falling in love with a married woman. And have you seen her? She does that awful thing with her eyebrows that they're all doing these days where they take the whole lot off and then draw them back on with a pencil to look like caterpillar droppings. I don't know what he sees in her.'

Winifred Mills leant over the worktable and said in a

stage whisper, 'I heard she learned special tricks when she stayed at a brothel in the Far East, and she's enslaved him with her bedroom shenanigans.'

Mrs Grimshaw was quick to bring them all back down to earth with a less romantic probability. 'I heard it was all just a smokescreen to cover up the fact he was getting the boot because the government didn't like him being a blackshirt. He got too friendly with Adolf Hitler and as long as we might end up at war with him and all the other fascists over there the government can't risk having a fascist spy sitting on the throne.'

'Oh, what nonsense!' Margaret Tweddle piped up. 'Everyone's against the Blackshirts and it isn't right; Oswald Mosley is the only man talking common sense and he's being vilified because people at the top feel threatened by him. They can see he's got the people on his side and they know it's only a matter of time before he's running this country, and they'll all be out of jobs.'

'If he's got "the people" on his side, why did "the people" throw eggs at him when he marched down Cable Street? Answer me that.'

'That's just the *Fabians*, those rich Liberal folk who can afford to take the day off work to stand in the way of democratic progress.'

'Democratic progress my eye! I had to go to Wakefield a week last Saturday to collect a postal order and I had three of those young scrotes wearing British Union badges shouting every kind of obscenity at me because they thought I looked Jewish. I shouldn't have to put up with nonsense from the BUF every time I walk out my front door.'

'You can't blame Mosley for some silly youths—'

'I can and I will! I'll blame him for the bad weather and the pain in my hip if I feel like it. Bloody Oswald Mosley and his bloody blackshirts, they're everywhere and we can't seem to get anything done without someone telling us that Oswald Mosley would do it better. I'd like him to come down here and make Gooseberry Creams for a shift and see if he still thinks he's so clever. I bet he couldn't tell one end of a piping bag from another, let alone keep the fondant off his sleeves.'

'Some days I worry that we won't get a royal visit at all.' Siobhan Grimshaw had been quiet until then.

'Don't you worry, love. They'll keep us on for the royal visit, you'll see.' Her mother-in-law put an arm round her shoulders and gave her a reassuring squeeze.

'I don't mean that, I mean the King.' Siobhan sighed with the difficulty of expressing her fears. 'I read the papers same as everyone else and the blackshirts are always talking about how they support the old king and not the new one. What if they do all the things they keep threatening they're going to do? What if we have a revolution? What if they throw out this king? What if they put his brother back on the throne and make us fascist like they've done in Italy and Austria and Germany and Greece and Spain? Isn't anyone else worried we'll go the same way as all the other countries?'

The spirit of lively gossip which had kept their discussion bobbing along seemed to seep away as though a chill wind had blown through the room. Mrs Grimshaw saw the fear in her daughter-in-law's eyes, and she tried to find something to say. 'Spain hasn't fallen yet, love. There's still all sorts of folks going over there to fight the fascists. I heard three lads from Crossley's Carpets ran away there last week, vowing to put an end to the whole Spanish Civil War with nothing but pluck and Yorkshire pragmatism.'

'But it *will* fall, won't it?' Siobhan pulled a cotton handkerchief from her overall pocket and mopped at an angry tear which had begun to fall down her cheek. 'All the other countries have, and then it will be our turn. And we're all worrying about whether we get to make the King's Toffee!'

'I think you'll find there is one significant difference in our case.' Emily Everard was not going to allow her workroom to dissolve into tears and melancholy. 'To place the Duke of Windsor back on his former throne would require his consent – and he has refused that consent while his younger brother, our present king, is still living. As long as King George lives his brother will not permit a revolution. And now, if we've all quite finished, it is time to change over the starch trays – and if half of you don't lend a hand, and half of you don't move out of the way, we're going to have starch powder everywhere and you know what a cloud of mess *that* makes.'

The married ladies reluctantly acknowledged that Emily Everard was right and pitched in to change over the starch trays, ready to mould another three hundred Gooseberry Creams before the end of their shift. Some of them had been more than a little disquieted by what Siobhan had said about the possibility of revolution in England – after all, it was happening everywhere else in Europe. But, as always, Emily Everard had taken charge and they felt better for it. As long as King George lived they were safe. They did not know then that a casket of their own choco-lates, with the king's coat of arms emblazoned on them, was abroad in Halifax and neatly glazed with poison, and that they were about to be thrown into chaos.

Diana had spent a productive morning solving employment problems, and responding to Mrs Wilkes' correspondence. She had also secured Mrs Wilkes' permission to coordinate factory support for Mrs Hunter's sponsorship of Spanish children affected by the civil war in their country. Diana had a cashbox and a clean new accounting ledger, and she had already typed memoranda to several departmental managers, informing them that should any of their employees wish to contribute to a fund sponsoring Spanish infant refugees to come to England, then she would be available to receive donations during office hours. Diana had modest hopes that, with time and effort on her part, she could raise enough money to bring one child refugee to England, and to safety from the war in Spain. However, this was not her principle reason for setting up the factory fund: if she was raising funds for one of Mrs Hunter's good causes it would give her a legitimate excuse to visit her house in the week, and so see Gracie more often.

Content with her morning's achievements, she now had to tackle what she thought of as The Norcliffe Conundrum, and she had arranged to meet Reenie Calder in the staff canteen before the lunchtime rush to talk it over.

Diana usually had to steel herself to exercise patience with Reenie Calder because the girl always reminded her of a Labrador puppy jumping up with enthusiasm at the idea of being involved in everything. However, Diana knew better than most that when you were in a fix you couldn't be fussy about who you took help from. She didn't understand just how Reenie's mind worked but she was not above asking her for advice if she wanted an unusual solution to a problem which had already stumped her. Now she looked directly at the younger girl. 'Reenie, do you honestly believe that there's a job for everyone?'

Reenie thought about the question. 'In a factory there is; everyone finds their place here.'

Diana pursed her lips. She knew as well as anyone how lucky Reenie had been to 'find' her place, and how many people had stuck their necks out for her to help her to keep it. Then again, Reenie was good at showing her gratitude so Diana didn't begrudge her it. And Diana supposed that, in a way, she herself had found her place in the factory, as much as there would ever be a place for her anywhere.

Reenie was conciliatory. 'I know you don't like Dolly Dunkley, and I don't like the way she throws her weight around either, but she'll have learnt her lesson – and like you said, she'll have taught a lesson to all the other girls too.'

'It wasn't Dunkley I had in mind,' Diana was frowning in thought, 'it was Bess Norcliffe.'

Reenie was surprised. 'Do you think she's well enough to come back to work?'

'As much as she ever was.' Diana had reluctantly helped Mary to cover up for her sister's shortcomings as long as they'd both thought that Bess was weak because she was expecting a baby out of wedlock. When Bess's weakness was revealed to be nothing more earth-shattering than anaemia, Diana had been irritated that she had wasted so much time helping them. 'I can't put her anywhere without her sister because she's an accident waiting to happen, so I'm not convinced there *is* a job for her, but I've got to find her one if I want her sister to help me out somewhere else. Have you ever seen *anything* she's good at?'

Reenie became animated. 'Organizing the flowers for other girls' weddings. She does very well at making things look pretty. And if there's ever a friend who's having a party she'll dress their living room lovely. Maybe you could put her in the box-making department and she could glue the tassels to fancy caskets.'

'No. She'd be just as bad on that as any other line. The box-making department might need more care and artistic flair, but you still have to be fast and work to piece rates; Bess can't keep her mind on a task for the time it needs to work on a line. She's a dreamer.'

'What about decorating the factory for the visit of the King? Who's doing that?'

'At the moment I fear it may be a free-for-all, with every department arguing over how far their territory extends, and then putting up things which don't match.'

Reenie was delighted by the thought of this decorative anarchy. 'Well, there's your answer! Get her to help organize the decorations. She's good at making sure everyone sticks to the same colour scheme for weddings and birthdays. You could put her in charge of all that.'

'I don't suppose she could go far wrong with giving out bunting and that would at least keep her out of trouble and keep her from slowing down a line.'

There was, of course, the other problem: that Bess wanted a baby so badly that if they weren't careful she'd be having it away with the first unsuitable rake to give her a smile. Diana thought that if she left her with the Salesmen's Department there would be much less chance of that. However, she did not anticipate that Bess would still manage to get a baby – and not in the usual way.

Chapter Seventeen

Diana took the tram to the Norcliffes' house. As it clattered to a heavy stop, Diana hopped down onto the cobbles. She knew the Norcliffe girls' house well enough – she'd visited once or twice, but never for longer than she had to. Diana was not a social animal, and the Norcliffe sisters were hard work at the best of times.

'Bess, Diana Moore is here to see you.' Mary, who looked cross, shouted up the stairs to the bedroom as she invited Diana in.

'You can show her in. She won't mind standing.' Bess's cheery voice was like tinkling bells ringing down the hallway, and Diana thought she'd rather do business with her miserable older sister Mary – at least you knew where you were with the miserable one.

Mary looked a silent apology at her colleague. It was both infuriating and embarrassing to have to watch her younger sister holding court from their bed like a dignitary.

Mary showed Diana up to their shared bedroom where

Bess was sitting up in a dressing gown talking to two equally silly girls of the same age who had stopped by to visit.

'Well, I said to Edith, I said "Bess gets a lot of visitors, but she's always glad to see a friendly face." So I told her I'd bring her with me to meet you. You don't mind, do you, dear?' The silly girl in the royal blue dress gestured to the silly girl beside her in a peony pink dress in a way that suggested to Diana that the pink dress was Edith, but they were so alike she wasn't sure it mattered.

'Not at all, chuck; you know I get so bored stuck here all day. It's been a terrible trial,' Bess sighed.

'You were at the trial?' Edith in pink bust out in excitement.

'Don't be silly, she wasn't at the trial,' the blue dress chastised the friend with a roll of her eyes, 'she was in the hospital for *weeks* afterwards. And we all thought you'd die,' she said to Bess gravely.

'Well, I thought I would die! Thank goodness for Lady Mackintosh being so kind to me in my convalescence.' Bess made the most of this opportunity to be as melodramatic as possible for this new, and less jaded, audience.

Diana was irked by Bess's melodrama, but she couldn't imagine that her older sister Mary was too happy about Bess's unhurried recovery either. Mary and Diana had been forced to bite their tongues in the weeks after the factory fire as Bess gloried in a reputation as something akin to a wounded hero, having her picture appear in the local newspaper, and being the daily recipient of kind letters and little gifts from wellwishers. Mary wasn't quite sure how her sister managed to always come up smelling of roses; Bess had been a feeble factory hand, had indulged in a highly dubious fling with an even more dubious young criminal, had gone for a ride with him in a stolen car whilst shouting 'Lady Mack's a strumpet!' out of the car window, had damn near caused the fire that had nearly brought the town to its knees, and had since come up with at least eight conflicting versions of what had happened that night. The sisters were so alike, but so different; they both had the same tiny strawberry mark high up on their cheek like a fairy kiss; they were both slight in build and delicate in appearance; and they both had too much imagination for their own good. Mary used her imagination to think of all the things in life which might go wrong for her and her family. Bess used hers to think of all the wonderful experiences which might fall into her lap. Behind their backs the pair were known as Bad Queen Mary and Good Queen Bess; this had always seemed unfair to Diana because while Mary might have a foul temper, and Bess might have a sweet disposition, Mary was the one who you could trust to do the right thing, and to care deeply about it.

Diana coughed conspicuously and the pink and blue dresses turned to see the much older girl, stony-faced and intimidating to such young factory girls, looming behind them in the doorway with Mary. The young visitors made their excuses and made themselves scarce.

Mary sighed in exasperation. 'Honestly, Bess, what goes on inside your head?'

'There's nothing going on inside my head.' Bess was bemused. 'I didn't bang my head. It was my ribs and my shins that got bashed; don't go insinuating things about my head.'

Diana gritted her teeth. 'Talking of Lady Mackintosh,

we've found a nice job you can do that will particularly please her if you do it well. You would like to please Lady Mackintosh, wouldn't you? How would you like to help with decorating the factory in time for the visit of the King?'

Mary looked horrified. 'You're letting her do what?'

'I know,' Diana said to Mary, 'but just hush, would you?' Then to Bess she said, 'Bess? What do you think?'

Bess turned her wide eyes on Diana. 'Oh, I don't know. I'm still very weak . . . I was terribly injured during the accident and I just don't feel ready to be back on my feet. I mean, I suppose if Lady Mackintosh wanted me to come and greet the King and Queen, just for a moment, I suppose I could come down in a car. I wouldn't want to disappoint Lady Mackintosh.'

Diana stood in the shabby, one-up-one-down and wondered who Bess thought would be sending this car to collect her. She suppressed her irritation and tried again. 'You wouldn't be expected to decorate the entire factory yourself. The company salesmen, who dress all the shop windows, are going to work together to decorate it and you're going to help distribute the bunting and things and organize some costumes. We've decided that all the girls who work in the Tour Guide's Department will be dressed as Miss Sweetly, the lady from the top of the Quality Street tin, and all of the gentlemen from the Salesmen's Department will dress as Major Quality. There's a dress-maker booked to sew all the costumes and your job will be to take the measurements from all the lady tour guides and send them to the dressmaker and then, when the costumes come back in boxes, you'll distribute them and make sure all the guides are nicely turned out on the day.'

'What about the salesmen? Will I need to take their measurements?'

Diana supposed she should have expected that Bess would try this on. 'That won't be necessary, Bess. They will all know their own measurements because they can ask their tailors. However, you will need to get them to write their measurements down for you so that you can send them off to the dressmaker, and then hand out their costumes when they arrive at the factory. I would hope that you won't be occupied with this all day long, and the rest of the time you'll help the salesmen to get the decorations ready for the inside and the outside of the factory.'

Bess thought for a moment, then asked, 'Are any of the salesmen very handsome?'

Diana bit her tongue 'I dare say some of them are.'

'Oh, well then, if Lady Mackintosh needs me to supervise them then I mustn't let her down.'

Diana didn't comment on Bess's rather shallow change of heart, her delusion that Lady Mackintosh gave a monkey's bum what Bess did, or Bess's assumption that she was the supervisor and not the dogsbody.

'What kind of decorations? Do they want grand banners and bunting and the like?'

'Yes,' Diana tried to keep a patient tone, 'all that sort of thing. The Estates Department will be painting all the buildings inside and out, but the sales department are planning banners to hang from the outside walls.'

Bess twitched her pretty little nose. 'I've had some initial thoughts. Do you want to jot them down for me?'

'Not particularly.'

Bess didn't notice the snub but carried on talking. 'I

134

think I'd like them to paint the outside of the buildings in a nice lilac, and then paint the cornices in red, white and blue to honour the King and Queen. And then for the banners I think cloth of gold . . .' Bess hummed, evidently feeling much stronger and healthier than she had three minutes earlier.

Diana ground her teeth and took a long look at the ceiling before asking, 'So am I putting you down for factory work back on the production line with your old job, or decorating the factory for the royal visit?'

When Diana rose to leave Mary offered to show her out. Diana could hardly get lost between the bedroom and the front door, but she was an honoured guest and Mary wanted to show her the respect that her sister had not. They stood on the doorstep of the Norcliffe girls' house.

Diana looked at Mary with seriousness. 'I've found somewhere to put Bess as I promised. Now will you definitely stay in the confectioner's kitchen and make a casket for the King? We're depending on you, Mary. Seriously, we've got no one else to turn to.'

Chapter Eighteen

'I've called this emergency meeting of the Senior Managers because we have had an edict that we need to cut costs immediately – and each of your departments is losing twenty per cent of their capital expenditure budgets.' Director Hitchens was brusque, but some of his colleagues could see that it was part of his attempt to save face.

'You don't mean we're cancelling His Majesty's visit, do you?' It was typical of Cynthia Starbeck that she should be more interested in seeing the King than having enough money to maintain machinery in good order.

'No,' Director Hitchens mopped his brow with a broad handkerchief, 'we need to cut costs to *pay* for the visit.'

'Why?' Amy Wilkes asked. 'How much are we spending on this visit?'

'Everything we have.' Mr Hitchens was grave as he watched the room fall silent in shock.

'But that's madness!' Major Fergusson was as patriotic as anyone else at the factory – he had fought for the old queen in his boyhood – but he could recognize a fool's errand when he saw one. 'We're already struggling to recover from the destruction of the fire.'

'It's the only way,' Mr Hichens said flatly. 'The fire damaged our reputation and because we weren't able to keep up supply to our customers, while we were down on our luck our competitors took a share of the market from us.'

Cynthia Starbeck turned up her nose at what she, in her ignorance of market forces, thought of as a preposterous idea. 'I can't believe that our competitors would be so underhanded, especially as our three major ones are Quaker firms.'

'They didn't do it deliberately; it's a natural by-product of a situation like this one. People go into shops to buy sweets and if the sweets they wanted aren't available they don't wait until they've been ordered in – which they might with a book they particularly want to read, or a suit of ready-to-wear clothes in their particular style – so for every shop we couldn't stock after the fire we lost good custom to Rowntree's, Cadbury's, Fry's and Terry's. We have no choice but to extend ourselves; this year will be make or break for Mackintosh's.'

'Aren't sales of Quality Street making any headway? Surely, with such a strong product, we can afford to bide our time.'

'Quality Street was a good idea – we've made something more affordable than a box of chocolates but more luxurious than a tin of toffees – so Sir Harold's idea was inspired. But it isn't enough to have a good idea; we need to build our sales and our customer loyalty or we'll go the way of Fry's and be swallowed up by a competitor.'

As usual, Cynthia Starbeck appeared to be under the impression that money grew on trees. 'I suppose, if this doesn't come off, we could always ask the bank for a loan to tide us over next year?'

Director Hitchens shook his head. 'We've already mortgaged the factories to the hilt. When I said we were spending everything we have on the royal visit, I meant it. We will transform the factory, the workforce, and the product. Everything will have a new livery and everyone will be aware of it. There won't be a housewife in Britain who won't see our factory on the Pathé newsreels in the cinema; this is the biggest advertisement we'll ever make and we're giving it everything we have.'

Amy Wilkes felt as though she was banging her head against a brick wall; was she really the only member of staff who could see that all their plans would come to nothing without the right people to execute them? 'But can we get the staff to do it? We're struggling as it is and this will take a hell of a lot of skilled workers.'

'We've lifted the marriage bar; that should be enough.' Mrs Starbeck made the most of her opportunity to tell Amy Wilkes how to do her job. 'There are plenty of married former workers who are glad to come back while we need them.'

Amy took a deep breath and prepared to say something she had wanted to say for a long time, but had not had the forum. 'I'm not sure that can work. Married women have children and homes of their own that need their attention; they get called away from the line to look after sick children, or children who have been sent home from school, or locked out of the house because they've lost their latchkey. Married women with children come with a different set of personal complications which need accommodations in the workplace. Without giving proper thought to how we accommodate them—'

'You will have to tell them not to bring their personal complications to work.' Cynthia Starbeck wrinkled her nose in displeasure and cut Amy Wilkes off before she could stand up for her married workers. 'They need to be told that the factory is a place for work, and home is a place for children – and that when they cross the threshold of Mackintosh's they must forget that they are mothers until the whistle blows to end their shift. For those mothers who need additional accommodations – they are not for Mackintosh's.'

Amy Wilkes was not in a position to press her point further because this odious woman appeared to have too many of the other managers on her side. She had to be satisfied with the knowledge that, whatever Cynthia tried to do, the Major would always be there to step in and make sure that allowances were made for mothers who were willing to make the personal sacrifices necessary to get to the factory and help it. Without Major Fergusson her job would be impossible. But Amy knew that without the talents and determination of the mothers on the Quality Street line, the rebuilding of the factory would have been impossible too. She resigned herself to the fact that some of her colleagues' minds would never be changed, and she only hoped the next generation would be more enlightened. She also hoped the Major would never leave.

Chapter Nineteen

'I bloody love it when Emily Everard sticks her oar in. I'm not kidding, it's better than watching the pictures.' Doreen Fairclough was watching from a distance as Emily Everard berated a production manager who was visibly shrinking inside his starched shirt collar.

'What's she bangin' on about now? Not enough sugar in her tea?'

'No, the production manager told Winifred and Pearl they could go home because they were too old to work on his line, and it's on shutdown anyway while he waits for a fitter to fix a machine. Winnie offered to take a look at it instead of calling a fitter out, and he patronized her within earshot of Emily Everard.'

'Oh my God! This I need to see.' Doreen scooped up her cup of tea and her break time biscuit which she had bought from the tea trolley and carried it over to the scene of the trouble, the better to hear Emily Everard give the young man a piece of her mind.

'They were building boilers out of tin cans under enemy fire before you were even born!' Emily Everard took in a breath to bellow her criticism. 'That's the trouble with lads who didn't serve in the war, they've got no idea that women did war work an' all! I'll have you know that Pearl can strip down four different kinds of military vehicles—'

'Five,' Pearl interjected casually.

'Pearl can strip down *five* different kinds of military vehicles and put them back together again blindfolded.'

'Not entirely blindfolded.' Pearl didn't like to boast.

'Look, I'm sorry.' The production manager was a lad who had been promoted rather sooner than was usual as a result of the sudden shortage of staff and the huge upheaval involved in rebuilding lines, but aside from his youthful foolishness, he was not a bad lad. 'I just can't let a married woman do a fitter's job. It's against regulations. We're short on fitters and engineers at the moment and we just have to wait until we can get one out to look over the machine. I don't make the rules, ladies.'

Emily Everard wasn't going to be brushed off so easily. 'What is it that you're worried about specifically? Is it that she's not qualified enough? Or that she'll get hurt? Or are you worried about her wanting to get paid a man's wage if she claims it as overtime? Because that wasn't what she was offering – she was offering to do this free just so that we can get the line up and running again as fast as possible. We're all on piece rates, you know, and every minute this line isn't running we're losing money.'

'I'm not saying she's not qualified, and I'm sure it's very kind of her to offer, but rules is rules: I can't let a woman do this on my line.'

Emily Everard looked around at her fellow factory workers who were all mentally calculating what a loss of one day's piece rates would cost them in the long run. For the younger girls who still lived with their mothers the loss of one day's work could sometimes be a boon if the weather was nice and they fancied a day's unpaid holiday, but to these women their earnings weren't pocket money and every day counted toward something they needed to save for in the limited time they had left at the factory. Losing one day of piece rates felt like the end of the world – little did they know they were about to lose much more.

Chapter Twenty

Lara and Gracie had put their kittens into their cardigan pockets, but they found that they had a tendency to pull runs in the knit with their claws and so they tried to find them a basket instead. On the whole the kittens were very good about not clawing things, but the tortoiseshell with blue-green eyes was a curious little muffin and she was intrigued by the pattern of woollen stitches on the girls' matching clothes.

Lara and Gracie had begun dressing alike almost as soon as they met. Other children might have exhibited jealousy when told that their parents were adopting another child, but the Hunter children did not have the same fears most children do. There was no scarcity of love or resources and they had no fear of sharing their own abundance. For them, a little sister would be a valuable additional playmate, and as Gracie was the same age as Lara they became inseparable. They could have been mistaken for twins, which was what they had decided they were from then on and when anyone asked, they said they were twins. Gracie loved having siblings closer to her own age, and she loved joining in with all of Lara's usual activities. Lara had a regular routine of lessons with their governess and charitable work with her mother for which she had found a new enthusiasm now that she had the novelty of sharing them with a new sister.

It was a red-letter day for the Hunter girls because they had been left to play in the garden under the watchful eye of Cook for the first time in weeks, and Cook had told them that they had been very good girls. This meant that they could now finally have a sweetie from the casket which they had kept wrapped in a very large cotton napkin on top of the dresser in their bedroom since Diana's last visit. They had wanted to give it to Diana, but she was obviously tired of chocolates and toffees in her job, and she'd told them that they could eat them for her next time Cook told them that they'd been good.

'Mother says you get lots more enjoyment from giving something away than keeping it for yourself,' Lara told Gracie as they sat on their bedroom floor holding back the kittens from the exquisite casket of chocolates they had collected in their basket from Kirkby's shop. 'But we have already had the joy of offering it to your big sister, so now I don't know if that still counts. Maybe we can eat one because we've been good for Cook.' Lara was wise beyond her years and Gracie looked up to her. Perhaps it was because Lara had grown up with older siblings that she was so talkative and so good at puzzling things out.

The pair of them sighed and lifted the lid of the casket again. They lifted it carefully because they didn't want to leave marks on it – Nanny had often told them off for spoiling the pages of books with jammy fingermarks.

Lara furrowed her brow and made a pronouncement, 'Actually, I don't think we should have one.' She sat up very straight in the way that she did when she wanted to seem very grown-up. 'I think we should save it in the cupboard and wait until we've thought of something really good to do with it. It's a good box so we should give it to someone who has been good.'

Gracie agreed. They had lots of nice things, so they would enjoy giving this one away.

Mrs Hunter was hurrying past the girls' room on her way out to a museum committee meeting and popped her head around the door. 'Gosh, that is a rather exquisite box. Whatever do you keep it?'

'Macintosh's toffees. Very special ones.' Gracie beamed.

'Ah, something else from Diana's factory, I might have known.' If Mrs Hunter was surprised that Diana hadn't told her about such an impressive gift, then she didn't show it. 'Just make sure you don't spoil your dinner by eating sweets.'

'Oh no, they aren't for us, they're for someone who has been very good,' Lara explained.

Mrs Hunter nodded, agreed, and, mentally already on her way to her committee meeting, missed her chance . . .

Chapter Twenty-One

'You've been lucky, Dunkley.' Diana had escorted Dolly Dunkley to the office of the Head of Cleaning and brought her employment file along with her.

'My name is either *Miss* Dunkley, or Dolly; I'll thank you not to be saucy with me and make my name sound ridiculous.'

'You manage to do that very well for yourself. I've seen your employment file and you weren't christened Dolly, your real name is Verity. Now, I'm letting you off your rudeness, your arrogance, your insolence and your patent incompetence because we are absolutely desperate for workers just now. However, don't think this means that I won't sack you in a heartbeat if you give me any more trouble or lip.'

Dolly squared up to Diana. 'One day very, very soon I'm going to be your manager, and then we'll see who's insolent.'

Diana didn't move away, she merely smiled, standing

her ground with the cool confidence of one who has eaten bigger troublemakers for breakfast and still settled down to a hearty lunch. 'That's as may be. But for the moment you're working as the most junior cleaner there is, and if you walk out I don't care. I dare say you *will* walk out when you see what kind of jobs they have for you to do. But here it is, your only chance to work at Mack's. Take it or leave it.' Diana indicated the room full of women in tan-coloured overalls and thick, scuffed boots.

'But I should be managing these people, I shouldn't be working in amongst them! I'm Dolly Dunkley and I have a letter from Lady Mackintosh!' Dolly was looking at her new colleagues in the cleaning department with contempt.

For a girl of nineteen, Diana thought, Dolly had precious little sense of how to make herself liked. She couldn't decide if her behaviour was babyish or old maidish, but in all honesty she didn't care. If the girl thought she could do better than Reenie Calder then let her prove herself where Reenie Calder proved herself – in a junior position. 'I don't care if you've got a letter from Clive of India. I'm your recruiting manager and this is where I'm putting you. *I* make the decisions, and I'll decide if you're ever suitable for promotion to the level of Junior Manager.'

'I have a matriculation certificate from a grammar school. I didn't come here to work, I came here to tell *other people* to work. Either you take me to my real office or I'll report you to Lady Mackintosh.' Dolly was not speaking in a whisper and since they had entered this factory corridor just as the whistle sounded for the tea break there had been no noise of factory machinery to drown out what she was saying. Several of the women in the cleaner's break room heard her, and it wouldn't be long before all of them knew what a high opinion she had of herself, and what a low opinion she had of them.

All of a sudden the throng of girls on their break burst forth from the workrooms and the factory corridor was a sea of white aprons and white cotton caps. Girls from all over Halifax dreamt of working at Mackintosh's one day, and to the girls sitting at the conveyor belts of gleaming toffees, this was the most beautiful place in the world, the place that saved them from going into service, or marrying a young man they didn't care for, or chafing their fingers raw in a laundry, or going without work at all. The girls on the line loved their jobs with a passion and Dolly Dunkley clearly didn't deserve the opportunity she was being given. She'd have been better to leave and take the 'genteel' work her father had offered to secure for her, but to the detriment of everyone whose path she was about to come across, she had a perverse desire to prove Diana Moore wrong, and to stay in work at Mack's until she had spoken to a director.

Diana returned to the Women's Employment office with a sense of achievement. She couldn't think why the Dunkley girl was so determined to have a job at Mack's, but she thought that Major Fergusson was right and that a stint as a cleaner would probably make Dolly leave of her own accord. With this satisfying thought in mind she checked the in-tray on her desk for the latest memoranda, checked Mrs Wilkes' appointments diary to see when her next meeting would finish, and then settled down to go over the ledger of factory donations to the Halifax branch of the Basque Children's Committee. She needed to enter the amounts of the three modest donations which had been sent to her through the internal postal system while she had been away from her desk, and lock the money away in the cash box.

The work she did for the fund was simple, but satisfying at the same time. Mrs Wilkes had kindly suggested that she might be allowed to do a little of it during office hours if she ran out of things to do for the Women's Employment Department, but Diana's principle motivation for volunteering had been the opportunities it would afford her outside the factory offices. Volunteering to coordinate donations for the fund helped Diana to kill some time in the evenings, but it also gave her the chance to report regularly to Mrs Hunter at her home on the fund's progress, because Mrs Hunter was chair of the Halifax branch of the Basque Children's Committee. Diana kept the locked cashbox on her desk when she was in the office, and locked it away in the small departmental safe when she was not. The entries in her ledger were neat, clear and ordered by date, which she could not have known then would be surprisingly useful to her before the month was out.

Diana's productivity was interrupted by a brusque knock at the door, followed by someone who did not wait to be invited in.

'Diana Moore? I'm Mrs Starbeck. I'm here to look over some work you're doing. I take it you can spare the time?'

Diana did not look up from her ledger; she could tell that Cynthia Starbeck was game playing. They had met before, but the older woman was obviously trying to cultivate an air of superiority by affecting not to remember

Diana. 'No, I'm coordinating the Mackintosh's factory donations to the Halifax B.C.C. fund. They're sponsoring Spanish child refugees to escape war.'

'I really don't think company time ought to be wasted on an enterprise like this; it's all ridiculous anyway. The children ought to be cared for in their own country by their own parents. If their parents weren't prepared to care for them during difficult times, they shouldn't have chosen to have them in the first place.' Mrs Starbeck was huffing in exasperation while moving her gold pendant delicately up and down the chain it hung from around her neck. 'Now, if you can bear to tear yourself away from all of this for a moment to talk to me about the proper business of the firm . . .'

Diana leant back in her chair and folded her arms. She could see that Mrs Starbeck had intended to wrong-foot her and make herself seem more important than Diana in order to get her own way at something, but Diana was wise to that trick and waited in silence to hear what it was that the other woman wanted.

'I've come about the visit of His Majesty the King.' Cynthia Starbeck paused for effect, but when her words appeared not to have had the effect she'd hoped for she pressed on. 'I understand you have been asked to type up the itinerary for the visit and I wanted to make certain that you have all the details correct.'

Diana did not move. She remained seated with her arms crossed while Mrs Starbeck stood awkwardly, evidently struggling to maintain whatever air of superiority she had thought to bluster her way in with. Diana waited another moment, sighed, and then said, 'I'm not just typing it, I'm planning it and writing it. An awful lot of the jobs for the King's visit have been delegated to me. I suppose all the most important people around here must be fully occupied with the proper business of the firm. Which details was it that you wanted to check?'

Mrs Starbeck appeared to be trying to change tack from self-important bluster to simpering charm, but that wouldn't wash with Diana either. 'Look, I don't want to create extra work for you, I just wanted to make sure that you've heard that I'll be one of the party of managers who takes His Majesty on the tour of the King's Toffee line. I've spoken with Lady Mackintosh and she thinks it would be rather nice for her if she could introduce me to the King because we have a family connection, you see?' Cynthia Starbeck lifted a delicate thumb and fore-finger to her collar and lifted her gold pendent for Diana to see. Diana had seen Mrs Starbeck fidgeting with it in staff meetings before, but she had never seen it up close and now she realized that it wasn't a locket as she had originally thought; it was a heavy gold fob with some old-fashioned insignia on the base. 'My ancestor on my mother's side came over with William the Conqueror and we still have the family seal. You see? There's a family connection.'

Diana remained impassive, only a slight twitch below her right eye giving any indication that on the inside she was trying not to laugh.

'Aren't you going to take a note of it? Or check the itinerary you have?' Mrs Starbeck was losing her charm.

'No, thanks. If Lady Mackintosh is writing to me about it I might as well hang on for her letter. I'm sure it's in the post.'

Mrs Starbeck was about to give Diana Moore a short

reply when the unmistakable voices of Major Fergusson and Mrs Wilkes reached them from just beyond the door of the office.

'Ah, Mrs Starbeck!' Major Fergusson always sounded as though he was delighted to see everyone. 'Delighted, delighted. And what brings you down to the Women's Employment office? Not applying for a new job, I hope?' And the Major chuckled at his own joke.

'No, I was just, er . . .' Mrs Starbeck looked at Diana and seemed unsure for a fraction of a second how she should respond.

Diana wondered if it had been a lie about Lady Mackintosh; it had felt like a lie, or perhaps an exaggeration. Yes, with Mrs Starbeck it would be out of character, Diana thought, for her to tell that sort of brazen lie, but it might be an exaggeration. Perhaps she had bumped into Lady Mackintosh at a society event in Halifax and had mentioned in passing how much she would like to tell the King about her dead Norman ancestor, or perhaps she had written to Lady Mackintosh and hadn't received a reply yet. Either way, she looked embarrassed and evidently didn't want to tell the Major the real reason she had stopped by. Diana wasn't going to help her.

'I came to make a donation to the fund I heard was being organized for the refugee children. So terribly important for us all to do everything we can to help them.' Mrs Starbeck's lie surprised Diana, but the Major and Mrs Wilkes appeared taken in.

'Capital, capital! Glad to hear you took my advice, Diana. Good use of your time, that. Very good.' And he and Mrs Wilkes went on to continue their discussion behind the closed door of Mrs Wilkes' office.

Diana sat forward in her chair and began writing Mrs Starbeck's name in her ledger and asked, smiling, 'How much can I put you down for, Mrs Starbeck?'

Cynthia Starbeck was clearly angry to have been so ridiculously caught out, and to have had to offer support for a charitable endeavour she so thoroughly despised. She glanced up to make sure that the door to Mrs Wilkes' office behind Diana's desk was closed, and then ground out, 'A penny.'

Diana pretended not to notice as Mrs Starbeck flounced out of the employment office, and instead wrote in careful, clear figures the nice round sum of one penny. It was the most enjoyable donation she had received. Although she couldn't know then, that Cynthia Starbeck's penny would change both their lives.

Chapter Twenty-Two

Reenie knew exactly what to do. The whole chocolate fudge line was running stop-start because there was a problem with one foil and band machine. The workers couldn't see it, but Reenie could. It was thought that the problem was the girls themselves – they were bickering – and the Women's Employment Department had been asked to split them up for the good of the production line. But they didn't need to be split up and they didn't want to be. They had a genuine affection for one another and, although most of them were only girls with a couple of years' experience, they had worked well together in the past. They knew one another's rhythms and they insisted that the problems were down to a jinx.

Diana had told Reenie to go and take a look and Mrs Starbeck told Reenie not to get involved because it wasn't their department's problem and she didn't want Time and Motion resources wasted on a problem that the Women's Employment Department should already have fixed.

Reenie decided to compromise and go along in her dinner hour, which was her own time, but this just irritated Mrs Starbeck further as she complained that Reenie wouldn't come back from her break rested, and if she didn't come back rested she was causing problems for Time and Motion because she wouldn't have the energy to help them with their work.

'Why didn't you take the overlooker's job they offered you?' Reenie asked Diana as they stood on the balcony looking down across the whole production line. 'I mean, I'm not saying you're not good at this one, I just think this one is an awful lot of extra work and trouble, and if you'd taken the overlooker's job you'd get to sit on a high chair all day and boss girls about.'

Diana shook her head. 'The trouble with being an overlooker is that you're being pulled in every direction, and you've got to do as you're told just as much as the girls on the line. You're getting told by the factory manager how he wants everything run, then Time and Motion come and tell you something different, then Women's Employment say your experienced girls are getting took away from you to go on a new line and you're getting inexperienced ones but you have to keep up the same speed, and then the Sales Director orders double the output because his men are selling the sweets as fast as you can make them. The overlooker's job is as much about being bossed about as it is bossing, if not more so. The Women's Employment job is different because you get to make strategic decisions. You get to talk to all those other departments, and when they pull you in one direction, you get to pull back.'

Reenie could see why Diana was better off under Mrs

Wilkes. Being bossed around had never suited her, and she had an intuition for the temperaments of the girls and where they ought to be.

'I can see what's gone on with your fudge line,' Reenie said. 'It's that foil and band machine.'

'No. I've spoken to the overlooker and the fitter and they both say the machine hasn't broken down once. Betsy Newman keeps complaining that it's faulty, but they haven't seen a fault yet. They think it's an excuse to get them all off the charge of bickering, which is the real problem.'

'No, I know Betsy Newman and I could see exactly what she was doing. The overlooker and the fitter are looking at the line from the shop floor, so they only see one tiny section at a time. From up here you can see down across the whole line and it's plain as day.'

'Well, I haven't got the time or the genius to watch for it meself, so can you just tell me?'

'It's like this; they've got an old Rose Foregrove foil wrappin' machine and it's taking up the fudges, wrapping them, then sending them down the chute. It's working beautiful. Next the foil wraps are shaken down into the new Baker Perkins machine what flips the fudge round and wraps it in a paper band – and that machine is a useless piece of junk. They've tried to do something fancy with this machine and it's a pig's ear. It would jam up every five minutes if Betsy weren't keeping an eye on it. She's waiting until she sees it's about to get clogged, slows the machine down, signals the girls behind her that they need to slow and then they end up with a backlog of fudges waiting like a wave at the floodgates. Further down from Betsy you've got girls shouting that they're losing their piece time because the flow of toffees has stopped and they've got nothing to pack into cartons. And it's all because Betsy Newman is too good. Anyone else wouldn't know when the machine was about to jam, but she's got an engineer's eye so she keeps it going. Personally, I'd let the thing break down and send it back. It's brand new so we'd get the money back.'

'That's all very well and good, but it doesn't solve my problem, does it? We need the line to run, and if we let the machine break so that we can send it back we have to go to hand-wrapping which will take a week to set up and won't be anywhere near as fast. Not to mention we haven't got the girls.'

'To be fair, I think you just want a cigarette machine.'

Diana had hoped for better from Reenie. 'I don't think that a cigarette vending machine would solve the problem. Aside from the fact that cigarettes are banned in the factory on hygiene grounds.'

'No, I don't mean give everyone baccy to keep them from bickering – I mean a cigarette wrapping machine is better for this kind of job. It's what we always used to use before the fire. Then the insurance money came along and Baker Perkins saw pound signs. They scrambled to come up with some fancy new machine we didn't need, and the bosses bought it because they thought newer must mean better. Bin it off, tell the production manager to get out one of the old machines we've got in store, give it a blast clean tonight and whack it on the line tomorrow. You'll solve all your problems: you'll increase efficiency *and* you'll get the company their money back on a machine that should never have been made. And give Betsy Newman an extra piece-time bonus because she's hung on all this time with everybody giving her an earful, but she knew what she was doing and kept at it.'

Diana surveyed the production line. Reenie was right. That one change would have a knock-on effect for the whole line. 'Reenie, I want you to go through every line and do what you've done here. See where we can make changes and write me a report. I want to know *all* the places where I can get spare skilled girls.'

'I don't think Mrs Starbeck would let me.'

'Then don't get caught.'

Chapter Twenty-Three

'That's just the final straw; that really is the final bloody straw.' Siobhan Grimshaw was turning away from the neatly typed notice on the changing-room wall which had appeared since their last shift. Other women were crowding around the notice to get a look when Emily Everard pushed past them, tore down the notice, read it to herself quickly, then read it aloud:

'Casual Staff will please note that piece rates on the Gooseberry Cream line have been removed on a permanent basis commencing this day, Monday 14th June 1937. Casual staff are reminded that they are still expected to work at the speeds set for them on this line by the Time and Motion Department. Weekly rates of pay will continue as per the department minimum of fifteen shillings per week.'

'Does that mean what I think it means?' Winifred asked.

'Yep. They're cutting our pay. We're all expected to work at the same speed, but we're not being paid for the extra piece work we do. We're being paid our minimums.' Siobhan Grimshaw took off her white cotton mobcap, threw it to the floor and plonked herself down on one of the benches where she usually put on her shoes so enthusiastically at the start of a shift. 'This is just the last straw!'

Her mother-in-law sat down beside her and rubbed the palm of her hand between Siobhan's shoulders. 'How near are you to getting the money together for your Julie's school uniform?'

'A damn sight further away than I was yesterday! Michael broke his rib playing Sunday league and that's all the money going on the doctor. I've got to start from scratch and how am I ever gonna' save it if they're cutting the piece rates? I tell you, I honestly don't know if it's worth me coming in any more. I'm run ragged.' Her voice faltered as the injustice of her situation weighed heavy on her.

'Why didn't you tell me? I'd have been straight round!' Mrs Grimshaw could see that her daughter-in-law had been trying to spare her the worry until she could tell her that it was all settled and that her grandson was recuperating, but still, she'd have liked to have been there to help. 'No wonder you look so pale. Have you been up all night with your Michael?'

Siobhan nodded. 'I don't know whether I'm coming or going. I'm trying to hold the whole family together; I'm trying to fit washday into two nights a week; I'm trying to keep four kids fed, clothed, watered, and safe; I'm cooking when I can, but we're eating more basin meals from Cowie's cook shop than I care to admit to you ladies; and when am I meant to sleep? Tell me that, when am I meant to sleep?'

'Don't you beat yourself up, lass.' Pearl had married young and her children had long since flown the nest, but she remembered the sheer bone-deep exhaustion of caring for a family and never having the time to care for herself. 'You don't need to apologize to us for getting supper from Cowie's – he makes a lovely mince and mash which I'm rather partial to myself.'

'Yes, don't be hard on yourself.' Winifred was offering her own crisply laundered handkerchief. 'I'm sure there's something we can do.'

'I'm already doing it,' Emily Everard announced from the back of the cloakroom where she was hunched over a tiny notecard with a stub of scarlet pencil. 'I'm sending a note to the Worker's Union Shop Steward to ask him to intervene today, and then I'm sending another to the local branch of the Women's Cooperative Guild to request they vote on sending a deputation to petition the Factory Manager. I think we can have this matter resolved swiftly.'

Pearl was most amused. 'Do you always carry notecards in your handbag?'

'Of course not.' Emily Everard sniffed with dignity. 'These are my calling cards. At a pinch they will have to do as postcards, but if there's going to be any more of this nonsense about stopping our pay I think I will bring in a reticule with some of my Basildon Bond correspondence things so that I can always be ready to strike while the iron is hot.'

Mrs Grimshaw was not the only one to smirk in amusement at Emily Everard's love of formality. 'Did you just say that you were going to strike?' she asked, pulling the other woman's leg.

'Oh no! I would never—'

'I'm sure I heard you say the word strike, Emily.' Pearl winked at Winifred who joined in.

'I think you're quite right. I'll strike with you, Emily – that is, if *you're* running the picket line.'

'I really don't think . . .' Emily Everard became flustered at the suggestion that industrial action might be taken without due process. 'I really can't emphasize strongly enough . . .'

'We're yanking your chain, Emily.' Pearl pulled on her work shoes, ready to get back onto the production line for the start of their shift. 'You write your letters, we'll be right behind you.'

'There you are,' Mrs Grimshaw told her daughter-in-law, 'we'll put it right together.'

The factory whistle sounded and the mothers of the Quality Street line reluctantly steeled themselves to go back to the job they loved but were no longer being paid for. It felt like a slap in the face after all they had given up to come back to work and support their factory during their darkest days. They did not hurry through the double doors to the production line, and the slowness with which they filed through made all the difference to Doreen Fairclough as she bounded through the cloakroom door from the factory corridor beyond.

'Oh my God, I thought I was going to be late again.' Doreen gasped to catch her breath, perspiring from her dash from the bus stop to the cloakroom. 'Hold the door for two seconds, I need to put my cap on.'

'Where have you been?' Mrs Grimshaw looked over her shoulder to make sure they weren't attracting the attention of their overlooker or they would both be for it. 'The whistle sounded half a minute ago!'

'I know that.' Doreen stuffed her handbag and outdoor shoes into the pigeonhole beneath her coat peg. 'Why do you think I ran so fast?'

'What did the kids do this time?'

'Shaved the dog.' Doreen followed Mrs Grimshaw through the door and onto the line. 'I didn't recognize it at first, so I thought we'd got hold of someone else's and I tried to shoo it away and went in search of ours for ages before I found my pinking shears and a pile of fur. I tell you, the sooner I can get my speed up to earn those piece-time rates, the sooner I'm paying for them to have a sitter.'

'Bad news, chuck,' Mrs Grimshaw took a place on the Gooseberry Cream line beside Doreen, 'we're working for minimums now.'

'We're working for what?' Doreen hurried to her place on the line, and in her astonishment to hear their news she forgot to clock in.

'I'll be honest with you, Mrs Wilkes, the married women don't want to go out on strike, that's not why they've asked for my involvement. These women love their jobs and they've relished the chance to come back to work even if it's only temporary. However, saying all that, my other members,' and at this the Worker's Union shop steward gestured to the male porters who stood by the door with their arms folded and their caps on, 'have said that they want to walk out in solidarity.' Mr Booth didn't make the threat of a walk out lightly; he felt Mrs Starbeck had pushed him into it and an appeal to the Head of the Women's Employment Department, who outranked Mrs Starbeck, was his best bet to resolve this quickly.

Amy Wilkes listened carefully before answering with restraint. 'Although I fully appreciate your point of view, Mr Booth, and I respect your position, I must correct you on one important point: this is not my doing. This is a decision which has been made by the Time and Motion Department.' Mrs Wilkes didn't add, '*And I wholeheartedly disagree with it*' because she was far too canny to allow her personal feelings to let her show her hand in a negotiation before she knew all the facts. Amy stood at the corner of a busy, gabled workroom on the third floor where temporary workers handmade the creams with piping bags over starch moulding trays, and enrobed the solidified centres in chocolate by dipping them into mixing bowls with special wire forks. The women worked quickly and with an admirable efficiency – Amy Wilkes had to hand it to the mothers who had come back to work the Quality Street lines; they really knew how to get a job done with an awful lot less fuss than the fourteen-year-olds she was forced to take on. 'The change was made without our knowledge and I have sent Diana Moore to the Time and Motion Department to ask them to send someone to explain.'

'I don't think we really need them to explain; it's pretty clear to me that the company has decided to save money by cutting the piece rates on this line.' Mr Booth was speaking directly to Amy Wilkes, but his booming voice was easily reaching the assembled porters at the back of the production hall who had still not started work and were muttering to one another.

It surprised Amy that the women to whom this injustice was being meted out appeared to have the patience to seek redress through such slow, formal channels, but the men in their workroom were on a hair trigger. 'As I understand it, production lines evolve and workers speed up as new machinery is brought in to assist them. If the natural baseline speed of the line increases, then it is only to be expected that piece rates will not be given out for slower work.' Amy Wilkes was trying to sweep the situation under the carpet, but she could smell a rat; Cynthia Starbeck was very keen on cutting piece rates and this was probably her doing. That said, Amy Wilkes didn't like to get involved in the work of other departments if she could avoid it; she had enough work of her own to do and the Time and Motion people were not her responsibility.

Doreen Fairclough had been working her place at the end of the production line, expertly pressing rows of plaster of Paris shapes affixed to a wooden slat into the tightly compacted starch powder which was then moved down the line to be piped. Doreen was within earshot of the conversation which was going on beside her and she could listen no longer. She gestured to the woman further down her line to wait a minute before sending her any more; she had to correct them.

'If you'll forgive me, it's nothing to do with the line getting better with new machines.' Doreen waved a hand across the production line, trying to hold back tears of frustration and anger at the idea that they could so easily be cheated like this. 'We're one of the last lines at Mack's to still be one hundred per cent handmade; they haven't rebuilt our mechanized line yet since the fire, so everything you see here is still emergency handmaking.'

Amy Wilkes narrowed her eyes. 'This seems very fast for a handmaking line.'

Doreen laughed, but it wasn't with amusement. 'We're faster than they were on the mechanized line before it burned down.'

'How are you able to manage that? What do you have that the regular workers don't?'

Mrs Grimshaw, passing with a stack of wooden trays pressed tight with white starch powder, said, 'Age and experience.'

That sounded about right to Amy Wilkes; the fourteen-year-old girls on the production lines just didn't have the emotional maturity that these older women brought with them, and they were certainly working wonders on this line.

Chapter Twenty-Four

Diana Moore could be seen following sedately behind a quick and agitated Major Fergusson, and a disgruntled Mrs Starbeck, the latter muttering something to the Major who appeared very concerned. Arriving beside Amy Wilkes he dispensed with pleasantries to get straight to the point. 'Booth, is this true? Are you planning to lead a walkout of your union's members?'

Mr Booth shook his head. 'Only as a last resort.'

Amy Wilkes saw an opportunity to pass the entirety of this problem over to the other head of department so that she could escape the noise and heat of the enormous workroom. 'Major Fergusson, I understand that all piece-time rates have been abolished in this workroom and that the women are working for a minimum rate without any incentive to work faster—'

'If you'll excuse me, Mrs Wilkes?' Cynthia Starbeck purred out a polite interruption. 'I think we have a nasty case of a storm in a teacup here. This is one of *my* production lines and I made the alteration to the pay rates in line with company policy. Although the women might not like it, I don't think it's a good idea to summon the most senior members of the Time and Motion Department down to the line to answer for their decisions every time some married women find themselves dissatisfied with their lot; it is a waste of everyone's time. A simple memo from you, through the usual channels, asking to see my report into the matter would have been more than sufficient, and I would have been happy to send it to you promptly.'

Amy Wilkes narrowed her eyes at Cynthia Starbeck; she'd never liked the woman. They came from similar backgrounds, but where Amy's modest family money had been used to further her education, to endow scholarships for other bright girls at her old school, and to care for their family servants in their old age, the Starbeck family money was splashed all over the Starbeck family members in delicately tailored clothes, sparkling jewels, and the light suntan of sailing weekends in fashionable places. 'You haven't responded to what I said, Mrs Starbeck: have these women been reduced to working for the minimum salary?'

Mrs Starbeck smiled rather too broadly to be convincing. 'Any and all alterations have been made in accordance with our company policies—'

'I wrote those policies, Mrs Starbeck.' Amy Wilkes' voice was flat and uncompromising, 'And I did *not* write a policy which allowed women to be reduced to working for a minimum with no prospect of advancement through hard work. Major Fergusson, I trust I can leave this in your capable hands?'

Major Fergusson was a peacemaker by nature, and the kindest of men. He was not pleased by his colleague's decision, but he believed that everyone made mistakes at one time or another and that, although he ought to have words with her about it, this was neither the time nor the place. 'Thank you, Mrs Wilkes, I'm confident that whatever misunderstanding has taken place can smoothed out through frank and open discussion.'

Amy Wilkes knew that the Major did not believe in allowing workers to struggle for minimums in his factory; the Mackintosh's piece rates were some of the most generous in their industry and he was proud of it. The caps for the maximum amount of work a girl could do before she had reached her maximum amount of piece work were set incredibly high so that, when they were lucky enough to employ prodigies like Reenie Calder or Mary Norcliffe, they got the best from them. Amy also knew that the Major was trying to help one of his managers to save face so that he could speak to her privately later. Mrs Wilkes was just about to summon Diana Moore to return with her to the Women's Employment Department offices when Cynthia Starbeck spoke.

'There hasn't been any misunderstanding. This line was working at a faster rate than the usual line and the women appear to need no encouragement to work as hard as they are able and so I removed the piece-rate payment. The minimum payment is more than sufficient for the work they're doing.' Mrs Starbeck had seen that the Major wanted to pander to the Employment Department, but she would not allow it. 'That's the trouble with these women, they all think they should be given an incentive to work hard, but the incentive is having a job at all. They don't realize how lucky they are to be in work and to have such a well-respected employer.'

Major Fergguson composed himself to contradict her with politeness, even though he was her department head. 'Mrs Starbeck, I know that you are very proud to work for Mackintosh's, and it is only natural that you would want to see that same pride in your colleagues, but the piece rates aren't there to encourage hard work – they are there to reward skill and speed. We pay more to the best workers so that we may retain the best.'

'These women are married, Major, so we can't possibly retain them. They'll be gone in a month or two when the need is over. What's the use of paying them more to keep them here when they are already willing to stay, and we don't want them to stay permanently? We're getting what we want from them, and they're willing to give it. You don't honestly mean to tell me that they would have the temerity to walk out because we've stopped the piece rates when we've kept them on longer than they could ever have hoped?'

Mr Booth respected the Major for his evident compassion in trying to keep the peace in every situation, and he respected Mrs Wilkes for her valiant defence of the company's policies, but he thought Mrs Starbeck was a nasty old widdop and was jiggered if he was going to pussyfoot around her to let her save face as the Major was doing.

'I tell you this for nothing,' he said, 'if these ladies don't want to strike, I feel like striking for them. Have you got any idea what they've given up to be here? They're run ragged working twice as fast – no, three times as fast –

as your usual girls on this line. And that's not working faster under the same conditions, that's working faster under conditions that you couldn't even begin to hope a new girl could find her way around. You should be thanking your lucky stars that they've found people to watch their kiddies so that they can even be here. They deserve to be paid for what they're doing and they deserve to be paid, at the very least, at the same rate as the women they replaced – if not more as a recognition of their superior skill, experience, and speed.'

'These women are already paid far too much. If we paid them a great deal less they would have to tighten their belts and plan their spending more carefully, then they'd realize the value of money, for a change. I'm of a mind that if you paid them less they might actually save more for their futures and be less of a burden on society in general. Paying them too much muddles them and leaves them spending carelessly and without proper scrutiny of their household accounts. I stand by my decision and—'

Cynthia Starbeck was cut off mid-sentence. Unbeknownst to her, Diana Moore had been listening to every word she said with a growing belief that if the woman was allowed to continue there would be a riot in the workroom. The married women were valiantly continuing their work, but they could not help but hear Mrs Starbeck's strident rant and Diana had noticed that one or two were working with clenched teeth or whitened knuckles. Diana knew this production line very, very well, and with almost no effort at all she was able to casually redirect the woman pushing the hopper full of used starch moulding powder down the wrong aisle, release the brake on a wheeled trolley of empty trays – and cause a collision which looked spontaneous. The hopper of starch moulding powder toppled just feet away from Mrs Starbeck's back and, although her colleagues saw what was happening and were able to dodge out of the way in the nick of time, Cynthia Starbeck was caught full in the back of the legs by the soft white powder and shrieked indelicately as she leapt forward to avoid being subsumed. She was physically unharmed, but her shoes, stockings, and skirt were thick with snowy dust.

The nearby members of the office staff hurriedly stepped forward to ask if she was quite all right, but not before a look had passed between Mrs Wilkes and the Major which seemed to seal her fate. Major Fergusson had defended her for too long, and the job in Germany had been her last chance to change her ways. Amy Wilkes only hoped that he'd dismiss her as soon as he'd got her back to his office, and not wait until he felt the time was right as he usually did. Amy Wilkes didn't think she could tolerate the woman in her factory another moment, but it wasn't her department, it was the Major's – and that was going to be a bigger problem than she could have anticipated.

Chapter Twenty-Five

Ruffian had still not returned to the Calder family farm and the Calders were having to make do with the loan of Black Wanderer from their neighbours. Ruffian, partially shoeless, frequently shiftless, and almost toothless, remained stubbornly by Reenie's side – or as close by as could be reasonably achieved when she worked in a factory and lived in a boarding house – and was contentedly listening to his mistress and her friends enjoy their dinner hour in his stable while he stood guard over them like a faithful hound. Reenie occasionally wondered if the trouble with Ruffian was that he thought he was a dog instead of a workhorse – that would have explained a lot. His stable for the moment was a borrowed one; the new factory ones were in daily use by the factory horses who towed goods around the complex day and night, but the old stables behind them, a dilapidated Victorian affair with a cobbled courtyard which had been built when the factory was still a carpet mill, were now only ever used for storage. In light of Reenie and Ruffian's heroics on the night that the factory burned down, the head of the factory stables had awarded Ruffian the freedom of the stable yard and put one of the disused Victorian stalls at his disposal for 'whenever he happened to be in town and needed somewhere to dine or to rest the night'.

Ruffian's stall in the old stables was a roomy one and Reenie, Mary and Bess had taken to sitting in it during their dinner hour to get away from the din of the over-crowded staff canteen. The old stables were to the north of the factory complex, near to the postal warehouse and the boiler house which generated electricity for every part of the factory. Its enormous, gleaming white art deco chimney was smoking that day, which they had been reliably informed that it should not do because it ran on gas, and one of the steeplejacks would be up there before the royal visit to polish the whole thing white again, no doubt.

Ruffian shuffled in his stall and Reenie gave him an affectionate pat on his shoulder while she listened to Bess tell them all about why she thought she wasn't allowed to work on a production line with the married ladies.

'No, they keep the married girls separate from us because they're worried they'll tell us about . . .' Bess mouthed the words 'marital relations' like a thrillingly dangerous magic spell.

'Don't be a dolt!' Reenie laughed at her friend as they sat on hay bales. 'That's not why they keep them apart from us; they keep them apart because they're all on temporary work and they know that if we all worked together we'd get upset when they had to leave. If they

174

didn't want us to know about marital relations they wouldn't let us have a union lending library.'

Mary was horrified. 'Do they have books in the union lending library about . . .' Mary nodded her head in an insinuating little twitch, reluctant to mention 'marital relations' in case the words conjured them and one of them found themselves in the family way. Mary was already on edge at the thought of all the rules they were breaking by coming out to sit in the stables in their dinner break, despite the fact that the dining hall was thronged with workers while the factory was at capacity and it would have been too loud and crowded to spend any length of time there, even if they had wanted to.

Reenie was pragmatic about both marital and certain extra-marital relations; she'd grown up on a farm and the reproduction of animal life was not alien to her. 'I'm sure they do. You can learn about anything in the union lending library, that's how Diana knows so much about politics and geography. Marital relations is probably in some of the novels, but I think they've got instructional books about family planning as well.'

'It's not in the novels,' Bess sighed with disappointment as she ducked past Ruffian's bridle to decorate one of the high wall sconces with flowers she'd collected, 'I've checked.'

Mary was horrified. 'Which ones have you checked?'

'They've got Marie Stopes,' Reenie said matter-of-factly. 'I've read that one.'

'Oh no, I don't think I trust Mrs Stopes. Not after what I've heard about her.' Mary did not trust everything she read, even if it was written by a renowned doctor. 'You know the rhyme everyone used to sing at school . . .'

'I know it,' Bess piped up.
'*Jeanie, Jeanie, full of hopes,*
Read a book by Marie Stopes,
But, to judge from her condition,
She must have read the wrong edition.'

Reenie did not approve of using the superstition of the playground to test the merit of the learning in the union lending library. 'Well, I don't agree with that. The Women's Co-operative Guild have had ladies from the Fabian Society up to give talks on family planning and they all talk about Mrs Stopes's pamphlets. They give them out for free. I reckon I could get one for Bess.'

'No!' Mary was emphatic. 'I do not want Bess reading about *marital relations*!'

'Oh Mary, I already know about marital relations. I'm pretty sure that ship has sailed long since. I wouldn't say no to reading about it, though.' And Bess confided to Reenie, 'We've got no wireless at home.'

'Maybe it would be a good idea for you to read one of Mrs Stopes's books, Bess. Then Mary would be less worried about you getting yourself in the family way because you would always know how to take precautions.'

'Oh, I'm not worried about being in the family way,' Bess sighed dreamily, 'I'd *love* a baby.'

'But you'd have to give up work at Mack's.' For Reenie this was the worst threat in the world.

'So will you when you and Peter settle down.' Bess was smoothing her fingers through Ruffian's forelock and nuzzling her nose against his. He was tolerating this unsolicited and undignified show of affection with barely concealed disdain. 'Is he still asking you to marry him?'

'Yes, but he says he'd want a long engagement. He wouldn't make me leave Mack's yet.' Reenie liked to keep all decisions regarding her future beyond the factory at a safe, almost mythical, distance. 'But we have an understanding.'

'Oooh, does that mean you're having relations?' Bess's eyes lit up in enthusiasm.

Mary said, 'Do not answer that question!' evidently fearing that her friend would answer in the affirmative and give Bess more ideas.

'Of course we're not having relations. Do I look like I was born yesterday? As far as I can tell, "relations" is asking for trouble. Peter can make do with a kiss and a cuddle in the cinema – if we don't fall asleep in there after doing a double shift on the line.'

Bess had more questions. 'But has he tried to press you for more? Is he a very passionate young man?'

Reenie folded her arms, sank back in her makeshift hay bale settee, and scowled in perplexity at the newly swept floor of Ruffian's stable. 'Well, I've always thought he was, and I've always told him that I wouldn't tolerate any funny business, but . . .' Reenie hesitated.

'Don't mind Mary, you just tell us how you feel.'

'Well, I thought he would try it on a bit and then I could relent a bit – not a lot, just a bit – but he doesn't ever try it on so I can't do any relenting whatsoever.'

'Well, that's lucky for you, Reenie Calder,' Mary said, 'because I doubt your landlady would tolerate anything unseemly.'

'Oooh, no. Mrs Garner is very broad-minded.'

Bess was already thinking about what she might have to do to secure a room in Mrs Garner's boarding house where the landlady was broad-minded. 'Does Mrs Garner really allow gentlemen callers?'

Reenie shrugged. 'She does if they're respectable, but I think it's because she has her own gentleman caller – who you both know well.'

Mary and Bess's eyes lit up at the prospect of hearing gossip, and both asked at once, 'Who?'

'Major Fergusson. He calls round and brings her flowers. We're all clearing out tomorrow night so that they can have the best sitting room to themselves to listen to the radiogram.'

Bess was in raptures. 'That's the most romantic thing I've ever heard. I *love* Major Fergusson.'

'But isn't he very old?'

'Old people can fall in love too, Mary. And they aren't old really, when you think about it.' Then, with a dreamy sigh, Bess asked Reenie, 'Do you think they really are in love?'

Reenie nodded and grinned. The blossoming romance between her landlady and her favourite manager was one of the bright points in her life at that moment. She had heard about it all first hand from Mrs Garner who had met the Major at the Methodist Church soup kitchen where they both volunteered their evenings to feed the needy. After that Reenie had needed to exert a herculean effort not to meddle and give them encouragement. No matter how much work piled up, no matter how many double shifts she had to work, no matter how many times she fell straight into bed without her supper because she was too tired to eat, through all of it was the joy of seeing two of her favourite people in the world find a happiness which they thought they had missed their chance at. Reenie watched Bess floating about the tatty old stable, putting up little posies of flowers on shelves formed by protruding bricks, pasting up glossy pictures of film stars cut from magazines, and tucking an old tangerine tweed blanket round their makeshift hay-bale settee, and thought how lovely their life at the factory had become. She breathed a sigh of happiness and leant back, rested her head on the freshly whitewashed wall behind her and looked out at the yard beyond the stable, sharing a bag of misshaped Toffee Pennies.

Ruffian sneezed loudly and Bess patted him fondly, saying, 'Bless you, Ruffian!'

'We were lucky that time.' Mary looked knowingly at Reenie, who nodded with relief.

'Lucky about what?' Bess gave Ruffian a hug which the peculiarly ugly horse did not appear to relish.

'He's got wind,' Reenie said apologetically. 'I think someone's been feeding him onions and now oftentimes when he sneezes he lets rip. Please don't let him near onions, Bess.'

'Let who near onions? What are you hiding here?' The appearance of someone else in the old stable yard surprised the three girls, but more surprising was the squeaky yet nasal voice of Dolly Dunkley. Bess had not met her yet, and although she was surprised to see so much make-up, so badly applied, and all on one individual, she was still her usual, chirpy, welcoming self. Reenie and Mary, on the other hand, were a little more reserved. They recognized the new girl only too well and were a little more on their guard than they might have been with any of the other factory workers.

'We're not hiding anything,' Bess said. 'This is where

Ruffian lives when he's at the factory. Do you want to come and meet him?'

'I don't think that's a good idea.' Reenie stepped forward and addressed Dolly directly. 'You're new, aren't you? Are you lost? Can we help you find your way? I know the factory can be a bit of a maze at first, but you'll find most people very helpful.'

'Of course I'm not lost, don't be ridiculous. It's just a factory and I'm intelligent enough to work out where I need to be.' Dolly said it derisively and even kind-hearted Bess was a little taken aback by the new girl's rudeness. 'You're hiding something in there and I'm going to see what it is.' Dolly strode past them and put her face in at the door of the stable. 'It stinks!'

'I did warn you,' Reenie muttered.

'What is this?' Dolly flicked at the variety of pictures and decorative flourishes which Bess had added for fun. 'Have you made yourself a clubhouse? I'll be reporting this.'

'There isn't anything to report.' Reenie was trying to remain patient, but it was a trial and she found herself unconsciously gritting her teeth as this girl invaded their privacy uninvited. 'We've got permission from the head of the factory stables to keep him in this old place that no one's using anyway.'

'You've been eating toffees!' Dolly squawked indignantly at the sight of a Toffee Penny wrapper on their makeshift settee.

'What's wrong with that?' Bess asked in innocence. 'We do work in a toffee factory.'

'You all humiliated me in the factory because I ate one toffee, and now here you are—'

'Oh no you bloody don't!' Mary interrupted the girl. She had remained silent up to that point because she knew that Reenie liked everyone to be kind and friendly to each other, but Mary wasn't going to let anyone talk to her friend and her sister like that. 'Don't come the hard done by with me. You humiliated yourself on the line by insisting on having a go at something you knew nothing about and then doing it badly. Eating toffees in the workroom is unhygienic and against the rules – and if I remember correctly you littered the place up as well. We are perfectly at liberty to eat misshapes we've bought from the staff shop out here away from the work-rooms, and we're also at liberty to sit here in our lunch breaks if we change all our overalls before we go back to work. What else we do here is none of your business because you're not wanted, you're not welcome, and you're not allowed to wander the factory between shifts without a pass out. So, unless you want me to report you for wandering, I suggest you go on your way.'

Ruffian took the opportunity to whinny in agreement and to turn as best he could and give this unwelcome interloper a fierce look. Dolly may have been intimidated by the horse, the threat of being reported, or the realiza-tion that she was outnumbered in a deserted stable yard, but she turned on her heel and stalked away muttering something about the regret they would feel very soon when she was made their manager.

'Oh dear,' Bess said with some pity and compassion for the poor girl who didn't appear to have much going for her.

'And that,' Reenie said, 'is the one who threw a strop at Mary on the line.'

'She wants sacking,' Mary said as she sidled back into her seat beside Ruffian. 'She's not got any aptitude for anything.'

'Have you got the bag of toffees?' Bess asked. 'Can I have one?'

'I thought you had the toffees.' Mary looked around in vain for her bag of misshapes and the other two stood up and looked around too until finally Mary stopped looking and said, 'That scheming sod! I think she's nicked my toffees!'

Chapter Twenty-Six

'Now what have you brought that basket for?' Diana asked it kindly and softly in the voice she reserved for Gracie, which now extended to Lara when she had them both for the afternoon to take to the shops with her. 'We can't carry that all round town, it'll be cumbersome.'

'It's the basket we carry our kittens in.'

'And I suppose, because you weren't allowed to bring the kittens with you, you at least wanted to bring your new basket.'

Gracie and Lara looked at one another and then back at Diana with wide eyes. They said nothing because they desperately didn't want Diana to lift the white cotton napkin which covered their secret.

Gracie and Lara had talked at length about who to bestow their casket on, and they had finally decided. They would give it quietly to Mrs Garner, Diana's landlady, as a thank you, not just for the gift of their beloved kittens, but also for taking such great care of Gracie's big sister Diana who had a nice warm place to stay and her meals cooked for her. The little girls had a soft spot for Mrs Garner, who was sitting smiling fondly at them, and they had both agreed she would be the perfect recipient of the casket, minus one tray of the confections which they had decided to keep for themselves.

'I tell you what,' Diana was checking the pockets of her coat for a pair of gloves which she supposed she'd left in her room, 'why don't you show your basket to Mrs Garner while I fetch my hat and gloves from my room? And then, if you ask her nicely, she might look after it for you while we're out at the shops.'

Gracie and Lara nodded, waiting until Diana was out of earshot before whispering at once, 'We've got a present for you, Mrs Garner.'

'A thank-you present,' Lara whispered.

'Yes, it's a secret present which Diana must not know about, to thank you for looking after my big sister, and for giving us our kittens.' Between them they lifted the casket gently out of their shopping basket and offered it up to Jane Garner, the soft tea cloths they had carefully wrapped it in falling away.

Mrs Garner was touched, and a tear stung her eye. 'Well, aren't you kind!' She took the casket gently, admiring it at arm's length, and carefully lifted the lid to reveal an assortment of sweets with an unusual sheen, as though they had been painted with sugar. 'Now, would you look at that. How lovely. They look right fancy.' Mrs Garner realized immediately that Diana must have given the girls the casket and its contents and that they didn't want her to know that they had given it away. She heard

Diana's bedroom door slam shut and quickly put the casket away in the sideboard.

'Are you two ready?' Diana gave a knowing look to her landlady, which her landlady completely misinterpreted – and that was a fatal mistake. 'Now leave that basket here with Mrs Garner and we'll fetch it when we come back.'

Mrs Garner beamed at them, and then said to Diana, 'They're such lovely girls, I'd give them anything.'

That evening Reenie was to leave the boarding house at the same time as Diana. It was a Saturday night and they both had places to go to. Peter had asked Reenie to be ready a little earlier because he was impatient to share some news with her – news which he wanted to tell her over dinner, which worried Reenie slightly because they never 'went to dinner', but she tried to tell herself that it was just Peter's fancy East Anglian ways.

Diana hadn't said where she was going, but this wasn't unusual; as always, she didn't like talking if she could possibly avoid it.

This was usually the time when Mrs Garner would get under their feet trying to be helpful, offering them extra hot water or the loan of a little piece of costume jewellery, or a little plate of cucumber sandwiches to line their stomachs because, she always said, 'You don't want to go out on an empty stomach because you'll only get a headache and cucumber will make you smell sweet.'

But tonight it was different; tonight they had the joy of seeing the landlady they loved getting ready for her own romantic evening. Mrs Garner hadn't stopped telling them that the Major was going to pay a call, but that she would be leaving the door to her sitting room open and that it was nothing untoward. Not that Diana or Reenie would ever have thought there would be anything but innocent, gentlemanly courtship from the Major. She was so excited and it was wonderful to see the kindest woman they knew finding happiness with the kindest man. Her face glowed with girlish joy as she excitedly cleaned the house and put on her best clothes. They were a little out of style but it didn't matter because they were reminiscent of her younger days and made her appear younger too.

The Major had found a new record that he thought they would like to listen to together on her radiogram. And there was a program on the BBC Light Programme about the King's visit to Belfast which they had seen in the *Radio Times* and were looking forward to listening to together.

When the Major pulled at the doorbell, Reenie and Diana dashed to the top of the stairs. They looked down over the bannister and saw Mrs Garner smoothing her hair and her skirts before taking a deep breath and opening the door wide. The Major was waiting on the doorstep with a bunch of peach-coloured roses and a beaming smile, radiant with happiness. He was so elegantly turned out he looked as though he could have been a matinee idol in his youth. He had come straight from his barber and he smelled of good cologne. Reenie sighed happily and Diana squeezed her hand to warn her against attracting attention, knowing they should not intrude on this moment. They crept backwards to their own rooms, not wanting to intrude any longer on the lovebirds and finished getting ready.

Reenie heard the faint sound of voices and footsteps from below as Mrs Garner took the Major down the stairs to the scullery to find a vase for his beautiful roses, then they made their way back up to the sitting room. A few moments passed and what she could not see was her landlady happily offer the Major the gorgeous casket of sweets, see their smiles as they each chose one. Upstairs, Reenie gathered up her gloves and her best handbag, ready to leave with Diana for the tram, then went out and stood quietly on the landing, waiting for the other girl. Suddenly she heard a crash of furniture followed by something thudding on the ground and, moments later, a bloodcurdling scream, glass shattering, and another thud.

As Reenie stood frozen, Diana thundered past her, neither of them understanding what they had just heard. Diana had left her shoes beside her bed and run down in her stocking feet. She pulled up short at the doorway to the parlour. Mrs Garner was lying face down on the sitting-room floor beside the vase of fresh flowers she had knocked to the ground when she had collapsed. The Major lay perfectly still on his back and his eyes, which were wide open, were filled with agony as he clutched at his throat.

Diana jumped over the pool of fresh water and broken glass, the rough weave of the carpet catching at the soles of her stockings when she landed. Major Fergusson lay on the floor by the radiogram, dainty little sweets scattered all over the carpet, and the casket which had held them upturned. Seeing that Mrs Garner was not breathing, but that the Major appeared to be, Diana wasn't sure what to do first but she dropped down by the Major's side and tried to loosen his collar and tie, calling out his name in desperation.

By this time Reenie was in the doorway and staring in confusion at their landlady.

'Reenie, fetch a doctor! Run!' Diana shouted. 'And tell them to call for an ambulance!'

Reenie didn't need telling twice and Diana heard the front door bang behind her.

Chapter Twenty-Seven

Mr Helliwell Pickles, the editor-in-chief of the *Halifax Courier*, was a red-faced man with a walrus moustache, a cigar-chewing habit, and the constitution of a gluttonous Hanoverian prince of the last century. He barked orders from his desk at all and sundry, whether they worked for him or not, and gave the appearance of having not listened to a word anyone said to him. He had an instinct for a story, an instinct for people – and his staff were loyal to him to a man.

Chester 'Sleepless' Parvin had never seen his editor with a healthy complexion; in all the years he'd known him it had vacillated between red and purple (depending on the ferocity of Mr Pickles's speech to the newsroom that day), and the criss-cross of scarlet spider veins on his nose glowed like the embers of a fire. Something was wrong that day, Sleepless could tell. He saw his editor pick up the telephone receiver on his desk, bark some response to the person on the other end, turn a brighter shade of mauve while the person speaking to him attempted to make their own voice heard, and then all of a sudden he was white, horribly white.

One by one the rowdy staff in the newsroom fell quiet. The rapid fire of typewriters and the guffaw of messenger boys ceased as, one by one, they looked up and saw their chief as never before. Something was very, very wrong.

'I quite understand,' Pickles told the speaker on the other end of the line in a hushed tone, 'I shall make sure the staff know it, sir.'

That final 'sir' made several ears prick up; if their editor was calling someone sir then either pigs were flying, or someone very important indeed had telephoned.

'Sleepless, Dewhurst, Priestly – my office.' What Mr Pickles called his office was, in fact, the news conference room because Mr Pickles chose to occupy a desk at the head of the office hall where he could hear all that was going on among his staff, the easier to bark orders. Conferences were not often held behind closed doors, but when they were you could hear a pin drop across the rest of the building, and more than one employee could be caught out trying to read the lips of the people in the conference room through the glass panelling of the walls. On this occasion, as his three most senior reporters followed him through the open door, Pickles closed the blinds on the rest of the staff.

'God rang.' Pickles always referred to the paper's owner as God. 'A story is breaking which we will cover, but the details are such that the owners of every publication in the county have agreed to a temporary embargo.'

Parvin's eyes widened. 'Does this have something to do with the visit of the King?'

'In a manner of speaking.' Pickles twitched his thick moustache. 'There's no easy way to say this, so I'm just going to out and say it: by tomorrow morning Major Fergusson is likely to be dead.'

The staff were aghast. Miss Dewhurst asked, 'Not our Major Fergusson? From Mackintosh's?'

'The very same. And there's a woman, a Mrs Jane Garner – local philanthropist he met at the soup kitchen. She's in an even worse state than he is. Both removed to St Luke's.'

There was a silence. They took in the news, and then Sleepless Parvin took a deep breath and asked, 'How did it happen? Has there been an accident at the factory? Was anyone else hurt?' Sleepless had been the first reporter on the scene of the Mackintosh's fire only six months before and he would never forget the sight of the smashed Hillman Minx Magnificent, blackened amongst the ruins of their toffee town. Another fatal accident was unthinkable.

'They were poisoned last night.'

There was an audible gasp from Mr Priestly who was not known for being highly strung, but this was a man they had all known and liked for many years.

Sleepless asked, 'Deliberately?'

'It seems so. He had a casket of toffees which had been painted with a varnish of rat poison. He apparently brought them home from the factory to share with his lady friend – and the casket had been made for the King.'

Sleepless was shocked. 'Was someone attempting to assassinate His Majesty?'

'This is what the police suspect, yes.' The colour was returning to Pickles's face, but he was still paler than they had ever seen him. 'And if someone is attempting to assassinate the King it is likely that they will make other attempts. This will be a difficult investigation – whoever has done this dreadful thing will have planned their work very carefully and they obviously have little care for the risk to anyone else's life.'

Sleepless nodded. 'How much is under embargo?'

'The poison. The police don't want the perpetrator to know that his casket of chocolates did not reach their intended target. If the would-be assassin thinks the toffees are still waiting to be presented to the King he may not try again. It will be impossible to keep it a secret forever – the factory are planning to issue a product recall – but the least we can do is keep a lid on it from our end.'

Miss Dewhurst cut in. 'And what of the Major? He is a noted public figure, active in many philanthropic causes. Surely this news can't go unreported.'

'Heart attack.' And as Pickles said it he never looked so close to one himself. 'We will report a sudden heart attack brought on by the strain of work and the rebuilding after the fire. Nothing need be said about Jane Garner at present. Miss Dewhurst, do we have a biography of the Major on file?'

'I'll go and look.' She jumped up and scurried out of the room to look through one of the large filing cabinets in the main pressroom.

'Priestly, go down to the print room and tell them to expect a two-column opening for a special edition this evening. Tell him Sleepless will be down in ten minutes with the story.'

'Yes, sir.'

'Sleepless, take this down: "Yesterday evening at seven

o'clock an ambulance was called to the boarding house of Mrs Elizabeth Jane Garner of Horton Hill Road. Major Antony Fergusson, who had been paying a call on the widowed owner of the boarding house, was seized with a heart attack while winding a gramophone."'

Chapter Twenty-Eight

Amy Wilkes and Diana Moore sat in silence; they were temperamentally well suited in that respect. Elsewhere in the factory and around the town people were talking about how they couldn't believe the news, or how good the Major had been to them, or how devastating was the tragedy; but there, in the seclusion of Amy Wilkes's office, the sentiments were expressed a different way, with numb desolation.

'How are we meant to face all this without him?' Diana didn't lift her unfocussed gaze from the empty fireplace which Amy had kicked once and viciously when she had heard that her favourite colleague was unlikely to live.

'I can't even think about that yet; I still don't believe anything like this could happen to him. Something keeps telling me that it's a mistake and any moment he'll come back to work.'

There was a long silence before Diana shook her head and said, 'I saw him. How ill he was.'

And Amy Wilkes said, 'I know.'

Neither of them moved from their chairs before the cold cast-iron fireplace; neither of them looked up at the other; neither of them spoke for a long time. In the case of Amy Wilkes she had a great many things she needed to force herself to think about, and in the case of Diana Moore she had just as many thoughts she wanted to blot out. The Major had touched the lives of many people in the town, but at various points in Amy and Diana's careers the Major had provided a lifeline.

'The first problem is who replaces him.' Amy didn't need to say that Cynthia Starbeck would make a power play while the Major's life was hanging by a thread – they both knew it. 'As far as I can see, everything we are about to face as a business will be worsened or improved by whoever takes the post of Head of Time and Motion.'

'What do you think we're about to face?' Diana knew that they were mortgaged to the hilt and that the factory was on capacity production, but she hadn't seen anything worse on the horizon than the departmental infighting they were used to.

'Isn't it obvious? There'll be a police inquiry at the very least. You heard what Director Hitchens said – the police surgeon has tested the contents and every one contained poison.' Amy signed in desperation. 'Diana, are you *certain* that the casket was from Mackintosh's? Is there any chance it was from somewhere else?'

'The sweets didn't look like anything that I've seen Mary and Herr Baum making in the kitchens here, but the casket was undoubtedly one of the ones we had made here earlier in the year, the ones old Birchy had been working on before he was sacked. There's no doubt about it, the Major must have brought it home from the factory because that casket wasn't available for sale to the public, so it could only have come from here.'

'If you're right and he was poisoned by sweets which he brought home from our factory, then this place is about to be thrown into a worse chaos than we're already in. There are only two possibilities: either we have an accidental contamination on our hands – which you and I both know is highly unlikely in a factory as stringent as Mack's – or this was a deliberate poisoning. If it was accidental we'll have to tear this place apart to find the source and make the product safe. If it was deliberate – well, the police will tear this place apart to establish who poisoned the sweets and, more importantly, to establish who the intended target was.'

Diana looked up. 'You don't think the Major was the intended target?'

'No. And I doubt the police will either. There is a more obvious candidate.'

Diana was confused. 'But the Major wasn't planning to give them to anyone else; he planned to share them with my landlady.'

'Yes, but you told me they wcre emblazoned with the royal coat of arms; you said this was a *royal* casket.' Amy was a shrewd woman and it was rare that an important detail escaped her.

'I'm certain it wasn't one of the caskets we have ready for the King's visit; I've seen those. This was an old one, made by the last confectioner. Perhaps it turned up in a cupboard somewhere, but it definitely wasn't one of the ones intended for the King.'

'Yes, but an outsider making an attempt on the King's

life wouldn't know that, would they? They would see the coat of arms and they would take their chance.'

Diana sat back in her chair and took a deep breath, trying to suppress a feeling of rising nausea. She had thought that this situation couldn't get any worse, but now she saw that the ripples of horror spread even further than she could have imagined.

'If there's even a suggestion that the toffees might have come from us then we'll have to do a recall.' Director Hitchens had cancelled all of his engagements to put himself entirely at the disposal of the police investigation into Major Fergusson's poisoning. As he and the factory manager stood united in their grief for a long-time colleague who had been such a friend, they hoped that the police would give them something to do. The news from the hospital was not good, and it was now certain that they would lose their colleague.

'We don't have any proof at present, so we're not making an accusation of Mack's.' The Chief Inspector was conciliatory, but he was privately relieved that the factory directors were treating the matter so seriously.

'No, Inspector, you don't understand; we can't wait until there's proof. We're a food factory and we have a code of conduct which holds us to a higher standard than the law. If those are our toffees then we're announcing a recall and we're going onto emergency measures in the factory to shake down every department.'

The factory manager nodded in agreement; it was the only thing they could do in all conscience, but it would near bankrupt them. As a business they were already sailing perilously close to the wind with all the extra staff and the rebuilding project for the fire damage which hadn't been fully covered by the firm's insurance. This was a matter of conscience and any self-respecting food factory would make the same decision; it was simply that in this instance the decision might mean the end of their business.

'I'll inform Sir Harold.' The director and the factory manager were clearly of the same mind; they would both rather end their careers early by doing the right thing than keep going with a poor choice on their conscience. 'Is there anything we need to do in the meantime to assist the police with their enquiries?'

'If you would be so good as to keep a telephone line open for us to reach you directly.'

'I'll make sure every member of the factory management is available by telephone day or night.'

Chapter Twenty-Nine

'He was poisoned with cyanide.' The factory manager
was clearly trying to break the news to them with sensi-
tivity, but they couldn't escape the facts. So soon after
the distressing news of his illness, they now had the news
that it was confirmed not to be from natural causes.

'But who on earth would want to poison the Major?'
The question was asked by a man from the Time and
Motion department who Diana rarely spoke to, but who
she knew by sight. They had gathered a select group of
the company's most senior managers together to hear
this news, but it was standing room only. Two of the
Mackintosh family members had flown in early that
morning in their small private aeroplane, along with
two other managers who would relay the news to the
senior Norwich staff personally, and on a need-to-know
basis.

'We don't think the Major was the intended target. The
poisoned toffees were in a casket made here – and this

is top secret, not to be spoken about – they may have been intended for His Majesty the King.' There were gasps of shock around the room, and many questions, but he silenced them with a wave of his hand which he stopped abruptly when he realized to his distress that it was one of the mannerisms of his old friend Major Fergusson. A lump caught in his throat, but he mastered his emotion and continued, 'The Major was in possession of a casket of toffees emblazoned with our crest, and the royal coat of arms. It is one of a kind and could only have come from our factory. The only reason *we* have been informed, and are permitted to inform you in the strictest confidence, is because the police have instructed us that we now must be vigilant. If a poisoner is abroad in our factory they can only be unmasked with our help.'

'When were they made?' another department head called out.

'We don't know precisely. As far as I have been able to ascertain, this is the casket which was made by our own former confectioner, Mr Birchwood, and which we believed had been destroyed when he left.'

'Do you think Mr Birchwood stole it when he left and tried to poison the Major as revenge for his part in his dismissal?'

'It is one of a number of possibilities which I'm sure the police will be investigating, but there are two more we need to consider. It is possible that this casket was poisoned as an assassination attempt on the King and that the Major unwittingly became a victim. To that end the Home Office are sending special investigators to the factory and I am confident you will extend them every courtesy.' The room became more animated. An assassination attempt on the King through their factory was unthinkable.

'Where was the poison?'

'It was on every single confection.' The factory manager took off his glasses and rubbed the bridge of his nose. 'Which is why we also cannot rule out contamination in the factory, and why we must issue a full product recall and institute our emergency procedures. We must face facts: it *is* possible that the Major was deliberately targeted and it *is* possible that some assassin is attempting to kill the King – but it is far more probable that we have an accidental factory contamination on our hands and I have summoned you all here to begin a recall.'

The room erupted in noisy discussion and Diana watched as these business-like and sober people tried to remain calm while they came to terms with what they had to do next: without letting anyone know that they were looking for a poisoner they had to begin the withdrawal of every Mackintosh's product from every shop across the country. Diana had seen a recall before, but never on this scale. It was a bold move, a cautious move – and the right move. Although it would put the business at dreadful risk when they were already on the brink of bankruptcy. How could they survive? And how could they ever find the source of the poison when the only person who knew where the casket came from was a man on the brink of death? It never occurred to any of them that the casket might not have come from the Major at all, but from someone who had never set foot in the factory.

Chapter Thirty

'You've got to come home, Reenie. There are plenty of other jobs – tell her, Arthur, there are plenty of other jobs.' Mrs Calder was looking imploringly to her husband who had just come into the kitchen from the farmyard on seeing his daughter arrive unexpectedly with their newly shod horse.

Reenie sat huddled in her father's chair beside the kitchen range, shivering beneath a blanket her mother had fetched her, and sobbing uncontrollably. When she had arrived she had been utterly insensible with tears and Mrs Calder had wanted to go and fetch the doctor because her daughter should not have been shivering on a warm June day, but both her other children were at school and she didn't dare leave Reenie alone. Knowing she had to wait until her husband came in from the top field, she did her best to comfort her daughter and, by degrees, she worked out that something had happened to a colleague at her place of work,

202

and she was now very worried for her daughter indeed.

'You found someone to shoe Ruffian, then.' Mr Calder shook his muddy boots off and shuffled across the flags to the scrubbed kitchen table, surveying his wife and his eldest daughter. Mr Calder assumed that there had been some altercation at the factory and that Reenie had answered back and was facing another ticking off. He stood beside his daughter and squeezed her shoulder. 'Don't you listen to what that factory lot say – you're the best worker they've ever had and it would serve them right if you left and got a job elsewhere. Come back to the farm and don't give them another moment's thought.'

Mrs Calder shook her head at her husband over and they exchanged looks. 'Reenie's not in any trouble.'

This stopped Mr Calder in his tracks and he looked down at Reenie and then back up at his wife in puzzlement. 'It's not your Peter, is it? If that lad has disappointed you I'll—'

'No, no Dad, it's not Peter. It's Major Fergusson. He's in the infirmary. They say he's going to die. And my landlady Mrs Garner too. It's so horrible, it's all so horrible. And we're not meant to tell anyone what's happened because the police said it's important.'

'They've both been poisoned,' Mrs Calder whispered over her daughter's head to her husband, 'and the police have been at her lodgings. I don't want her going back. I don't want her in town any longer.'

'You don't understand, Mother! I want to be with my friends, I want to be at the factory, I want us all to be together. And the King is coming to visit and there's more work to do for it than anyone ever thought there would be and not enough workers to do it. They need everyone and I can't leave them now, I just can't.'

'Oh, but Reenie, love, we can't let you go back. Can't you see that you're more important to us than any visit from the King?' Mrs Calder looked to her husband for his opinion.

Mr Calder had expected his daughter would find trouble, but not this sort of trouble. He'd never known his daughter so happy as she was when she worked at Mackintosh's and he worried it would break her heart to leave, but this was horrifying, far beyond his realms of experience.

Chapter Thirty-One

'And you didn't make this casket of toffees yourself?' The man who asked as he pointed to the photograph did not wear a policeman's uniform, and he appeared to outrank the Chief Constable who had introduced him to Mary, Albert and Mrs Wilkes as Detective Inspector Anderson of Scotland Yard. It was, he had explained, only natural that a case like this would make use of the expertise of a Scotland Yard man, and the gaunt figure of the southern policeman with his southern ways immediately frightened Mary.

The big confectioner's kitchen, which had become a safe haven to her, suddenly felt very small and insecure now that it was being invaded by outsiders with questions and notebooks. Mary understood that questions needed to be asked, but the distress she felt at knowing she was, in some intangible way, connected with the imminent death of a person, mingled with the vague fear that somehow her Mr Baum might get the blame and so she did what she always did when she was afraid: she turned into Mardy Mary, the girl who, before Reenie Calder had befriended her, had been renowned in the factory as a rude, fierce defender of herself and her own.

'They've got nothing to do with us and we don't know where they come from!' Mary snapped in the general direction of all the figures of authority who waited patiently to see what she could tell them about the casket of sweets in the photograph they had brought.

'It is quite all right, Mary. These men want our help because we are experts; we cannot deny them our expertise when it would help so much.' The calmness Mr Baum displayed reassured Mary as nothing else could have done. He then addressed the policeman. 'I did not make any of the confections in that casket, no.' Mr Baum was confident in his answer. 'You cannot have failed to notice that I am a foreigner and I only arrived in this country a short time ago. My papers are in order and reflect my date of arrival. I have not had sufficient time to make a full casket of chocolates but I believe they were indeed made by a master confectioner. In addition, they are a mixture of toffees and chocolates, and I have only been working on chocolates here.'

The detective eyed the confectioner for just a fraction longer than was polite and made a note in his pocket notebook before saying, 'I was aware that you took over the post of confectioner some weeks ago; do you know if the casket was here in the kitchens when you arrived?'

'The kitchens were in disarray and my assistant Mary and I had a great deal of work to do discarding old refuse, but I do not remember seeing anything of this sort.'

He handed Mary the photograph of a richly covered casket containing exquisitely piped chocolates of which only two were missing. A lump formed in Mary's throat.

'Do you recognize that casket?'

'No, sir.'

'Have you ever seen one like it in this room?'

'No, sir. The casket for the toffees we're making is wide and flat to prevent them sticking to one another in the warm weather. This is narrow and deep for chocolates. I'm certain I've never seen this casket in this kitchen.'

'How do you account for the fact that it bears the Mackintosh coat of arms and that of His Majesty? And that there is nowhere else in the factory where it could have been produced?'

Mary was panicked into silence; she didn't know how to answer that question and she could feel the threatening fingers of suspicion tightening around her throat.

'We do not have to account for it, I think.' Mr Baum was calm and reasonable as ever, and Mary thought she might cry with relief that he was there beside her and that she was not facing this alone. 'If you can find some more information to prove to us that the casket was here contemporaneous with us, then we will be very interested and we will talk more on the matter, but for the moment we can only tell you that this is not our work and this is not an object we discarded.'

The policeman nodded. 'You make a fair point, Mr Baum. We've no evidence these things were made here; I suppose they could have been made anywhere and disguised with the Mackintosh's insignia. But this doesn't help us to discover how the casket came to be in the possession of Major Fergusson.'

'I agree, sir, it does not.' Albert Baum looked the policeman straight in the eye as he said gently, 'But Major Fergusson is a very dear friend to my assistant here, and I would ask you to remember that she is very worried indeed.'

Chapter Thirty-Two

Mrs Starbeck did not wait long before moving from her desk to Major Fergusson's. She was technically the most senior manager in the Time and Motion Department, and it made logical sense that she would take over the workload of her Head of Department. The Major wasn't dead yet, but all the news implied it was only a matter of days, possibly hours before he was, and Mrs Starbeck was nothing if not prepared. Mrs Starbeck had a reputation for making assumptions strategically, and in this case it was to force the hand of the Mackintosh's directors to give her the Major's job rather than face the embarrassment of telling her later that they were advertising for other applicants and that she would have to move back to her usual place.

Major Fergusson's desk was as neat and orderly as the military man himself, but it was not without personal touches; beside the amber Bakelite inkstand was a gilt-framed photograph of his late wife who had died young, and in the desk drawer Mrs Starbeck found a miscellany of personal papers, including salary slips and cheque books. She wrapped up everything she thought had belonged to the Major in a parcel of manila paper and tightly bound cotton string and sent for one of the factory messenger girls to deliver it to Amy Wilkes with a memorandum requesting that she arrange for it to be sent on to the Major's solicitors for safekeeping until the inevitable happened. She was marking her intention to take on the role as the new Head of Time and Motion. Once the awful news came, and of course she was very upset herself, it would be much more difficult for them to dislodge her if she was in his place already.

It was with annoyance, then, that Mrs Starbeck discovered the Major's savings book on the floor beside his chair after the girl had left. She thought she had put it into the parcel with the other items, but it must have fallen out when she was turning the parcel over to wrap it with string. It didn't matter; as all would become clear when his will was read, the Major planned to leave the majority of his estate to the Confectioners' Benevolent Fund, and as long as the Major was still alive she didn't see any urgency in sending it on. She would pay a call on Major Fergusson's solicitors and deliver it in person when she had the time. She dropped the savings book into her purse and for several hours thought no more about it.

Reenie returned to work to find that everything had changed in the Major's absence. All the plans that he had put in place were being overturned by Mrs Starbeck. Reenie found that her first job was to go down to the

Gooseberry Cream workroom and tell the married ladies on the line that they would not be given the chance to transfer to the King's Toffee line as they had been promised; instead, that line would be reserved for the fastest unmarried girls and the women of Gooseberry Cream would stay where they were 'pending review', and Mrs Starbeck's edict removing their piece rates would be reinstated. This was not what the Major had intended, and it pained Reenie to see it. Reenie suspected this was Mrs Starbeck's way of getting revenge for the starch hopper incident on the line after she had tried to cut the married women's pay the first time around. Now the woman was cutting their pay and taking away their chance to work on the production line which the King would visit – it was a double blow.

Reenie did not relish the thought that she was about to be the bearer of bad news, but she decided to go early and catch the ladies in the cloakroom before their shift began. She was lucky and she found that all of the women bar one had arrived early for their shift, as they did each morning, and she could talk to them all together. The ladies of the Gooseberry Cream line were welcoming enough, but they were in no mood to go meekly. Emily Everard wanted to know precisely how long the company would continue to allow them to work, and what their plans were to maintain the level of piece rates for the casual workers who needed to earn more to counteract the insecurity of their jobs. They had agreed not to go out on strike because they were loyal subjects of the King first and foremost, and this was partly about the King's visit, but they were still unhappy and they seemed to think that Reenie could do something about it.

'But just imagine it was you!' Emily Everard said. 'How do you think you'd feel? You work hard, you learn the ropes, you get good at something for once in your life after years of your school teachers tellin' you you're not worth a damn, and then you do the natural, honest, God-fearin' thing and marry, and you're out on your ear, never to come back.'

'But you're here now,' Reenie tried to sound optimistic, 'that's something, isn't it?'

'And how long's that supposed to last, eh?' Old Mrs Grimshaw could not trust to providence the way Reenie did. 'They said they'd lift the marriage bar while they rebuilt the factory, but as soon as they're back onto machine working they'll reinstate the bar and we'll be back to how we were.'

Emily Everard had touched a nerve when she'd asked Reenie to imagine how she'd feel if she had to leave when she married. If Reenie was honest with herself, it was one of the things she secretly feared. Peter was keen for them to marry one day, hopefully in a year or two when they'd saved up plenty for their bottom drawer, and Reenie could suddenly see herself in these women; she, too, had been useless at school, she had worked hard to learn the ropes at the factory, and she had found something for the first time in her life that she was really good at. Reenie dared to ask the question that she was afraid to hear the answer to. 'Don't you find once you're married that you don't really miss it? Don't you like being a wife and a mother better than being a factory lass?'

The look on the women's faces said it all: there was no comparing the two and they were torn in a way Reenie could see herself being torn. The love she felt for her job was visceral, and although she was sure she'd love her family and her home when she settled down to marry, she'd couldn't imagine being parted from her job with anything but bitter heartache. Reenie had always assumed that it was just her, that she was the first girl to feel like this about being a factory lass, that being passionate about what she did at Mackintosh's was one of her many oddities – but now she saw the sparkle in the eyes of these wives and mothers, and she knew that the fire burned in their hearts too. 'But what can I do about it? I'm just one person. I'm a junior manager and I don't—'

'Keep us here as long as you can. We're clubbing together to buy Siobhan Grimshaw's daughter a school uniform and we need the best piece rates you can get us. If we can't earn them on this line, then help us get transferred to another one.'

The Gooseberry Cream ladies were about to launch into the details of their scheme to get their colleague's daughter into the grammar school when a clatter at the door of the cloakroom caused them all to look round – Doreen Fairclough had tumbled through the doors, out of breath and almost out of time to start her shift without another late marker against her employment record.

'Was it the kids again?' Mrs Grimshaw threw her a mobcap from the coat hook above her.

'I turn my back for less than a minute – *less than a minute* – and Fred's eaten a bee. What are you even supposed to do when they eat a bee? Do I call out the doctor?' Doreen Fairclough was looking to the older women in the cloakroom for authoritative advice as they had raised children of their own and she hoped they would have answers. 'He seemed all right in himself and it was his sister who was upset.' There were nods of understanding from other women who were putting on their own mobcaps, ready to go onto the line – they had evidently found themselves in comparable situations. 'But will he need the doctor later, that's what I want to know? Am I a bad mother for sending him to school when he seemed all right after ten minutes and nothing bad happened?'

Winifred and Pearl were about to offer practical advice but deferred to Mrs Grimshaw as the eldest of the mothers in their department, and therefore the most experienced. 'I've got good news and bad news for you, love: the good news is that no one knows what they're doing when they raise kids, and we're all making it up as we go along, so you're probably doing as well as anyone would in your shoes.'

Doreen hurried into her factory overalls and tucked her hair into her mobcap. 'And the bad news?'

'The only thing any of us really know how to do is factory work – and this very nice young lady has come to explain that they may now be taking all of that away from us after all.'

Chapter Thirty-Three

'The news isn't good, we've been sifting through your father's affairs carefully. I think you were already aware that your father was in financial difficulties.' The solicitor tried to be compassionate, but he didn't want to become too embroiled in a case which would take up a lot of time and pay nothing.

Cynthia Starbeck's look of shock told the solicitor that he had been mistaken. 'My father was a successful businessman, an investor, he was . . .' Her voice trailed off as she struggled to grasp what he had been. What *had* he been? She had never fully understood. He had been a Member of Parliament for a term, and there had been board meetings and a house full of purple-faced, cigar-smoking men, but what had his line of business actually been?

'But you took out loans for him, considerable loans. Were you not concerned that he was in need of money?'

'I don't know what you're talking about. I've never

taken out a loan in my life. I own a flat in Hipperholme, and I have some money in some investment trusts which my father arranged for me. I didn't involve myself with the details, but some of my salary each month went into the fund, and—'

'If I may, Miss Starbeck, how much is in this fund, and to whom was it paid?'

'Well, I arranged a standing order from my checking account of £6 per month to my father's—'

'Those are loan repayments, Miss Starbeck; your father had you sign an agreement to borrow money on his behalf against your flat. You were to pay off the interest on the loan at the rate of £6 a month.'

'But that can't be! My father would never have—'

'Your father had sizeable debts, Miss Starbeck. It seems the money he asked you to borrow against your flat was to invest in a high-risk scheme which, if it had come off, would have given him enough money to keep his creditors at bay a little longer – but the sum was lost. I regret to inform you that your father has died without the wherewithal to even pay his funeral expenses or for the administration of his estate.'

'But what does this mean? Will I have to use the money he invested for me to pay off this loan?'

'Miss Starbeck, he didn't invest any money for you. The money you gave him was paid to a lender against the interest of the loan.'

'But where is the investment trust money? How much do I have in trust?'

'Nothing.'

'That's impossible! He's been investing my money for me all my working life, I—' And suddenly the reality of what her father was washed over Cynthia Starbeck and she felt cold and empty and alone – and she hated the man.

'I can keep his creditors at bay for a little longer to allow you to settle your affairs—'

'Why would I need to settle my affairs? They were *his* debts, they're nothing to do with me. I may not have the investments I thought I had, but I have my own flat and a job which pays me well enough to keep myself and put by a little money in savings. It's been a long time since my father gave me an allowance and I used my late mother's money to buy the flat; I am self-sufficient and have been for a considerable time. I'm disappointed that he has left me with the cost of his funeral, but I shall manage quite well without him.'

'I don't think you fully understand, Miss Starbeck. You no longer own your flat, your creditors own it. Your father asked you to sign forms which were actually those for taking out a mortgage on the flat, and you have been repaying the interest, but not the residue of the loan. The time has come now for all the debts to be paid, so the flat will be repossessed and the contents auctioned. I can give you a little time to find somewhere within your means, but you will have to make repayments towards the other loans which—'

'What other loans?'

'Miss Starbeck, I will need to know your exact financial situation because you will be ordered by the courts to repay as much of these debts as your salary can stretch to. Please prepare yourself because you will need to make some severe changes to your style of life; there is no other way.'

Chapter Thirty-Four

Bess had always loved the idea of being a secretary. She had seen them on films at the pictures and occasionally read about them in thrilling stories they published in *The Girl's Own Paper*. The idea of messing about with a typewriter ribbon and telling people that she was 'busy' had an intoxicating appeal for the silliest girl in Halifax who had always known in her heart of hearts that she would make a beautiful secretary. Working on the production line was fun for the other girls, but it was ever so tiring for Bess; she had to stand up quite a lot of the time, and she had to pass people things and fetch things, and it was so *noisy*. Being a secretary, on the other hand, would be heavenly. She'd sit up at a desk and make sure she sat at an angle where her colleagues could admire her profile, and she would keep her desk pretty with a nice posy of fresh flowers on it every morning, and when the tea lady came round with her trolley at break times Bess would make cheery conversation with her; she'd find out her name and make sure she was given a chance to take the weight off her feet. Being taken to see her new workplace by Reenie and Mary was raising hopes for Bess of a glamorous existence in an office on these terms.

'Do I get my own office?' Bess was curling a ringlet of her golden hair around her finger as she skipped along behind the two other girls.

'Of course you don't.' Mary was marching on ahead. 'You're in a warehouse out the back of the postal goods yard.'

'But do I get my own office in the warehouse?'

'I tell you what,' Mary was sardonic, 'we'll give you your own chair and your own inkstand, and, if you're very, very lucky, we'll write your name on the inkstand.'

'Oooh! And what kind of a chair am I getting? Is it one with big arms like a throne?'

Reenie opened her mouth to answer Bess, but Mary gave her a warning look that said *don't get drawn in, we don't have time*. Reenie stepped ahead of them to open the rattling door of the Water Lane postal goods warehouse, with its corrugated glass roof which cast a pretty pattern of light onto its painted blue concrete floor. The place wasn't as bad as Reenie had remembered; the main warehouse was drafty, but Bess would ostensibly have her own annexed office in the front corner, with a desk, chairs, a small stove, and a lavatory through another door. It was typical of Bess that she should land on her feet even in a remote warehouse at the far end of the factory complex. Reenie suspected it wouldn't be long before Bess had made it cosy.

'All right, Bess, pay attention because I don't think

I'll have time to come back here and explain this to you again. You've got to try to remember that you're not responsible for how the decorations look on the day of the King's visit and you're not responsible for ordering the decorations, or for choosing what gets ordered – all that has been done by Mr Conricode in Sales and he has allocated space on every wall to different departments to decorate. He has listed every department in this ledger, and he has allocated a precise quantity of decorations. These decorations will arrive in boxes in the warehouse and your job is to wait here for each department to send a representative to collect their allocation.'

'How should I look while I'm waiting? Should I look unobtainable?' Bess tossed her pretty hair over her shoulders and pouted like a Hollywood starlet from *Picturegoer* magazine.

'No!' Reenie was feeling rather frustrated with Bess, but she knew she didn't mean any harm and that the best way to deal with her was to appeal to her imagination. 'You know those advertisements for mothers who feed their children malted milk?'

'The ones where the mothers have got their hands on their hips and they're all capable, like?'

'The very same. Have a go at looking like one of those capable mothers.'

Mary rolled her eyes and Bess tried to imagine her way into her new role. 'Well, I'll do my best, but—'

'I knew we could rely on you, Bess. Now, listen carefully. When people come down to the warehouse you will have to look them up in the book Mr Conricode has drawn up and give them the *exact* amount of decorations from the boxes which have arrived corresponding with Mr Conricode's instructions, and give them a permit slip which says exactly where they are to decorate.'

Mary was watching Bess's expression of vague interest and thought she ought to make sure she really understood. Mary had an ominous feeling about this job. A lot could go wrong if Bess was merely left to run a bath, but Mary thought leaving her sister to run a warehouse full of decorations for the King was asking for trouble, so she said, 'Take a look in the book for me and see if you can see the entry for the staff canteen . . . Yes, you'll need to flick through it but—'

'Oooh, I've found it, I've found it!' Bess was enthusiastic about her accomplishment, as if this was the sum total of what was expected of her and she had succeeded on her first try.

'Very good, Bess. Now, can you look and see which space they've been allocated to cover? It should be in the column next to their department name.'

'It says 8,000 square feet from the west canteen to the stairway gate.'

'Very good. Now, in the next column, what decorations does it say they should have?'

'Um . . . 1,500 yards of bunting, 700 yards of crepe, three banners, four garlands, and a tarpaulin.'

'Very good. Now, when they come to collect their decorations what do you give them?'

'I don't know, I haven't got any decorations.'

'Well, you will have shortly because they're going to arrive in boxes. Your job will be to go through the boxes and pull out *exactly* what is on this list and no more because otherwise there won't be enough for the other departments. They've ordered just the right amount. Now, the most important thing, the thing you really, really must not forget, is that you need to remind them of exactly where their territory is, and impress upon them that they must not decorate anywhere else, or *with* anything else, do you understand?'

Bess nodded and repeated back, 'They mustn't decorate anything else and I've got to tell them that when I give them the bunting – and I mustn't give them too much bunting or there won't be enough to go around.'

Reenie and Mary breathed a sigh of relief. Bess understood perfectly. They both went away feeling a little guilty that they were so hard on Bess – she really wasn't as silly as all that. They tended to assume that she would make a mess of everything, but that was unfair.

'Now, I can give you your bunting, but I've got to be very strict with you and remind you that we are using this to decorate for the King's visit and you're not to decorate anywhere else. No using this to decorate your house for the FA Cup – you're decorating the factory for the King's visit and that is all.' Bess was running her fingertips along the edges of the boxes and dithering over which to open first. It was fortunate for Bess that the two young men from the factory stables, who had been sent to collect their decorations for the factory horses, were too much enamoured of the pretty girl to be put out by her patronizing speech, or irritated by her slowness and general inefficiency in distributing the items they had come to collect.

'I tell you what,' one of them suggested, 'how about we open up all those boxes for you and take the tops off them so you can take out what you want without any trouble?'

Bess's eyes lit up; now she could just look beautiful while young men did her work for her. Nothing could have pleased her more.

Chapter Thirty-Five

Mary sipped her sugary cup of tea and looked straight ahead of her out of the window as her sobs slowly calmed to gasps.

The confectioner's kitchen was in disarray. Broken shards in various sizes of a smashed yellowware mixing bowl were strewn all over the floor, and amongst them the splattering of molten chocolate toffee. There was a lot of clearing up to do, but also apologizing. Mary lowered her cup and looked to Mr Baum to say something, but he did not give her the opportunity.

'Not yet, there is much to say,' Albert Baum was reassuring her, 'but not yet. I told you, you must sit here, you must drink all of your cup of tea, and then we will talk.'

'But—' Mary wanted to say how sorry she was, or how keen she was to get on with the cleaning up, which would be nothing but trouble because the sugar was cooling and the toffee was sticking to every surface it had reached; and it seemed to Mary that it had reached everywhere.

'You need strong, sweet tea, and a sit down.' Albert Baum had made himself a cup of tea also, but seemed more interested in the cup which Mary held. 'Everything will be quite all right, I assure you.'

Mary didn't see how anything could ever be right again. Old Major Fergusson, one of the best people she had ever met, lay dying in the hospital because he had probably been poisoned with sweets from her kitchen; she had been separated from her trusted friends who she felt she saw so rarely now compared to their old days on the line; she and her sister had left the simple jobs they understood and felt safe doing, to take on jobs which seemed far beyond their abilities – and now she had ruined everything with the manager who she thought the world of by showing herself up as clumsy in the kitchen and breaking company property.

She had allowed a ridiculous thing to upset her – but if she was honest with herself, she knew that she had been in a nervous mood before she arrived in the kitchen. She had woken up late, missed her breakfast, missed her tram, run most of the way to the factory, then Dolly Dunkley had bumped into her in the factory corridor and been insulting in a way only Dolly could be, insinuating that foreigners like Mr Baum wouldn't be able to stay at the factory much longer. Mary had been very upset by this and she had arrived at the kitchen fuming but also light-headed, and tried to rush through the work of the morning.

But this morning's work had been delicate and had needed care and consideration. Mr Baum had asked Mary to show him how to make traditional Halifax toffee, the kind which Mackintosh's were famous for, but which they did not make in Germany. Mary had overcomplicated matters by trying to make the toffee – which she had seen made once by old Mrs Todmorden – but also invent a new flavouring at the same time. And it had caught fire. Or rather, one of the pans which she had left on the stove while she checked on the two cane bowls she had waiting on the warmth of the tempering table had caught fire, and Mr Baum had quickly put it out. When Mary saw that her first batch was ruined she lost all faith in her ability to remedy the situation and clumsily dropped the first of the cane bowls on the floor where it bounced off the corner of a chair, sending its contents splattering even further. That was the moment she had been sure that not only was her career at Mackintosh's at an end, but that her beloved Mr Baum would never respect her abilities again.

Mary had sobbed uncontrollably while she waited for Mr Baum to tell her that she was dismissed and should never come to the factory again, but instead he had walked calmly to the stove, removed the burnt pan, replaced it with a tea kettle, and rummaged in their cupboards for cups, saucers, a teapot, and the battered tin of tea leaves. By the time he had brewed Mary a steaming cup of tea her panic had ebbed away and she was left with miserable guilt. Who was this man who was so kind to her and so patient when she was making everything more difficult? He made her laugh, he had made everything better when she cried, and he made her better at her work than she'd ever thought she could be. She desperately wished they could stay working together in the kitchen forever, but her heart was breaking at the thought it would all end very soon because Mr Baum had to go home to his children.

Albert Baum saw that Mary's teacup was empty and, instead of offering her the chance to apologize for her actions, offer an excuse, or suggest a plan to clean up the kitchen, he asked her about the one topic which had been on her mind all day, bubbling away in the background. 'You are still thinking about your Major Fergusson,' he said, 'yes?'

Mary had to work hard to hold back more tears. Not only had she been thinking about the Major constantly, she had also been turning over possible ways his poisoning might have been her fault. None of them were even within the realms of possibility, but it was in her nature to look for a way in which the situation might be something for which she could heap blame and recrimination upon herself. 'I don't understand who he could have got them from. Surely he must have known that there was something wrong with them?'

'Perhaps they were given to him by someone he trusted. Perhaps he didn't question their judgement.'

'But then that must mean that they came from someone we know. Someone who is still here at work.' Mary shuddered. It was too horrible to contemplate. 'It feels as though there is poison everywhere.'

'In the people, or the confections?'

Mary stopped short and suddenly realized that Mr Baum had hit upon her fears precisely; Mary was fearful of the very tangible poison which had found its way into that box of confections, but she was also afraid of the less tangible poison which was even more pervasive. She was afraid of the poison which had got into the people in Germany and was making Mr Baum's life there more and more perilous; she was afraid of the poison which had got into people in Spain and was driving countless children from their homes as refugees; she was frightened of the poison in people like Mrs Starbeck who she had heard was trying to do everything in her power to have Mr Baum removed and returned to Germany early because she did not believe the King's Toffee ought to be made by a foreigner. Suddenly, Mary felt a little better knowing what she was afraid of and how to articulate it, and the fact that Albert Baum had helped her to realize it made her feel all the more attached to him. It was as though he understood her thoughts better than she did herself.

'I'm afraid of both,' she said, and Mr Baum nodded sagely, as though these were both very sensible things to be afraid of, and that he too had a healthy fear of them.

'But we have another problem, do we not?' Albert Baum looked around at the burnt pan and the smashed mixing bowl. 'Your king is coming, and Mackintosh's want a new toffee for him. But I think we have learned something valuable today – neither you nor I know how to make this toffee.'

And Mary realized that this meant that either she or Mr Baum would have to be replaced with someone who could do the job, and even if she hadn't dropped the mixing bowl this moment would still have been the parting of the ways.

Chapter Thirty-Six

Reenie, Peter, Mary, and Bess were all sitting round Ruffian in his stable wishing they could do more. It was a dull day, and as the summer rain spattered down on the cobbles of the old factory stable yard the four friends thought how glad they were that they had somewhere quiet and dry to sit together in the dinner hour. Since their friend the Major had been taken to the infirmary they had felt even less inclined to brave the noise and crush of the factory dining hall; it felt obscene that so much life could continue when they were so close to losing someone so dear to them.

'Well, I suppose it's a good job we put down blankets in here and got it fixed up while it was dry.' Reenie looked around Ruffian's stable with little pleasure. 'I honestly didn't think he'd be coming to the factory much after I'd moved to Mrs Garner's house, but it is so useful to ride him from and to the farm each day.'

'How is Mrs Garner?' Mary asked.

'I don't know,' Reenie said truthfully. 'The last thing I heard was that she wasn't expected to last through the night – but that was two days ago and I don't know who to ask for more news.'

'Poor Mrs Garner.' Bess had never met the woman, but she was heartbroken at the thought of Reenie's landlady and the Major missing out on their chance for love. 'It's a shame you can't live in town for the moment, but it's nice for us to see Ruffian every day. Where are all Mrs Garner's other boarders living?'

'Most of them have stayed on,' Reenie said. 'Diana has written to Mrs Garner's family and taken charge while they all wait to see what will happen next.'

Mary shook her head. 'I'm never going to have a dinner hour again at this rate! I've got that much to do, I'm all at sixes and sevens. I've got to learn how to do a hundred things a day; there's no toffee confectioner; we've had a thief in the kitchens taking sweets; Mr Baum is only allowed to stay for three months – and the key to the kitchen broke in my hand this morning and now I've got to leave the place on the latch! And that's only if I'm allowed to stay at all . . .' Mary's voice cracked with emotion. 'I talked to Mr Baum this morning and I think they might be about to replace me and send me back to my old job on the line because I'm not a master toffee maker.'

Reenie tried to console her. 'Yes, but at least you've got us, Mary. If you ever need us to come and help you, or if you need to talk about how difficult the work is you know that you always have us. It's Mrs Garner I feel most sorry for; I wish there was something we could do for her. I hate being so far away from her and so powerless at a time like this.'

Peter was sitting with his arms crossed and his brow furrowed in disapproving thought, 'But we shouldn't be letting the King visit at all – this whole enterprise ought to be cancelled. Not just as a mark of respect to the Major and Mrs Garner, but knowing how they were both poisoned it seems like madness now to press on with it. Surely someone, somewhere, must see the danger in letting him come here? I've been thinking about it; these sweets were specially made – and the casket. What if someone is out to get him and those sweets were meant to be given to the King?'

The girls looked horrified

'No,' Reenie said, 'no one here would do that! It's madness! If we do a thorough recall and a thorough sweep of every factory building we could find out where the poison came from and settle the whole matter. There's no assassin planning to poison the King, it's just a simple accident and we need to find out how it could have happened.'

Peter didn't usually contradict Reenie, but they were under a great deal of strain and emotions were running high. 'You know as well as I do, Reenie, that there isn't a single place in the entire factory where that could have happened by accident; there is no risk of poisoning anywhere – and if there were, you and I would have been the first to see it on a line and report it. The whole of Europe is falling apart and we're decorating the factory so that we can give the King a box of toffees that we can't find anyone to make, and all this during the worst product recall in the history of the firm.'

'Well, that's why we need him here! The King's visit will publicise Quality Street and it will save the factory.'

231

'You're living in a dream world, Reenie; *nothing* can save the factory now.'

There was a strained silence as Reenie tried not to burst into tears and Peter tried not to snap at her for looking as if she might. They were all upset and worrying about the Major and Mrs Garner, and they were frustrated that the hospital wouldn't allow them to visit while they were both so gravely ill. It felt doubly hard that the one person who they turned to for advice in these situations was the very man who they were about to lose.

'We have a problem, I think, Mrs Wilkes.' Albert Baum had not burst into Amy Wilkes's office as some of her colleagues might have done but had politely sent a memorandum requesting an urgent interview with her at her earliest convenience. Amy had hoped it wasn't anything to do with Cynthia Starbeck; she was only too aware of the troubles Mr Baum had experienced in Germany and she didn't like the thought that Mrs Starbeck was adding to them. She knew that Albert Baum had already been assured by the Head of Men's employment that he was not in any way suspected by the firm of having had a hand in the poisoning of the chocolates which had killed Major Fergusson, but she had a horrible suspicion that Mrs Starbeck would be doing her best to sow the seeds of doubt against the foreigner in their midst.

'I hope it's nothing too serious, Mr Baum.'

Albert Baum calmly lowered himself into the seat in front of the employment manager and said pragmatically, 'You will need to find a new confectioner; I am not suitable for this task.'

Amy was shocked but tried not to show it. 'I think

you're eminently suitable, Mr Baum.' She hoped this was merely a matter of frayed nerves and that she could talk the man round, because the last thing they needed was to be left without a confectioner once again.

'I have spoken with Mary Norcliffe and it has become apparent that I cannot continue here as your confectioner, you need someone else.'

This came as a surprise to Amy Wilkes and she showed it. Of all the people who she had expected to be difficult Mary was not one of them. 'Has Mary behaved in some way that—'

'No! No! Maria... I mean Mary, is excellent, an excellent woman. I think very highly of her. It is a pleasure to work with her. My concern is regarding the casket of confectionery for His Majesty, King George.'

This sounded to Amy as though he had been listening to complaints from Cynthia Starbeck and she inwardly cursed the woman. 'It really isn't a problem that you aren't English, Mr Baum.'

'But it is, it is a problem. You need an Englishman.' And before Amy could dismiss any of his concerns as easily solved, Albert Baum delivered his hammer blow. 'I don't know how to make your toffee. Halifax toffee is not like anything we have in Germany. Our toffee is like your humbugs; it is brittle, it smashes like glass when you throw it to the ground. Your Halifax toffee is of a special kind, invented by Violet Mackintosh; you know this. It is soft, but not so soft as caramel. It has a different flavour and many different qualities. I do not know this well enough to make it for the King so soon. Mary has tried to show me what she learned from one of your retired ladies, but she is not a master toffee maker; she cannot be expected to know all she needs to in order to do something so momentous as invent a new toffee for your king.'

Amy sank back into her chair; she hadn't thought about this. Of course Mackintosh's toffee was utterly different – and they couldn't leave it out of the King's casket because it was the great distinguishing feature of their firm. 'Wouldn't it be possible to learn? I don't wish to be rude, Mr Baum, but we brought you here because we understood that you were a trained confectioner. Can't a trained confectioner learn how to make any confection if they have the recipe to hand?'

'I must correct you, Fräulein Wilkes; I am a trained chocolatier in the Swiss tradition. I specialize in the manufacture of products from the cocoa bean, but sugar confections of the nature you are looking for are a different discipline. And yes, I could look at a recipe and attempt to make a Halifax toffee with the apparatus we have, but it will not be the finest toffee to have ever left the Halifax factory. You want a toffee fit for a king, yes? You will need one of these old ladies who makes things in barrels when they have no pans.'

Amy Wilkes tried to resist the temptation to rest her head in her hands and give up. 'Very well, Mr Baum, I will attempt to find someone who can make Halifax toffee to the standard we require. If I find a suitable candidate will you do us the pleasure of staying on to make the chocolates for the rest of the casket?'

'But of course, if you wish it.'

'Is there anything else you need, Mr Baum?' It was an almost sarcastic question, born of not uncharitable exasperation, but Albert Baum took it literally and answered with gratitude.

'Yes, thank you. I would like a full-time cleaning lady in the confectionery kitchens. We have many vessels and implements to wash after we make a batch of chocolates, but I do not want Mary to do all of this cleaning – I value her skill too highly to waste it on pot washing.'

Mrs Wilkes could not help but smirk at the German's use of the Yorkshire expression which she assumed he had picked up from Mary Norcliffe. 'Very well, Mr Baum, you leave it to me. I'll find you a toffee maker *and* a cleaner.' And she ushered the man out of her office before he could ask for anything else.

Once she was confident that he was out of earshot she opened her door and summoned Diana to vent her spleen.

'Oh well, that's just wonderful,' Amy Wilkes said, pacing up and down her office in annoyance. 'Now we have to find a toffee maker immediately; a general confectioner to start work in a few months' time when Mr Baum leaves; and a cleaner for the confectionery kitchens who comes with impeccable references and can pass the Home Office test. And not only that, they need to be full time so we can't get a mother to do the job.'

Diana listened impassively. 'I think I have just the girl.'

'I thought you said there wasn't anyone left in Halifax who could satisfy the Home Office criteria?'

'That was before I met Dolly Dunkley. She's a vicar's daughter – and I think she'd be delighted to clean up after Mary Norcliffe.'

Chapter Thirty-Seven

'There's a girl. Victoria. She might, possibly . . .' Sir Harold trailed off. He had called his head of Women's Employment to his office because he had hoped that he might have the solution to their problem of who would make the toffees for the King's casket, but it was a long shot.

Amy Wilkes could see that the head of the firm was hesitating, but she was quick to seize on any possible solution to their predicament, 'What is holding you back, sir?'

Sir Harold took a deep breath. 'The girl is blind.'

It wasn't what Amy was expecting him to say, but it wasn't the worst thing he could have said. 'Is she a good confectioner?'

'Yes. Exceptionally so. Her father was the confectioner who trained my mother before she started our family business. She can run rings around anyone.'

'And the only obstacle is that she's blind? Because that isn't an obstacle. We have Mary Norcliffe to assist her.

Wherever she is we should hire her. Does she live in Halifax?'

'There's another obstacle.' This time it was Diana Moore who spoke up from her reserved place as notetaker beside Amy Wilkes. 'If you'll forgive me, Sir Harold, I've already seen Vicky Geall; she's an old acquaintance of mine.'

'The obstacle?' Mrs Wilkes asked.

'Insurmountable,' Diana said, with a look that told her manager that she would explain later.

'Then,' Sir Harold sighed, 'it looks like I'll have to make them myself. Not that I ever had my mother's skill, but needs must if we really can't get anyone else.'

'I'll talk to our Norwich factory confectioner, Sir Harold, and see if they can help Mary to make them; she's made Toffee de Luxe on the production line before, so she already has some of the skills necessary. I think we can find a solution.'

'Very good, although I think you'll have the same trouble there. The Norwich factory are a chocolate factory, not a toffee factory. My offer stands: if it's necessary I will come down to the confectioner's kitchen and make toffee. However, my preference would be that we found someone else because I have a lot to do in preparation for a royal visit.'

'Yes, Sir Harold.' Amy Wilkes took the indication that the discussion was at an end, and Diana could see that she was keen for them to get away so that she could hear what the obstacle was to bringing in Victoria Geall. Out in the hallway, as they made rapid progress toward the stairs, Amy Wilkes asked her junior, 'Tell me the worst – why can't we have this confectioner?'

'Vicky Geall has a baby.'

'Well, that is insurmountable.' Amy was deflated. 'No amount of Mackintosh's money is going to make her strong enough to start work again if she's just given birth. I'm not above begging centenarians to put their overalls on and make fudge in a barrel if I think they'll enjoy it for a bit, but let's not sink to the level of slave drivers.'

'To be honest, that's not the trouble.' Diana had already turned over all the options and dismissed them. 'The baby is seven months and Vicky's happy to have a part-time bit of work to pitch in to if it isn't permanent. The problem is what we do with the baby.'

'Can't we pay a neighbour to mind it?'

'Not when it needs to be fed. The baby needs his mother, and I thought it would be indelicate to explain to Sir Harold that she needs to nurse it herself, and a wet nurse is out of the question because if Vicky doesn't nurse the child herself she'll lose her ability to nurse him very quickly.'

Amy Wilkes nodded in thought as they weaved quickly in and out of gates and gables. 'I don't know much about these things. How frequently . . .?' Amy's reserved nature meant that she shied away from saying the words 'breast feed' in a crowded corridor of factory workers.

'As much as he needs. The baby would need to be here somewhere at the factory, and I didn't mention it to Sir Harold because I thought I knew what would happen – he'd suggest we let her keep the baby in a Moses basket in the kitchens – which wouldn't be safe for the baby or hygienic for the kitchens – or he'd say we should we hire a nanny to mind her in his office and carry him to the kitchens every hour when he needs a feed, which would set a precedent for other married women who want to come back to work and want Mackintosh's to pay for someone to look after their children.'

'You were right not to mention it to Sir Harold; it is too difficult.' Amy Wilkes arrived at the door to her office and held it open for her junior. 'But I still think we're too hard as a business upon the mothers who want to work. Why shouldn't Mackintosh's pay people to look after their employees' children while they work for us? It's not as though children are a hobby or luxury goods.'

Diana shrugged, concealing the emotion within. She wanted to tell her manager how much she agreed with her, because if there had been anyone at all to care for her daughter while she worked, then Diana would not have had to give her up. But she said nothing and tried to think of a way to get Vicky Geall back to work.

'Can't you just enjoy the excitement while it lasts?' Reenie sat in the stable on a hay bale beside Ruffian as she watched Mary pace the floor with nervous energy. It was a shame that Mary had to be so anxious about everything because it would have been a balm just then to have indulged in happy speculation on the King's visit to distract her from the constant sadness which clung to her while she waited for news of her landlady and Major Fergusson.

'How can I enjoy it? I've got my sister telling me every five minutes she wants a baby, in a matter of weeks when Mr Baum goes home I'll have no manager, and . . . and . . .' Mary tried to come up with a third reason why she should be worrying, but Reenie interrupted her.

'But just think, you're going to be making sweets for the King!'

'Exactly! I've got to make them and I know I'm not experienced enough. I know they're going to be bad.'

'I think I'd just be happy that I was getting the chance to help.'

'You'd be happy if they put you in charge of cleaning the loos. *You're* happy with anything.'

'I don't understand why you can't be happy too, when good things happen to you. You never seem to be able to enjoy anything.'

'How can anyone be happy when there's so much to worry about?'

'But there'll *always* be things to worry about. If you look at it from that point of view you'll never enjoy anything.' Rennie heaved herself up from her hay bale and patted Ruffian's warm, soft muzzle. 'Is there anything I can do to make it better?'

Mary was quick to answer. 'Put a guard on my sister. Make sure she absolutely cannot get pregnant. She's working out in that warehouse and she could have any number of assignations without getting found out. She needs watching.'

Reenie considered for a moment. 'And you're sure it's the baby she wants and not the assignation?'

'Well, knowing her it will be six of one and half a dozen of the other, but yes, it's a baby she keeps going on about. It's not right, you know; there are people with babies who can't work and who would tell Bess how lucky she is to have this time now to herself, and then there're girls like Bess . . .'

'Oh, but having babies is natural,' Rennie said, 'so it's absolutely natural for her to want a baby.'

'You know Diana Moore found a trained confectioner

who can teach me to make Halifax toffee? Someone to supplement the chocolate work Herr Baum is doing.'

'Did they?' Reenie was surprised she hadn't heard about this already. 'When does he start?'

'*She* doesn't; she's got a baby.'

'Oh.' Reenie still didn't understand why a solution had not yet been found to the age-old problem of being a parent, and at the same time wanting to earn a living. It wasn't as though this was a recent development in the history of mankind – and if human beings could prevent smallpox, build a canal to join two oceans, and create machines to take flight, then surely they could find a way to keep an eye on a baby while the mother worked.

'Her father was the confectioner who first employed old Mrs Violet Mackintosh all those years ago, and she was running his shop till she sold up to get married. She's perfect for the job, but she's said she can't come because her baby's not weaned yet and it can't be left.'

'Couldn't she find another mother nearby to mind it?' Reenie asked.

'Not likely – they're all working here.'

'But if someone minded her baby she would come and show you what to do?'

'Don't go getting any ideas, Reenie Calder. You don't know the first thing about babies and even if you did, the factory can't afford to have you go off and mind a baby for a fortnight while they're setting up new lines. Take my advice and don't get involved.'

But Reenie was determined to get involved; this sounded like just the kind of problem she could solve.

'But if I did find someone to mind her baby, someone

nearby, would she be able to leave the kitchens often to check on it?'

'Well yes, I suppose so, we'll be there – that's Mr Baum and I – but to be honest, I'm starting to worry that he only wants another confectioner so that he doesn't have to spend as much time with me because I'm so much bother. He's said he's going to get us a full-time cleaner to work in the kitchens on pot washing and the like, and he's always finding excuses to send me off to the other side of the factory to get something, or to go out on an errand himself, so we're hardly in a room together any more. We got on so well at first and now I don't know what I've done wrong.'

'I'm sure you haven't done anything,' Reenie said automatically, her mind already turning over a possible solution to two problems at once.

Chapter Thirty-Eight

Peter had waited as long as he could, but the news he had for Reenie when he had come to collect her the night Mrs Garner and the Major were taken to the infirmary couldn't keep any longer. That dreadful night he had booked them a table at a restaurant on Horton Hill and planned the gentlest way to break the news to her, but now Peter had no time left and the gentlemanly plan had to be replaced by the necessary one. He caught Reenie outside the noisy canteen and pulled her in and sat down with her at the end of one of the long tables, turning away from the others there so that they couldn't be overheard.

'I had a letter from home, Reenie.' Peter was holding the letter to his chest with both hands. It seemed to be a shield against the criticism which he knew was coming.

'Your parents are making you move too, are they?'

'Move?'

'My mum and dad don't want me to live in town any more; even if I find another boarding house they don't want me to leave home again. They nearly told me I had to leave the job as well, but I pleaded with them to let me stay.'

'You really love it here, don't you?'

'You know I do.' Reenie began to look worried. They had talked until the cows came home about how she didn't want to marry young if it meant leaving the factory, and Reenie had thought that they had reached an understanding, but it felt as though everything in their lives had changed since they had lost the Major.

'My cousins are going to Spain.' He said it quietly; looking the girl he loved in the eye.

Rennie was naturally worried for these lads even though she'd only met them in Norwich a couple of times. 'Won't that be dangerous? Will they be where the war is?'

'They're going to fight the fascists, Reenie; they're going looking for the war.'

Reenie placed her hand on his arm and gave it a little squeeze; she wanted to reassure him that although he was worried about his cousins, she was hopeful that they would be all right in the end.

Then Peter said, 'They've offered to take me with them, and I want to go.'

Rennie gasped; she had been worrying about their jobs, and being tired from riding in to the factory each day from her parents' farmhouse, and working all the hours she could to help them get through this difficult time. She'd kept telling herself that if they could just get to the other side of the royal visit then she could rest and they could be happy together, but she had never thought in all this time that Peter would be her biggest worry. Steady, reliable, kind Peter; who wanted to go and put himself in danger when she desperately needed him here.

'Have you told anyone at the factory?' Reenie asked. 'Do they know you're thinking of going?'

Peter shook his head. 'I talked to the Major about it in passing and he said that I should tell you first before he presumed to give me advice . . .'

'Will you do something for me?' Reenie didn't know what to say, or how to go about talking Peter out of this terrifying thing, but she knew that there was one practical, pragmatic person whose opinion she valued almost above all others. 'Will you tell Diana Moore what you're planning to do? You'll have to hand in your letter of resignation anyway, and you might as well hand it in to Women's Employment now the Major isn't . . .' Reenie didn't need to finish her sentence because Peter had put her arm through his and she knew that he sorely missed the presence of Major Fergusson in their lives just as much as she did.

'And what makes you think you're so special, Peter McKenzie?' Diana was in a worse mood than usual and she didn't have time for nonsense about leaving Mack's to fight for Spain. 'Have you got some soldiering experience that Mack's doesn't know about? I've seen your file in the employment office and there's no mention of you being an army cadet.'

'No,' Peter was embarrassed, but he was not dissuaded, 'but I'm a man and I've got a duty to fight to protect women and children. The Spanish are bombing their own citizens and it's women and children who are suffering the most. I have to do something.'

'Then buy them milk tokens, or sponsor one of my refugees.' Diana thought she knew what this was about; it was about what had happened to the Major. Major Fergusson had been a champion of Peter, and he was completely shaken up and questioning everything in his life. Now that there was no one at Mack's to tell him that what he did was worthwhile, he wasn't sure it was. 'There are women and children suffering here in Halifax too and they don't need a lad with no fighting experience to volunteer as cannon fodder for someone else's country, they need someone with your experience, in your position, to create jobs and keep them working.'

'But this is life and death—'

'*Yes*,' Diana was emphatic, 'yes, it is. And do you know how many people die of poverty in England these days? Too many. The Spanish people need all the help they can get – but if you want to hear some home truths there are plenty of girls who'd make better fighters than you, Peter McKenzie. Heather Roger's father went to prison for poaching, but only because she ran faster than he did, and if they're looking for a marksman Heather Rogers can hit a rabbit in the dark at thirty yards. Then there's all the women on your own production line who served as Wrens in the Great War, I bet they could teach you a thing or two about battle. And let's not forget Mary Norcliffe, who nursed her father and two elder brothers when they died at home. This factory is full of women who would not only survive longer than you in Spain, but would be a damn sight more useful. And all of them want to stay here for their families, and all of them need *you* to stay here for their families, because some days you are all that stands between them and poverty. Get more married women on the line and you'll be saving women and children, I promise you. The Major wouldn't have abandoned the factory at a time like this if he could help it, and he is a trained soldier!'

There was a strained silence as they both felt they had gone too far and had roused too much feeling. Finally Peter broke it by saying quietly, 'Where do you need me to help; where can I make more jobs for the married women?'

Diana said nothing for a long time as she regained her composure and tried to save something of her precious dignity. 'I went too far.'

'No, you did right. If I can help here then I need to know.'

'I was angry. We're all angry . . .' Diana faltered and then said, 'In all honesty I think we're employing all the mothers we can; to get any more in we'd need to start our own crèche. If you want to help now, then prioritize the King's Toffee line. I need the fastest girls there. Replace them with married ladies, but keep an eye out for the fastest girls, or girls who could be fast if you changed a line to suit them.'

'I'll talk to Reenie about it straight away.' Peter turned to leave but Diana stopped him.

'Peter—'

'Yes?'

'The Major would be so proud of you if – if he knew . . .'

Chapter Thirty-Nine

'How much do you want a baby?' Reenie was whispering urgently to Bess having slipped cautiously inside the warehouse door and looked around hurriedly to see if there was anyone else about.

'Oh,' Bess sighed with wide-eyed enthusiasm, 'more than anything.'

'Would you be willing to take someone else's baby?'

'Do you mean like a widower who is terribly tragic and needs me to adopt his children if I really love him?' Bess's eyes shone at the thought of being a romantic heroine.

'No, I mean would you look after someone else's baby in the warehouse here while the baby's mother works in the factory with your sister? It would be a very good way to prove to your sister that you're good at looking after babies, and it would help her get her job done at the same time.'

'Yes, but where would I find one that fitted that description? It's difficult enough to—'

'Leave it with me,' Reenie said as she raced off with an air of a girl on a mission, 'you might be about to save the day!'

Reenie had decided, when she heard Mary talking hopelessly about the confectioner with a baby, that she herself would find a way to help her back to work. She knew that Bess had very little to do out in the postal warehouse and she thought she would make an excellent nanny. Reenie's imagination had even stretched so far as to think up a way that Bess's corner annexe in the warehouse might be kitted out to allow her to care for a clutch of little ones and allow even more former employees to return to work at the factory. She was convinced that this was an excellent idea, and that it was likely that Diana wouldn't see it that way because she was naturally pessimistic. Reenie had enlisted Peter's help, and – with thoughts of his recent telling off from Diana, and her instructions to help married women back to work still ringing in his ears – they had gone around the local Sunday school halls asking to borrow play pens, toys, and any spare apparatus they could find which seemed conceivably connected with childhood.

'What do you mean, you've got someone to watch her baby?' Diana did not look up from the filing cabinet where she was putting correspondence away. She was used to Reenie bursting into her office with brilliant new ideas about how she might solve unsolvable problems, and stopping work to listen was now the exception rather than the rule. 'Have you spoken to Victoria herself about this? Does she approve of this person who you have found to look after her child?'

'Am I allowed to go and ask her?' Reenie seemed surprised.

'Well, I would have thought the first thing you would do would be to check with the mother.' Diana sensed that something about this latest plan of Reenie's was too good to be true and she looked up from her filing to fix Reenie's eye with her own. 'This isn't going to turn out to be one of your madcap schemes, is it, Irene Calder?'

'Oh no, I've definitely learnt my lesson, honestly I have. This is a very reliable person, very nearby, who has offered to mind the baby and possibly the children of some other mothers who want to work in the factory. But the confectioner's baby gets first place.'

Diana appraised Reenie's level of enthusiasm carefully; usually the higher the enthusiasm the more madcap the idea was. This time Reenie only seemed fairly enthusiastic, and that boded well. Besides, Diana told herself, it was up to Victoria Geall who she left her baby with, and if she met this person and approved of them it would be a private matter between them. Diana did not usually allow her desperation to find a solution lead her towards something she considered unwise, but on this occasion turning a blind eye might be wise so she said, 'Very well. Go and speak to Mrs Vicky Geall of 48 Burr Bank Lane. And don't tell her that I've recommended this – she has to make her own mind up, it's nothing to do with me.'

'Just through here . . . Yes, not much further now. It's definitely only a short walk from your new kitchen.' Reenie emerged into the postal warehouse to greet Bess with not only Peter, but also a perambulator, a baby, and a blind toffee maker who was sniffing the air and frowning in suspicion. They moved quickly through the open warehouse space and into Bess's office annexe, where their stockpile of borrowed Sunday school sundries were waiting to welcome an infant who was far more wriggly than Reenie had anticipated.

'Bess, this is Mrs Geall who has come to work with your sister Mary, and this is her baby Simon. Mrs Geall, this is my very good friend Bess, who has volunteered to look after your baby here during your shifts. You'll be able to step across here to see to him as much as you need to.'

Mrs Geall was running her fingers along the walls and surfaces, and Reenie worried that this boded ill for their plan to find Mary a Master Confectioner. 'What is this place?' Vicky asked. 'It's very quiet for Mackintosh's. What's on the floor?'

'It's my crèche,' Bess said with a confident self-assurance that took Reenie's breath away. 'I don't have any babies yet, but I've got two play pens, a box of books, two boxes of toys, and a tricycle.' Bess behaved as though this were the most natural thing in the world, and that all these items had sprung fully formed from the ground she stood on, and hadn't, in fact, been gathered by Reenie and Peter as they rode round in a trap pulled by an ugly and somewhat irritable horse. 'Now, how old's this little chap? He can sit up in his pram so he must be what, eight months? Is he weaned yet?'

'He can eat a Farley's rusk if it takes his fancy, but I still feed him.' Vicky Geall reached out for the perambulator with muddy wheels and shabby carriage which Peter had been pushing. There was a sack hanging from the handle and Vicky Geall offered it to Bess. 'Do you know what these are?' It was clearly a test.

Bess opened the sack and rummaged inside. 'Of course I do. It's terry cloth nappies and muslins to line them with. Oh, look at him!' Bess rubbed her nose lovingly into the baby's chubby cheek as he tried to flop over the side of his perambulator. 'He's such a pudding!'

Reenie watched Mrs Geall's reaction closely. There was further discussion of the space; where the stove was and how it was fenced off (baby Simon was a crawler); where the toys had come from, and if they had been cleaned with Milton (baby Simon was a chewer); and how often the door was left open (baby Simon was an all-fours escape artist). As far as Reenie could tell, Bess had passed muster.

'I'm looking for someone to watch him from nine until half past three. How does that sound to you?'

'Just fine. I'll need a written outline of his daily routine,' Bess sounded uncharacteristically capable, 'and any medicines or special toys he can't do without.' This answer seemed to please Mrs Geall.

Reenie had known that Bess liked babies, but she hadn't expected this level of apparent prior experience. While Vicky Geall gave her son a cuddle, Reenie whispered to Bess, 'How do you know all this?'

'I'm surprised you don't. Do you never visit your neighbours when they've had babies?'

'Our neighbours have lambs and foals; I don't see a lot of human babies.'

Bess, taking baby Simon from Mrs Geall, said, 'Oh, I love babies. They're just so roly-poly, aren't they?'

Reenie agreed with Bess to save time. 'Is everything

you need in this bag?' Reenie said, offering a large draw-string sack which had been swinging under the perambulator carriage. 'It's got clothes in, and . . .' Reenie trailed off, not really knowing what half of this apparatus was: babies were not as appealing to Reenie as machines or horses.

'And a shawl,' Vicky Geall put in, 'though he'll probably not need it in this weather, and extra terry cloths.'

Bess rummaged through the bag with one hand, while holding the baby on one hip with the other. The move-ments seemed more natural than any work Bess had ever done in the factory; there was skill there and Reenie recognized it. 'This looks like everything.' Bess turned to Mrs Geall. 'Do you want me to soak the nappies before I send you home with them, or just wrap them up in newspaper like fish and chips?'

'Best soak them if you would. I'm being ferried around in one of the Mackintosh's cars, so it's no skin off my nose to carry them home in a bucket.'

'Fair enough.' Bess considered, 'Reenie, you'll need to bring me a bucket.'

Reenie looked worried. 'A bucket?'

'Don't look so horrified, Reenie, it's quite natural. I'll need to put all the baby's napkins in it to soak whenever I change him.' Bess cooed happily over the baby, then became as matter-of-fact as Bess ever could be. 'Mrs Geall will want them all back to launder at home and it's not good to let them sit un-soaked. Have you got any Milton? The bucket could do with a dash of Milton. You don't want to carry a bucket of bad smells home if you can help it.' Bess did not appear to notice that Reenie and Peter were looking at her with unconcealed amazement.

Reenie was wary of letting herself get too excited but it really seemed as though she had found the one job which Bess was good at – and it was exactly what Reenie needed her to be good at, at exactly the right time. Reenie had almost forgotten that the last occasion she'd got involved with Bess's work, the other girl had helped to burn the entire factory to the ground, plunging them into the crisis which they were now struggling to emerge from.

Chapter Forty

Lara and Gracie sat in the garden of the Hunters' home watching their kittens gambolling on the lawn. Lara had not forgotten that they had a tray of their beautiful sweets left, nor that they had been told that they could eat one if Cook told them they had been good.

'Cook has said we've been good three times this week.' Lara had a pleading note to her voice. She was usually the natural leader in their relationship, given Gracie's place in the household as a recent addition, but the sweets had been Gracie's idea, and she had saved up most of the money, so there was an agreement that she was in charge. 'What if we just had one of the sweets and we asked Cook to cut it in half for us and we had half each?' Thinking that the suggestion would appeal to Gracie's altruistic nature she added as an afterthought, 'We could offer one to Cook at the same time as a thank you for looking after us.'

Gracie was not unmoved by the suggestion; she too had

been thinking about the sweets, and now that they had given away the lion's share of them to the lady who had given them the kittens there was a part of Gracie which felt that they had earned the rest of those sweets in their entirety, not just half of one. 'I suppose we *could* give one to Cook, but then wouldn't we have to give one to all of the servants? I don't think we've got enough.'

Lara didn't like the direction this was headed; she didn't mind giving one of their sweets to Cook, but she didn't want to give them *all* away to the servants because then she would almost certainly miss out altogether. Lara had a sweeter tooth than Gracie and she was tempted to reach into their basket when her new sister wasn't looking and to take a sweet.

A dove fluttered down from the dovecote to pick up some juicy insect mortal from the lawn and the kittens bounded for it. The flurry of tiny claws and angry feathers distracted Gracie for a moment and she trotted off down the garden to scoop up both felines.

Lara looked into the basket and turned aside the large cloth napkin which the last tray of sweets was wrapped up in. Lara had been the one who had said that they mustn't touch the sweets because they would put fingermarks on them, and her elder brother Steven was always complaining about them passing him food at picnics with their sticky fingerprints on. Lara saw the gloss of the chocolates and toffees – the unnatural, enticing gloss – and tried to decide which one to take. It was not an easy decision because they were all so different. There were some in plain chocolate with a prancing pony embossed on the top; there were others whose little pieces of glacé fruits indicated the flavour within; and some were coloured like a rainbow of exotic jewels to tempt the eater. Lara's hand reached into the basket.

'What are you doing?' Gracie cried as she returned with a kitten in each hand. 'You've taken the napkin off the sweets! You've stolen one!'

'I have not!' Lara jumped to her feet. 'I can look at them without taking one. I'm allowed to look because they're mine too.'

'You were *going* to take one, I saw your hand in the basket.'

The girls' bickering reached such a pitch that Steven, who had been reading a novel in a hammock further up the garden, came to intervene. He wasn't listening to the details of the argument, just gathered that it had mostly to do with which sister was allowed to put their hand into the basket they shared. As he reached them, without investigating the cause further, he picked up the basket and took it into the hall where the very top of the huge grandfather clock made an excellent shelf for it, well out of the reach of both his younger sisters. 'You can have it back when you've learnt to get on better,' he told them. Then he went on to the kitchen to see about a cooling glass of lemonade to slake his thirst, and thought no more about his little sister's silliness over little things.

Chapter Forty-One

Reenie arrived at the factory to the worst possible news: Mrs Garner had died in the night. It was news that they had all been expecting, but it was devastating all the same. Mrs Garner had been a true one-off and Reenie knew she would miss her terribly. The Major was still gravely ill and wasn't expected to survive either. It was all so horribly unfair.

Reenie was beside herself; she felt she needed something to do, some way to be useful or good at a time when life was making her feel so helpless, and she remembered the fudge wrapping line which Diana had shown her which was still such a problem. Perhaps she could set up the fix she had been telling Diana about? It would only be the work of an hour or so to get the factory fitters to set up the old wrapping machine beside the new one that didn't work properly, and then she could get it running and save a whole department a mountain of worry.

Her only problem was that it was something Mrs

Starbeck had told her not to do, but she was confident that once Mrs Starbeck saw how much better Reenie's plan made everything she would be forced to agree that it had been an excellent idea.

Reenie had carefully planned in the machine changeover with the engineers and the fitters, and after six months working at the Mackintosh's Norwich factory planning the layout of new Quality Street lines, this felt like a doddle. Particularly as Reenie wasn't designing a new line; she was just restoring an old one with a machine she was confident would do the job. There was a certain satisfaction which came from doing something she knew she was good at and which would have a measurable benefit to her colleagues and the business as a whole.

She had also come up with another bright idea: she had chosen some incredibly fast married women from the Gooseberry Cream line to come and work on this one. They were glad to move across because it would mean they were on a line where they could get piece rates again, unlike Gooseberry Cream where Mrs Starbeck still had them working for minimums.

The changeover of machinery was complete and the married women got to work on the same line with the unmarried girls and they appeared to be having the time of their lives. The noise of their laughter and hoots of encouragement roused Mrs Starbeck who was in the office on the balcony. She looked down and saw Reenie doing the very things she'd told her not to.

'Overlooker,' Mrs Starbeck called out over the din of the machines, 'stop that line!'

The overlooker let her hand hover reluctantly over the switch that would bring the entire line to an emergency halt, but another look at Mrs Starbeck's face made her press it.

'What is going on here? Reenie Calder, why are you on a line which you have not been assigned to work on? And why is the old wrapping machine back in production beside the new one we had specially commissioned?'

'Well, it just works better.' Reenie was at a loss for any other way to put it; the truth might be inconvenient for Mrs Starbeck, but it was the truth.

'We have spent a great deal of time and money on commissioning that new machine from Baker Perkins and I do not want to see it wasted. Fitters, remove the old machine and reinstate the Baker Perkins update. I will have no more of this ridiculous nonsense on my watch. And what are these women from the Gooseberry Cream line doing here? We do *not* mix married and unmarried female workers. Return all these women to the correct production line.'

'But if we do that,' Reenie interjected, 'there won't be enough people on this line and it will *definitely* break down. I've sent Betsy Newman and some of the other girls down to Gooseberry Cream where they don't mind losing their piece rates for a bit if they get an easy life for a change. Then I've brought the fastest ladies from Gooseberry Cream up here. So you see, the company isn't paying out any more money than it was before, but it has happier workers, more efficient production lines, and a new machine it can send back for a refund. This way everyone is better off.'

'I would say that you have overstepped your authority, Reenie Calder, but I would remind you that you never had any authority to start with. You were not given permission to work on this line and that is a disciplinary offence.'

'I *was* given authority,' Reenie blurted out without thinking about the consequences of what she was about to say. 'Diana Moore asked me to fix all of this because—'

'Enough!' Mrs Starbeck didn't like it when these factory girls answered back. 'I will be speaking to Amy Wilkes about this. In the meantime, Overlooker, restart the line with the machine I have instructed you to use.'

A fitter in worn blue overalls piped up, 'But this is working much better than the new one. The new one is holding everyone up; it wants sending back.'

Mrs Starbeck smiled. 'No, this one has been made specially and at great expense and we're going to use this one. Overlooker, restart the line please on *this* machine. And you ladies from Gooseberry Cream, you need to leave and return to your correct production room immediately.'

The married women choked back rage at the injustice of their situation, lining out to collect their possessions from the cloakroom before returning to their old jobs. The remaining girls hurried to their places and braced themselves to take on the line with even fewer workers than they had had before.

The fitter tried one last time to reason with Mrs Starbeck, who he knew outranked them all. 'Madam, we really can't run this line with so few people.'

Mrs Starbeck looked affronted. 'It's talk like this that's damaging our country. Overlooker, I insist you restart this line.'

The overlooker glanced round at the line, and when she judged that her colleagues were as ready as they would ever be, she pressed the large red button which caused the first of the machines to whirr into life. Mrs Starbeck gave a satisfied nod and then turned away in the direction of the Women's Employment Department, intent on a row with Amy Wilkes over Diana Moore for allocating work to one of her own employees.

However, without Betsy Newman to run the new, troublesome machine it was only a matter of minutes after Mrs Starbeck had left that it clogged, jammed, and began to billow smoke which had a smell of burning tar to it. The fitters were on hand to stop the machine and to prevent a fire, but at the sight of smoke some of the girls panicked and tried to evacuate the line. In the ensuing chaos not all of the machines were stopped immediately, and foil and fudges spilt out all over the floor.

'You know, the Major would love all this.' Peter sat down beside Reenie, and without turning to look at her face he reached out for her hand and squeezed it. She was sitting beside the faulty Baker Perkins machine in the deserted production hall now that the whistle had sounded for the end of the shift and her colleagues had escaped as soon as humanly possible

Reenie wiped tears from her cheeks with the flat of her hand and was glad Peter had diplomatically chosen not to see. 'What? Me setting fire to a machine, or me getting Diana Moore in trouble with Mrs Starbeck?'

Peter breathed out a little laugh and said softly, 'You know what I mean. He'd have seen how you tried to help, and how you found a solution that made everyone happy for a while, and he'd have flattered Starchy Starbeck into thinking it was her idea so that she'd leave you be.'

'You didn't just call her Starchy Starbeck!' Reenie gasped in delight.

'I did. She's a right starchy knickers, she is. I bet they crackle when she sits down in the morning to have her perfect breakfast egg.'

'Oh Peter,' Reenie sniffed and laughed and hiccuped and wiped all her tears away and said, 'you're incorrigible.' Then, with seriousness she asked, 'Why do you think she won't let me make things better? I can understand her wanting to follow the rules, but why does she want to follow them if they make everything worse?'

'Because she was the one who commissioned that new machine. She planned it with Baker Perkins, gave the specifications to our engineers to give to the designers, and so she is ultimately responsible for the fact that it's never worked. If she lets you come up with a better way of doing things it just shows that she got it wrong, doesn't it?'

Reenie's eyes widened in surprise as she fought to put aside her naive belief in the innate goodness of all people just long enough to see that Mrs Starbeck was a cow.

'Not everyone wants to do what's right, Reenie. Some people just want to do what's right for them, and she's one of those. If Diana were here I think she'd be telling you to watch your back for knives.'

'Do you think I'm for the sack this time?'

'In all honesty, your guess is as good as mine this time. If Mrs Starbeck is going up against Mrs Wilkes then there's no telling who will win out. But I meant what I said about the Major – he'd have been proud of you today.'

'Oh, I do wish he was here. He always stuck up for me.'

'Me too.'

'Do you really think we'll never see him again?'

'Things look pretty grim in light of Mrs Garner,' Peter replied.

They both sat and thought about this for a moment, then Reenie said, 'What do you think he'd tell me to do if he was here?'

'Probably to do half as much. You've tried to help everyone and you've done a good job – but you can't spread yourself too thin or there'll be nothing left of you. Sometimes I wonder if we'd be better to step back and let events take their course . . .'

'Says he who wants to go and fight in Spain. Tell me, Peter Mackenzie, how would it have helped anyone if I'd stepped back and let events take their course? That wouldn't have done any good; Betsy Newman would have been sacked for troublemaking, and the other girls would have been split up for bickering, and no one would ever have realized what the real trouble was with the line and it would have carried on being trouble. Look, I know this is a mess and I'm in a lot of trouble, but it's not a mess because I helped – it's a mess because Mrs Starbeck had the chance to help and didn't.'

'You know, I've been thinking about what Diana said to us. I think I've seen a way that we can help the business stay afloat and get more married women to work.'

'But would it get us in trouble with Starchy Starbeck?'

Peter was casual. 'Oh, certainly. In fact, I'd say it would guarantee we'd both be sacked if we were caught. But then again, you're in trouble anyway, and we both know that without the Major back here as our champion we won't last long, so we might as well be hung for sheep as lambs.' Peter grinned at the thought. 'I think we should get even more mothers into the factory. I think we should see if we can borrow even more toys from the church hall and find a couple of volunteers to help Bess, and make a regular crèche for the children who are too young to go to school but whose mothers want to work. If Bess can mind one baby it can't be that hard to mind half a dozen, can it?'

Chapter Forty-Two

Word had reached the factory manager and the production manager of the chaos on the line where Reenie had attempted to replace new machines with the old ones. The ensuing problems had caused them delays all over the factory and they were astute enough to realize that the problem had a root which went beyond Reenie or Mrs Starbeck.

'We can't do this with the staff we've got – all the most skilled girls are working overtime as it is,' said the production manager.

'I'll talk to Mrs Wilkes in Women's Employment about hiring some more local girls.'

'With respect, that's no good to me. Any local girls will be untrained and we don't have the time or the people to train them. We need to talk to our overseas factories and see who they can spare for three months.'

'That's impossible.'

'It's not. I happen to know that Mrs Roth is in

Dusseldorf as we speak, trying to recruit us new confectioners who can come over.'

'She already has; she's found scores of good workers Dusseldorf think they could spare for a few months – but the Home Office won't give them permits. It's the same everywhere; we can't get entry permits for people to come here because the government don't want to let any foreigners in unless they can help it. With Moseley's lot crying foul every five minutes, they can't be seen to let anyone in. Besides, we've got to think of the publicity; how would it look if we brought in foreigners to make sweets for the King of England in an English factory? We should be hiring more girls and training more girls so that we never face a shortage like this.'

'We can't just hire any old girls and train them up. This is skilled work, they have to have a very specific aptitude for it. I don't think anyone realizes that Reenie Calder and Mary Norcliffe are once-in-a-generation talents. Well, twice, in this instance, but I heartily agree that we should be training more girls and giving them more opportunities.'

'What about our Irish factory? I know they can't make our toffees there any more, but could they send us some of their people temporarily?'

'If only. Haven't you been reading the papers? They have a General Election on the first of July *and* a plebiscite. This is the most important vote in the history of their isle and the flow of workers into England has stopped almost completely because they all want to be at home to vote. I don't blame them, but it's a shame for us because the girls from the Dublin factory could make toffee in their sleep while singing.'

*

'Well, I think it would be nice if we could make a toffee in the shape of a crown and press four little dried redcurrants into the top to make it look like the velvet on the one the King wore at the coronation.'

Dolly Dunkley was working in the most important place in the factory: the confectioner's kitchen where the King's Toffee was being planned. And although she was there as a cleaner, typically she couldn't keep her opinions to herself. This was the first opportunity for Mary and Mr Baum to meet their new toffee-making colleague but it was Dolly who was holding court.

'. . . and I was reading that the King likes ginger-flavoured things, so we really ought to flavour it with ginger. I've discussed it with my father, the vicar, who knows Lady Mackintosh very well, and we're agreed that this is exactly the sort of thing the King would like. My father says he can arrange to have your samples tasted by Lady Mackintosh when you have some ready to give to me.'

Dolly had not noticed that Vicky's face was unimpressed and that Mr Baum was shaking his head.

'I am only a chocolatier and not a confectioner of sugar,' Mr Baum said, 'but this sounds very complicated for something we must transfer to the production line. Is it possible to make a confection like this on the line with speed and still place this fruit in this special arrangement?'

Mary liked the way Mr Baum was kind enough not to directly contradict Dolly, or point out that she was there to do the pot washing; it felt like the kind of thing her friend Reenie would do and it was one of the reasons she thought she always felt so reassured by his presence.

'Dunkley,' Vicky refused to use the nickname Dolly had adopted for herself, 'why do you think you are here?'

'To make a special toffee to celebrate the King's coronation year, and his visit,' Dolly chirped confidently.

'No. Why do you think you've been assigned to the confectioner's kitchen? What do you think your duties are?'

'Well, obviously to give you advice about the sort of thing the King would like, and to give you little ideas. I've had the benefit of meeting some very important people and the directors have obviously realized how valuable it would be to you to have an observer who knows how the quality behave.'

'No, Dunkley, you're here to clean up after Mary, and Mary is here to learn from me. Mary, tell me what we've got to work with.'

Mary stammered, 'I'm sorry, I don't . . .'

'Go ahead, Mary,' Mr Baum encouraged her, 'don't be nervous.'

Vicky squinted in Mary's direction. 'They told me that you had four years' experience on the factory line and you're meant to be my eyes. Tell me what kind of toffee kitchen they've given us. Tell me what kind of equipment we've got.'

Mary looked around and opened her mouth to answer, but Dolly interrupted her, 'Oh, I've got factory experience too, I've been working here for three weeks. I can tell you. We've got one marble table, two metal tables, lots of drawers full of little implements for making sweets, shelves of lovely tin moulds, a very technical-looking cupboard (but I don't think we'll need to worry about that for *this* project) and a . . .' Dolly hesitated; she wasn't sure what she was looking at, but she was confident that it was useless '. . . well, a little copper font.' She laughed it off nervously, but Vicky wasn't laughing.

'Mary, am I to assume that the "marble table" is a middle-heated tempering top?'

'Yes.' Mary was confident. These were questions she could answer easily and she felt a weight lift from her shoulders. 'Heated from the central hot water supply. The metal tables are a vibration plate, and a plain stainless-steel-topped work bench.'

'And I take it the copper font is our boiling pan. Is that on the hot water supply, or do we have to kindle our own fire like witches on the moor?'

'No, it's fully plumbed in. It's a very well-equipped kitchen; they've bought all new things since the fire, so anything that can be electric is electric. Except the ovens and the little hob, they're on the gas.'

'Thank God for that! There's nothing worse than these new electric cookers. You know where you are with gas.' Vicky pulled herself up at the stool beside the long work-bench which sat like an island in the middle of the kitchen. 'What do you think, Mary; anything missing? We're making toffee and you've made toffee on the line.' There was a pause. 'It's not a trick question – you won't be in trouble with me if you can't think of anything, I just thought I'd ask on the off-chance. We've got a handsome budget, we might as well use it.'

Mary hesitated. 'We've got no toffee cutting table, but I suppose we could make do with—'

'There's no making do if we don't have to. A toffee cutting table's an essential. Mary, tell Dolly what happens if you try to cut toffee on a normal table.'

'It ends up on the floor,' Mary said matter-of-factly.

'It ends up on the floor, Toffee is molten sugar, butter, and whatever else we put in it. Without a lipped table we might as well just pour it on the floor, because it will roll off the edges. Mary, send a memo to the factory manager and ask him if he's got a cutting table on the way. It's not like him to forget necessities.'

'Well, what do you want me to do?' Dolly sounded affronted.

'For the moment you're just paying attention. Oh, and hang about, I do want your advice. Dolly, tell me, how clean are our new kitchens? Do they meet with your standards?'

Dolly became animated at this. 'Well, actually, no, they don't. I mean, they look clean, but in my opinion—'

'Good.' Vicky cut her off. 'Start cleaning them. Mary, it's time for you to take me to my meeting with Sir Harold Mackintosh. He's an old friend and is the eldest son of my father's last apprentice. I don't like to keep him waiting.'

Dolly was left gaping like a fish as Mary led her new tutor away by the arm with all the caution and care in the world because Mary thought the woman was wonderful.

Chapter Forty-Three

Mary had some ground almond left over from a batch of marzipan Mr Baum had taught her to make and she knew that it wouldn't keep. Not wanting to waste it, Mary decided to attempt one of the more exotic-sounding recipes she'd come across in the book Mr Baum had told her to read – Lebkuchen. They were soft and light, little pillows of delicate flavour, the lemon zest in perfect balance with the cloves, cinnamon, and fresh ginger. The butter was of the best quality and she had managed to bake them so that they melted in the mouth.

Mary laid a plate of them on the tasting table in the confectioner's kitchen with the pot of fresh coffee she always had ready at eight o'clock in the morning when she started the day.

Dolly often grumbled about the tribulations of working life, and how awful it was to have to tell her stepmother to wake her early so that she could get out of bed in the cold and then get the tram 'with the great unwashed' all the way to the factory to work like a skivvy for 'the blind old cow' as she called Mrs Geall, and 'the rotten kraut' as she referred to Albert Baum.

Mary would listen to her complaints in silence, knowing that they were the only bad things in her otherwise wonderful days working in the confectioner's kitchen with her two new managers. Mary always had been an early riser and, until now, she'd woken in panic at all she had to do, but now she woke in excitement, eager to be in the place she loved best, with the employers who were teaching her more than she had ever imagined possible.

Mary and Bess used to walk to the factory. They'd walked in all weathers and had even had to dig themselves out of snowdrifts. But now they were picked up by young Mackintosh's salesmen who drove them in company cars and competed for the affections of pretty Bess. And now Mary could even leave early without worrying that her sister would stay at home in bed or sneak off with some unsuitable young man.

Mary had been trusted with the keys to the kitchen and would sometimes come in early to warm the room and the equipment, and to delight in the place.

The kitchen looked beautiful to Mary that morning as the strong June sunlight streamed through the windows and blushed the marble surface of the tempering tabletop. The motes of dust in the air sparkled in a shaft of sunlight and the air smelled of warm spices. Mary was careful to wrap her hands in a thick cotton cloth as she opened the steaming hot oven door to slide out another tin tray of treats. The cloud of steam from the oven hit her eyelashes and made them curl.

'What do you think you're playing at?' Dolly Dunkley's

voice grated on the air and took the beauty out of it. 'If you want to bake things you ought to be doing it at home. You shouldn't be making a mess in our kitchen – this is for sweet making.'

Mary knew that Dolly was only complaining because she was lumbered with the cleaning duties, although Mary had hoped to have finished and cleared up after herself long before Dolly arrived. Mary had been looking forward to painting the Lebkuchen with icing sugar and beaten egg, and to enjoying the sight of the glistening mixture gradually crystallizing to a matt finish as it cooled. Mary's heart sank at the idea that she would have to work around Dolly; her plan to have the dainties beautifully arranged as a surprise for Albert and Vicky when they arrived might now be ruined. Mary slid the little biscuit cakes onto the cooling rack and tidied away. 'I'm making a traditional German recipe.' She was tight-lipped and cold; Dolly Dunkley could go hang, she wasn't going to get a rise out of Mary, even if she had ruined her morning by coming in early. Mary made a mental note to keep herself locked in the kitchen in future, and Dolly Dunkley locked out – although she'd have to get the door lock repaired first because she still hadn't been able to get the piece of broken key out of it and she didn't like to admit she'd snapped it.

'I never do any baking myself.' Dolly threw her coat untidily over a stool by the door and wandered over to the window to look down at the gates where early workers were beginning to trickle in. 'That's why one has a cook to come in each day. Of course I can make a few little things – one must have domestic accomplishments – but one doesn't learn these things so that one can do them oneself, one learns these things so that one can oversee the cook and make sure she's doing it properly.'

Dolly really was labouring under the misguided impression that she was Lady Muck, when in reality she was only the daughter of the vicar from Stump Cross. Mary would have found it funny if it hadn't been so irritating. Dolly moved back from the window and looked across at Mary. 'I don't suppose you have a cook, do you?' It was said with a sneer which was as ill-judged as it was ill-concealed, because at that moment Mr Baum was leading Victoria through the door which Dolly had carelessly left open.

'Are we all early this morning?' Victoria let go of Mr Baum's elbow and walked round the room, her finger running lightly beneath the rim of the bench.

'Something smells excellent.' Mr Baum was hanging up his light summer jacket and putting on his kitchen whites, ready to begin work for the day.

Dolly saw her opportunity to make herself the centre of attention. 'Well, I was—'

Victoria cut Dolly off mid-sentence. 'Yes, I'd gathered you were here, Dunkley. Norcliffe, what are you up to with those ground almonds?'

It pleased Mary to know that she was working with a confectioner so talented that she could detect the aroma of even the least of ingredients on the air. 'Well, we had three ounces left over from the batch of marzipan we made yesterday and I didn't want it to go to waste, so I tried one of the recipes in the book of Christmas sweetmeats from around the world. I think I might have found something we could adapt for the casket chocolates, but I haven't tried them yet.'

'Very good, very good.' Mr Baum pulled himself up

onto a high stool at the bench in the centre of the room where they usually sat to taste samples and discuss their work. 'I think Diana found us a good apprentice, don't you think so, Mrs Geall? Mary likes to learn – but she can teach herself as well.'

Mary murmured her thanks. 'I was just about to paint them with icing but you can try one now if you like. I made them for us to use the leftovers.'

'Thank you, Mary,' Albert said, looking into her eyes with sincerity. 'That's very thoughtful of you.'

Vicky Geall pulled up a seat at the same table, picked up one of the morsels from the plate Mary slid in front of her, and then took a bite. She tilted her head slightly, thinking, assessing. 'They're like a cross between a marzipan, a biscuit, and a cake, but they taste like Christmas. They're interesting, what do you call them?'

'Lebkuchen,' Mary said, 'they're German.' And she and Mr Baum caught one another's eyes but tried to look away quickly and pretend the look hadn't happened.

'And pretentious.' Dolly put Mary down with such confidence that she was clearly expecting the other two confectioners to agree with her when they saw her point of view. 'What's wrong with a normal cake, or a normal biscuit? Why do you have to be pretentious and do something foreign with a fancy name?'

'There's no such thing as pretentious in this kitchen.' Vicky took a second Lebkuchen, 'We're making sweets fit for a king and there are no holds barred. If I fancy putting gold leaf on a toffee, we'll do it.'

Chapter Forty-Four

'I don't understand why a recall means you've got to cut costs. Doesn't a recall mean you just stop the toffees you've made from going to the shops?' Reenie's sister Kathleen had a lot of questions about the working of the factory, but she did seem to genuinely want to understand what was going on.

'It's worse than that; when you have a recall you put notices in all the papers telling people that you're recalling a particular batch and you ask them to check their cupboards and see if they've got that particular one and then take it back to the grocer they bought it from and get a refund – even if it's half-finished and they didn't think there was owt wrong with it!'

'So what do you do, put a notice in the paper saying that anyone with a royal-looking casket can take it back for a refund? There can't be many of them doing the rounds.'

'How did you know it was meant to be a royal-looking casket?' Reenie was aghast.

'Oh give over; everyone in the Calder valley knows that.'

'But it's not been in the papers.' Reenie had genuinely believed that if she wasn't blurting out the news to all and sundry, then none of her colleagues were either.

'That's not really how news travels, is it?' Kathleen gave her a look which suggested she had a network of contacts which spread far further than Reenie could ever imagine. 'Everyone knows you're doing a recall on posh caskets.'

'It's not just the royal caskets, it's everything. We've got no idea where the poison came from and no idea if there was more in the factory. The whole place is being shaken down. I'm on double shifts going on factory sweeps to make sure we strip down and mould wash every bit of machinery, every workroom. Even the cloak-rooms are being searched and scrubbed down. It's like we're trying to find a needle in a haystack – but there might not be a needle.'

Mrs Calder interrupted her daughters to ask with concern, 'Are you telling me that Mackintosh's is recalling everything they've ever made?'

Reenie huffed in exasperation at her mother. 'Yes, that's what I said in the first place.'

Mrs Calder glanced up at the two-pound tin of Carnival Deluxe with quiet concern. 'So that tin up there on the dresser with four toffees in it – could I take that down to Kirkby's Fancy Goods and get my money back?'

'Yeah, that's about the size of it. But don't, because I got those from work for free and I'll get in trouble if you go for a refund.'

Mrs Calder wasn't interested in the refund, she was

worried about what might be in the toffees. 'But that's not what I mean. I mean should we throw those away, Reenie?'

Reenie hesitated. If she was honest, she didn't really know what the company hoped to achieve through the recall. The police had taken a photograph of the casket of sweets which she and Diana had found beside their landlady and the Major, and they could see as well as she could that this was a selection of handmade sweets, so the other, mass-produced lines weren't likely to be contaminated, but they were not willing to take that risk. 'No,' she did not sound convincing, 'I brought those home myself, they're fine.'

Mrs Calder looked her daughter in the eye for a moment, then snatched down the tin and threw the contents straight onto the fire where the sugar blazed away ferociously. In homes all over Yorkshire, worried mothers were doing just the same thing.

Chapter Forty-Five

'You can have one bath a week but you have to book it in with me, and don't expect me to cook you any dinners. I do not permit hotplates in the rooms, or food or drink of any kind; it makes everything smell.' The old woman hauled herself up the stairs by the balustrade with a grunt over every creaking stair. The ragged stair carpet released the pungent odour of age, poverty, and cats. 'You're sharing with Violet Whittaker who—'

'No!' Mrs Starbeck blurted out rather louder than she'd meant to, but she was shocked at the idea of having to share with anyone else. She recovered her composure and said rather more politely, 'I wasn't expecting to have to share a bathroom with anyone; mightn't I have a room on a floor with a bathroom that I could have to myself?'

The old woman gave her a look of withering disgust. 'What do you think this is? The Majestic Hotel, Harrogate? You're sharing a twin bedroom with Violet because there aren't any single rooms and there certainly aren't any private baths. There's one bathroom and water closet for the whole house and everyone shares it. If you want to take extra baths you can go down to the public baths and pay by the hour like everyone else. I expect all my lodgers to keep themselves clean, but you have to fetch up your own basin of water of a morning because I'm no housemaid. I expect rent to be paid every Friday, a week in advance with four weeks in hand. The front door is locked and bolted at eleven and if you're out after that it's your lookout.' The old woman stopped outside a door with peeling paint and banged on the panels. 'Violet! New lodger!'

The door swung open slowly to reveal a smirking, garishly dressed woman who reeked of sickly sweet cheap perfume and stale nicotine. 'All right, all right, no need to bang doors off their hinges.' The saucy young woman smirked confidentially at Starbeck. 'And I thought this was a genteel establishment.'

It was clearly a joke which she thought very funny and which the landlady thought very old, and without offering proper introductions she sniffed derisively at her lodger, gave her a withering look, and sulked away muttering about prompt payment of rent and observance of the house rules.

'Don't mind her; she's quite lenient with gentleman callers if you give her an extra three bob for the privilege.' The young woman shut the door behind Cynthia Starbeck who was carrying her cases into the room gingerly. 'Not that I'd ever have one without tipping you the wink, dearie; I'm not that sort. Have you got a friend you can stay with some nights? If I leave a vase in the window to let you know when I've got a gentleman caller? I can do the same for you when you've got one; these beds push together without any trouble.'

Cynthia Starbeck was horrified; this was far worse than she'd anticipated. Sharing a room was distasteful enough, but with someone who would bring a man back to her own bed and expect her to let him sleep in hers was beyond the pale. In an over-hasty moment she blurted out, 'I'm Methodist; I'd rather not.' It was a flimsy lie and she didn't like the thought of being caught in it later, but she wanted an excuse not to have to allow the sullying of her bed for gentleman callers, or any callers.

'Oh, well that's fair enough.' Violet Whittaker looked put out but seemed to rally when she saw that Cynthia had two suitcases. She darted forward when Cynthia unlocked one. 'What have you got in here then? Anything good for going out in? All my stuff's just about worn to ribbons and I never take very good care of my stuff so it doesn't last long before I get a fag burn in it.' She talked rapidly as she fingered Cynthia's expensive silk and satin dresses. 'Oh, now these two are ritzy, I'll definitely borrow these. And you've got just my size feet too – I'm down to my last pair so you couldn't have come at a better time.'

Cynthia recoiled in disgust – the thought that she would lend out anything of hers was too horrible to imagine. This, she told herself, was why she hated working-class women; they were all like this and none of them had earned what they had but took it from hardworking people like her. The remembrance that the money for her tailor-made clothes had come from her mother's legacy, and that her mother's legacy had come from a family coal mine worked by other people was not something that ever troubled her.

Cynthia Starbeck had no choice but to stay in the lodging house that night; she'd clearly picked the wrong place and she resolved to begin looking for another room immediately in the morning – anywhere would be better than this. She was relieved to remember that her suitcases were expensive enough to have good locks on them and she could leave all of her clothes locked up rather than unpack. She laid out one outfit of clothes to wear to the factory in the morning, left her office shoes under the bed and her wristwatch on the nightstand beside her bed. She would talk to Violet about not borrowing her clothes when she came back from work; although, if she was fortunate and negotiated well with the landlady, she would be moving straight into another house before she passed another night in this stinking hovel of iniquity.

Cynthia slept fitfully and only drifted off in the small hours. The sleep she finally achieved must have been very deep indeed, because when she woke she found that Violet had taken her watch and her shoes while she slept . . .

'But she's stolen my watch! I want the police!'

'You're not stopping here if you're going to be the type to cause trouble and bring the police to my door. I'll warn you once and then not again: you sort your own squabbles out and don't bring them to me, I'm not here to be bothered with all your fallings out. She hasn't stolen nothing off you, she's borrowed it and she'll bring it back. People borrow things from people they live with, it's normal.'

'It's theft! I want you to summon me a policeman.'

'I'm not your servant, I don't summon anyone for you. If you're at death's door and you need a doctor you summon him yourself. I'm your landlady and you'll show me a bit of deference.'

Cynthia Starbeck held back angry tears and returned to her room to take out a different pair of shoes to wear to the factory. She needed to leave here at all costs, and she realized, to her chagrin, that it would cost her a great deal because this landlady had insisted on four weeks' rent in hand. She still had jewellery that she could pawn, and good clothes that she could sell, but why should she have to? They were *her* possessions and it maddened her that she should be placed in this position. Still, she could see a way that she could get the money to leave these lodgings and keep her remaining possessions – but she would need to keep her nerve.

'Sadly, the Major has died.' It was a lie, but she knew that it would only be a matter of time before it was the truth; Cynthia was just pre-empting the inevitable event. The Major's life hung by a thread and very soon she would be called on to execute his will, so what did it matter if she began early? If anyone questioned her she could claim that she had been incorrectly told he had died and that she did not realize she was acting prematurely. However, she felt confident no one would question her.

Cynthia Starbeck had presented herself at the office of the credit union where Major Fergusson had been depositing his savings for many years, a short train ride outside Halifax. It was in a town not far from Hipperholme, which made things easier, and though she had been forced to take a morning of leave from Mackintosh's in order to travel to the office of the credit union during their opening hours, her employers were understanding and assumed she still had some personal matters to attend to relating to her father's death.

'I am one of the executors of the Major's will, and he made several bequests to charity which I must see to. I will be withdrawing the full balance.' Cynthia Starbeck said it confidently enough, but the words made her feel sick. She hated sinking to this level.

'I'm afraid we wouldn't be able to raise this sort of money in cash for several days, Mrs, erm—' The credit union clerk looked over the detailed pile of official-looking papers that the smart and respectable-looking lady had brought with her.

'Starbeck. *Miss* Starbeck. As you can see I have served as the treasurer for several local charities which is why Major Fergusson appointed me to manage his affairs. He was a close personal friend and it has been a terribly sad loss.' Not as sad as the loss of her own flat, Cynthia Starbeck thought to herself.

'Well, we're a credit union, not a bank, so although we'll be able to issue you with a cashier's check for the balance of his account, we will need at least a week to make our own plans. This is a very large sum for us, though it might not be for a bank.'

'I quite understand.' Cynthia Starbeck felt her skin itching with the danger of what she was doing, but told herself that if the Major were able to, he would have helped her; he had promised her as much. He had told her before that he was leaving his estate to the Confectioners' Benevolent Fund – and what was the fund for, if not to help women like her support themselves when they fell on hard times through no fault of their own? As far as Cynthia Starbeck was concerned, her case was just the sort that was entitled to help from the fund. She told herself that she would repay the money to the Confectioners' Benevolent Fund quietly when she was in a position to do so – and she believed it. 'When would be convenient for me to come back?'

'Shall we say a week tomorrow?'

'I'm afraid I'm at work during the week. Would it be possible to see you outside of office hours?'

'Well, we open our office for two hours on a Saturday morning once a month; would a week on Saturday suit you?'

'That would be fine.' And Cynthia smiled as broadly as she could manage despite the thought that she would shortly have to decide which of her possessions to pawn in order to afford to leave her lodging house and find another.

Chapter Forty-Six

It was the morning of Mrs Garner's funeral and Mary was ashamed to be attending in her mother's old dress. It was a very hot day and Mary had realized only that morning that her funeral clothes were for winter, and if she wore them she'd be so hot she'd probably faint.

Mary and her sister had not been close to Mrs Garner, but they knew that Reenie and Diana had been, and they wanted to go with them for moral support.

'Mary Norcliffe, look at you!' Reenie greeted her friend with hushed enthusiasm as they met at the tram stop at the appointed time. Reenie had spent a sleepless night crying at the thought of saying her goodbyes to her beloved landlady, and she was glad to have the chance to distract herself with the opportunity to praise a friend. Mary looked startlingly chic in her mother's black silk dress, and though the style was old it was beautifully cut and fitted Mary's tall figure flatteringly. Reenie was used to seeing her friend in overalls, or frumpy make-do-and-mend affairs, but this was quite a different Mary and it took her by surprise.

'It was my mother's and I had to wear it because it's so hot. I wasn't trying to show off!' Mary was just as embarrassed about wearing a dress which so conspicuously suited her as she would have been about wearing an ugly one.

'I didn't mean anything by it.' Reenie squeezed her hand reassuringly; she understood that Mary was not mean-spirited by nature – she just showed her worries by getting snippy. 'You look nice, is all.'

Peter arrived, smartly dressed in his best summer suit with a thick black mourning band around his upper arm. 'Are you three ready?' he asked.

'As we'll ever be.' Reenie linked arms with Mary and Bess, and they all walked towards the church.

Once inside the cool of St Aiden's nave they were faced with the problem of finding somewhere to sit. Mrs Garner had made many friends in Halifax through her charitable work, and the girls noticed that there were a lot of Mackintosh's employees in attendance too. Mary supposed they were there because their friend the Major could not be and from the far end of the nave she caught a glimpse of Mr Baum. He turned and saw her and their eyes met. For a moment he appeared surprised, but then he nodded in a gentlemanly, old-fashioned sort of bow, and she nodded back in acknowledgement.

'Oooh, guess what?' Bess whispered to Reenie as they shuffled down the aisle at the side of the church. 'I think I just saw Mr Baum make eyes at our Mary.'

Mary hissed at her sister in horror, mingled with embarrassment, 'Don't say things like that, Bess!'

'But it's true. And you look knockout in that old dress of Mother's – you wouldn't know it was dragged out of the attic this morning.'

Mary huffed as they finally found a pew where the four of them could all sit together and squeezed in to their spaces. The edge of Mary's dress caught on the brass umbrella hook at the end of their row but she managed to untangle herself, luckily before any damage was done, for the material had become brittle with age; she breathed a sigh of relief that it hadn't torn.

Mary leant across Peter to whisper concernedly to Reenie on his other side. 'You don't think people will be noticing my dress, do you? I don't want anyone to think I'm dressed inappropriately at a funeral.'

'No one would think that of you!' Rennie patted her friend's hand reassuringly. 'You can stop worrying and just go back to being normal funeral miserable. You don't need to add any extra miserable, or specialist worry. Just the standard grief is fine.' Reenie said it in a friendly way because she loved Mary, and she often wished she could take her worries away.

Mary leant across Peter again, this time straining a little further to whisper to Reenie that she was particularly worried that people would think she had dressed up to catch the eye of Mr Baum specifically, but as she opened her mouth to speak all that came out was a gasp of fright. She had felt the old silk dress tear at the seam and realized that the dress had practically dissolved from her underarm to her hip, and the only thing which stood between her and exposure to half of Halifax was her sister who was sitting to her left, looking with wide eyes at the offending article of dress.

'Oh Mary,' Bess said to her sister, looking down at the very visible gape where the dress had rent its seam, *'that's* not going to mend itself.'

Reenie was only taken by surprise for a moment before she began problem-solving. 'Stay right where you are and slide up into the corner of the pew so that you're up against the wall.'

Mary rolled her eyes at the contradictory advice. 'Well, am I staying where I am, or am I sliding up the end of the pew? It's one or the other.'

'Slide up the pew; Bess will have to swap places with you so that you can move to the end and then no one will have direct line of sight.'

Bess clambered over Mary in an undignified manner, which brought the frowning attention of Diana Moore from the other side of the church. Bess sat down on her sister's right-hand side and Mary gingerly slid to her left while holding tight to the gaping seam under her left arm. Mary tried to look nonchalant, looking directly ahead as though everything were perfectly normal; and it was because she was looking straight ahead that she didn't notice that Bess was sitting on the folds of her skirt. They only realized it when they heard another rip. Mary and Bess looked down at her side in alarm; the rip which now appeared ran across her right bosom and down to her hip; the means by which the dress had been held up was now seriously undermined and Mary was struggling to keep the whole flimsy thing from sliding off her shoulders.

'Now look what you've done, you total doylum! It's half off me!' Mary hissed at her sister.

Reenie saw what had happened and quickly changed

places with Peter so that she could be next to Bess. 'Don't panic, it will be all right, we'll have you fixed in no time.'

'With what?' Mary was still speaking in a hoarse whisper, but she was becoming hysterical. 'We'd need a barrel of pins and an hour of time, and unless you hadn't noticed we've got neither and we're surrounded by the quick and the dead!'

Mary had worried about looking conspicuous in a winter dress so she had worn an old one; then she had worried about looking conspicuous in the old dress when it had turned out to suit her; then she had worried about looking conspicuous when she had torn one seam; but now she was beside herself because she was certain that the whole damn thing was going to drop off in the middle of the church, and she was going to go down in Halifax history for streaking through a kindly widow's funeral. 'Hold that bit, there,' Mary instructed her sister, who was grasping at the shredded material of her sister's bodice. 'Not that bit, the shoulder bit! Hold it up!'

'I know, let's put you in Peter's jacket.' Reenie turned to her young man. 'It's all in a good cause, come on, off with it.'

'Erm . . . well . . .' Peter blushed red as he found himself caught between the embarrassment of being thought the sort of uncouth young man who would remove his suit jacket in church and the embarrassment of sitting near a girl whose dress was falling off but he duly handed over the jacket.

'Here, put this on, and then slide down onto the kneeler so that people can only see the top of your head.' Reenie passed the jacket down the pew to Mary and pointed at the stout-looking oblong cushion decorated in thick cross-stitch which hung from a hook under the pew in front of them. 'You'll just look like you're praying.'

'I can't look like I'm praying through the whole service!'

'You can if you're Roman Catholic. Hang on, take these.' Reenie unwound a long string of black malachite beads from her own neck and put them into Mary's hands. 'From a distance they'll look like a rosary. Trust me, I've got a papist auntie. If you close your eyes and hold onto some beads you can have a snooze through the whole service and no one will think the worse of you. Crouch down.'

Mary pursed her lips in distaste at the ridiculous panto-mime that Reenie was getting her to perform, but she acquiesced for want of a better plan. While holding onto the principle sections of her mother's dress for dear life, she wriggled cautiously into Peter's loaned jacket, and then attempted to lower herself piously onto the rough church kneeler while at the same time looking around to make sure no one saw her dress. But as Mary lowered herself forward, Bess budged down the pew a little so that she could reach forward and squeeze her sister's shoulder reassuringly and managed to put her foot on the folds of her sister's skirt this time. The final rent in the old silk was the worst so far. Mary sighed in despair, clutched her friend's string of beads as she knelt down on the floor of their pew, then turned to Reenie in final acceptance of her undignified position. 'What do Roman Catholics say?'

Reenie shrugged. 'Jesus wept?'

The service for Mrs Garner was bitter-sweet. The mourners were saying goodbye to someone who had brought them much happiness and even the brilliant sunshine beyond the cool walls of the dark church interior seemed to proclaim that she deserved a day of bright gaiety. St Aiden's church was full not just with people, but with floral tributes bursting with colourful life: simple bunches of sunflowers rested alongside rare hothouse blooms professionally arranged into bursts of ruby red, and lapis blue.

Mary had taken the death of Mrs Garner and the serious illness of Major Fergusson particularly to heart; the knowledge that she had lost one of the people who they could turn to when things went wrong, and the feeling that she had never properly thanked the Major for all the times when he had been kind to her, and now might never get a chance to, all combined to overwhelm her with a fearful kind of grief. She was also upset about her torn dress, and worried about how she could avoid drawing attention to herself, but since she had caught Mr Baum's eye on entering the church, all she could really think about was how reassuring it would be to talk to him now, how much solace she would get from his calm and logical way of speaking; how much she wished he was wrapping her up in *his* jacket and taking her back to their kitchen where he would hide her away from all the world.

The service ended and there was a low rumble of voices, a different quality of hush to the one which had preceded the service, and the mourners began to make their way out into the sunshine. Mary, Reenie, Bess, and Peter stayed where they were and watched people leaving the church from the vantage point of their pew; they all four of them knew that they would need to wait until everyone had left before they could sneak Mary out to spare her blushes.

'Oooh, don't look now,' Bess piped up with an inappropriately cheery expression, 'Mr Baum is coming over to see Mary. Isn't he lovely? He's so attentive to our Mary and I think they'd make a *lovely* couple.'

Reenie and Mary followed Bess's somewhat daft gaze and saw that sure enough Albert Baum was trying to make his way through the throng to the other side of the church, signalling to Mary to stay where she was.

'Oh no!' Mary was still kneeling on the prayer cushion on the floor, clutching Reenie's string of malachite beads as though they could bring her a miraculous deliverance from her current situation. 'Reenie, don't let him come over! Don't let him see me with my dress half hanging off, I can't let him see me like this!'

'Don't worry, we can just shuffle you out of the church squashed between us if we all four leave in a bunch. No one will properly see what you're wearing if we're crowding round you.' Reenie tried to discreetly look around for the best exit to take. 'Sidle out this way with Bess on one side and me on the other and Peter can walk in front of us.'

They huddled together and walked, crablike, down the side of the pews towards the vestry door which stood ajar, their faces tight with concentration. Mr Baum was making rapid progress towards them and seemed frustrated that they were not paying heed to his gesticulations and were instead taking Mary further away from him. Mr Baum was in better luck than Mary, because just as he needed them to, a group of mourners moved out of the church and let him pass and he was able to catch up with his assistant.

Albert Baum cut a smart figure in his suit of cedar brown silk with his simply coiffured black hair. His dark good looks could so easily have made him a magnetic movie star villain, but he had such an honest face and ready smile that they would have totally contradicted such a character; one only had to look into his chocolate brown eyes to see that he was honest to a fault. To Mary Norcliffe the sight of Albert's smiling face was balm in a world of worry and for a moment her heart leapt to see him approaching; then she remembered that her dress was falling off and she went white with annoyance at her sister, herself, and the world in general.

Mary clung to her dress seams beneath Peter's jacket and tried to slink backwards between her friends, but it was too late – Mr Baum had caught up with them.

He nodded polite and rapid greetings at Reenie, Peter, and Bess, before checking on Mary. 'Are you quite all right?' he asked her. 'Are you too cold?'

'No, no, Mr Baum, just fine. Going home now. Goodbye. Come along, Bess.' She took another two steps backwards, pulling her shoulders inwards within the jacket to make herself as small as possible.

'But you are wearing your friend's jacket, I think, yes?' Mr Baum seemed genuinely concerned for Mary's comfort. 'If you are very cold we should take you out into the sunshine where you will get warm. You must not risk catching a chill. Chills can be very dangerous. Perhaps I could escort you to—'

'No!' Mary and Reenie both exclaimed in unison as Mary began to adopt an even stranger backwards walk which combined crouching with intermittent leg crossing while she clutched at her dress with a handful of the necklace whose beads were starting to flake off their colour in her coldly perspiring hands.

'We have to go now, Mr Baum,' Reenie said a little too loudly to sound natural, throwing her arm out in front of Mary in a rather over-protective gesture.

'Don't you worry, Mr Baum,' Peter said with suspicious awkwardness, 'I'll make sure they're quite all right.' And he took a step backwards too, shuffling closer to the vestry door.

Albert Baum watched in confusion as the four friends kept reversing, three of them looking both embarrassed and concerned and Mary's younger sister with her pretty blonde ringlets looking delighted, but not altogether bright.

'Maria, I would very much like to walk with you outside—' Mr Baum persevered.

'I must go, Mr Baum. It wouldn't be proper for me to walk out with you.' She ducked in through the vestry door followed by the other three and Reenie shouted a quick apology to the confectioner before she shut the door in his face. The four friends looked round in relief at having gained the safety of the vestry, but surprise and embarrassment overcame them at seeing the look of shock on the face of the curate who had been tidying up, and who had been startled by Mary's appearance in a frag-mented dress.

'Sorry,' Reenie said to him as they made for the back door, 'it couldn't be helped.'

Back in the nave of the church Albert Baum silently reprimanded himself for having been so foolish as to think that Mary Norcliffe might have been willing to entertain any acquaintanceship with him outside their working hours. He knew that he was not a catch; he was a widower with two young children, neither of whom spoke English; he was Jewish and so unwelcome in his native Germany that he could not hope to offer a comfortable life to any girl anywhere, because no country on earth seemed to want him. Mr Baum had hoped to tell Maria the news he had just received, that he would be returning to Germany sooner than planned because he had had news that the permits he had hoped to obtain for himself and his children had fallen through and he would not be able to return Britain; the news that he had secured more staff for the confectioner's kitchen so that her workload would be lighter; the news that he loved her.

All this and more he wanted to pour out as they walked in the sunshine and she wore the striking raven black dress which had diverted his attention when he had seen her across the church. The imminent loss of their colleague and the talk of the life of goodness his lady had caused Albert to think about his own life and how little time he had left with Mary, how he ought to seize the day and tell her what an honour it had been to work with her, how much he had enjoyed her company. Then she had looked so startled and her friends had tried to hurry her away. He kicked himself for having been deluded enough to believe that Maria might have been able to overlook his background and his situation, and he went home to his boarding house where even his own landlady was suspicious of him.

Chapter Forty-Seven

'It's a matter of some delicacy, Mrs Wilkes.' The gentleman from the office of W. H. Boocock, Solicitors shuffled in his chair.

'I am no stranger to matters of delicacy in my profession, Mr Hodges. Please be frank, I think it will save us both time.'

'Well, we wish to know if you have found a savings book among the belongings of Major Fergusson. Perhaps he had an office with a desk drawer which has not yet been turned out, or . . .' His voice trailed off as he struggled to think of alternatives.

'What would it look like? Which savings bank was the book with?'

'Well, we don't know for certain that he had one. We have his account book and the deeds to his property, but from what he'd said to his regular bank clerk it was understood that he had a savings account with one of the credit unions.'

'That does sound like the Major. He would save with

a credit union to help those less well-off than himself, even if it meant he missed out on a higher rate of interest. Which credit union does the clerk think it was?'

'That's the trouble, he doesn't know, and so long as the Major is too ill to look after his own affairs we have been arranging them for him. It wouldn't do for him to recover and find that his rates had gone unpaid, for instance. We have checked the usual sums he transacted, but there is one unaccounted for. The clerk said he'd take out the same sum once a month to pay into his savings account in cash and in person, but we've written to the managers of the branches of each of the credit unions represented in Halifax and none of them have a record of the Major's account. We can't write to every credit union in the country – that wouldn't be feasible – but it is possible that if he did have a savings account it might be with a branch in a neighbouring town, perhaps somewhere where he had a family connection, or a former residence?' Mr Hodges hoped that this might elicit some suggestions from the man's colleagues, but none were forthcoming. 'To be perfectly honest, Mrs Wilkes, we've come up against this sort of thing before.'

'What sort of thing? I'm afraid I don't follow you.'

'Vice, Mrs Wilkes. I won't mince my words, because you've asked me to speak. I have known other gentlemen who were in the habit of withdrawing a certain sum of money each month and in order to save embarrassment with the clerk they would say it was for a savings account with another institution, but in my experience that is very seldom the case. Was your Major Fergusson a man you would consider prone to vice?'

'He was not. And for the avoidance of doubt, he was not *my* Major Fergusson.' Amy Wilkes had not expected this. 'Which vice in particular did you have in mind?'

'Erm . . . well, not to put too fine a point on it, gambling, madam.'

'It's Miss.' Diana enjoyed joining forces with Amy Wilkes to wrong-foot the man who had insulted the reputation of their friend, but she didn't show even a hint of it. 'I think that's highly unlikely. The Major's principle weakness, if weakness it can be called, has always been charity. I know that he made gifts of money to sick employees in the past, or to widows without pensions. I think it far more likely that he was giving the money to the needy. The only time I ever heard him quote the Bible was to warn an apprentice lad against wasting money on a flashy suit of clothes – he told him to store up his riches in heaven where moths couldn't get it, instead of on earth where it might well get robbed.'

'Yes,' the man said, 'I'm familiar with the scripture from the gospel according to St Matthew, although I haven't heard it rendered quite like that.'

'I think we've answered your question, Mr Hodges. If you wish to write to the various credit unions of Yorkshire you are welcome to do so, but we passed all the Major's personal papers to your office after you contacted us. Major Fergusson's colleague, Mrs Starbeck, was most thorough when she parcelled up his possessions.'

Diana nodded. 'I don't think there is an employee in the factory more thorough than Mrs Starbeck.' And in her haste to prove the solicitor wrong, she did not wonder for a moment that there might be a savings book; she did not connect this visit with the reference request on her desk, and despite what she thought about Cynthia Starbeck, she did not question her integrity.

Chapter Forty-Eight

Reenie and Mary were agreed that the time had come to tell Diana about the success Bess was making of her new position in the postal warehouse looking after not only Vicky Geall's baby, but the children of a handful of other women workers besides. There had been a few teething troubles to start with, but Bess, contrary to her usual daftness, had given instructions to Peter about help or supplies she needed, and he did his best to find them. It had come as a complete surprise to them both that Bess was doing something which was both useful and too difficult for anyone else, but they weren't about to question their good fortune. As Reenie always said, when the gods gave you a gift horse, it was unwise to let them see you counting its teeth.

It was an ideal situation and they were almost convinced that Diana would see it from their point of view once they revealed what they had been up to without her entire knowledge. Reenie and Mary had agreed that if they just explained it to Diana in the right way she would see the practical benefits of allowing one of Halifax's silliest girls to look after the children of essential employees in secret in a postal warehouse with no proper facilities for child-care.

At the door of Diana's office Mary knocked politely, if a little timidly.

'Leave me to do the talking,' Reenie said with a smile.

'No, *I'll* do the talking; I know what we need to say to not get up her nose,' Mary countered.

'Yes, but I'm a natural problem-solver, so it will be better coming from me.'

'I can hear you both, you know.' Diana's voice reached them from the other side of her office door before she opened it. Her sour expression threw them completely from their prearranged plan.

'Erm . . . We've come to talk to you about Bess and about the job she's doing,' Reenie faltered.

'She'd better not be causing any trouble, because that's the last thing I need.' Diana looked from Reenie to Mary, waiting impatiently to be told why they were there, taking up valuable time. 'Is she doing the work I gave her to do?'

Mary tried to answer but was cut off before she could explain that Bess had diversified into a new line of work, on top of her warehouse duties.

'And you two? Are you doing *your* jobs? I know what you're like, Reenie Calder, and I don't want to hear that you've been taking on extra work for all and sundry, do you hear?'

'Yes, Diana. Although I think I might—'

Diana didn't let Reenie finish what she was saying.

'Don't do any thinking – it only gets you into trouble. And Mary, I want to see you watching your back for knives. You need to be extra careful of your reputation. Dolly Dunkley wants your job and she's trying to get you out of it by complaining to me and anyone else who will listen that she would make a better confectioner than you do.'

Mary was taken aback. She knew that Dolly Dunkley had grumbled about her after their run-in on the cellophane wrapping line, and their stand-off in the stable yard, and possibly even their bickering over her work in the kitchens, but she hadn't thought it would get as serious as complaints to Diana. 'None of the things she says are true, I promise you they aren't.'

'Of course they aren't,' Diana shrugged. 'She's a rotten little widdop and she makes things up to get her own way because she's not capable of working for anything for herself. You can ignore everything she says so long as you watch out for knives and keep your nose clean.'

Reenie was not convinced. 'I don't think she's after Mary's job, I think she's after mine.'

'Dolly Dunkley is greedy and she wants everything she sees. She wants to organize the decorating for the royal visit instead of Bess; she wants to make the sweets the King will eat; she wants to be a junior manager like Reenie so that she can lord it over girls her own age; she wants to plan the new production line like Peter, and she wants the power to interview new girls the way I do. She wants *all* our jobs and she's too stupid to realize she can't have them all because she can only do one job at a time – and she's barely managing that.'

'Well, what are we meant to do?' Mary was already

panicking that her job was under threat. 'You're acting as though it will all sort itself out, but it won't.'

'I think you'll find it will resolve itself quicker than you might imagine. She's vain as well as greedy. If I keep giving her menial jobs she'll soon tire of the indignity and quit the factory. If she doesn't, I'm quite sure her greed will trip her up, just wait and watch.' Diana herded the two girls back out of her office door. 'Now, I hope that's all for today, because if you hadn't noticed we are rather busy. If you've got anything else to tell me it better be good.'

Reenie and Mary exchanged nervous looks before Reenie replied, 'No, no, really, it's fine. We just thought we'd tell you how well we're doing. Nothing else to report.'

'Good, then don't bother me again unless you're bringing Martini cocktails and a handsome man.' Diana closed the door on Mary and Reenie and they felt even more uneasy than they had when they had arrived.

'Do you think we should go back in and try to tell her?' Reenie asked.

'Good grief, no. Didn't you hear what she just said? We've got bigger problems to deal with. Dolly Dunkley is out to get all of us!'

Chapter Forty-Nine

'This is typical of what you get when you employ fourteen-year-olds.' Amy Wilkes was rolling up the sleeves of her cream silk blouse, ready for a morning of frantic meetings and difficult decisions, hurriedly drinking a cup of cold tea at her assistant's desk before they both went on to brave the day. 'They stage elaborate dramas in the toilets, usually crying about something they think that a boy thinks about them, and get all the other girls sneaking off the line to check that they're all right, and then before you know it you've got half the line huddled around the sinks, weeping for no reason, or consoling the ones who are weeping, and if you try to get them back to work they all sulk because you don't understand the import of their situation. Not turning up to work without letting anyone know where they are is also typical.'

Diana Moore said nothing because she knew that her manager did not need her to say anything; she simply needed someone to vent her frustration to, and to hand her the morning's correspondence and internal memoranda.

'If you ask me,' Amy said and she put her gilt-edged Mackintosh's teacup in its saucer with a rattle, 'we shouldn't be employing them this young; if the Home Office weren't so bloody-minded about labour permits we could have plenty of workers from Ireland, or Spain, or Germany. Just think of all the Jewish people in Germany who would jump at the chance to work here, and who would benefit? *We* would because we would have a vastly better output at the factory and we could leave the minnows at school another year at least.'

Diana heard a tread in the corridor beyond and smiled to herself – it was her old friend Laurence Johns and he had clearly hurried to see them.

'Have you heard?' Laurence burst in without ceremony.

'About the girls?' Amy asked. 'Yes, they've not come in to work because there's rain forecast and every farmer in the valley needs to bring their harvest in.'

'But this is terrible.' Laurence slumped into a chair, the strain of their recent troubles clearly taking its toll on him. 'What are we going to do without them? We can't run lines like this. In some places they're missing a third of their workers.'

Amy Wilkes sighed. 'Whatever we do there is no easy solution. And with Mrs Starbeck as acting Head of Time and Motion I fear we will have an even less straightforward time of things.'

'But she's not acting Head of Time and Motion any more; haven't you heard the bad news from Sir Harold?' Laurence looked to both of his colleagues with surprise.

'Oh God.' Diana put her hand to her mouth. 'It's not the Major, is it? He's not—'

'No, no,' Laurence was quick to reassure her, 'it's not that. The last I heard was that the Major is still gravely ill, but he's still with us. No, the bad news is that Sir Harold doesn't think it wise to leave Mrs Starbeck in such an exalted position despite her experience. He's appointed another acting head of department until they can find someone who knows what they're doing.'

'Well, who is it?' Amy Wilkes didn't think anyone could be worse than Mrs Starbeck.

'I'm afraid it's me.' Laurence Johns had turned white as a sheet. He was a cocoa buyer who had risen to the Head of International Affairs and claimed to know nothing at all about Time and Motion work. He had taken over a line briefly after the fire, but at the Major's instruction he had let the married women in his department run themselves; this was going to be far more challenging.

'Well,' Diana picked up her teacup, 'that's not the worst news I've heard all week.'

'But you don't understand! I have no idea what an acting Head of Time and Motion does. And I've got my own job to be doing! What should I do?'

Amy Wilkes shook her head. 'It's up to the factory manager, but I'm on my way to see him now to tell him the news and I suspect he's going to say that we move the married women on to electric lines and shut down all the handmaking until we've got the girls back. It's the only way, and as long as we give the electric lines priority, we can at least make something. This is our best chance to maximize our output in the circumstances.' Amy, however, was now thinking about the supply of electricity itself. 'Diana, do you know any of the workers down in the factory power plant? We don't need to worry about any of them running off to their family farms, do we?'

'No fear there, Mrs Wilkes,' Diana spoke with confidence, 'they're not farmers, they're mostly part-time Rugby League players and Halifax are already out of the challenge cup so there's no worry that they're going anywhere. As long as no one needs them to kick off they'll keep the power plant fires burning.'

'Good,' Amy said, 'then we need to give priority to any line connected with the royal visit and simply shut down the rest, Mrs Starbeck be damned.'

Chapter Fifty

This must be how ballerinas felt before going on stage to perform, Mary thought to herself. She was nervous, but excited too. She knew that she was about to do something that no one else in Halifax had the skill to do as well as she could, and if all went well she would be saving the day for her factory.

The confectioner's kitchen looked even smarter than usual; every stray utensil had been tidied away, and every piece of machinery not in use had been carefully covered with a crisp, fresh dust sheet and bound with a clean cotton cord. The surface of the metal-topped worktable shone like a mirror where they had scrubbed and polished it the night before, and sheets of waxed paper lay neatly arranged down the length of the table, their corners precisely lined up by Mr Baum who had straightened them, and re-straightened them every time he walked past the table and caused a draft of air to make the papers flutter out of place. The smallest of their freestanding copper boiling pans was ready with a quantity of violet toffee, gently heated by the steam which ran through the pipes around it. Vicky Geall had given careful instructions for the temperature they needed to keep it at, and she stood by, sniffing the air for any indication that it had become too hot and was scalding the sugar and fat.

After much experiment and long deliberation Vicky Geall had decided that the King's Toffee would be purple, and should be made to look like an old seal of wax on a royal charter. By making the toffee purple they were using a colour with royal connotations, but also giving a nod to Violet Mackintosh who had invented their first toffee. Vicky was even going to give the King's Toffee the lightest violet flavouring in their founder's honour.

The instruments they needed were primed and ready, the ingredients carefully measured and neatly arranged, their aprons and overalls clean, starched, and dazzlingly white. Mary, Vicky Geall, and Albert Baum waited eagerly for nine o'clock and the arrival of Mrs Starbeck, Mrs Wilkes, and – most importantly – Sir Harold Mackintosh himself. Sir Harold did not attend the trial runs of every new sweet, but this was the King's Toffee and he had taken a particular interest in it.

Mary had never seen a handmaking trial run in the kitchens before, but she knew that Reenie had worked on a few of them. The handmaking trial runs were an important stepping stone on the way to creating a mechanized production line. First the confectioner would be commissioned to invent a new sweet, and would spend some time working on a small scale with recipes and experiments to create a sweet which looked and tasted the way they thought it ought to. Then the confectioner would start thinking about how the sweet could be made on a large scale by hand on a production line and change the recipe accordingly. Only then did they create a miniature production line in the confectioner's kitchen using the same type of equipment the handmakers would have on the line.

The trial runs on this miniature line could be make or break for a new product; if the recipe reached the trial stage but created too many complications, the confectioner could have their product cancelled and be sent back to the drawing board to invent something entirely different.

'Don't pull that face, you're making me nervous,' Vicky said.

Mary did a double-take, 'How can you tell what kind of face I'm pulling? I thought you were meant to be blind!'

'I can hear it,' Vicky said, grinning. She was clearly looking forward to their demonstration, but Mary thought it was all right for her because she wasn't doing any of it. Vicky could manage very well on close detail when she was seated at a table and working with care. But this job would require a different kind of skill; Vicky was an artist, but this was a job for a factory girl.

Mary heard animated chatter in the hallway before she saw them at the door: Mrs Starbeck had come along as the most experienced manager in Time and Motion to see what sort of line they would be required to set up, clearly still smarting from her demotion from her illegitimately assumed position as acting head of department; Mrs Wilkes was there because she would need to know what skillset was needed from the girls her department would be recruiting for this line in the longer term – and she was followed by Sir Harold himself, who held the door open to her.

Mary took a deep breath; she had come a long way to this time and this place. There had been the worry about her younger sister's possible pregnancy out of wedlock, then the worry of Bess's injuries and slow recovery after the car crash which she had been lucky not to have been killed in, and now that she was there she had to tell herself to fight back the worries that tried to clamour in.

'Mrs Geall,' Cynthia Starbeck spoke before any of her colleagues had a chance to begin proceedings – another trick she had been known to use to jostle herself into position as chair of any meeting, 'how nice to see you.'

'I wish I could say the same for you, madam.' Vicky smirked as she knew her sarcasm would not be lost on Sir Harold and she would be allowed to get away with it while Starchy Starbeck bristled with indignation. 'Do we have everyone here? Shall we begin?'

'Yes, yes.' Sir Harold was in good spirits. 'Where do you want us to stand? Will we block out your light if we stand along the wall by this window?'

'You won't block out my light,' Vicky said, 'but you'd best ask Mary as this is her big day. Mary, where would you like your audience?'

All eyes turned to Mary Norcliffe. 'Erm . . . yes, yes, that's . . .' Mary was about to follow the path of least resistance when she caught Albert Baum's eye and felt a surge of courage knowing that he was there to support her if she needed him. 'Actually, no, you *will* block the light there. I'd like you to all stand in a line to the left of Mrs Geall. She won't be part of our demonstration today.'

Mrs Starbeck smiled sweetly, but sniffed in distaste that they were being addressed by a junior assistant. 'Mr Baum, I understand that you will be leaving us earlier than planned to return to Germany. You must be relieved that you're not being kept away from your own country for quite so long.'

Albert Baum had wanted to tell Mary in person that he was leaving earlier than planned, but when he had tried to speak to her at the funeral she had seemed so skittish that he had assumed she was avoiding him; now he saw the look of shock and disappointment on her face and realized that he had been wrong, that he should have tried harder to make her listen to all that he had to tell her.

'On the contrary, Mrs Starbeck,' he said, 'I think I will miss your company very much. Perhaps you could write to the Home Office for me and request they consider me for permanent leave to remain? I would be very glad to take up a permanent position at the Halifax factory, if my sister and my two children can join me here.'

Mrs Starbeck was seething, but she had to keep her spite in check as long as they were in the company of Sir Harold; she was not so stupid as Dolly Dunkley, and although she thought that some of her wrongdoings were justified, she was not so foolish that she was not fully aware when she was sailing morally close to the wind. Her rage at being demoted from her temporary position as acting head of department – and to someone with virtually no experience of the work of the department

– had put her in an even more spiteful frame of mind than usual.

The skies beyond the factory were darkening with a gathering storm and Albert Baum went over to the light switch in the doorway to turn on the electric light. There was a high, round window in the door of the confectioner's kitchen, and through it Albert caught a glimpse of someone waiting in the corridor beyond. It was a Mackintosh's messenger girl and she appeared to be in two minds about knocking on the door. Albert opened it and put his head out. 'Can I help you?'

The girl looked down at the internal memorandum she held in her hand and then back up at the doorway.

'I-I've a message for Sir Harold.' The girl was overwhelmed by the importance of her mission.

'He is here, I will take it.' Albert took the memorandum and sent the girl away before returning to the trial line and passing it to the head of the firm.

'I'm sure this can wait,' Sir Harold said, his bushy, bird-of-prey eyebrows knitting together in interest at the confectionery line laid out before him, uninterested for now in what the unopened memo was about to reveal. 'Let's begin. Young lady, when you are quite ready.'

Mary nodded nervous assent, took a deep breath for courage, picked up the hand depositor, and then began to lower the copper boiling pan on its hinges until it poured a deep, violet confection, thick as volcanic lava, into the tin hand depositor she had at the ready. The heady aroma of sugar, butter, and delicately mixed violet filled the room, and as Mary began her work it became clear why it was so important to get a local confectioner to run this trial; Halifax toffee was a difficult substance to work with, but

Mary Norcliffe made it look not merely simple, but graceful too. The gentle roll of her wrist and the flick with which she brought the depositor back up, caught any drips, and then dipped in again had a hypnotic quality; there was nothing faltering or hesitant in Mary's movements, because when she made confectionery she was more herself than at any other time, and in that moment she felt it.

Moving along behind her at a steady pace was Albert Baum; they made an exceptional team and Mary wondered if it was usual for colleagues in a confectioner's kitchen to be so attuned to one another's actions, and whether she would ever be able to return to her old life which had no Albert in it.

Mr Baum gave the toffees a few moments before pressing the specially made seal into the cooling sugar to create the look of blobs of sealing wax bearing an ancient coat of arms. The stamped toffees had a deliberate and very slight irregularity – Mary and Albert had, between them, managed to create the illusion of imperfection in a perfect batch just like a real collection of wax seals on royal documents, and it was exactly what the King's Toffee ought to be.

In the main the spectators were transfixed by the ebb and flow of the handmade toffee line Mary had created, but every so often Mrs Wilkes's eyes would drift to the memorandum in Sir Harold's hand and she hoped it didn't contain what she suspected.

The demonstration was finished and Sir Harold initiated a round of applause which made Mary blush with embarrassment; she had been prepared for everything to go wrong and to receive a reprimand from somewhere – but she had not expected to be lavishly praised.

'Excellent work, Mary,' Sir Harold said, beaming. 'Truly excellent. My mother would be very proud to see a violet toffee being made for the King; it really is wonderful that you've incorporated her into your work, quite wonderful. And such skill! You must be very proud of your apprentice, Victoria.'

'Oh, I am, sir.'

'If you will excuse me?' Sir Harold waved the memorandum and intimated that he needed to take a moment while he opened it. The assembled company did their best to disguise their mounting curiosity and talked among themselves about the plans to begin production on the new, temporary handmaking line for the King's Toffee.

'It will have to wait, I'm afraid,' Sir Harold said.

'The discussion?' Amy Wilkes asked.

'No, the line itself. This is a memorandum from the factory manager; it has been decided that the opening of the King's Toffee line will be suspended indefinitely while our shortage of staff is chronic.'

Sir Harold turned to look out of the window at the rooftops of his factory and his town beyond; the world was changing and tasks which had seemed simple a year earlier now seemed herculean. Sir Harold tried to give Mary a smile of consolation. 'These toffees you have made today will not go to waste, and the work you have done on them so far will all have been worthwhile; however, instead of making a new sweet for every tin of Quality Street we will use this batch for the King's Casket and the other important visitors. You will still have made toffee for the King, I promise you.'

The room was silent; they had worked such long days and late nights to perfect this recipe and this method –

and it was all for nothing. But what surprised Mary most was that she cared much less about this disappointment than she did about the loss of Albert Baum. Troubles would follow her all the days of her life, but for a glorious moment she had felt that she could bear them better because Mr Baum was there with her. Now she felt as though the world was falling down around her and nothing would ever be safe again.

Chapter Fifty-One

'I wouldn't bother her just now if I were you, Reenie.'
Bess smiled amiably at their friend while behind her the
sister she always claimed was even-tempered kicked seven
bells out of her bicycle in the bike sheds.

'She's not looking happy. What's happened?'

'She's just heard from Diana that they can't keep Herr
Baum here as long as they had planned. There's been a
problem with his work permit.'

'Mary!' Reenie called out tentatively. 'Are you all right?'

Mary looked up with a scowl. 'No, I bloody am not!'
And returned to kicking her bicycle which she had been
so proud to buy on the H. P. from Bulmer's second-hand
warehouse with her wages when they went up at Easter.

'Is there 'owt I can do?' Reenie was always confident
that for every problem there was a solution, and she
found that the solution to most of Mary's troubles was
kindness and friendship.

'Get rid of Mrs bloody Starbeck! I never want to see her again!'

Ruffian neighed agreement at the suggestion that Mrs Starbeck was a bad sort and stamped the hoof which he had only recently been trying to kick a shoe off. Mary looked up at the peculiarly ugly horse and burst into tears. Reenie had been intending to give Mary a hug, but Mary threw herself onto the horse's neck instead and hugged him, sobbing.

'What's all this about then, eh Mary? What's the old crow done now?'

'It's Mr Baum's papers to let him stay in England.' Mary rubbed at her tears with the back of her arm. 'Someone from the factory wrote to the Home Office and told them that he wasn't needed here because they've already got a local lady doing the job.'

Reenie was taken aback. 'But surely Mrs Starbeck wouldn't do that, would she? I know she doesn't like foreigners, but everyone knows that Vicky is a married mother so she can only be temporary. There must be a mistake; I'm sure they'll fix it and you'll get your Mr Baum back.'

Mary shook her head. 'I heard Mrs Starbeck gloat about it and then Diana Moore told me after I'd done my toffee-making demonstration for Sir Harold. She said that Mrs Starbeck wrote a letter to the Home Office. She's deliberately trying to stop him staying, or bringing his children.'

Bess was conciliatory. 'I'm sure Mrs Starbeck knows what's best. She seems like a very clever lady – and she wears lovely blouses.'

Reenie opened her mouth to explain to noodle-headed Bess that the loveliness of a person's choice of blouses bore no relation to their ability to make positive moral choices, but Mary stopped her before she could waste her breath on the matter.

'The worst part is that he says he thinks if he goes back he might be in trouble for working in England. He's frightened of what his country has become, and I just don't want him to go. He understands me – and hardly anyone understands me.'

The skies over Halifax had darkened deeply by lunchtime and were now a deep, ominous, wild indigo. All through the factory electric lights had been lit, giving the summer factory an October feeling. Distant rumblings told Diana that a storm was on its way and she wished it would hurry up and break so that they could lift some of the humidity in the air. Her colleagues were becoming fractious, and to Diana's mind it wasn't just the anxiety over the royal visit, or the natural distress over the recall and their colleague's dangerous condition in the infirmary; there was a summer ague and a cooling storm would give them all some respite from the foggy-headed madness of the stiflingly hot offices in summertime.

Diana had been summoned to the factory dining hall where a dispute over royal decorations had broken out. According to one quarter the factory dining hall resembled nothing so much as a Hallowe'en gala since the cleaning department had put up some grotesque decorations which were most certainly not from the factory's own supply. A distant flash of lightning blazed across the violet sky as Diana arrived at the site of the dispute. A rumble of thunder followed moments later and in the eerie darkness of the storm Diana could see why the contraband decorations were causing so much consternation.

'Well, blow that for a game of soldiers, I'm not budging!' Mrs Hebden, the chief of the cleaning staff, was clutching an effigy of the King which she had made, life-size, from waxed paper toffee wraps. It was as ugly as it was painstakingly detailed, and there was no knowing whether the King would see it and be insulted – or intimidated. Mrs Hebden had evidently meant it as a token of esteem, but it was exactly the kind of inexpert monstrosity that Diana had wanted to guard against when she had given Bess the job of keeping an eye on decorations.

'You can't put him up in my canteen! Get your own place to decorate!' Mrs Carol, the chief cook, did not want her area of work to be associated with this gigantic voodoo doll. Another crack of thunder rattled the canteen window-panes and was closely followed by a blue-white fork of lightning.

'Everywhere is our place! We clean this lot for you day in and day out and we've got just as much right as anyone to put up the decorations we've made to greet the King.'

Diana watched from a safe distance. She had already guessed what would happen next, and she hoped it would happen sooner rather than later and spare her the tiresome effort of banning the offensive item. Sure enough, in a fit of rage, Mrs Carol the cook reached over to the effigy of King George VI and pulled his head off. It was worse than Diana could have predicted – the stuffing of sweet wrappers burst out like confetti and an even more undignified spat broke out between the matrons.

'Ladies . . .' Diana cleared her throat and watched as the grown women ignored her to fight over the crumbling handicraft. Diana was not about to raise her voice; she disliked the indignity of raising her voice if she did not have to, and she was confident that if she waited a moment longer she would have her chance to intervene.

A simultaneous bang of thunder and fierce flash of lightning outside gave the scene a dramatic quality which Diana did not feel the ridiculous farce deserved, but she didn't care so long as the storm broke the muggy feeling which was hanging about them all and making people fractious. The shuffling, scuffling dispute continued for a moment more until a sound on the window ledge gave everyone pause: hail the size of pigeon's eggs was hammering down on the exterior walls of the canteen. One or two of the bystanders ran to the windows to look out and others followed, watching as the hail collected in the guttering, rattled down on the cobbles in the yard, and formed banks of strange shapes instead of melting into the earth. The guttering overflowed and Diana wondered how rusted the old Victorian pipes were and if they would take the unexpected weight of so much compacted ice.

The walls of the canteen gave an audible groan; it was a kind of hum in reverse and the women who did not have electricity in their homes looked around in panic, but Diana recognized it only too well – they were having a power cut.

The lights in the canteen went out with the briefest of flickers, and the stormy gloom left them staring at one another in anxious silence. Diana took charge. 'There isn't any need for alarm; it'll be back on in a minute. We generate our own electricity here so the men in the boiler house will be working away to fix whatever the trouble is. Storms do funny things.' And in the window of surprised silence Diana took the opportunity to say what she had been sent to say all along. 'But to the business in hand, ladies,' she said, addressing the two women who were respectively clutching the head and the torso of King George, 'you should each have been issued with a Mackintosh's permit when you went to collect your decorations from the postal warehouse. That permit will tell us which section of the factory you have been asked to decorate, and which decorations you have been allocated. Do you have them to hand?'

'But what about the storm?' Mrs Carol's eyes had widened and she was looking perplexedly at the lifeless light fittings. 'How will we do anything if—'

'Come now, Mrs Carol,' Diana said, 'I don't think at your age you can possibly tell me that you've never seen a storm before. And there is no danger to life or limb in a power cut, it is merely an inconvenience.' Another flash of lightning illuminated the garish features on the face of the wax paper effigy of King George. 'Now, do you have those permits to hand?'

'We don't have no permits. Who said anything about permits?'

Mrs Hebden tried to scoop up some of the stuffing from the King's wax paper innards which were littering the canteen floor. 'No, I asked about that when I went to the postal warehouse, and the girl in the warehouse said that we'd need a permit if we wanted to take company decorations home, and she wasn't going to write any permits for anyone because she wasn't letting anyone take their decorations home.'

Diana thought this had a ring of truth; it would be typical of Bess to be such an utter noodle-head that she'd completely fail to understand her own system. 'Ladies, there has been a misunderstanding. Each section has been allocated an area to decorate,' a crack of thunder broke through Diana's words and she ignored it as though not even the storm could disquiet her, 'and a supply of decorations which match all the other decorations around the factory. I'm sorry, Mrs Hebden, but your beautiful work of art can't go on display on this occasion.'

'It can't go on display at all because this . . . this . . . *woman* has ruined it!'

'Who you calling a *woman*?'

'You! And I'll call you worse!'

'I'll tell Mother!'

The women's faces were illuminated in the quick, blue light of the storm and Diana spotted the family resemblance; she remembered now that chief cook and chief cleaner were widowed sisters. 'Mrs Hebden, you've done a beautiful job,' Diana lied with easy charm, 'but I'm afraid we can't have this work of art on display in the factory because the other departments would be jealous.'

'I could make some more of them.' The storm cracked in horror at the suggestion, 'and put them round the place, like?'

'I will be quite frank with you, Mrs Hebden. I think you should take this to the Town Hall. I think they need to see this.'

'Do you really? Do you think it's good enough for them to display?'

'I can't think of anywhere else worthy of it.' Diana held a dim view of the town corporation and she hoped the gruesome effigy terrified the life out of them instead of giving her a headache here in the factory. Duty done, she made her way towards the postal warehouse and the bone she had to pick with Bess Norcliffe.

324

Chapter Fifty-Two

A knot of workers stood inside the open double doors at the end of the main factory corridor, looking out onto the hail which was smaller now, but still falling heavily. There was no sense in Diana walking all the way up to the postal warehouse in this weather – she'd be soaked through before she got there at best, and bruised to buggery from the hail at worst. The warehouse Bess was in had been given a telephone line and Bess had been taught how to use it, so Diana accepted that she would have to make do for the moment with giving Bess a flea in her ear by telephone.

She dashed across the yard under cover of the wooden, shingled awning which joined the Albion Mills building to the smart office block, and wended her way back to her desk, walking past clusters of excited factory workers speculating that this was the worst summer storm the town had ever seen. So long as the storm didn't knock their electricity out all day, Diana didn't care if it was the worst storm they'd had since Noah floated his ark. She settled herself down at her desk, picked up the heavy Bakelite telephone receiver, tapped the brass hook three times to reset the connection to the factory switchboard, and prepared to ask to be put through to the silliest girl in three counties.

A pantomime of confusion, principally originating with Bess who didn't fully understand who was telephoning her, despite it being explained to her by both Diana and the girl from the switchboard, eventually resolved itself and Diana was able to impress upon Bess that the project of decorating the factory was in chaos, and she was the reason for that chaos. To Diana, Bess sounded relieved that she wasn't being told off for something utterly different, and this felt ominous to Diana, but she didn't have time to investigate further. Knowing Bess, she had probably been holding assignations with some young man in the warehouse and this was why she had taken her eye off the ball and let the factory decorations go to pot.

'Bess, I don't think you understand that the whole point of your job is to stop this from happening.'

'Stop what from happening?' Bess hummed happily while twisting her end of the telephone cord around her finger end.

'You're meant to make sure that each department puts up the decorations that they have been given. You are giving out the decorations the salesmen have organized, you are keeping track of each department in your book. It is so simple a child of five could do it.'

'I have done it. Everyone has got their decorations on time. I got the porters to help me distribute them. I know everyone got them because I ticked them off in my book. And then when I got to the end and I'd run out of decorations I asked the salesmen for some more and they made some more.'

'But you were supposed to make certain that each department only used the decorations they had been given, and stuck to the area you had allocated them to decorate.'

'Yes, but some people wanted to add extra things they'd made, and some people didn't have enough space so they wanted to put their decorations up in other places.'

'This is the very thing you were supposed to stop! This was the entire purpose of your job. It's a mess and it all has to be taken down. I don't have time to go from department to department fixing your mess – I want you to go back and do the thing I asked you to do in the first place.'

'But does that mean we can't have any decorations? Am I meant to take them down, or am I meant to tidy them up?'

'You can have decorations, but you have to use the decorations the salesmen told you to use, in the places they told you to use them.'

'I don't think anyone is going to like that much. Some people have worked very hard to make extra things for the King, and if you tell them to take them down there'll be a lot of bad feeling. It would have been better if you'd told them before now that they couldn't put them up – it would have saved everyone a lot of trouble.'

'It's times like these that I can see why your sister is permanently on the verge of hysteria.' There was a sudden yelp in the background and Diana thought she realized why Bess had been so disorganized, and so concerned that she was in trouble for something else. 'Is that a dog I can hear in the background?'

'No, there's no dog here.' Bess said it a little too quickly, and with a rising tone in her voice which sounded like a blatant lie.

Diana sighed and leant her forehead in her hand; perhaps it was no bad thing if, for some mad reason, Bess had taken in a dog at the postal warehouse. It would keep her occupied so she would be less likely to seek out trouble in other forms, and she was so far away from any food production lines that it couldn't cause contamination. It was the least of her troubles, if it *was* a dog . . .

Chapter Fifty-Three

'Reenie, do you know if anyone else has noticed that it's a three-tier casket?' Peter was sitting beside Reenie on a bale of hay in Ruffian's cool, shady factory stable, and was frowning at the photograph of the royal casket which the police had given to the factory manager. When the casket had been removed by the police from Mrs Garner's boarding house they had decided to take a photograph of it before it was sent for chemical analysis and give the photograph to the factory for identification. The good news for the police at the time had been that it was a unique casket and not something which would ever be sold in the usual line of business; however, the bad news had been that this had brought them no closer to uncovering the mystery of how the casket had reached Mrs Garner and the Major, or how it and the sweets had come to be covered with poison.

It had been difficult to look at when they were first offered the chance to see it by the policeman who asked them questions about their colleague and their work, because the sight of the photograph could only remind them of the Major and cause a jolt at the heart, but as time had gone on Reenie and Peter had become more and more determined to understand how the Major had got hold of them, and now they did little else when they were together but talk over possibilities. The Major had been in hospital for a week and a half, but it felt a great deal longer.

Reenie snatched the photo from his hand and scrutinized it. 'There's a tier missing! You're right – that's a three-tier casket with a tier missing!'

'I know, but have you heard anyone say that there's a tray of sweets missing from the poisoned box? Do the police know?'

Reenie couldn't remember even a suggestion that anyone thought there might be a tier missing. 'We can't be the first people to notice it, surely?'

'That wasn't what I was thinking; I was thinking of the recall. If the person who poisoned these sweets threw that top tier away, or abandoned it somewhere, or gave it to someone, it might have found its way to a shopkeeper. Someone might have taken it to a shop to get the money on the recall. Someone else could be poisoned!

'I think we need to go and visit some of the shops in Halifax, Reenie. I think we need to investigate and see if we can find out something that the police haven't. Perhaps even prevent another tragedy.'

'There's good news and there's bad news.' Mrs Wilkes threw a manila employment file across her desk to Diana Moore who had come in to take her morning dictation of correspondence and memos from her boss.

Diana maintained her composure. 'About time too. Are we getting to keep Mr Baum?'

'I'm afraid not; however, Mrs Starbeck is about to become less of a thorn in our side.' Amy Wilkes allowed herself the shadow of a smirk. 'I don't flatter myself that I have any large influence over Sir Harold, so when I have his ear I use it sparingly, but in this instance I decided that needs must. I suggested that a replacement needed to be found for the Major as a matter of urgency – and he has appointed his cousin, Mr Jed Sinclair, to the position. He'll be coming over from the Dublin factory just as soon as they can get a local man to replace him.'

'Well, that's a relief.'

'I thought you'd be pleased. There is of course the problem that he knows almost less about the science of Time and Motion than our friend Laurence Johns, but at least this gets Laurence off the hook and he can focus on running International Affairs.'

'Is that the bad news? We have a new head of department but he doesn't know anything about running his own department? It wouldn't be the first time it's happened here that I can remember. Laurence Johns isn't exactly a factory man either.'

'Oh no, I'm not worried about that. That department are all pretty sound, they'll manage their own work. Long-term strategy will falter while he finds his feet, and he'll need to be able to keep an eye on Starbeck and her feuds, but he has the telephone numbers for the secretaries of the Time and Motion managers at each of the other Mackintosh factories, so he can always arrange a call if he needs direction. And it's not forever – he's made it plain that he doesn't want a career with the family firm.

The main thing is that he's a Mackintosh, even if not in name, and Starbeck wouldn't dare cross a member of the old clan.'

'Then what's the bad news?'

'I might need to second you to him for a while when he arrives. I want eyes and ears in his office. You might not have as much time for your Spanish Refugee charity, because you'll be working for both of us.'

'That's fair enough, I can do that in my own time. Has there been any news about our other refugees?'

'Mr Baum? Yes, Sir Harold says he will personally pay the bond for all four of the Baums to apply for permits to live in England.'

'Well, that will save us having to find another confectioner.'

'Only if the papers are approved. Mr Baum has to be in Germany when he applies for the change of permit to the embassy. He has to go home first, apply, and then return with his children and his sister.'

'Should we be worried?' Diana read a lot of newspapers and she wasn't sure how much to believe about Germany; their present regime sounded too awful to imagine.

'Not yet.' Mrs Wilkes appeared to be trying to persuade herself. 'Not yet.'

Chapter Fifty-Four

'I don't have time to deal with this. Can you go?' Mrs Wilkes was clutching a pencil-scrawled internal memorandum which had just arrived with the messenger girl. 'I trust you to handle it as well as I would, although I haven't the first idea what we can do about it.'

Diana took the memo from her manager. It had been sent as an urgent communication from the north gate watchmen's cabin and it explained that the heavy hail had blocked the storm drains between two of the warehouses and a lake of rainwater was now forming between them, cutting off the north gate to pedestrians and cyclists and warning them that they would have a lot of late workers on the line because they were having to turn them away at the north gate and make them walk the full perimeter to the next entrance along.

'They lifted me up on the wall so's I could climb over the roof of the stables.' Olive, the messenger girl, stood proudly in her Mackintosh's postal department uniform, clutching her satchel of memoranda for delivery. 'They said I had to run and to leave all my other messages until after I'd delivered this one.'

Diana frowned. 'What's wrong with the telephone? They've got one in all the cabins.'

'They're flooded out of the cabin. The plumbers were already on a burst pipe job at the postal warehouse so they were just arriving when they sent me off with the message. They said you'll need to know that you'll have a lot of lines starting late this morning, and they'll riot if you try to dock their pay.'

Diana's hackles went up; this was exactly where she had left Bess Norcliffe, minding the postal warehouse, and combined with the news that she had been letting all and sundry do as they pleased with the very decorations she had been employed to police, she had a strong suspicion that Bess would have something to do with it. 'Did they say what they thought had caused the burst pipe?'

'It was nappies.'

Amy Wilkes and Diana exchanged surprised looks and Mrs Wilkes said, 'It was *what?*'

'They said it was nappies; you know, the cloths you wrap babies' bottoms in? The girl up there who's running the new crèche said that she'd been dangling the dirty ones in the lavatory and holding them there while she gave it a flush so the water would give them a bit of a clean off before she put them in the nappy bucket to soak, but she let go of one by accident and it went whoosh up the U-bend. She said she'd had some go that way before, but this was the first one that had caused bother. The plumbers said that all the waste water from her burst pipe is flooding the storm drain from the overflow below, and then you've got the hail blocking it all on top; it's biblical!'

Diana took in a restrained breath and asked, almost afraid of the answer before the words left her mouth, 'What is the name of this girl who is running the crèche?'

'Oh, I don't know, I'm afraid. I'm only on my second week here.' Betty the messenger girl had high hopes of graduating from the messenger pool to the typing pool, and thence to the secretarial pool.

'Can you remember what she looked like?'

'She looked a bit like a tiny Betty Boop, but with very fair hair and a little red mark on her cheek which might have been a birthmark, or it might have been rouge she hadn't rubbed in, I'm not that sure.'

'Bess Norcliffe! It would be.' Diana clenched her teeth; could anything else go wrong this day?

Amy Wilkes was of the same mind as her assistant. 'Not satisfied with burning the factory down, she now tries to flood it out. Can you take care of this, Diana? I don't think I can trust myself not to wring her neck.'

'I'm flattered you think I could manage not to do that myself.'

Diana had expected some hare-brained schemes from Reenie, but this was a level of incompetence and disobedience that even she could never have predicted. The bunting which Bess was supposed to have issued to the canteen had not been issued because she had knotted it into the shape of ragdolls and given it to toddlers to chew. The tablecloths were being used with some old chairs to form a den for children who looked to be close to school age, and a pile of souvenir copies of the company

335

magazine had been used as colouring-in pages by a child who had been let loose with a red pencil. There was ink and jam on every surface – and Bess was dancing a waltz in the centre of the room with a toddler on her hip. Three other girls in their early teens were feeding, herding, and entertaining children. Diana didn't recognize them, and was confident that she herself had not hired them for any job in the factory.

Diana rolled her eyes and said, 'Elizabeth Norcliffe, I want to know why this warehouse is full of babies.'

Bess shrugged. 'Isn't it obvious?'

'Please to God don't tell me one of them is yours.'

'Well, I only specifically asked for one of them – the others were just presents, really, when you look at it.'

Reenie burst through the door, out of breath and clutching a memo for Diana. 'I can explain!'

'I should have *known* you'd have something to do with this! Who do these children belong to?'

'Married women! I promise you they belong to married women! And one of them's Vicky Geall's baby who I said I'd find someone to mind, and if you remember you said it was up to Mrs Geall who she chose to look after her baby and it wasn't anything to do with you.'

'Reenie Calder, you beggar belief! You did not, at any point, even *suggest* that you might be leaving our confectioner's baby with the silliest girl in Halifax who – if you had forgotten – already had a job I wanted her to do. And who, pray tell, trusted Bess Norcliffe with these other children which have magically appeared?'

'They were all women who we needed to work on the line, but who couldn't work unless someone minded their bairns and they just all happened to mention it to me in passing and I told them to see Bess – just as a one-off – and then word got round, and you did tell me that we needed to do everything we could to get more workers, and you told Peter and me that the best thing we could do was buy milk tokens for Spain and—'

'Has Peter McKenzie been involved in all this?'

'He got the loan of the toys from the church hall, and—'

Diana held up a hand to signal that she'd heard enough; she realized in that moment that she had just reached the end of her tether. She could blame Reenie Calder for this as much as she liked, but she knew very well that she herself should have investigated the convenient childcare arrangements which Reenie had so vaguely proposed, and which she had suspected at the time were too good to be true. If there was going to be trouble, then it would be coming her way.

The door to the warehouse clattered open behind Diana and a mother with a new perambulator wheeled in a singing toddler. 'Is this the place where I can leave our Ted?'

'Yes, just park up there next to the others,' Bess answered cheerily, oblivious to the telling-off she had just received from Diana.

'You've got no idea how glad I am to be back,' the lady with the toddler said. 'We've all been that jealous of the mams with older kiddies who can come back to work to help, so when I heard you'd opened a crèche for the little ones I was back like a shot. I'm gonna' tell all the girls who used to work on my production line – we've all got kiddies the same age and I know they'd all come back if they thought there was a crèche.' The young mother paused in her effusive gratitude as she began to detect a coolness in the atmosphere of the room. 'Is it just you three then, running it?'

Bess was about to answer, but Diana got in first. 'Yes, just the three of us for the moment.'

'All right, all right, I can see that we need a crèche,' Diana said after the mother of little Ted had left to find her new workroom in the factory, 'but that doesn't mean you're forgiven for all of this, Reenie Calder.' Diana could see that the firm had a dilemma; they could not run the King's Toffee line without more workers, but there were plenty of skilled workers who would come back at short notice if they were running a crèche. Diana looked around her at the abandoned prams and sticky-fingered toddlers; it was an accident waiting to happen but there could be a solution to the problem here, though not under the unconcerned management of Bess Norcliffe and the three teenaged girls who had materialized from God knew where.

'Reenie, you have to stay here and supervise Bess until I get back.' Diana was already mentally planning how she would explain this all to her own manager. Sir Harold would love the idea, but if they were short of workers for the line it wasn't going to be any easier to find workers to run a crèche. 'Bess, don't flush any more terry cloths down the lavatory, don't take on any more babies than the ones you already have here – and whatever you do, don't take your eyes off them. You have got toddlers and they are the *worst* kind.'

Reenie waited until Diana was gone, and then dashed out behind her. Reenie was meant to be meeting Peter to divide the list of grocers' shops they planned to visit between them. As far as Reenie was concerned the children in the crèche were perfectly safe, but the grocers of Halifax might not be. Reenie and Peter had plans to carry out investigations of their own, and possibly prevent another tragedy. 'Bess, do you think you could do without me for a bit?' Reenie looked in the direction of Bess's eminently qualified-looking volunteers who had been recruited from among the babysitting pool of Bess's acquaintance.

'Of course.' Bess shrugged. 'What do you think could go wrong?'

Chapter Fifty-Five

Cynthia Starbeck had found the preceding fortnight to be the worst in her life. She had been forced, through financial and practical circumstances, to stay in a lodging house where her clothes were stolen and damaged by the very woman who slept beside her, and where she had no recourse in law to object. She lived in a kind of sickening terror at all times and it was with relief that she heard that a room had become available in a respectable boarding house in Halifax.

Cynthia had never thought she would sink so low as to live in Halifax, or even in a workers' boarding house, but after her experiences of the last few weeks, she was willing to accept almost any alternative. The new room would have considerable benefits; she would be close to the factory and wouldn't have to spend on train fare to and from Halifax each day; the room was a single one, and baths were permitted each day. She would even have her meals provided. The only problem was the cost, which was slightly higher than her present budget as so much of her income was swallowed by repayments on the loans her father had taken out in her name.

Cynthia Starbeck would find she had a lot of pride to swallow, but she was ready to do it in order to escape her current predicament. What was more distasteful was the money she would have to take from the Major's savings account. She assured herself again and again that once she was settled she would find a way to pay it back and make it appear that it had never happened. She was, after all, one of the Major's executors, and when the Major passed away she could take her time about executing his wishes so that no one would ever notice that the money was missing unless they went looking for it.

The office of the Credit Union was crowded that Saturday morning with factory girls who wanted to deposit part of their Friday wages as savings as quickly as they could, and mothers who needed to borrow to feed their families for the week because, once again, their husbands had drunk their pay packets before they'd reached home with them.

Cynthia Starbeck waited her turn to be seen and when she was called over by the manager made a show of looking pleased to see him. She stepped into his office – and that was when she realized that she would have to *sign* for the Major's money. Cynthia's heart skipped a beat, but she didn't show it. She proceeded with her plan as though there were nothing unusual about it in the world.

341

Chapter Fifty-Six

'And what did you think you were doing, visiting Mackintosh's customers with this fanciful scare story?' Mrs Starbeck's tiny diamond earrings glittered in the streak of lightning which blinked through the office window behind her and made Reenie jump. Reenie had been nervous enough when Mrs Starbeck had summoned her but the sudden loss of electric light through the factory corridors had given Reenie an ominous feeling that worse was to come.

'We just wanted to make sure that none of the shop-keepers got poisoned.' Reenie, in her naivety, still thought that if she just explained that her motives were pure, this whole misunderstanding could be politely resolved.

'We? Who is this we? Have you been doing this at more shops with other girls?' Mrs Starbeck's elegant nose wrinkled into a snarl that gave her face the look of a vicious dog.

Reenie hesitated; she didn't like to lie, but she also

342

realized that she needed to protect Peter; especially as he could now be their only chance to visit the other remaining shops. Reenie swallowed and prepared to make herself sound stupid. 'It was the royal we. Everyone calls me Queenie Reenie.'

There was a disgusted silence from Mrs Starbeck, and a silence laced with self-loathing from Reenie Calder; she had been told off by grown-ups many times in her life, and she had frequently answered back with tall stories or white lies, but this, Reenie thought to herself, was an all-time low point, even for her.

'If it were up to me I would have dismissed you a long time ago, and I certainly consider this to be a dismissal matter. However, as Mr Sinclair insists on handling all employment matters personally, I shall be referring this to him.'

Reenie held her breath and tried not to look as worried as she was. She knew only too well that if this was passed to Mr Sinclair it would also be passed to Diana and then she would get a right rollocking. 'Does this mean I can carry on until he has—'

'No, it most certainly does not. You are forbidden to speak to any more Mackintosh's customers. This nonsense about missing sweets ends here, do you understand?'

'But—'

'But me no buts, Reenie Calder! You cannot imagine the cost to the business of a recall of this nature; there isn't merely the financial cost but the immeasurable cost to the firm's reputation. It will take a great many years to rebuild, and your fictitious scare stories can only make it worse.'

'They aren't scare stories! Anyone can see that there's

a tray of sweets missing in the photograph! And we did it in our own time in the evenings, not company time, so it shouldn't have anything to do with—'

'Are you trying to tell me that you think you are more observant and more astute than every senior Mackintosh's employee who has looked at these photographs? Every Scotland Yard policeman? Every palace official with concerns for the safety of the King?'

Reenie's eyes stung with tears when she realized that this was *exactly* what she had thought, and that Mrs Starbeck had a valid point; of course the police would have realized if there was a tray of sweets missing. They had probably taken it away themselves to test in a laboratory somewhere. Reenie was being cut down to size and all of a sudden she felt that she deserved it. She had dragged Peter into trouble again and it was more serious than anything they had been up against before.

'I knew that you were conceited, Reenie Calder, but this is the limit.'

Reenie realized that she needed to find Peter and tell him to stop visiting the shops on their list; they had split up to cover more ground, but now she wished she'd kept him close.

Chapter Fifty-Seven

Diana stood beside the window in her manager's office, looking out on the main factory gates where scores of factory workers were arriving for the start of their shifts. Diana wondered how much longer those workers could expect to keep their jobs; if they didn't go to war then the factory might go under anyway, but if they did go to war the consequences would be so much worse. Only two months ago they had all been filled with hope as the business seemed to be entering an exciting new chapter: they were preparing for a visit from the King, they were launching a new sweet for Quality Street, and they were rebuilding their factory to be far better than it had been before. For Diana herself there had been heartache, but also the hope that she was giving her daughter a chance at a better life and a future where they could both be safe.

Now everything seemed to be collapsing around them; they had nearly lost the Major and might still do so, they had lost their workers, they had been forced to shut down the factory without electricity, they had been forced to bear the cost and workload of a recall, and worst of all there was still a possibility that they were responsible for the death of a woman through poisoning, and they had not yet established how, or made certain that it could not happen again.

'Just the girl I wanted to see!' Mrs Wilkes had returned from a meeting with Sir Harold. 'I have such good news. Major Fergusson's condition is improving. He has been able to speak a little, and his doctor is hopeful for him.'

Diana couldn't believe what she was hearing. 'Do you mean he might live?'

'Yes, there's real hope now. He's asking for Mrs Starbeck and I've been charged with getting the message to her, but apart from that all seems better.'

'Cynthia Starbeck? What does he want with her?'

'Heaven only knows. His doctors have informed Sir Harold that he is still too weak for any other visitors, but Mrs Starbeck's presence is requested.'

Diana hadn't dared to hope that they'd hear such wonderful news. It made her feel more optimistic about everything.

'Have you found out what the fuss was all about with the – what was it? – a crèche?'

'I found it, and it's partly my fault.' The news about the Major made Diana feel very slightly more inclined to take the blame for Reenie's actions. 'One of the girls had told me she'd found someone to mind Vicky Geall's baby, and I didn't ask enough questions. Bess Norcliffe has ended up minding half a dozen children while their mothers get back to work.'

'Have you shut the crèche down?'

'No.' Diana thought for a moment about how best to convey her own change of heart. 'We are desperate for workers, and there are skilled workers who are willing to come back to work for us, the only obstacle being someone to care for their children. I think if—'

'I think you're quite right.' Mrs Wilkes took Diana by surprise. 'Sir Harold would be delighted. How many more children can they take?'

'None at the moment. I'm not even sure Bess ought to be trusted with the ones she's got.'

'Very well, get in touch with Mrs Sanderson at the W. I. and see if she can drum up some volunteers to come and run a crèche. Maybe try your Mrs Hunter, too. She's always organizing charitable ventures and might have an idea. Leave no stone unturned, Diana. I want as many mothers in the factory as you can get me.'

Cynthia Starbeck made her way through the echoing, seemingly never-ending hospital corridors, her palms cold and clammy with panic. *What had she done? What had she done?* She had been so certain that the Major would die and that no one would ever know that she had taken his money, but now here she was taking slow and shaking steps through hallways that reeked of coal tar soap, invalid food, and the overbearing medicinal odour of TCP. She had heard that he was awake, and that he was asking for her, but what would she find?

She was afraid. Afraid of what she had done; afraid of being found out; afraid of confrontation and as yet unnamed consequences . . . but she was also afraid of what she would find. Would he look horrifying? Would he make demands of her as sick people do? Would he contaminate her with his spittle, or his touch, or his breath? Would she think herself lucky if she arrived and found that she was too late, and that he had not survived long enough for her to speak to him?

Cynthia Starbeck passed the door to the grand, gothic hospital chapel, trying not to meet the eye of the Victorian angel who looked down at her from stained glass. She slowed her steps; she had decided that the Major would not get his dying wish, that she would make sure that she arrived too late for him to see her.

'Are you lost, dearie?' A cheerful hospital porter pushing an empty bath chair came up behind Cynthia and tried to gauge whether she needed directions or sympathy.

'Ah, I think I might be.' Cynthia Starbeck didn't want to admit that she had been dawdling deliberately, but she did realize that if she asked directions to the wrong place she could kill some more time before arriving too late at the Major's bedside. She opened her mouth to ask directions to the admissions ward when the porter pointed at the note she was holding in her hand.

'You're off to E Ward. That's where I'm off to, so I'll take you there myself. Ward Sister's birthday there today and I know one of the staff nurses brought in a cake. Love a bit of cake, I do.'

The porter led Cynthia Starbeck to the nurses' station in the ward where she looked around in panic when one asked who she had come to visit. The porter pointed to the note in Cynthia's hand, which the nurse took from her in a kindly way; she was clearly used to visitors who were overwrought.

'Oh, Major Fergusson!' the staff nurse said to Cynthia

as she put down a patient chart beside an open biscuit tin. 'He hasn't been able to see any visitors because he's been so poorly, but he's doing really well now and Dr Waller is ever so pleased with him. Is he expecting you?'

Cynthia choked on her words. She didn't know what she had been trying to say, but whatever it was the words would not come out. The nurse led her to the far corner of the ward where a face she barely recognized smiled up at her from beneath layers of crisp, clean bed linen.

The Major was clean-shaven, and the loss of his large moustaches heightened the effect of the weight loss in his emaciated cheeks. His skin was grey, and around his eyes were tiny scarlet dots like measles. The nurses had wrapped him up to the neck in a dressing gown and kerchief, and his hair had evidently been combed for him because it went very slightly against his usual parting. He raised his eyebrows as though they might help to lift the corners of his mouth into a smile; he was weak, but he was definitely very much alive.

'Cynthia, my dear.' The Major's voice was a hoarse, reedy whisper. 'Do not distress yourself. I shall be quite well.' And with weak, shaking movements he very slightly reached out his hand to her. Cynthia Starbeck could not have failed to see the great effort he had put into that gesture, and she could not pretend to have missed it. She was now in the embarrassing position of having to hold his hand as she sat in the visitor's chair beside his bed.

'You asked . . .' Cynthia Starbeck's voice failed her for a moment as she realized that there was no doubt now that she would be found out. 'You asked to see me, Major.'

'You'll remember some years ago, when I was chair of

349

the fete committee, and you were treasurer, you kindly—'
The Major broke into a fit of racking coughing again,
then waited for it to subside, took two deep breaths, and
continued, 'you kindly agreed to be the executor of my
will. During this time there are certain of my bills which
must be paid on time, practical arrangements to be made
while I am indisposed . . . Would you, Cynthia, take over
my financial affairs until I can—' Another fit of coughing
bent the Major double and Cynthia panicked that she
was about to lose her only chance to come up with an
excuse for all the money she had taken from the Major's
account to pay her own rent and keep up her own style
of living. There was no way to cover it up now, only to
make excuses for it, and in her panic she blurted out the
first one which came into her mind.

'Oh Major, I'm so sorry, but there was a terrible misunderstanding. I believed you were already dead, had been
told categorically that you were already dead, and I
remembered, of course, that I was your executor and
I took steps immediately to take money from your account
and give it to the urgent appeal for child refugees in Spain
that you had been so emphatic in your support of. I am
so relieved that the news I heard was wrong and that
you are quite well – and I will pay the money back to
you from my own salary – but oh, Major, I was so
distressed by the thought that you were lost that I wanted
some good to come out of it.'

Cynthia Starbeck turned on her tears, sobbing loudly.
She knew her story was weak, thought how much simpler
this would all be if the Major had died, but there was
nothing she could do now except lie, and lie, and lie some
more.

Chapter Fifty-Eight

Mr Kirkby kept a jar of fresh coffee beans under the counter in his shop, and whenever a customer walked through the door he'd knock a couple onto the ornately decorated terracotta floor tiles and crush them slowly under the heel of his shoe to release the aroma just as the customer approached. It was a habit he'd learnt from his mother, who had claimed to have sold much more coffee that way.

A young man appeared at the door and Mr Kirkby's hand hesitated over the jar. Was this a customer or a salesman? He had a determined look about him, and he was carrying a worn leather satchel which might contain order forms, but any salesman who served Kirkby's tended to bring a suitcase with dummy products. He wore a nice suit of clothes, but he was not so smart as the Hunter lad who came into the shop with his little sisters, nor so rough as the labouring classes who tended not to use Kirkby's Fancy Goods as often as Mr Kirkby would have liked them to.

Mr Kirkby decided to hazard a guess and throw down some coffee beans and welcome the golden-haired young man with a genuine smile. It was a quiet afternoon and he had all the time in the world. 'Good afternoon, sir. And what can we do for you today?'

The young man pulled out a visiting card which identified him as a Mackintosh's employee.

'You're the new salesman? I'd wondered when we'd be seeing you. Mr Carstaff emigrated to Canada, didn't he? Any word of him? I do hope he's doing well. We've been sending in our orders at the end of each week, but I've not seen one of your men in months.' Mr Kirkby wasn't complaining; on the contrary he was delighted to meet his new Mackintosh's man.

'I'm sorry, Mr Kirkby, I'm not your new salesman. My name is Peter McKenzie and I'm here because I need your help with a Mackintosh's matter which is very urgent. Is there somewhere we could speak privately?'

Mr Kirkby looked surprised, then said, 'Of course, of course. Marilyn, you take over the counter while I show Mr Mckenzie into the back.'

Pretty Marilyn Parkin walked rapidly to her place at the counter, crushing tiny pieces of coffee beans underfoot as she went.

The back of the shop was dark, cool, and crowded with newly arrived stock in fresh pine crates. Mr Kirkby led Peter to a little parlour where there was a rough table and a handful of chairs. A deep blue willow pattern teapot and teacups sat on the tabletop, remnants of the family's earlier break.

Mr Kirkby offered Peter a chair and took one himself.

'Is it connected to the recall? I can assure you we sent everything back and we've been very vigilant.'

Peter opened the satchel on the table to pull out a selection of five photographs; one was the photograph the police had given to the factory of the casket which had nearly poisoned Mrs Garner and the Major, and the others were caskets which were available through the Mackintosh's catalogue. There was a chance that if he only showed the man one photograph he might say that he remembered the casket when in fact he just remembered seeing one very like it. Peter had to be sure.

'Do you recognize any of these caskets?' Peter did not expect the reaction he got.

Mr Kirkby fell back, white-faced, his hand to his mouth. 'Dear God!' His eyes were locked on the photograph of the King's casket.

Peter gently pushed the photograph towards Mr Kirkby. 'Tell me where you've seen this casket, Mr Kirkby.'

'Is this what caused the recall? Is this what everyone has been looking for?' The urgency and fear in Mr Kirkby's voice made him sound breathless, and he reached forward to pick up the photograph of the casket of sweets which he had so carefully poisoned all those weeks ago. 'This can't be! It can't be! I destroyed it! I know that I destroyed it!'

Peter felt a rush of excitement. 'Tell me where you've seen this casket, Mr Kirkby. I'm not a policeman, I just need to know where the tainted sweets came from.' Peter was gentle with the man who was quite obviously frightened.

'This is the casket Mr Carstaff gave me to put in the window before he left for Canada. This is the casket I destroyed. I put it in a rubbish sack when I was clearing out the old window display, and all the rubbish sacks were taken by the binmen.'

'Can you be certain that this is the same casket, Mr Kirkby?' Peter looked at him with well-meaning concern. 'Is it possible that this is one that simply looks similar?'

'No, no, it's not possible.'

'How can you be so certain?'

'Look at the photograph. You see that loose strand of silk cord hanging from the centre of the lid? There was a silken tassel there which I cut off before I threw the casket away. So this photograph was taken *after* I threw it away.'

'And you're certain you're not remembering a different casket with a tassel? You could have cut one from a different casket.' Peter offered the lifeline, but Mr Kirkby shook his head and produced from his pocket the shop keys, which were held together with a steel loop, decorated with a silken tassel.

Tears filled Mr Kirkby's eyes. 'I know that those are the sweets I painted with poison. And I can see that there are a great many missing . . .'

Cynthia Starbeck knew that she only had two options, and one of them – the course of total honesty – was unthinkably galling to her. She knew all she could do now was attempt to cover her tracks as best she could. She wished that she had been better prepared for her meeting with the Major and had taken the time to come up with a far more plausible lie. One of her biggest regrets, bigger even than having borrowed his money in the first place (and she had convinced herself that she only meant to borrow it), was that she had allowed herself to blurt out a flimsy falsehood in the panic of the moment that placed her in more difficulties than she had been in to start with. Now she had to find a way to make it look like she had made the donation to the Spanish refugee fund, just like she had told the Major she had.

Selling her pendant had been the only way out. She had taken it to a pawnbroker but the sum she could raise against it as a loan was not nearly as much as she had thought it would be. Selling it outright to a jeweller beside the Borough Market, along with all her earrings, her dress watch, and her mother's pearls was the only way she was able to raise the amount she had taken from the Major's account.

If it were a matter of putting the money back where she had taken it from she would have done it, but it was not that simple. The Major's saving's book had a written and stamped record from the credit union which would show clearly that she had withdrawn cash. If she wanted to return it the record would show the date of its return and she would be forced to explain why she had taken that specific sum and then returned it. There was always the option to admit what she had done, explain that she had used the money to pay for her rent in a new lodging house after she had left an unsatisfactory one without giving enough notice to reclaim her bond, and beg forgiveness, but that would mean admitting to a weakness on her own part which was too abhorrent to contemplate – she would far rather be thought a muddle-headed fool who had tried to help a charitable cause rather than a morally weak character.

Cynthia's plan was simple: she would to go into Diana

Moore's office when she was not there, put the cash into her cashbox, alter the record of her donation in the ledger so that it looked as though she had donated a larger sum, and then slip away unnoticed. Except Diana Moore did not leave her cashbox unattended or unlocked because she was not a fool. Cynthia Starbeck knew that she would need an accomplice, and she knew that there was only one person she could use. Dolly Dunkley . . .

'Verity, my dear.' Mrs Starbeck had deliberately chosen to invite Dolly Dunkley to see her in her office at just the time of day when she knew the tea lady would be passing her door with the trolley. Strategically, Mrs Starbeck had thought that offering the girl a cup of tea while they talked would almost certainly act as a short cut to intimacy in their conversation. However, when Dolly had arrived and Cynthia Starbeck had offered to buy her anything she liked from the tea trolley, she hadn't expected Dolly to plump for the largest iced currant bun they had, and to then insist that she didn't mind eating it without a tea plate. Cynthia watched with carefully concealed disgust as her potential accessory to crime sat in the velvety forest green upholstered chair opposite her desk, and dusted sticky, fatty crumbs over every nearby surface, while spilling the tea she slurped loudly into her saucer.

Cynthia Starbeck had thought over her predicament carefully and she knew that if she manipulated this girl into acting as her accomplice she would have to keep her close from now on to guard against her giving the game away to anyone else. However, the thought that she would be bound to this girl for good or ill, possibly for a very long time, was repugnant to her. Cynthia

Starbeck operated on a guiding principle which she had never fully explored, but which floated murkily in her consciousness at all times: it was the idea that when Oswald Moseley finally rose to power in Britain everything would be 'sorted out' and this was an influencing factor in her decision to plough forward with her plan of deceit: she was going to tell some small lies, but once the British Union were in power, they would make everything all better.

'It's Dolly. Everyone calls me Dolly.' Dolly said it through a mouthful of doughy currant bun.

'Oh, but Verity is such a lovely name, and really, if you have ambitions to become a junior manager – you do still want to become a manager here, don't you?'

'That's what I've been telling everyone! I was always meant to be a manager. I was never meant to be a cleaner.' As Dolly said this Mrs Starbeck noticed a fleck of Dolly's spittle and icing sugar land on her skirt.

'I quite understand your frustration.' Mrs Starbeck put on all her best efforts to charm. 'I shall definitely talk to Major Fergusson about offering you a position within our department, but he is still very ill at present, so I need you to be patient a little longer. You can be patient for a sick man, can't you, Verity?'

Dolly sighed with a loud harrumph. 'I suppose so. If he doesn't take too long about it.'

'I promise you that all your sacrifices will be worth it in the end. You know, until you *are* promoted to manager, I think there is something which I could do for you – how would you like to be part of the welcome party for King George?' Dolly's face filled with excited glee and Cynthia Starbeck smiled; she had Dolly hook, line, and sinker. 'I know you've been working ever so hard in the confectioner's kitchens, and that is a hugely important contribution towards the work they've been doing. I believe you have been just as instrumental in making the casket's contents as Mary Norcliffe, and I thought I might arrange for you to present the casket to the King with Mary. How does that sound?'

'Oh yes!' Dolly nearly dropped her iced bun. 'I definitely think that when you look at it like that I did help to make the casket for their majesties—'

Cynthia didn't let Dolly continue; time was of the essence. 'Now Dolly, I can trust you, can't I?' Dolly nodded. 'I thought as much. I know you're a dedicated member of the British Union – I've seen you at meetings – and I know that we're of the same mind about some of the rather liberal things that have been happening at the factory lately.' Mrs Starbeck decided not to ask for a favour, but to make it sound as though she were offering one to Dolly. 'I have an opportunity for you to start doing some things to help the British Union with their work. You want to help the British Union, don't you? You'll have heard that Diana Moore has been collecting money for those Spanish children who have been bombarding our ports? Well, I need to get a look at the ledger to see exactly who has been donating to this Communist fund so that we can keep an eye on them, so I need you to keep Diana busy while I look through the ledger on her desk for a few minutes. Do you think you can do that for me? I knew I could count on you,' she said when Dolly nodded her head eagerly. 'But you know that the work that you and I do for the British Union must remain very secret – our country depends on us.'

Dolly nodded again, delighted at the thought of under-mining one of the managers she disliked while at the same time ingratiating herself to the more sophisticated members of her new favourite club.

Chapter Fifty-Nine

'We wanted to thank you for looking after us.' Gracie
and Lara proffered their carefully wrapped handkerchief
parcel of travel-worn sweets to Bess Norcliffe. 'We had
a whole box full, but we saved these.'

After the call to arms had gone out among the women
of the W. I., several had offered their services in the
Mackintosh's crèche and Mrs Hunter had volunteered
the services of her family's new nanny and their new
governess, insisting that Gracie and Lara could go along
to the factory crèche for a few days to meet some other
children and have a change of environment. This was
how the two little girls had come to be under the watchful
care of Bess Norcliffe and offering her a tray of poisoned
confections.

Bess knelt down to accept the gift with all the grace
of a queen receiving tribute. 'These are lovely! I shall
enjoy them with my afternoon cuppa. Do you mind if I
share one with my friend the tea lady when she brings

her trolley? She has to make a bit of a detour to come out to the warehouses and she's always glad of a sit down and a natter in here.' Bess thought it good manners to ask permission – she had a philosophy of deferring to children when one was put in charge of them; it seemed to make them much more amiable companions.

Gracie and Lara conferred before Gracie said, 'We don't mind if you share them.'

Bess was about to ask them about the rest of the box and where they had got them from, but a toddler had fallen and she needed to see to him. Bess hastily folded the handkerchief back over the tray of sweets, putting them on her table next to the telephone receiver, and an hour later Mrs Parkin trundled round to the makeshift crèche with her tea trolley to have a break of her own. She liked Bess Norcliffe who was always welcoming and warm.

'My goodness, am I glad to see you!' Bess was rubbing the back of an unhappy baby who was resting its head on Bess's shoulder and being sick down the back of her wool cardigan. 'I'm gasping for a tea. Come and sit yourself down . . . no, you take the chair beside the telephone, I won't sit down until this little chap settles a bit. He's had rather an exciting day with all the toys and other children to play with, haven't you, poppet?'

Mrs Parkin poured scalding hot water from the urn and brewed up a pot of tea. As she laid out the cups and saucers along the edge of the table Bess could see that the hastily wrapped handkerchief parcel had caught her eye. The sweets, which could be glimpsed through the gaps, were stunningly beautiful and had a pristine sheen that seemed undiminished from so much carrying around.

'Well, those are fancy!' Mrs Parkin leant over to lift the corner of the handkerchief to reveal more of the lacework-piped confections beneath. 'Did your sister make you these?'

'No, no, these won't be hers; everything she makes is bright purple, she's shown me.' Bess's dreamy voice was tinged with uncertainty. 'But I don't think we should touch them – they don't look like normal sweets to me. I think we should wait until Reenie has been down here with Mrs Geall the confectioner and then she can take a look at them.'

Mrs Parkin liked Bess, but she didn't think it was beyond the realms of probability that she was too dim to have noticed that the famously blind confectioner could not take a look at these sweets. 'What do you want Mrs Geall to take a look at them for, love?'

'I don't want Mrs Geall to look at them, I want to show them to my friend Reenie; she knows everything. I've got this funny feeling that they've come out of a bin. The little Hunter girls over there, they gave them to me wrapped in this big handkerchief and they said they'd come from a bigger box of chocolates and these were left over – but look at all the smudges on the handkerchief; it's filthy dirty.'

'But the Hunter family are very well-to-do – surely their mother wouldn't let them take things out of bins.'

'You'd be amazed what little ones can get up to; well, you'll know yourself, won't you?'

Yes indeed, Mrs Parkin remembered one of her children trying to eat a beetle in the garden many years ago and taking great offence at being told not to eat insects.

'I make a rule to never eat anything a little one has given me until I know *precisely* where it has come from.

Little ones are angels in disguise – but you do need to watch them with food and animals.'

'I suppose you're right.' Mrs Parkin wasn't that fussy, but the dirty handkerchief the sweets were wrapped in did not look very appealing. 'Well, if they turn out to be all right you'll save me one, won't you?'

'Of course I will; I'll save you as many as you like because we've got a whole tray load.' Bess pulled back the cloth to reveal the satin-covered tray with long ribbons on either end for lifting in and out of the casket. On the side it was emblazoned with a lion and a unicorn in gold and Mrs Parkin began to feel suspicious of the confections herself.

'I tell you what, I'm taking the tea trolley over in the direction of the Time and Motion Office; I'll let Reenie Calder know you're after her. They're all that busy over there getting ready for the royal visit day after tomorrow that they probably wouldn't pick up the telephone even if you had time to wait for a call to be put through. You leave it to me, I'll get the message across.'

'Oh would you, Mrs Parkin? You're a saint!'

Diana Moore could not believe her eyes; there on the counter in front of her in Lister Horsfall's jewellers was the gold pendant she had so frequently seen around Mrs Starbeck's neck. Diana was not in the habit of entering jewellers' shops, let alone dropping everything at the office to race across to the Borough Market to inspect their contents, but on this occasion she had felt compelled to do so. Among the correspondence in the eleven o'clock post had been a routine reference request from the owner of one of Halifax's most trusted family businesses. In her position as a junior manager in the Women's Employment Department she often had to reply to reference requests from prospective landlords, or bank managers signing up an employee for their first current account. It had been with growing interest that Diana had seen the trail of correspondence trickle in for Mrs Starbeck, and it had not told the story she had expected it to. Diana would have anticipated that the woman would be well-established in her expensive flat in Hipperholme and would want for nothing, but this did not appear to be so. At first there was a request from the County Court for details of her salary so that they could calculate affordable repayments on an outstanding loan; this happened occasionally with Mackintosh's employees, and Diana sent an answer in confidence and filed away the request. Next there was a request for a reference from a landlady, who shortly afterwards wrote to complain that Mrs Starbeck had left without giving notice and that she wanted it known that she wouldn't be getting her bond back. A little later a lodging house in Halifax wanted to know if they could confirm that Cynthia Starbeck was in their employ, and at around the same time a credit union asked for the same confirmation. This latest development was the most unexpected; Mr Horsfall from the jewellers had already parted with his money, but something had been nagging at him, and before he sold the jewels he had bought from the respectable-looking lady he wanted to check that she was who she had said she was, and so he had written to her employer for confirmation.

'I wasn't expecting anyone to come around in person.' Mr Horsfall looked startled when Diana proffered his letter. 'There's no law against selling one's own jewellery,

I just wanted to verify that the lady was who she said she was.'

'Yes,' Diana said, 'she is one of our employees. I recognize some of these; they were hers.' This did not appear to put the jeweller's mind at rest very much, but that wasn't why Diana was there. 'How much are you selling this one for? Can I buy it back?' Diana pointed to the unmistakable heirloom; the gold pendant.

Mr Horsfall perhaps assumed that the young lady intended to return the item to its original owner, so he did not inflate the price very much, 'Fifteen guineas for that one. It's one of a kind, you know, a genuine antique.'

'Yes, I know.' Diana thought about the money sitting uselessly in her building society account, growing by the day as she continued to live as simply as she had when she had been poor and struggling to raise her daughter. 'I'll take it,' she said.

It was all Reenie could do to keep herself from shaking Bess. Bess had been looking at these things for hours on her desk and she hadn't called on anyone to let them know.

'But you know what these are, don't you?' Reenie was fuming.

'Well, I can't say I've seen them before, but I am almost certain that Mary didn't make them. I'd know them if Mary made them. I just felt a bit iffy about them, really, because they didn't look like proper sweets.'

'Iffy? Iffy! Oh, you total doyle! These are the sweets everyone's been searching for which were missing from the casket which poisoned Mrs Garner to death!'

'Well, I didn't think *I* was meant to keep an eye out

for those sweets – I thought someone else would find them. Does that mean that these ones are poisoned?'

'Yes, very probably. You didn't touch them, did you?'

Bess looked thoughtful for a moment, although the level to which she could be said to be thinking at any time was doubtful. 'I didn't touch them, but I have felt very weak all afternoon.' Bess adopted an air of melo-dramatic invalidity and staggered back to her chair, which she sank into with a sigh. 'I suppose I will have to go back to the hospital where the handsome doctors were. It will be terribly sad if I am poisoned, but I will try to bear it with dignity.'

'Oh give over, we don't have time for all that. Where did you get them from? Who's been paying you courting calls in here?'

'No one. Diana's little sister gave them to me.' Bess pointed to two little girls sitting below the window arranging a dolls' tea party with great interest. 'She brought it to me wrapped in a handkerchief.'

Reenie's face turned pale as she remembered the night her landlady and the Major had been poisoned; the little girls had been at the boarding house that afternoon – what if the Major hadn't brought the casket with him? What if Mrs Garner had offered them to the Major and he had eaten one? 'Have you talked to them about it?' Reenie asked Bess urgently. 'Have you asked them where they got them?'

'Well, I started asking, but then I got interrupted. Do you think it's important?'

'Yes, Bess, it's important. It's life and death.' Reenie walked over to where the little girls were sitting cross-legged on the floor, feeding their dolls imaginary cake.

She was painfully aware that she did not have a gift for speaking to children and she tried to conceal her own emotion so as not to frighten them into clamming up. 'Hello. You're Gracie, aren't you? I know your sister. Is that your doll?'

Bess sighed sadly for Reenie's incompetence with children and sat herself down on the floor beside Gracie and Lara and tucked her feet under her skirt. 'Hello, my little darlings,' she said lovingly. 'Aren't you absolute peaches to be giving your dollies such a gorgeous feast of a tea party? They look like they're having a lovely time. Are you two having a lovely time?'

Lara looked worried by the manic expression on Reenie's face, but Gracie was in a chatty mood and offered Bess some imaginary cake and told her that they had four different kinds of sandwiches on their tiny empty plates.

Bess pretended to eat a cucumber sandwich and then said, rubbing her tummy, 'Gosh, that was lovely. Do you think I've eaten enough sandwiches to have one of your lovely sweets for dessert, do you? They look lovely and I bet I can guess where you got them from.' Bess play-acted great thought. 'I bet you got them from . . .' Here she paused for dramatic effect and then burst out, 'The butcher's shop!'

Lara and Gracie both giggled. 'No, silly, you don't get sweets from a butcher's shop!'

Bess play-acted thinking of another guess. 'I bet you got them from . . .' Another dramatic pause, which the little girls enjoyed all the more because they were getting the hang of the game. 'The candlemaker's shop!'

Lara and Gracie became nearly insensible with laughter and shook their heads.

'Well, I'm all out of guesses,' said Bess. 'You win, you tell me where it was.'

Gracie said, gasping with laughter, 'We got them from Kirkby's Fancy Goods with our pocket money!'

And with that Reenie ran to the telephone, hoping she could find Diana before she had to telephone the police.

Chapter Sixty

Diana was desperately trying to resist the urge to race up the stairs to Gracie's bedroom, clutch her daughter to her and never let her go. Instead Diana was sitting as impassively as she could manage to appear in the drawing room of the Hunter family home as people around her talked over one another and fretted about the danger that the children had been in all this time.

'But why was the shopkeeper poisoning his sweets in the first place?' Mr Hunter was angrier than any of his family had ever seen him. He had returned home early from a business trip when his wife had telegrammed to tell him that a police inspector was at the house asking questions about how their youngest daughters had come to be in possession of cyanide. 'Surely there are laws against this sort of thing!'

'I honestly don't know how they got hold of them,' Steven Hunter, the eldest son and the young man who had been looking after the little girls on the day they went into the shop and picked up the poisoned sweets was beside himself with remorse. 'Truly, I was with them all the time and if I turned my back it was only—' His voice broke and he burst into despairing sobs; the teenage lad so close to man's estate was reduced to boyhood again.

'No one blames you, darling.' Mrs Hunter placed a gentle hand on her son's shoulder, but it shook a little with emotion, 'No one blames you. You couldn't have known.'

As the Hunter family, their nanny, their governess, their cook, and the police inspector all turned over the events that had led to the terrible accident, Diana decided she couldn't stay away from her daughter any longer. She had not seen her at all since the discovery of the last remaining poisoned sweets and every moment was anguish. When the poison had been discovered Reenie had telephoned Diana straight away, but to Diana's enduring regret she had not been at her desk; she had been in Lister Horsfall's jeweller's shop buying the gold Starbeck family pendant which she could only afford because her personal finances had improved so dramatically as a direct result of giving up her daughter six months earlier. Instead of being the first to see her daughter, she was the last. The little girls had been hurried away to the police station with their new nanny and new governess, and surrounded by strangers and strangeness until Mrs Hunter could return from one of her committee meetings and insist that any questions were answered at home, and with her husband present.

It seemed that the questions were all for the adults and not for the little girls themselves. Diana had been summoned, but from what she could gather she had been summoned as Gracie's sister during a time of family trial, and not to answer many questions herself. A police inspector was explaining which of them would be called to give evidence

As she watched the Hunter family become caught up in a knotty and emotional post-mortem she took the opportunity to quietly slip away and go in search of Gracie.

'I think if we give them something to scratch they won't climb up the curtain.' Gracie was sitting on the rug in the centre of the bedroom she shared with Lara, holding out a stick from the garden to a sooty black kitten, while Lara tried to disentangle her kitten from her cardigan pocket. Gracie looked up quickly as Diana put her head around the bedroom door, but instead of her usual enthusiasm, Diana saw fear in her daughter's eyes. 'Didi, are we in trouble?'

Diana fell to her knees beside her secret daughter and held her close, 'Of course you're not, my good girl, why would you be in trouble?' Diana put her arm around Lara who had run to her for reassurance. 'Some bad things have happened, but you're not to blame. You weren't to know.'

Gracie clutched Diana tight, 'We had to go to the police station and I wished you'd been there.'

'I promise,' Diana said, 'that you will see much, much more of me from now on. I'll be here at the house whenever I can. Nothing will keep me away from you again.'

Chapter Sixty-One

Dolly had worked herself up into a frenzy of self-righteous indignation at having been excluded from making the final casket of toffees for His Majesty, the presentation of which was just a day away. In her own eyes she had contributed more talent than anyone else to this project and it would never have occurred to her that she was lucky to have been given so many second chances, and that if the factory had not been under such strain she would have been dismissed long ago.

Instead of thinking on how lucky she was, Dolly had been lying awake thinking over all the ways that it was unfair that she was not more involved in the preparations for the royal visit, and rehearsing speeches to Diana Moore and that nasty German in the confectionery kitchen, telling them that she would leave them. *Then* they would realize how much work she had been doing for them, and be sorry that they hadn't worked harder to keep her. In the small hours of the morning, as the fresh summer air was waking the birds in their nests outside the vicarage to call for the dawn, Dolly Dunkley suddenly realized that there was a way that she could fight back against all the people who she perceived as having stolen away her rightful place in the factory.

Everyone knew there had been a huge recall because there was a risk that some of their sweets might have come into contact with a contaminant. What if some *more* sweets were contaminated? She could go into the kitchens when the other staff were out – she didn't need a key because Mary had broken hers in the lock and still hadn't got it mended – and she could spoil the special toffees.

Dolly lay in her large, comfortable bed. The household servants would soon arrive for the day and begin clattering around with pails of water for the family's morning ablutions; with Dolly's work overalls which were washed and hung out to dry by the char twice a week; with garden trugs to gather vegetables. Dolly decided that she would make it appear that Mary had spoilt her own work by leaving a window open and allowing the breeze to blow the contents of the royal casket onto the floor. Mary was always the last to finish work in the evening and she shut up the room behind her; she also had a habit of working with the window open during hot weather. If Dolly stayed behind after everyone else had gone – she could hide in the lavatories – she could knock all of the sweets onto the floor, then leave, arriving in the morning just in time to see Mary being blamed for carelessness. It would serve her right for all the times she had shown Dolly up and put herself forward. For the first time in months Dolly was up and out of bed before her step-mother could wake her; she would make her move that very evening.

Dolly's cold, clammy hands trembled as she turned the door handle and scurried inside the deserted confectioner's kitchen. She had waited all day for her chance and now finally all the confectioners had gone home for the evening. Faced with an empty room, Dolly closed the door carefully behind her and breathed a sigh of relief, a little light-headed at how well her plan was progressing. There, on the centre of their tasting table, were two thick card boxes, and Dolly knew exactly what they contained.

As she lifted the lid on the first of the two boxes it shuffled off with a scratching sigh, revealing a casket fit for a king. It was covered with watered silk in a champagne cream, and elegant little brass feet in the shape of lion's paws lifted it a quarter of an inch at each corner of the base. Caskets were usually trimmed with ribbons or lace-work, but this one had a band of tiny, hand-carved roses in a pale, soft wood. It was a fussy design for the age of Deco, but the quality of the craftsmanship was so exquisite that it would have outshone any more *à la mode* design.

Dolly unfastened the little metal clasp, also shaped like a lion's paw, and lifted the heavy lid. It was empty. The casket lining of rose-pink Japanese paper, lightly embossed with the Mackintosh's coat of arms, lay awaiting the treasure that Vicky and Mary had worked so hard to invent, craft, and refine. Dolly knew that she had to leave that box untouched; her plan was to make it appear as though the box of sweets had been left precariously close to the edge of a work bench beside an open window and had been knocked to the floor by a stiff breeze in the night.

Dolly took a deep breath. Her heart was beating faster now. She had felt excluded from this project for so long, and before she carried the box to the window to upend its contents it was tempting to open it and see the sweets she had longed to see when they were first made. With growing anticipation Dolly lifted the lid of the second, larger box. There before her was the top layer of a box filled with handmade sweets of the finest quality – and it was like seeing pirate gold. The glistening medallions of buttercup yellow toffees, the pink bonbons like fairies' kisses; and the specially invented King's Toffee, which had the look of a violet sapphire glistening in the box. It was the one sweet which Dolly had not been allowed to see, not been allowed to taste. She realized that if she knocked the sweets to the floor and let them scatter under the bench no one would be likely to notice if one toffee was missing . . . So she could take just that one and leave the others; she would still have made sure that Mary's sweets did not reach the King and that she had got her own back on all the people at Mackintosh's who had cruelly frustrated her ambitions. In Dolly's mind justice would be done; why shouldn't she also taste one toffee? Or perhaps more than one . . .?

It all happened before Dolly had time to realize what she was doing; she pulled open heavy wooden drawers until she found a thick paper sack, and then, with quick, trembling hands she began stealing sticky fistfuls of the sweets intended for the King.

Dolly Dunkley had not taken all of the King's sweets. She didn't need to take all of them in order to spoil the whole. Those which she left behind in her haste were scattered, smudged, ruined, and littered the floor below the window as she had planned.

Dolly had bundled as many as she could into her paper sack and scampered away like a bad fairy. This had not been part of her plan for the day, and so, looking for a quiet, hidden place she hurried through echoing corridors, down dark stairwells she didn't know, and then through a tatty little door which led her out into a courtyard. She was in the factory stables section and, as luck would have it, she was a long way back among the old stables which were rarely used, a quiet corner where she might sit unobserved on a bale of clean straw and enjoy her booty. There seemed a pleasing justice to Dolly in the idea that she would eat the sweets she had been denied, in the clubhouse that she had been kept out of by Reenie Calder and her nasty friends. Dolly didn't know what they saw in the place anyway, it was smelly and frightfully low, but for her purposes it would do. She lifted the latch on the rickety old door and slipped into the stable. The lone, ancient, knock-kneed and peculiarly ugly horse whinnied in irritation at being disturbed by anyone other than his mistress.

Dolly crouched down on the corner bale and opened up the paper sack. The sweet, earthy smells of the stable were overpowered by violet toffee, nut and butter caramels, and a tang of fruit creams. Dolly was not a connoisseur. Instead of tasting the sweets one at a time and really thinking about their flavour, texture, and melt, she grabbed three at once and forced them all into her mouth together with the flat of her palm and tried to swallow them, barely chewed, before repeating the disgusting spectacle for the benefit of the watching horse.

The horse stamped his hoof and gave a very pointed

snort. It was clear to the horse that this disgustingly greedy girl had not only insulted him by intruding upon his stable, but had also failed to introduce herself to him formally, or offer him any of the sugary things in her paper bag. He shuffled closer and Dolly climbed up onto one of the hay bales and looked over the partition into the next empty stable and wondered if she should climb into that one to scoff her sweets uninterrupted. But the problem with the next stall was that although it was full of old saddles it offered nowhere to sit, and she supposed she was better in this one with the smelly horse.

Dolly continued to wolf down her stolen sweets as she leant on the partition and looked down on the mess of old riding things stored below. She was eating the sweets far too hurriedly and was struggling to swallow them all down when a disk of King's Toffee lodged in her gullet. Dolly was trying to cough it up, but she couldn't take a breath in let alone cough the sweet out. Her face was turning a dark red as she strained for breath, then all of a sudden she felt a hard shove against her left buttock which caused her to fall forward and land with a jolt, stomach first, on a pile of horse tackle in the next-door stall. The force of the landing winded her, and the King's Toffee came shooting out of her mouth like a missile. She had been saved from choking to death on a stolen toffee by an undignified head butt in the bum. Ruffian was the master of the well-timed head butt, and on this occasion he had excelled himself.

It was late in the evening and Mr Baum had returned to the confectioner's kitchen to retrieve his watch. He was very methodical about taking it off before he started work, and laying it out beside the telephone on the desk he shared with Victoria Geall. That evening he had been preoccupied with thoughts of his children, his imminent return to Dusseldorf, and the assistant who he did not want to leave behind. He walked past their worktable in the twilight and did not notice that their work was in disarray. He retrieved his watch from the table, folded the leather strap around his wrist, and wondered if there was another way to get his children to England. The applications for permits were not simple, and even if one completed everything correctly there were many inexplicable obstacles which were designed to stem the flow of desperate Jewish people who wanted to escape to safety from a country ruled by Nazi fascists. Mr Baum had thought about going into hiding and overstaying his permit in England – but he couldn't bear to stay when he knew his children were not safe and there was very little hope of getting them out of Germany. Also, the risk of capture and prosecution by the British was too high. The papers were full of cases of Jewish workers who had overstayed their permits and been given hard labour.

Albert Baum was thinking over his impossible situation when his foot caught on something sticky on the floor. The room was not yet dark, but the sun had moved round sufficiently in the sky to leave the kitchen in a gloom. Mr Baum looked first at his shoe and then at the scattered sweets across the floor, and then at the boxes which had been opened and raided.

'Gott im Himmel!' Mr Baum said aloud as he looked around to see if there was any trace of the culprit. They expected the King to visit them in twelve hours – and it would take twenty hours to remake the chocolates.

*

378

'Are there any you can salvage?' Mrs Wilkes asked as her knuckles turned white with the ferocity of her grip on her teacup. She and Diana Moore had been working late on preparations for the following morning's visit, and Mr Baum had been lucky to find them there.

'Not one,' Mr Baum said. 'And I wouldn't risk it if I could. We don't know if they have been contaminated as the others were.'

'Mr Baum,' Amy asked, 'if you were to work through the night could you make replacements for the chocolates which have been destroyed?'

'Not in the time we have. We could make one type of fruit creme, perhaps, but there is no time to make the others and let them cool. We have only one choice I can see: we have to remake the King's Toffee tonight and fill the casket with them alone. There is nothing else to be done.'

'What will you need?'

'I will ask Mary and Vicky to return immediately to the kitchens, and you have another toffee confectioner up your sleeve, I think, someone who has volunteered to assist in the past. It is time to tell Sir Harold to put his apron on.'

Chapter Sixty-Two

By nine o'clock that night Mr Baum and Mary had managed to completely clean the confectioner's kitchen, fetch fresh ingredients from the factory stores and begin heating a new batch of toffee under careful instruction from Victoria Geall who had received assurances that her extra toffee-making assistant was on his way – but she had chosen not to tell Mary who he was in case she worried even more about what they needed to achieve that night.

'Sir Harold!' Mary gasped as she watched him march into the confectioner's kitchen, pick up an apron, and begin scrubbing his hands at the sink, ready for work. Mary had been worried before about making a mistake – now she was terrified; if Sir Harold was going to watch her at work then she would go to pieces. 'I didn't expect—'

'For tonight, my dear, you must call me Harry.' Sir Harold beamed. 'That's what I was known as by the last confectioner I assisted – my late mother. And I hear from Mrs Geall that you are just as talented as she was.'

'I'm sorry, sir, I don't understand. Are you here to check my work? Because we don't have any to check yet; someone destroyed all the toffees and we're having to work through the night to make them again.'

'He knows that, you daft ha'peth,' Vicky Geall chuckled. 'I've roped him in to assist you just for tonight. If we're going to be ready for morning then we need another skilled pair of hands at the boiling pan.' Vicky turned her face in the direction of Sir Harold Mackintosh and said, 'But honestly, I think she could have managed without us. Her standard of work is very high – she could do this blindfolded.' And she smiled in Mary's direction.

Chapter Sixty-Three

Cynthia Starbeck was convinced she had got away with it. Her tears at Major Fergusson's hospital bedside had distracted him from the flaws in her story; the accomplice she had found was a known liar and could be discredited if she broke her word and tried to talk about what Mrs Starbeck had asked her to do; and the ledger on Diana Moore's desk now showed a donation to the Spanish refugee fund from Mrs Starbeck which was equal to the amount which she had withdrawn from the Major's savings account.

She thought she had been very clever. Both the Major's savings book and Diana's ledger were completed with the date beside each transaction so she couldn't lie about having made the donation to the Spanish refugee fund before she had spoken to the Major in hospital. If he checked, the Major would immediately discover that her story didn't add up. All of the donations in Diana's ledger were listed in chronological order and there was no space for one earlier up the list where Mrs Starbeck wanted hers to appear. There was, however, an entry which she could alter – the donation of one penny that she'd made, and she'd got Dolly Dunkley to lure Diana away from her office while she was in the middle of working on the ledger and altered the number of that donation to reflect the amount she had taken from the Major's account, then put that same amount in cash in Diana's cashbox. Diana might suspect that something was wrong with the tally on her ledger, but she would never be able to prove it, and she would have a difficult time making anyone listen to her if the amount had gone up rather than down.

Helping Dolly to distract Diana had not been easy, and for a moment Cynthia Starbeck had thought she was about to be caught in the act, but with heart thumping she had managed to complete the fraud, return the ledger and the cashbox to where Diana had left them on her desk, and walk away with a look of innocence on her handsome face.

She stood now among the clutch of senior managers who were waiting to be presented to the King, bitterly feeling the loss of her jewels, most of all the pendant which had been in her family for so many generations. She had speculated over ways that she might get more money in order to return to the jeweller's shop and buy it back, but when she had passed the window the preceding day she had seen that it was missing. Cynthia Starbeck wore the finest suit of clothes she had. She wore her golden hair neatly plaited in twists around the crown of her head in the Bavarian style in marked contrast to the very British shows of patriotism which bedecked the factory walls. Mrs Starbeck and her colleagues among the senior managers stood in neat rows outside the door to the Mackintosh's office building, waiting for the King to arrive so that they could be presented to him. One or two were lucky enough to have been chosen to walk with the royal party through the factory itself in case there were any questions which they could answer. Standing below union flags, bright bunting, and banners of welcome, Cynthia Starbeck believed she was one of them.

There was a little scuffle behind Mrs Starbeck as another manager arrived and moved in beside her. She glanced upward to see who it was, then did a double-take; not only was Diana Moore standing beside her but she could see that she was very clearly wearing Cynthia's gold pendant!

Cynthia Starbeck gasped when she caught Diana's eye and saw her cat-like smile. She realized then that Diana must know something . . .

'Mrs Starbeck,' Diana glanced down at her clipboard where the itinerary for the King's visit was typed out neatly on sheets of brilliant white foolscap paper, 'there is a matter which requires your attention; would you step this way, please?'

In any other circumstances Cynthia Starbeck would have given the girl short shrift, she would have told her not to bother her with trivialities, she would have told her to relay any messages through her head of department as was fitting, but Cynthia Starbeck's eyes were caught by the sight of her own gold pendant hanging around Diana Moore's neck, and she knew in that moment that she too was caught. Cythia Starbeck cast one last desperate look up towards the bend of the road where her king would arrive from, and without the excuse of his presence to save her, she bit her tongue and followed Diana Moore into the office building.

'You are not on my list.' Diana handed her clipboard to Mrs Starbeck with a graceful, sinister flourish. She had chosen to lead her to the directors' stairwell at the side of the office building where, as there was no view of the road and the coming royal spectacle, she could be certain there would be no people. The chatter of excited specta-tors outside could be heard echoing within, but as Cynthia Starbeck took the clipboard from Diana there was not a sound to be heard from the stairwell.

Mrs Starbeck looked at the first typed sheet of foolscap, and sure enough her name was not on the list of managers who had permission to wait at the doors for the royal entourage. Ordinarily this would have been Mrs Starbeck's sole concern; she had been eagerly plotting how she would ingratiate herself with the King, but there was her pendant; absolutely unique and unmistakable, hanging around Diana Moore's neck and glinting in the sunshine which filtered through the skylight high above them. 'Where did you get that?' she asked Diana quietly.

'That's on the next page.' Diana nodded almost imper-ceptibly toward the clipboard.

Cynthia Starbeck lifted the day's itinerary, and below it was another sheet of tightly typed prose. This was an entirely different document, and at a glance she could see that it was a witness statement of some kind, labelled at the top of the page with that morning's date. Mrs Starbeck's eyes scanned over the words, taking in a clear and articulate account of how Diana Moore had come to discover that she, Cynthia Starbeck, had found herself in financial difficulties, then had fraudulently withdrawn money from the savings account of a dying man to pay her own rent, then had attempted to create an excuse for her actions by selling her jewellery and using the cash to create a false entry in a ledger of charitable donations. It was all there, all the things she thought no one else could ever know, but Diana had clearly found her out. Now Mrs Starbeck realized why it had felt so easy to distract Diana and interfere with the ledger and cash box she kept on her desk; Diana had wanted to see what she was up to so that she could catch her red-handed.

'I could give this to the police today.' Diana sounded untroubled; she often sounded like this but only now did Cynthia Starbeck realize that this was one of Diana's strengths; Diana gave away very little of what she knew, felt, or understood. 'But we both know that Major Fergusson is still gravely ill, and the worry of a police investigation could damn near kill him.'

'How did you find out these things? How could you possibly—'

'References. You have no idea how many people write to me for references.' Diana took back her clipboard and smoothly covered over her statement with the itinerary. 'Every lodging house you've stayed in has asked where you were employed and you have never thought to lie. They have each written to us for a reference. Then there was the Credit Union where you withdrew money from the Major's account; they wrote to us asking for confirmation of your employment and position because you claimed that you were employed by Mackintosh's and they don't simply hand money over to smart-looking women without checking that they are who they say they are. Everything you have done has left a trail of documentation behind it, and I have carbon copies of it all.'

The two women looked at one another in silence; all the power rested with the most junior. 'Does Amy Wilkes know about all this?' Mrs Starbeck's voice was as restrained as she could muster, but rage and fear were bubbling up and threatening to break her voice.

'No one else knows, and for the moment no one else will know.' But there was no kindness in Diana's voice as she said it.

'What do you intend to do?'

Diana looked her up and down, 'I am – until the property is sold – the de facto landlady of an exceptionally convenient boarding house. I have one vacant room, and I have decided that you are going to live in it.' The statement did not sound like charity, or mercy; it sounded like a threat.

'Are you blackmailing me?'

'No, I'm watching you; I'm watching you like a hawk. Your rent will be set at the same rate as all the other tenants. You will live where I can see you; you will work where I can see you; and you will eat where I can see you. You are at my mercy, and I have precious little to give.'

A strained silence stretched between them, and when she could bear it no longer Mrs Starbeck said, 'Presumably you wish me to hand in my letter of resignation.'

'No. You will stay. You will reinstate full piece rates for the married women working on the line, and you will stay in your old position to ensure that those piece rates are protected.' Diana did not wait for a reply. 'You may go now.' She gestured in the direction of the office door which would lead Cynthia Starbeck back to her desk, back to her work, and far away from the path of the royal visit.

'Excuse me?'

'You are dismissed.'

Cynthia Starbeck opened her mouth to object, but closed it again and turned away.

Mary stood outside the doors of the Mackintosh's palatial office block looking up at the famous Mackintosh's factory buildings, which were now covered in exquisite decorations which her sister had helped to distribute.

She could see that all along the railway platform, the bridge, the road above, and the windows of the overlooking houses and shops, people squeezed together with happy, excited faces waiting to see the arrival of the King. She knew that beyond those streets, and far up into the town, more crowds would be thronging every place the King was expected to visit, just to be near him and to cheer. And down in the basin between the railway line and the toffee factory there was an entirely different sight: hundreds of neatly dressed Mackintosh's workers in their whites and overalls stood calmly and proudly waiting to bow or curtsey in unison as the royal car pulled into the drive. They waited in neat rows like soldiers standing for inspection, and the dignity of it made her eyes fill with tears of pride.

Mary saw the movement of her colleagues before she saw the King. At the far end of the basin, just beneath the stone railway bridge, the first few white-aproned staff had dropped into a curtsey, and the motion rippled down through the staff like a wave on clear water. A gleaming car with the royal standard fluttering on its bonnet swung gracefully around, with two uniformed military men riding on either side of it, standing with one foot on the footplate, and a hand on the roof of the vehicle, like footmen riding on a horse-drawn carriage. Mounted police followed at a trot and another car pulled up behind the King's out of which stepped two remarkably tall men in smart suits with armbands on their sleeves with the stripes of Sergeants.

As the car pulled up at the doors of the Mackintosh's office block the army officers jumped to the ground and gracefully opened the rear doors of the car in perfect unison, like dancers at the ballet. King George alighted from one side, Queen Elizabeth from the other, and the crowds cheered and cheered. And then, unexpectedly, two more passengers appeared from inside the car, passengers the town had never dared to hope they would see. The crowds cheered again so much more loudly that Mary felt she could feel the noise in her chest, in the floor beneath her feet. The two unexpected guests were the little princesses – and the people of Halifax could see that, for all their differences in station, the King and Queen were just like them, with children who wanted to be taken out for a Saturday treat.

The King paused and held out a hand to his eldest daughter who walked carefully up to him. The eleven-year-old princess appeared to be asking him something as she looked around about her and he looked up and pointed to the spot on the side of the Albion Mills building where the fire had been last Christmas. The little princess nodded in acknowledgement and the crowds realized that the royal family had seen their plight last year in the newspapers or on the newsreels, and the princess was asking where the damage had been, and her father was pointing it out to her. In that moment they knew that the royal family knew of the struggles they had been through, and cared about how well they had recovered.

The King and Queen and their children disappeared inside the office building and Mary knew that they would be waiting for some time while the royal party promenaded through the smartest production lines and saw the King's Toffee being made according to her own method. Mary hoped that the straw-lined box where they were keeping the new casket kept the sweets from getting too hot because she didn't want to hand over spoiled sweets to the King.

The rush for the royal visit was almost over, and Mary knew that this would be her last day with Mr Baum before he returned to Germany and his children. He had told her that he hoped to come back to England with his family to take up the confectioner's job in the future, but he feared he wouldn't be allowed. She wanted to tell him how desperately she wanted him to come back, or even to take her with him, but she didn't have the words.

When the royal party returned Mary was so lost in thought that she didn't notice that Dolly Dunkley had squeezed past the official guard with Mrs Starbeck to stand at Mary's side to help lift the royal casket out of its case.

The casket was very large and flat and Mary was put in such a position by Dolly that she would have to hold one side of it while Dolly held the other, creating the impression that it was a gift from both of them.

As the King and Queen were returning to their motorcar,

Mary and Dolly stepped forward to present the casket which had caused so much trouble and sadness. His Majesty, who was possibly very used to receiving gifts, and was tired after travelling so far that day, asked simply, 'Hullo, what's this?'

Dolly took advantage of Mary's usual hesitancy and replied, 'Some chocolates that I made for Your Majesties.'

Mary's very natural look of hurt shock was not lost on the Queen who said, 'Oh did you now?' and gave Mary a wink.

Mary could not have been happier. She was consoled by the knowledge that the entire casket was lined with chewy violet toffees and nothing else and she was confident that the Queen would see this and remember that the girl who claimed to have made the contents did not know what was in it, and so a private understanding would exist between the two of them. The knowledge that she and the Queen had that secret bond, and that Dolly Dunkley had exposed herself as a liar to the highest in the land, meant more to Mary than if she had just presented the casket on her own.

The royal family departed the factory to go on to the town hall, but before they left King George told the Mackintoshes that he believed that their premises must be the biggest toffee factory in the world; a toffee town. The King, the Queen, and the two little princesses waved to the crowds one last time and were gone. All over Toffee Town workers let tears roll down their cheeks unchecked because they were so happy and so relieved that all the hard work and anguish had been worthwhile, and they had achieved all they had meant to.

There was a fond feeling among the crowd that they

had not just seen a head of state who needed to visit their town for strategically political reasons, but a father and mother who wanted to organize a treat for their two little girls. They might have a loftier pedigree, they might rule over an empire upon which the sun never set, they might be going home to a castle full of servants – but the workers of the Halifax factory felt a kinship with their king and queen. They were parents like themselves, and they too had to do battle with the knotty problem of how to go to work and at the same time do their duty to their children.

'You have seen your king and queen, Maria. How does it make you feel?'

Mary had returned to the empty confectioner's kitchen in the hope that she could find some more work to do, some tidying up perhaps, but everything was gone. The royal family had left the factory not an hour earlier and the bunting on the walls was already beginning to sag. Mary had to wonder what would happen to her now that the royal visit was over, and the King's Toffee had been made, presented, and consigned to history. Vicky Geall had collected her recipe books and said her goodbyes much sooner than Mary had expected, and she had feared that Mr Baum might have left without saying goodbye at all. But there he was, that twinkling smile that made her heart flutter, there to speak with her alone.

'I thought you'd gone already!' Mary's heart beat faster as she saw that Albert was carrying a suitcase and had his hat in his hand. She couldn't blame him for wanting to get back to his children and his sister; and he had only been waiting until they had finished their work for the King's visit, but Mary had hoped they might have a few more days together.

'I could not leave without congratulating you, Maria.' Albert smiled, but there was a sadness in his cocoa-coloured eyes. 'You have triumphed and I am proud to say that you were my apprentice.'

'You will come back, won't you?'

'I will try every day to return.' Albert Baum gently lowered his suitcase, placed his fedora hat on the kitchen worktop, and took a few paces closer towards Mary. 'But while I am away, try not to worry so much, Maria. You have so many reasons for happiness; seize them.'

'But I'll be worried about you.' Mary didn't dare say why.

'You don't need to worry about me. I shall be quite safe. I shall be very bored by much embassy paperwork as I apply for our permits to return to England, but I will be well.'

'But I'm worried that you won't come back. I'm worried that I won't see you again.' Mary gazed into Albert's eyes, her own brimming with unshed tears.

Albert Baum felt a lump catch in his throat. He didn't dare to hope that his Maria was telling him the one thing he longed to hear. 'I promise you that if I can come back, I will.' He reached out and took her hand, kissed it as though his life depended on it, then turned hurriedly to leave. As he stood at the door he said, 'I will come back for you, Maria.'

Chapter Sixty-Four

Reenie and Peter had been summoned to Director Hitchens's office to receive a private and personal thank you for the work they had done to track down the source of the poisoned casket and end the largest product recall in the history of the firm. Peter, however, knew without even asking Reenie, that it would be impossible for her to stand still and stay quiet for any length of time while she was thanked and praised, if she had another matter on her mind – and Peter knew that Reenie had been applying her mind to the problem of providing more work for the mothers of Halifax.

As they waited in the luxuriously carpeted hallway, the sun streamed through the magnificent rainbow-tinted skylight, turning Reenie's smartly pressed white overall into a kaleidoscope of colour. Peter could almost hear Reenie's mind humming with excitement at what she was going to tell the director now that she knew she had his ear for an uninterrupted moment. The director's secretary emerged from behind the ornate oak door which was decorated with carved acorns and manuscript 'M's to usher in Peter and Reenie for their appointed meeting. As the director looked up from his desk, piled with memos and production reports, he smiled in recognition at the young pair and was evidently opening his mouth to greet them when Reenie got started.

'I think we're doing it all wrong!' Reenie launched into her latest idea with unbridled enthusiasm and sat down in a chair at the desk opposite the director before he could invite her to do so. She leant forward with a beaming grin, excited to share the solution she had come up with, which in her mind was so perfect that it couldn't fail to be adopted. 'But I know exactly what we need to do.'

The director took a deep breath and braced himself.

'What she means to say,' Peter interjected, 'is that Reenie has had an idea about how we can improve the Time and Motion Department and make our work much more efficient than anything Mrs Starbeck has proposed.'

The director was interested; Reenie had a reputation for bringing fresh ideas to projects with her fresh eyes, and although she didn't always express it well it didn't matter – he thought of her as speaking another language and needing Peter as her interpreter. 'What sort of change does she suggest?'

'A new section which is entirely made for temporary, experimental lines, with a handpicked group of workers who are known for their flexibility and experience.'

'Half the time these girls on the experimental lines are new in,' Reenie piped up, 'and they don't know even the basics. We'd be better having a special troop of girls who only break in new lines, and then the breaking in will take half the time.'

'Do we have enough new lines to support a troop of full-time girls? I'm not convinced that we'd be able to keep them occupied all of the time. There'd be plenty of occasions where there were no new lines to build. And as I understand it, you really need to run your experimental lines in the evenings, when the rest of the factory is on shut down and the engineers are free to supervise and make changes. Aside from the problem of paying these girls to be permanently available for your troop, and aside from the problem of finding girls with the skill and experience to do this without cannibalizing the other regular lines, you'd also need to find girls who are willing to work evening shifts and forgo their chance to walk out with their young men. You would essentially be damaging their marriage prospects while costing the company more money and taking them from the regular lines.'

'Not if they're already married, sir.'

'How's that?' Director Hitchens was taken aback by Reenie's suggestion.

'Not if it's a troop of married women who used to work here, sir. I wouldn't need to take talented girls from other production lines if I only picked from the married women who've come back while the marriage bar is lifted. And you wouldn't need to worry about paying them to hang around if there aren't any new lines for them to break in because married women aren't entitled to permanent contracts anyway; they'd all just be casual like the seasonal workers. We could even plan in our experimental work around the school terms.'

'Yes, but what about their husbands? We can't be seen to take women away from their domestic duties.'

'That's why the married women are perfect, sir. We need evening workers, and the married women need evening shifts so that they can work after they've fed their husbands and bathed their children. I think this could be a way to help the problem you pointed out, Mr Hitchens.'

'Which problem, I don't remember—'

'You once said that the children of Halifax go unfed, unclothed, and unshod while Halifax feeds and clothes the empire. Let's employ the mothers, sir. Let's do what's in our gift.'

'With respect, Sir Harold, we need to change the Mackintosh's rule book.' Amy Wilkes had avoided speaking her mind openly on this topic for years, but that had been before the Major had almost been taken from them, when she had always known that he would intervene to make sure her workers were treated fairly.

Mrs Starbeck had been invited to the meeting as she was the principle challenge to Mrs Wilkes's endeavour, and the time had come to take the problem, and her suggested solution to the highest quarter. Mrs Starbeck sniffed delicately. 'But I'm not sure we need to go so far as—'

'We do.' Amy was tired of Cythia Starbeck's objections and now that she had Sir Harold's ear she was going to make the most of it. She addressed him directly. 'Sir, with respect, if we want your family name to survive in business then we do. Confectionery manufacture is an industry which relies on women – I know it, you know it, and our competitors know it. It is a truth universally acknowledged that a confectionery production line needs the fine motor skills of women workers, but we can't keep dismissing women when they marry and then starting from scratch again training fourteen-year-old girls who cry if they have to work next to someone they don't like. The argument against employing women who have children has always been that they bring their troubles to the workplace; well, in my experience so do the unmarried girls, because they simply don't have the maturity to work the way that mothers do. We're exchanging one type of drama for another.'

Mrs Starbeck was gently patronizing, as only one who stands for the status quo ever can be. 'But as I've said before, if these women want to have children—'

'Being a mother is not a luxury hobby! They are not being self-indulgent by raising children. If you'll forgive me for saying so, Sir Harold, many of these women aren't given a great deal of choice by their husbands in how many children they have. These are valuable workers who bring a host of irreplaceable skills to our business. They bring an example of maturity to the fourteen-year-old workers who benefit from working beside an adult. And, what's more, the needs of mothers are very simply and easily met; they need a crèche here in the factory complex where they can visit their children at regular intervals throughout the day. They need the flexibility to meet the needs of their families. Is it so much to ask?'

Mrs Starbeck wrinkled her nose. 'Having a crèche in a factory?'

'At present we have a ballroom, a lending library, an annual beauty pageant, a monthly cinema club, and a weekly meeting of the Temperance Society – a room in which some modestly paid women watch children eat soup does not seem so remarkable to me.' Amy Wilkes would have liked to see the end of the Mackintosh's Beauty Pageant – but that was a battle for another day.

Mrs Starbeck looked to the impassive Sir Harold to pooh-pooh the idea. 'And presumably you want all of this to be paid for by the company, Amy?'

Amy shrugged. 'Why not? If we have the budget for fourteen miles of bunting, six liveried horses, and an annual beauty contest for employees, why not?'

'Because we should not be paying for the choices and luxuries of women who have chosen *that kind of lifestyle*!'

Sir Harold chose this moment to interrupt after waiting and listening patiently to both his employees. 'Yes, indeed we should. The mothers of the Quality Street line are worth ten times the expense. This business was founded by a mother who made confectionery during the week and walked her children to Sunday School when she closed up her shop, and I know that if she had been made to give up work immediately after her marriage this factory would not exist, and we would not have the luxury of discussing this matter at all. I think that we should talk about creating a crèche somewhere in Toffee Town, and I think we could spare the second postal warehouse to be nicely converted. If changes are necessary to accommodate the best workers, then changes must be made.' Sir Harold paused gravely and continued in a different vein. 'However, I asked you here to speak with you about another matter. We received an invitation last year to attend a government briefing, and in the circumstances following our fire I requested that we be given leave to rebuild before taking up the invitation to co-operate with His Majesty's ministers.'

Whatever Amy and Cynthia had been expecting, it had not been this. Amy wondered if Sir Harold was talking about cooperating with ministers over the investigations into the poisoning, but surely that matter was now closed?

'The time has now come,' Sir Harold told them, 'when I need us all to show our willingness to help plan for war.

'I have received a communication from the Minister for the Department of the Co-Ordination of Defence. I'm sure you all saw the news in the papers last year – they have set up a Department of Food which will be responsible for the organization of supplies of food and feeding stuffs for defence purposes—'

'But surely that's only in the event of a war – and no one believes that we will have to go to war.' Mrs Starbeck made the mistake of interrupting Sir Harold mid-sentence and Amy was pleased to see the shadow of irritation cross Sir Harold's face.

'The department is at present completing their plans for the maintenance of supplies and for the control and distribution of food and feeding stuffs in all possible conditions of war. We have no way of knowing what the future has in store for us, but I suspect that if the war which is almost certainly coming is anything like the war I lived through as a younger man, then these are our golden days. The King's Toffee was intended as a last hurrah for Mackintosh's, and now it's time for us to begin to batten down the hatches.'

Sir Harold rose from his immense oak desk and moved thoughtfully to the window which looked out on the

Albion Mills building where they had worked so hard to create his brainchild, his Quality Street. They had watched it all burn a year ago, and then had fought hard to rebuild, and to put on their best livery for the King. 'I fully agree that we must begin to make provision for our married women, and I give my approval to a project to plan how we might better provide for them. But this must not be about propping up our existing infrastructure; this must be part of our plan for war, because we have been called to play a part in our nation's struggle, and we have left it too late already, and the enemy is at our gates. We will need men and women alike; and we will need to be ready for war no matter what.'

Chapter Sixty-Five

The cloakroom was almost as quiet as it was when it was empty. Mrs Grimshaw thought the overlooker would get a shock when she came in for the start of the shift. At this time of day the cloakroom outside the Gooseberry Cream production line was usually a flurry of white overalls, raucous laughter, and loud complaints about sleepless children or inconsiderate binmen who had stolen their well-earned sleep. However, this morning was different; it was the last morning that their line would operate, and when this final shift finished they would turn in their mobcaps and leave the factory with heavy hearts, knowing that they were leaving forever. They had all arrived early, and now, instead of racing through the changing rooms like whirlwinds to start work on the production line in the nick of time, they waited in silence, ready too soon to be let in to stand by their posts. Some of them sat on the benches where they would usually stop to lace up their boots, others leant against coat stands and gazed at the scrubbed steel floor tiles which caught the early morning sunlight here and there and had never looked so much like home. Arm in arm, hand in hand, they waited in silence, hoping against hope that this wouldn't be the end.

'This time back at the old job, this time with you all – it's been a gift.' Mrs Grimshaw knew that it wasn't really goodbye because these were all women that she had known since her girlhood; they were women who lived in her town, and sometimes in her street; she knew that she'd see them all again, and they would likely be in and out of one another's houses; but the feeling of all being back together again, at the work they loved again, that could never be recaptured.

'I didn't realize how much I'd missed it until they said I could come back.' Mrs Grimshaw's daughter-in-law fought to hold back tears, as though pulling her chin a little closer in towards her chest would disguise the redness of her eyes, the shake in her shoulders, and the wobble in her lip.

'Oh there now,' her mother-in-law tried to reassure her, 'you're still young; there could be lots of chances for you to come back. They'll have seasonal rushes now and then, and we'll make sure we keep an eye out for advertisements – and if you need to leave the kids off with me I'll be ready at the drop of a hat to take them. We'll make sure that if they're taking on married women again you're the first in the queue, carrying the best references and the toughest boots.'

'But it won't be the same, though, will it?' A voice they didn't recognize for a moment made them turn. Emily Everard, the woman they had always thought of as a battleship in human form was blubbing like a baby and burying her face in a powder-blue handkerchief. 'It won't be like this. They can't make us go, they can't, it means everything to us.'

Siobhan Grimshaw choked back her own tears, took a deep, calming breath, and crossed the cloakroom to Emily Everard. 'Mrs Everard – may I call you Emily?' The other looked up and nodded through her helpless, childlike sobs. 'Emily, there is no easy way to say this, but you need to think about doing something beyond the factory. Don't get me wrong, you're good. In fact, you're very, very good, but you've got a bossy way with you and I just think it's about time you thought about standing for parliament.'

Some of the other women in the cloakroom burst out laughing, and the bleak silence of the cloakroom was replaced by relieved humour at the look of shock on Emily Everard's face. Finally she composed herself to say, 'Do you honestly mean that?'

'I do.' Siobhan looked around her at the other women. 'I don't know about everyone else, but I'd vote for you.'

'Yeah, *I* would,' Doreen Fairclough said, nodding in agreement.

'You've got our votes!' Pearl called out and pointed at Winifred by her side.

Other women chimed in, and before long tears of a very different nature were welling up in Emily Everard's proud eyes. 'I must say, although I have never sought public office—'

This raised guffaws of laughter from the other women who had always said that Emily Everard only settled for running a production line because no one had let her run the country.

'I think our Siobhan's right,' Mrs Grimshaw said. 'We'll never be able to get this back, and even if we could we all know that it couldn't last forever. The school holidays are coming and there's not many of us who won't have children to mind. But if we can find something new, then I think I can bear the leaving – and I've got a feeling that pitching in on your campaign for election would be just the thing for all of us. What do you say, ladies? Vote for Everard?'

And the response from the factory lasses waiting in the cloakroom for their final shift was so loud that they didn't hear the whistle telling them their shift had started – and despite all being ready and prepared for so long, they were now late to work.

Kathleen and John watched the road from the farmhouse window, refusing all offers of other more profitable occupations from their mother, in favour of waiting for Reenie's young man to arrive. Reenie, on the other hand, had plenty to keep her busy, and wasn't going to get involved in some tomfool vigil for Peter who she saw every day at work, and who was only coming up the lane on his bicycle same as he always did for Sunday dinner.

'When he gets here,' Kathleen asked her mother, 'can I show him my banner that I sewed for the Sunday School procession?'

'That's not fair, I've got nothing to show him. I didn't get to be in a procession.'

Mrs Calder, whose hands were wrapped in a thickly woven oven mat, heaved a steaming joint of roast lamb from inside the kitchen range, and dropped it down on the scrubbed pine table with a clatter. 'You can show him his dinner, John. If you guard it from the cat while it's resting you can say you helped make it.' Their marmalade cat was circling ominously, and she didn't want a repeat of the 'Easter Incident'. Mrs Calder had insisted that they should have a good roast joint for Peter's first dinner with them since the royal visit because Peter was the hero of the hour. She had roasted it with soft, fresh stems of rosemary picked from the pots out in her kitchen garden, and she boiled up some of her husband's new potatoes and was about to smother them in glistening golden butter.

'Is that lad here yet?' Mr Calder had been tempted in from his work by the smell of roast lamb and Mrs Calder despaired of his appearance.

'Go and put something smarter on,' she told her husband, 'you can't sit down to Sunday dinner looking like that.' Truth be told it wasn't the day or the meal which influenced their choice of dress that day; it was their awe of Reenie's posh young man. Reenie did not encourage this, but it went on all the same.

'He's here!' Kathleen piped up from her place on the window seat, and she and her brother raced each other to the farmyard leaving the roast joint dangerously unattended in the presence of Marmaduke, the notorious dinner thief.

'. . . and is it true you found the man who poisoned them?'

'. . . and will you be in the papers?'

'. . . do you get a reward?'

'Would you two let him get in the door and take his bicycle clips off?' Mrs Calder gently led her two youngest away towards the table so that Peter could catch his breath. He was a shy lad and he took her children's questions in good spirits, but he didn't always have an answer. 'Reenie!' she called up the stairs, 'Peter's here!' She turned to Peter and said confidentially, 'Very well done on all that work you did for the King's visit. And that poison business; we heard it all from Reenie, you're quite the hero in this household.' And in a moment of enthusiastic fluster she reached out and shook his hand, which confused Peter but he returned the handshake anyway as a matter of good manners. Mr Calder, not to be outdone, and seeing that handshakes were the order of the day, reached forward and shook Peter's hand too, which then meant that Kathleen and John had to join in.

Reenie appeared at the top of the stairs just in time to see the chorus of awkward, but enthusiastic handshakes, and asked, 'What on earth is going on? I leave you lot alone for five minutes and you all go stark raving mad. Why are you all shaking Peter's hand? You've known him for ages; it's Peter.'

'They were just congratulating me, Reenie.' Peter looked like a startled rabbit appealing to Reenie to be rescued.

'Have you been telling people that we're engaged again, because if you have—'

'Are you engaged?' Kathleen's eyes lit up, while Reenie's mother looked elated, and Reenie's father clapped Peter on the back in delight.

'No, we are not!' Reenie greeted Peter with an affectionate peck on the cheek.

'Well,' Peter blushed and grinned at Reenie knowingly, 'perhaps not yet. I'll bide my time if you want to stay on at Mack's.'

Reenie smiled back at Peter. She loved him, but she

loved him all the more for understanding what her job meant to her.

'I got a message for you, Reenie, and it's good news.' Peter hurriedly pulled a note from his jacket pocket, 'The Major has asked to see us. He wants us to visit him tomorrow.'

'Oh my goodness! Is he all right?' Reenie gasped. She had been so certain that she would never see her friend again, but this news was the best surprise.

'He's getting better, and he can have visitors now.' Peter was hopeful, 'He wants to hear all about the King's visit.'

'He's not the only one!' Mrs Calder said, although she wasn't sure what she wanted to ask about first, the King, the Major, or the hint of a wedding. There was much to talk about, and all of it good. They had a hot dinner waiting for them, and a sunny Sunday afternoon stretching ahead of them; this day, thought Mrs Calder, is a precious gift.

Historical Note

Humbug Billy did not intend to kill anyone. However, a complicated series of misunderstandings caused him to sell 5lbs of sweets made with arsenic from his Bradford market stall in 1858. In addition to making himself and 200 of his customers gravely ill, he also inadvertently poisoned twenty-one people to death.

The lessons learned from the notorious Bradford Sweet Poisoning Case transformed the confectionery industry. Laws were eventually introduced to prevent food and drink manufacturers from adulterating their produce, and the sale of poisons and other pharmaceuticals became more strictly controlled. However, in 1937 lives were still being put at risk by the widespread use of cyanide as an insecticide and efforts were being made to force a change by law.

Although there are a few recorded cases from around this time of attempted murder by poisoned chocolate box, there were fortunately none during the real visit of King George VI to Halifax in 1937. Then again, there is no record of the king visiting the Mackintosh's factory or being given a casket of their sweets either. Royal visits to the major Quaker chocolate factories were almost a regular occurrence – and the visiting royal always left with an exquisitely crafted casket of handmade sweets. But when the king and queen visited Halifax it seems that the attractions of the Mackintosh's factory could not compete with the grandeur of nearby Shibden Hall. When the king visited the town on 20th October that year, he was taken to the former home of Anne Lister, where the newspapers reported he was 'told its romantic story'. This is intriguing for a 21st century reader, because we know that the story of the great romance between Anne Lister and Anne Walker – which became the basis for the BBC TV series *Gentleman Jack*, and which was lived out within its walls – was still locked away in coded diaries waiting to be uncovered by the post-war generation.

The royal visit to Halifax can still be relived in all its glory through the *Pathé* newsreel footage which has survived and is available to watch freely on the internet all these years later; it shows enthusiastic crowds, the stately progress of the royal couple, and the thick fog which caused so much trouble that autumn.

The fog was not the only problem in the new King's reign; he had lost a portion of his kingdom, and the people of the newly created Republic of Ireland had reclaimed their independence. Years later a Macintosh's manager wrote about this time and described how their Mackintosh's branded toffees had been taken from the shops and 'burned with the aid of paraffin'. The slogan 'burn everything except their coal' was a real motto of the independence movement in Ireland, and the effect of the trade war between the two countries even reached as far as our humble toffee factory in the town of Halifax.

The new king may have had fewer subjects by the end of his first year on the throne, but his kingdom's problems had only increased. There had been hunger marches the year before as starving men from the North East petitioned for government help; now the problem was a shortage of skilled workers to fill vacant posts. Questions were asked in Parliament about the problem, and one MP appealed to employment agencies and employers to consider hiring older men to fill their vacancies, so that everyone could have a chance to earn a wage.

Over eighty years later we could be forgiven for asking why the British didn't solve their problem by inviting in foreign labour; there were plenty of people who wanted to flee Nazi Germany but couldn't obtain the necessary permits to enter the United Kingdom. Even for those who did reach these shores there was the constant risk of being sent back or being sent to prison for overstaying your permit. Hansard records discussion of the case of a Jewish gentleman from Germany who came to England on a work permit. When his work permit expired he went into hiding rather than return to the Third Reich. He was caught and sentenced to six weeks hard labour in an English prison.

Meanwhile civil war was raging in Spain and committees were being set up in towns and cities all over Great Britain to raise funds to bring Spanish children into the country as refugees. The costs were high; not only did these committees have to raise enough money to bring the children across the channel, but they also had to raise enough extra money to satisfy the Home Office that the children would never become a burden on the state.

Great Britain was a troubled place that year and it bears an uncanny resemblance in some respects to the Great Britain of 2019. Europe was in turmoil, poverty had many citizens in its grip, and too many jobs lay vacant for a want of skilled employees. Fortunately, our British museums do not appear, in 2019, to be packing up their artefacts and sending them as evacuees to the homes of volunteers around the country. However, if they should ever need to, they will be able to draw on the experience of their predecessors who did just that in the 1930s, and who were preparing for war from the very moment Adolf Hitler took power in Germany in 1933.

There is one similarity between our story and the present day which is much more welcome: the Quality Street factory in Halifax are making a new sweet. At the time of writing, Nestlé (the owners of Quality Street and the Halifax factory since 1988) are making a Chocolate Caramel Brownie in a turquoise twist-wrap. This is not such a rare occurence, the Quality Street assortment has been evolving since its earliest days and of the current assortment only five of the sweets date back to 1936.

Gooseberry Creams – like the Apricot Delight – were only discontinued during my lifetime. Although I lament their passing there are plenty of Quality Street fans who were glad to see them go. This is, of course, the reason why they were discontinued; as consumers' tastes change so does the assortment. The manufacturers regularly review the sweets in the Quality Street selection, and if a sweet has fallen out of favour with the general public it is replaced with something they hope will be liked better. The assortment has said goodbye to the ginger and lemon flavoured Harrogate Toffee; the Peanut Cracknel; and the Malt Toffee, but we still have the Noisette Paté (the Green Triangle), the Golden Ingot (the Toffee Finger), the Hazelnut Caramel (the Purple One), the Caramel Cup (the Caramel Swirl) and the good old Toffee Penny. Sir Harold's original assortment may have changed to appeal to new generations of devoted fans, but I think he'd be proud to see that it is as popular as it has always been.

Acknowledgements

This book has been through more drafts than I've had Quality Streets, and many people have shown immense kindness and patience during a process which I had naïvely thought would be easier since I had a first novel under my belt.

Love and thanks are due first and foremost to Scott Leach (who is better known to my readers as Mr Thorpe); his support of me and my writing knows no bounds, even to the extent of carrying around an engagement ring in secret for ages because he wanted to wait until I'd met my manuscript deadline before distracting me with a proposal of marriage (I said yes).

Huge thanks are also due to my editor, whose natural instinct for a story saved me from poisoning the wrong character and gave a much-loved Mackintosh's employee an eleventh-hour reprieve. Without Kate Bradley this book would be neither finished, nor readable. Her expert coaching and kind patience allowed a completely different story to flourish than the one I had planned.

I continue to count myself lucky to have one of the world's most unflappable agents; when I am worrying more than Mary Norcliffe would think possible, Jemima Forrester saves the day with good advice and good humour.

My family have been enthusiastically supportive during the release of the first book and the writing of the second and I couldn't have got this far without them all. Even aunts, uncles and cousins rallied to the cause and did credit to the names of Hutchinson, Forrest, Walker, Baum and Copley.

Special thanks are also due to my friend and fellow writer Fiona McIntosh who has not only mentored me, but also made me laugh until my face hurt. Many friends were good enough to help me in my research and I'm grateful to John Thomson, the Edmundsons, Dejagers, Sprays and Tylers for all their help. Especially Lewis Tyler, without whom much of this writing could not have been done. I am also indebted to Beckie Senior and her family for the donation of their aunt's name. I am assured that the real Dolly Dunkley was lovely.

Independent booksellers were wonderfully supportive of *The Quality Street Girls*, my first book, and helped cheer me on while I was writing this one. Chief among them were Kirstie Lount of Fox Lane Books, and all the team at The Book Corner in the Halifax Piece Hall.

And last, but by no means least, I am so grateful to all the enthusiastic readers who have written to tell me what they thought of the first book. This second was only possible because they liked the first, and Ruffian only reprised his supporting role because he appeared to have his own fans. Ruffian thanks you for your letters.

If you haven't read
The Quality Street Girls yet,
keep reading for another
delicious taste of factory life.

Available now in paperback
and e-book

Chapter One

It was late, and the Baxter's store on the corner at Stump Cross was closed, but the lights in the main window illuminated a sparkling display of Mackintosh's Quality Street; the latest success from the sprawling factory they called Toffee Town. As Reenie rode her nag closer she could see that someone had taken the coloured cellophane wrappers from the chocolates and taped them between black sugar paper to make little stained glass windows. Between the tins and tubs and cartons were homemade tree baubles; an ingenious mixture of ping-pong balls, cellophane wrappers, glue and thread.

While there were plenty of other confectionery assortments that Baxter's could have chosen to feature, Reenie couldn't imagine they'd have had much luck making a stained glass window out of O'Neil's wrappers. Besides, Quality Street was the best, everyone knew it; plenty of girls from Reenie's school had left to work in Sharpe's or

O'Neil's factories, but it was the really lucky ones that went to work at Mackintosh's.

Reenie's enormous, ungainly old horse shuffled closer to try to nose the glass, the explosion of colour bursting forth from the opened tins on display had caught his eye and was drawing his curious nature to the window. Reenie didn't blame him; it was a beautiful sight and he deserved a treat when he was being so good about coming out after putting in a day's work in the top field. She had a great deal of affection for the old family horse, and she liked spoiling him when she got the chance, so she let him dawdle a while longer.

Reenie gazed at the window display, and dreamed of growing up to be the kind of fine lady that bought Quality Street, and had a gardener, and got driven around in an automobile. For the moment she would have to be content with being a farmer's daughter who had a vegetable patch and occasional use of her family's peculiarly ugly horse. Fortunately for Reenie, she found it easy to be content with her lot, she was an easily contented girl. As long as she didn't have to go into service she was happy.

'Come on, Ruffian. We've got a way to go yet.' Ruffian reluctantly allowed Reenie to steer him away from the bright lights, and continued up through the ever steeper streets of Halifax, over quiet cobbles she knew well. The night was cold for October, but she knew she had to ride out to get her father nonetheless.

Reenie didn't mind; Ruffian was technically her father's horse, and most fathers would not allow their daughter freedom of the valley with it, so she supposed she ought to feel pretty grateful. And it wasn't as though she had to come out to get her father very often, she thought to herself. He only got this blotto once a year when the Ale Taster's Society hired out the old oak room and had their 'do', apart from that she thought he was pretty good really. He was very probably the best dad.

Reenie's thoughts kept drifting back to the sandwich that was waiting in her pocket, wrapped in waxed paper and bound up with a piece of twine. The sandwich contained a slice of tinned tongue and some mustard-pickled-cauliflower that her mother made for Reenie to give to her father to eat on his way back. Reenie's stomach rumbled and she was tempted to take a bite out of it before she got to the pub, even though she'd had her tea. Her mother frequently told her that she was lucky to live on a farm where there was no shortage of food, but Reenie pointed out that there was no shortage of the same food: mutton, ewe's milk cheese, ewe's milk butter, ewe's milk curd tart, and ewe's milk. She rode in the dark past the Borough Market, there was a clamour outside The Old Cock and Oak. As she approached, Reenie didn't like the look of what she saw. Ahead of her, she could see brass buttons glinting in the old-fashioned gaslight from the pub, and the tell-tale contours of Salvation Army hats and cloaks. It was going to be another one of those nights.

Reenie knew before she'd even rounded the corner that this was not the regular Salvation Army, they would be off doing something useful somewhere involving soup and blankets. This was a Salvation Army splinter group, who the rest of the Salvation Army considered to be nothing but trouble. Reenie tried to feel friendly towards them as she wasn't in a hurry, but she did wonder privately why they didn't just go to the cinema when they got time off like everyone else.

'Think of your wives! Think of your children!' Reenie couldn't tell where in the throng of ardent believers the call was coming from, but she knew that they wouldn't be popular with the pub regulars. There were several other pubs along Market Street, but the faithful had chosen to cram into the courtyard of The Old Cock and Oak to protest against the annual meeting of the Worshipful Company of Ale Tasters. Reenie couldn't see what they were so fussed about, but this wasn't anything new.

Reenie decided not to dismount this time and walked old Ruffian as close to the pub door as she could, keeping a loose, but expert grasp on the fraying rope that served as Ruffian's bridle. 'Comin' through, 'scuse me, if you'd let me pass, please.' As the ramshackle old horse nosed its way through the faithful, the crowd parted, some out of courtesy but others to avoid being stamped on by a mud-caked hoof, or bitten by an almost toothless mouth. Ruffian may not have had the aristocratic pedigree, but like his rider, he encouraged good etiquette in his own way. Reenie was close enough now to see a few faces she knew guarding the doorway; exasperated men waiting for the do-gooders to move on, their arms folded. 'Is me dad in there still?'

'Now then, Queenie Reenie, what's this you comin' in on a noble steed with your uniformed retinue.' Fred Rastrick gave her a wicked grin as they both ignored the small, rogue faction of the otherwise helpful Halifax branch of the Salvation Army.

'Don't be daft, Fred, you know full well they're nowt to do wi' me. Now fetch us me dad, would ya'? It's too cold for him to walk home, he'll end up dead in a ditch.

420

Go tell him I'm here and I'm not stopping out half the night so he has to be quick.'

'Young lady! Young lady, how old are you?' Reenie recognised the castigating voice of Gwendoline Vance, self-appointed leader of this band of Salvation Army members who'd taken it upon themselves to object to most things that went on in Halifax, including the Ale Tasters annual 'do'. Reenie could have mistaken the woman's face in the dark, even this close up, but there was no mistaking the way she was harping on.

'What's it to you?' Reenie was not in a mood to be cross-examined by strangers, especially those in thrall to teetotalism.

'Shouldn't you be at school?'

'Well, not just now as it's half past ten at night.'

'Well I meant in the morning, shouldn't you be at home in bed by now so that you can go to school in the morning?'

'No, and I'll tell you for why. Firstly, I'm fifteen and I finished school at Easter; secondly, some of us would rather be spending our time helping our families than wasting it on enterprises that won't get anyone anywhere; and thirdly (and forgive me if I think this is the most important), because today is a Friday, and when I were at school they taught me that the day that comes after Friday is Saturday, and that, madam, is when the school is closed. Now if you've quite finished, I want me' dad. Fred!' Reenie had to call out because Fred had disappeared further inside the pub. The Salvation Army devotee blanched and choked on her words. Reenie ignored her and turned her eyes to the doorway of The Old Cock and Oak.

421

'He's here, Reenie,' Fred reappeared, 'but he can't walk.'

'Well then tell him he doesn't have to. I'm waiting with the 'orse.'

'No, I mean he can't walk. He's blotto; out cold.'

'Oh, good grief. Well, can someone drag him to the door, I don't want to have to get off the horse or I'll be here 'til Monday.'

'I'll have a go.' Fred turned to go back inside. 'But he's not as light as he used to be.'

'*Reenee*,' the do-gooder emphasised the Halifax pronunciation, ree-knee, and tried to assume an expression that was both patronising and penitent for her earlier mistake, 'may I call you Reenie?'

'No, you may not. Unless you're gonna help with m' dad.'

'We'd be very, very glad to help with your father; it must be terribly hard on you and your family. Do you think you could bring him with you on Sunday to—'

'No, I meant help lift him on the 'orse. Good grief, woman, are you daft? Fred! How's he looking?'

'Nearly there,' Fred called out through gritted teeth as he attempted to pull the dead weight of Mr Calder out to his horse and daughter, then turned to a fellow drinker 'Bert, can you give me an 'and throwin' him over Ruffian?'

Bert held up a hand and said, before darting back into the pub, 'You wait right there; I think I know just the lad for this.' Bert brought out a bemused-looking young man who Reenie didn't recognise, slapping him on the shoulder with friendly camaraderie and pushing him in the direction of the horse. He didn't have the slicked hair with razored back and sides that the other lads round here had. His hair wasn't darkened by Brylcreem;

instead, he had fine, golden toffee coloured hair that fell over his left eye and gave him away as a toff. Straight teeth, straight hair, straight nose, and a smarter suit of clothes than anyone else there; to Reenie, he looked hopelessly out of place among the factory workers and farm hands. It made her like him instantly for joining in with people who weren't like him. She might not have a lot in common with this posh-looking lad, but there was one thing; he looked like the type who would make friends with anyone.

'Reenie, Peter; Peter, Reenie.' Bert skimmed over the necessary introductions. 'We need to get Reenie's dad here over the 'orse.'

Peter smiled and nodded, and with what seemed like almost no effort at all, he gathered Reenie's father up and launched him in front of where Reenie sat, with his arms and legs dangling over the horse's withers on either side. The landing must have been a rough one for Mr Calder because, though unconscious, he still managed to vomit onto the military-style black boots of the nearest Moral League man.

The sudden eruption caused a shriek from the group's ringleader who turned to Reenie, 'Oh you poor child. You shouldn't have to see such things at your tender age.'

'Oh gerr'over yourself, woman. Everyone's dad drinks.' Reenie bent over to check on her father because although she was confident that he'd be alright, she thought it was as well to make sure. Her shoulder-length red hair dangled down the horse's side as she dropped her head level with her father's, reassured by his loud snore; *silly old thing, what was he like? Her mother would laugh at him come the morning.* Reenie looked up to thank the young man, but to her disappointment, he'd already gone. She had wanted to tell him that her father wasn't usually like this, and not to mind the Sally Army crowd because they weren't bad as all that if you weren't in a hurry to get anywhere. She had wanted to say so many things to him, but she supposed it was better she get a move on and take her father home to his bed. It didn't occur to her that the young man had gone indoors to fetch his coat and hat so he could offer to walk her home like a gentleman.

Reenie pulled on Ruffian's make-shift bridle and began to lead the horse away, then thought better of it and stopped to call over her shoulder 'and my friend Betsy Newman's in the Salvation Army and she says you six are pariahs! Go and help 'em with the cleaning rota like they've told ya', and stop botherin' folks who've had an 'arder week at work than you've ever known!'

Ruffian snorted, as if in agreement, and guided his mistress home.

PENNY THORPE

The Quality Street Girls

Three girls. One factory.
A Christmas they'll never forget